CALL OF HEIR AND SEA

THE SYREN SONGS

BOOK ONE

E . WILKINS

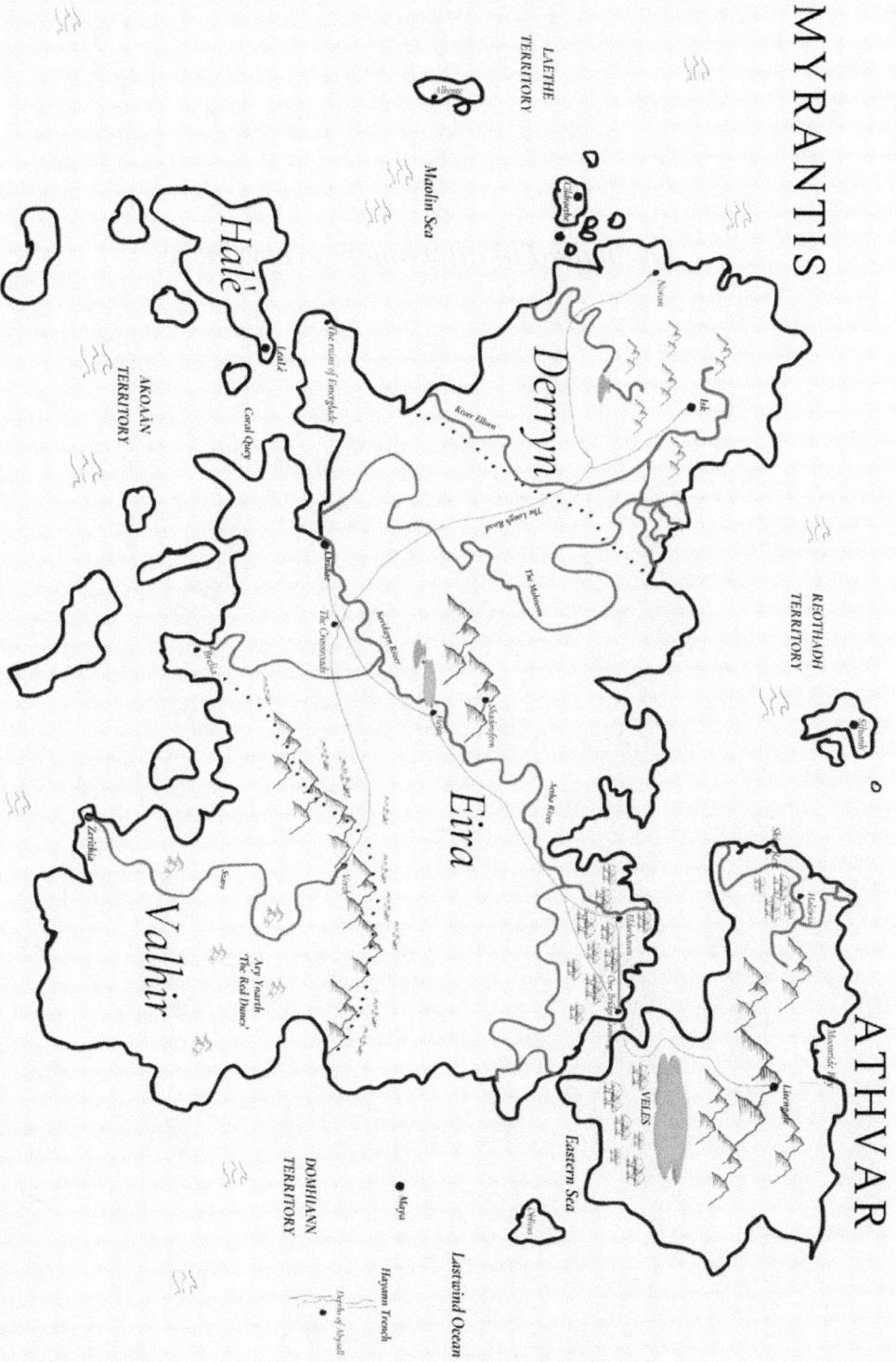

Dedicated to all women, everywhere.

Prologue
20 years before…

Death came on the swift wings of new life that night.
A summer storm was raging. The centuries-old fishing boat
creaked as it was thrown around in the maelstrom.
Huddled under itchy blankets, the small raven-haired boy, no
older than five, watched in terror as the strange men who put
him here shouted, struggling to keep the vessel from sinking.
To his right, holding the boy's newborn baby sister, the
Mother's Maid was praying while humming a song the little
boy did not recognise. She stopped rocking back and forth just
long enough to look at him and speak.
"You mustn't be frightened child, these strong men will not let
us sink, they have their Lord aboard. They will not let the
Syrens get us."
The strange men paid the boy no mind, pulling at ropes and
throwing buckets of sea filled water over the edge, trying in
vain to keep them all from sinking under the furious waves.
One of the strangers appeared braver than the others. The little
boy wanted to be like him when he grew up.
Just hours ago, that same stranger was in his little crumbling
home on the cliff tops.
The little boy thought back to the wails of his mother,
indecipherable to the howling of the winds.
What confusion the boy felt as she screamed out in pain.
He remembered seeing the very same Maid who was with him
now at the end of his mother's bed, covered in blood-soaked
rags and whispering to the strange men.
The boy was afraid. So terribly afraid.

He wished his mother was here with him to give him a cuddle and a kiss. To whisper in his ear what a brave boy he was and how much she loved him.

That was the last thing she had said to him not too long ago, before he was ripped from her, out of his home with his baby sister, heading for the docks.

But she wasn't here now, they had left her behind. The little boy heard one of the strange men say his mother had died. He had also heard them say the Laeth Syrens must be angry tonight to create a storm this savage.

Suddenly, the brave man crouched down in front of his face. The man was saying something to the boy and the Mother's Maid. She reached out and took the little boy's palm in hers, gripping it tightly to a point of near pain, but the little boy did not protest.

"The Syrens are here boy. You must cover your ears and not look over the edge. Do you understand?!"

The boy nodded his head at the man.

"Yes, Lord Rast."

The boy repeated what the man just said. "Yes, Lord Rast."

A large wet hand ruffled his hair. "Good lad."

Then, Lord Rast nodded once and proceeded to give the Mother's Maid a rope and a basket for his sister.

The first time the boy met Lord Rast was outside his home, not long after his sister was born.

The boy overheard him telling the Mother's Maid she was to accompany the little boy and his sister on their journey.

"The girl has only just been born and needs to have her blood tested. She may not be Damned," she replied.

Lord Rast just rubbed his jaw and sighed.

"'We've had our orders from the King. There is no one to hide them now, no one to look after them. Take him and the girl to the docks. It is time he went to Oblitus."

The Mother's Maid had gasped, and the little boy had wet himself. He knew of Oblitus from his history lessons with mother. It was where humans with no magic went to live, far away in the eastern sea. But mother had reassured him that even though he had no magic, he was still special and would never be sent there.

The little boy always liked to hear that.

The conversation had ended there and they swiftly left their grey, isolated home atop the cliffs. Afterwards, the boy was asked what he would like to call his new baby sister, but he did not know. It was his mother's baby; her choice, not his.

This made the little boy incredibly sad.

Nevertheless, on tippy toes he peeked at the baby held safely in a wicker basket, giving her the biggest smile any brother had ever given their sister.

"Aura."

The little boy liked that name. It was a name from his favourite book about the brave Fae, who lived a long time ago on Athvar.

He thought about that book now, as the icy waves splashed onto his urine-soiled trousers. The little boy did not feel brave or strong.

When the men started to scream, he started to cry. Little Aura did too; a tiny cry, like a kitten.

Then in the chaos, he heard a sound. The most beautiful song he had ever heard. Even though Lord Rast told him not to, the boy looked over the edge in the direction of the singing.

He saw a couple of the strange men in the water, dragged under by what could only be described as monsters. Human-like beings, but with eel tails and sharp claws.

Hairless, from what little the boy could see in the dark.

Laeth Syrens, if he recalled correctly from studying his books. Here, they were described as beautiful with long flowing hair.

There was no mention of sharp claws at the end of spindly white arms.

The Mother's Maid screamed, and the little boy turned around just in time to see the basket holding his baby sister being washed away by a giant wave.

He did not have time to react, as the same wave pulled the Mother's Maid and himself into the water too.

Even though it was Summer, the sea was bitterly cold. So cold it took his breath away. However, the little boy was a strong swimmer; his mother had taught him well. He tried to swim to his sister, who was floating further and further out of reach, but the waves were too strong. He despaired as he realised, he could not reach her.

The boy tried shouting for help, but water kept flooding into his mouth. The sounds of the crashing waves, Syren song and screams from the men drowned out his small cries.

A few frantic minutes passed, and as tiredness and cold overwhelmed his small body the boy did not think he could keep swimming anymore.

He wanted his mother and sister. Maybe if he just went to sleep, he would wake up and they would all be back by the fire in his safe, cosy house atop the cliffs.

As the little boy began to slip under the waves, large hands grabbed his collar and lifted him out of the raging water. He coughed and sputtered as he landed with a thump back into the vessel.

"Go go go! The syrens are distracted," he heard a man's voice bellow.

The little boy could just about peer over the edge of the vessel, to see his baby sister's basket still being tossed around the waves.

"No, my sister!" He tried to shout to the strange men over the deafening noise of the storm, but no one heard him. His wild eyes searched for Lord Rast, but he did not appear to be

onboard either.

The basket floated away, this time dipping below the surface of the water.

The last thing the little boy saw of his baby sister was her being knocked over into the torrent below.

The little boy was not brave or strong.

The little boy cried.

1

Keyara

Keyara awoke from a dreamless sleep in her scratchy bed. Her head throbbed in rhythm with the harsh daylight filtering through the small window.

She groaned, immediately regretting the copious amount of Akoaàn Wyne she had downed the night before at Gregory's. No surprise there.

She frequented the tavern so often that it had become her second home-much to the annoyance of the staff.

She knew she was a nuisance.

"*I don't deserve this headache*," she thought wryly, sitting up. Though as her toe made contact with an empty wine bottle, sending it rolling across the floor and under her bed, Keyara supposed the headache was warranted.

"Shit," she hissed, as the dizziness hit her like a punch, forcing her to clutch the edge of the too-small bed to steady herself.

She must have kept the party going after stumbling home, judging by the number of bottles scattered around.

Akoaàn Wyne was notorious for wiping out memories, and she had a vague recollection of toasting to no one in particular, alone in the night. Her sensitive eyes squinted against the midday sun burning through the curtains.

It was noon already.

"*Godsdamn it,*" she cursed internally, rubbing her temples. She was supposed to help prepare for the spring festival today, and her mother would be thoroughly pissed off if she didn't pitch in.

Her eyes fell on the other beds in the cramped room. Both were empty, the blankets neatly folded-a sure sign her mother and sister had already gone to the village.

Aura's side was as tidy as ever, with flowers, ribbons, and homemade perfumes neatly lined up on the windowsill.

Keyara's gaze lingered on the perfumes.

She knelt down on her sister's pink, faded sheets, dabbing a bit of lavender scent onto her wrists, all the while hoping Aura hadn't noticed how much the contents of one particular bottle had been disappearing.

Those sheets, though worn and stained, were a relic from their childhood-reminders of simpler, albeit poorer, times.

She added them to the long list of items in her head that needed replacing, once they had the money.

And they *would* have more money.

By the gods she would make sure of it.

She looked at her mother's cot, squeezed between her and Aura's beds. Neat, simple, and frill-free, just like their mother, a folded nightgown resting on top.

Keyara's lips curled in a smirk, thinking of her mother's fiery temper, which could easily rival her own.

If she didn't get moving soon, she'd be on the receiving end of it.

Keyara haphazardly cleaned up her mess-her books, empty bottles, all the various crap she had not yet put away.

Her precious daggers were slung over the end of the bed underneath her threadbare jacket.

It always made her smile to remember when she had swiped them from a drunk fae at Gregory's years ago, when she must have been no older than fourteen. Though she doubted her mother or sister would approve, Keyara cherished them.

Keyara did not want to be the cause of her mother's heart attack and Aura's disapproval.

They would both be shocked to know that she had been training in weapon wielding and fighting, for going on ten years.

Her brain ached just thinking about her training with Berran.

"*This is a bad one,*" she thought with deep breaths as she slowly padded over to the wash basin, splashing chilly water over her face.

Keyara kept her eyes half-open, lifting them fully was not an option, it was way too fucking bright.

Pressing a cold cloth to her face as she leant against the washbasin, she realised she could've used magic to warm the water, but maybe the icy shock would snap her back to reality.

Staring at her reflection in the rusty, crooked mirror – askew from her own efforts at putting it up on the half-rotten wall – she grimaced at the sight.

Red-rimmed, deep-set hazel eyes looked back at her, framed by a bird's nest of dark, tangled hair.

The sharp features of her face appeared even more gaunt by her unkempt locks. The long strands refused to cooperate with the laws of nature.

"Eurgh," she muttered, brushing out the knots. Strawberry blonde strands clung to the brush-a telltale sign Aura had used it recently.

"*One day,*" Keyara thought bitterly, tossing the brush under the bed where it skidded on the worn floor, joining the wyne bottle in a pathetic dance of failure, "*we'll have enough money for our own damned things.*"

Keyara made herself as presentable as possible under the circumstances, the sweltering temperature of the room fucking with her composure.

Gods knew how hot it would be in this room tonight when there were three of them stuffed in a space the size of a broom cupboard, with one window that did not even open properly-on account of, again, her own efforts to fix the damned thing.

She slipped on her favourite airy tunic, the pale eggshell blue fabric complementing her lightly tanned skin, a result of the warm spring sun. Her well-worn cotton pants skimmed her ankles, patched and repaired beyond recognition.

As her only pair of shoes were winter boots, she left the stifling cottage barefoot, pushing past the wisteria vines that scraped her face every time she went outside.

She threatened to cut it off or burn it every time her mother or sister annoyed her.

Which was often.

The sounds of laughter, hammering, and children playing drifted toward her from the village green, where preparations for the festival were already underway.

The brightness outside was blinding. Shielding her sore eyes with her hand, she started the short walk to the square, glancing toward the forest that stretched beyond the village-it felt like a barrier, keeping her trapped in this small, suffocating world.

Aura would need to use that magic of hers to make Keyara feel not so damned awful right now. The warm glow of her sister's power was a drug that she would gladly take.

Tall grass and wildflowers lining the path slowed her pace, but the shade from the towering oak trees provided some relief from the glaring midday sun, unusually hot for this time of year.

The trees were ancient, their roots embedded with coral-remnants of the Akoaàn magic that had first brought the syren ancestors to Eldorhaven thousands of years ago.

She made it to the village square, despite her aching head and the nausea still threatening to topple her over.

Villagers had already strung up delicate rose petal bunting and coral ornaments, no doubt crafted with magic by the Akoaàn descendants.

Across the green, children were playing, splashing each other with water as the Akoaàns laughed, their abilities no longer the powerful syren magic of their cousins out west in the coral sea, but something watered down and harmless.

Their hair didn't have the usual shocking brightness, nor did rainbows dance in their eyes, but they were still Akoaàn nonetheless.

A pang of sadness tugged at Keyara as she stared at their pale red, orange, and pink hair shimmering in the sun, remembering the lessons she barely paid attention to as a child.

They had first found refuge here in the aftermath of the Maolin Wars, after their home reef off the coast of southern Hale' had been decimated by the giant Skuidd that the Domhiann syrens commanded. Their numbers had dwindled, a legacy nearly forgotten.

All Keyara knew was that the Akoaàn ancestors who had made Eldorhaven their home were some of the best people she'd ever known, and they knew how to throw a damned good party, especially during the spring festival.

Tonight, they would tell stories through song, and she couldn't wait to hear them sing.

They would gather here, by the large boulder that sat in the centre of the green. Underneath her fingers, Keyara traced the bright pink dolphin carved into its side.

Those ancient syrens came here, to the other side of the continent, to forget.

To get as far away as possible, for the grief of losing everything was too much.

But the Akoaàns couldn't resist commemorating their old home.

Such a sentimental species.

The carvings on every building in Eldorhaven were proof of that-little reminders of where they'd come from and what they'd lost.

14

Her favourite carving was the one above Gregory's bar: a sea turtle with an absurdly large... appendage.

A recent, rather inappropriate addition to the original artwork, courtesy of a lifeday party that had gotten out of hand.

It always made her laugh, especially after a few drinks.

Across the green, a group of her drinking friends lounged on the wooden benches outside the tavern, waving at her.

Even from here, she could see one of them sported two wicked black eyes and an old scab slashed across his cheek. Keyara smirked and sent a small wave in return, knowing she'd probably add to those injuries during tomorrow's training session.

She fought without mercy-no one ever accused her of going easy.

Keyara knew she was a ruthless combatant, always heating her daggers with her magic to make sure her opponents thought twice before getting too close.

And when it came to hand-to-hand combat, she knew she was spiteful, targeting sensitive spots-groins, eyes, toes.

Her thoughts were interrupted by her sister's feminine voice calling her name.

"Keyara!"

Over where her mother stood at the small table, setting up candle holders and glassware, Aura was a vision in her simple, white linen dress-the one she'd sewn herself from old drapes Keyara had found dumped behind Gregory's last year.

The dress was torn at the bottom, the hem soaked with mud.

But on Aura, it still looked beautiful.

Her strawberry blonde curls grazed her waist, pushed back by a makeshift headband framing her delicate, freckled face.

Aura was pushing away a few unruly tendrils that had escaped to fall in front.

She was everything Keyara was not.

Gods, her sister deserved better.

Keyara walked over, her own aches and weariness momentarily forgotten. Aura was wiping her hands on her dress, while their mother was deep in conversation with their blue-haired neighbour, her expression serious. Whatever they were discussing seemed important.

"Morning," Keyara greeted them, her voice rough from sleep and the remnants of her hangover.

Aura smiled up at Keyara, and looked up at Keyara with her clear, sparkling eyes the colour of the sea-not quite blue, not quite green. "It's afternoon, Keyara. We've been working all morning while you've been lazing about in bed like a lady of the manor. Hungover, I'm guessing?"

There was a teasing lightness to her tone, and Keyara knew better than to bite.

Instead, she used it to her advantage. "Well, I'm here now, so if you want the best of me, you'd better help me out. I feel like shit and could do with being made to feel even slightly better."

Those ocean eyes rolled, a gesture she'd clearly picked up from Keyara herself. "Not that I mind Keyara, but I seem to be doing this more and more often."

Without bothering to reply, Keyara stepped closer and held her hands out. She craved the direct contact needed for her sister's magic to take effect. Aura's power was a soothing balm, flowing from her hands into Keyara's with a warm glow that spread through her body.

It felt like a mother's kiss-gentle and comforting, both inside and out.

She felt instantly better.

The headache eased, though it didn't disappear entirely, and her overall pain dulled.

Keyara no longer felt like she wanted to murder the sun for having the audacity to shine.

"Thanks," she sighed in relief. "Now, what do you need me to do? I'll help with anything-except painting, crafting, or anything that requires creativity. Maybe I'll just serve the Wyne."

"There's going to be an Heir's Rite," the blue-haired neighbour said with an air of excitement. "It was announced in Oridae five days ago."

Keyara snapped her head up from the feast on her plate as Aura, sitting next to her, went still, a goblet halfway lifted to her mouth.

The darkness of the night had overthrown the pale blue of late evening, and their bodies flickered from the candles that were placed along the banquet table.

Aura's voice was quiet when she said, "Really?"

Her mother turned her head and looked at Keyara with complete resignation.

"Yes," the neighbour continued, her blue hair bouncing with every word. "My brother lives in Oridae and told me when he arrived. He brought the letters of invitation himself. It's happening at the end of the spring-enough time for everyone to get to Shadowfern, and for the participants to receive their letters. I'm surprised he mentioned someone from our village being chosen."

Music and singing from the Akoaàn troop seemed to stop in Keyara's ears.

The festive atmosphere around them faded for Keyara, drowned out by the sudden rush of blood pounding in her ears. Her sister spoke, her voice measured, "Well, we all knew their Majesties do not have an Heir-we all knew this day would eventually come."

The neighbour nodded, clearly revelling in the gossip. "Of course, but many of us held out hope that a bastard might come forward, or some distant relative could make a claim. It's not unheard of in Eiras' history. Bastard heirs have taken the throne before when others were Damned."

Their mother spoke with a hard edge to her voice. "King Farhand would never have betrayed his wife."

"True," the neighbour agreed, "but I don't think anyone ever dreamed we'd see an Heir's Rite in our lifetime either."

Aura shifted uncomfortably. "It's a good thing that my magic is weak," she said, her words slow and thoughtful. "There's no chance I'd be called up. I don't think I could stomach it. I've heard they sometimes fight to the death in the final trials, sometimes they even tortured the competitors, just to see if they could handle it."

Her mother's face was gentle as she looked at Aura-who always seemed too good for the harshness of the world.

The soft spot for her adopted daughter shining on her ageing face.

Keyara knew Aura would never be chosen.

The Rite only called for the twenty most powerful humans in Myrantis, and Aura's magic was far too weak to make her eligible.

The pool of competitors taken from the sample of their blood that was taken at their birth. Being that she was adopted, her mother wasn't even sure Aura's blood had ever even been tested.

No such luck for Keyara.

She on the other hand, had been preparing for this day for as long as she could remember.

She had known since childhood that her magic was different.

The neighbour was giggling again, clearly entertained by the idea. "Imagine winning the Heir's Rite and becoming a king overnight. Moving into Oridae palace with your family."

"Or queen," Aura corrected softly, taking a sip of her drink.

"Well, not exactly overnight," their mother added. "You could be the heir for years. Some never even made it to the throne."

"Like Olave," the neighbour chimed in. "Didn't she die in the rebellion?"

Their mother nodded, but Keyara's mind had already drifted away. She barely heard the rest of the conversation, too lost in her own thoughts.

Images of the trials she would inevitably face, whorled around in her mind's eye, of her mother telling the story of her birth over and over again, of what it meant for her in the future.

The way her blood had reacted when she was born.

When her vial was taken, like every other human in Myrantis, it hadn't simply reacted like most-water magic turning to liquid or earth magic causing a small tremor.

No, her blood had heated to such extreme temperatures, that it melted the enchanted crucible used to contain it.

The burn had nearly blinded the midwife, and it had even melted part of the floor before evaporating into steam.

Keyara had been marked from birth as something powerful, and she would love to read what was written next to her name in the book the Mother's Maids recorded their findings in.

She could feel the weight of that power now as the conversation continued into the night.

"...maybe the letter is for Gregory, the old cad has shown me some power in his time."

Aura groaned with disgust, ignoring the wink the neighbour threw at her.

Keyara closed her eyes and heaved a sigh, her mother mirroring the release of breath.

They both knew who that letter would be for.

2
Keyara

Keyara sighed, staring up at the wooden beams of the ceiling. Telling Aura about the Heir's Rite felt heavier than any of the burdens she'd faced in the past. They had always been open with each other, never hiding anything-whether it was a silly secret like who ate the last apple or something as monumental as Aura's first time with Cal.

Remembering the sweet taste caused her stomach to rumble. But *fuck*, she thought, this was different.

The Heir's Rite wasn't just a secret to share; it was a fate that would change everything.

She could still remember on Aura's nineteenth lifeday, her sister had told her about Cal, blushing and nervous but laughing through the story.

Aura had been giddy, carefree, sharing the details of her awkward but sweet experience as if it were the most natural thing in the world. Keyara had listened, teasing her as older sisters do, but also feeling an odd mix of pride and protectiveness.

Cal was sweet, with an obvious deep liking of her sister, but she was not interested in pursuing a relationship with him. Though the poor guy was still hoping she would change her mind, always following her around, like a pathetic lovesick syren struck.

She was the first of them to lose her maidenhood.

Her sister was so open, so vulnerable, so trusting with her emotions in ways Keyara never allowed herself to be.

But that was Aura-the light to Keyara's shadow

20

Mother had already left for the green by the time Keyara awoke, rubbing her eyes as the weight of the inevitable conversation settled heavily on her chest.

The sun streamed through the window, casting a soft glow on Aura's sleeping form, and the soft whistling of her sister's snoring confirmed she was still sound asleep.

The rise and fall of her body in harmony with her breathing. The familiar hum of jealousy writhed within Keyara.

Aura's feminine curves were outlined by the thin blanket, soft mountains and valleys that drove men in the village crazy.

Her own body was lithe, willowy, with barely a hint of hips and breasts. Rolling onto her back, she stared at the ceiling.

"Godsdamned it", she breathed through a sigh, knowing she couldn't delay the conversation any longer.

The longer she waited, the harder it would be to break the news, and the last thing she wanted was for Aura to hear it from someone else.

She had to tell her sister about the Heir's Rite.

Today.

Keyara had seen the excited whispers and knowing glances from the villagers the day before; the rumours about the Rite were already spreading like wildfire.

It wouldn't be long before the letter arrived, and then there would be no avoiding it.

She stood and padded softly over to the crooked stairs, deciding to let Aura sleep for a little longer. There was no point in waking her before she was ready.

Clean-up from the festival would begin early, and Keyara really thought she should help her mother and the other villagers tidy up the mess.

But that required conversing with other people, and everyone would be annoyingly happy today, with the annual charity from Lord and Lady Corall distributed among them all.

Being not overly wealthy themselves, the ruling Akoaàn ancestors treated all who lived under them with a fair and generous hand, sometimes to their own detriment.

Downstairs, Keyara began pulling open their bare cupboards to prepare the lemon balm tea, her movements automatic as her thoughts churned.

Putting the beaten-up old kettle over the permanently flaming hearth, her body shivered from the constant chill that filled their home.

She loved her magic, but she cursed it at the same time.

It was as though the magic was stealing Keyara's own warmth to add to its own.

Fucking typical.

Aura always said Keyara was better suited for the desert climates of Valhir rather than the easily changeable seasons of Eira. Especially here in Eldorhaven, where the nights always had a nipping cold to it, thanks to the ocean current that flowed past from the icy cold waters of the north. Keyara was inclined to agree with her right now.

The blazing sun and large red dunes, spices, strong alcohol and shooting stars-her kind of place she thought, pulling a blanket around her shoulders as she stirred the tea.

Shame about some of their inhabitants though.

Godsdamned Vampyres.

Arrogant and egotistical. That was what she had heard anyway, as she had never met one.

Not that she wanted to.

The whistle of the steam interrupted her train of thought.

Picking up the kettle, she placed some fresh lavender into it, as she knew Aura liked it, and as she unbent from over the hearth, she spotted her in the garden through the kitchen window.

She was in her usual white dress, a stained pinafore that was tied around her waist, bending over the small Mottel garden she tended with care.

A delicate purple bloom with multiple tiny heads and a long stem, Mottel was Aura's favourite.

She watched as Aura weaved the flower into a braid at the top of her strawberry blonde hair, letting half of it down, tongue sticking out as she did so.

Aura always seemed so peaceful in moments like these, her calm nature reflected in the way she touched the flowers, fingers dancing lightly over the leaves as if in conversation with them.

It was as though the world around her calmed in her presence, bending to her will, but not through force-just through kindness.

And maybe a little magic.

Keyara couldn't give a shit about flowers. Particularly Mottel. The smell it gave off was so delicate and yet so strong, smothering the garden in its fragrance and polluting everything else around it.

The thought of telling her about the Heir's Rite, knowing it would shatter that delicate peace, made Keyara's stomach twist. But there was no avoiding it.

It would be better coming from her, gently broken over tea and soft words, rather than from the village gossip mill.

Keyara had always known she was destined for this-she had felt it in her bones since childhood.

Her fate was to rule, she was sure of it.

But knowing and accepting were two different things, and dragging Aura into that reality was something she had avoided for as long as possible.

Splinters stuck into her backside as Keyara leant against the kitchen table. "Oh, I didn't think you would be up until at least the afternoon, Kiki," Aura said with a smirk as she came through the door, placing the bunch of flowers she was holding down on the table.

"Yes, well I can't lay in bed all day". Keyara replied, ignoring the pet name Aura had given her when they were children. Grabbing Aura's tea, she handed it to her sister.

Taking the cup from Keyara's hands, Keyara caught the flicker of surprise as Aura noted the dark green and purple bruise on her arm near her elbow.

She hastily pulled the blanket further down over herself.

Neither of them said anything for a heartbeat, moments passed in uncomfortable silence before Aura gently said, "what have you been doing Keyara, and your hands…"

Aura put down the tea and went to grab Keyara's hands.

They were burning crimson.

In the winter, whenever they needed Keyara to heat the bath water or unfreeze the pipes, the tips of her fingers-up to just above her wrists-would turn a pale red, like they had been scalded from the inside. Any time she used her magic, her hands would look like they'd been submerged in icy water for too long.

It was usually barely noticeable.

Not this time.

Keyara snatched her hands away and turned toward the door.

"Nothing really, a man got too drunk at Gregory's last night and the silly fucker fell into the river. I had to warm him up. Gods, some men really can't handle their wyne."

The lie came out so easily, it surprised her.

"I'm not an idiot, Keyara," Aura said quietly. "I know that didn't happen. You left the festival before me, in the opposite direction of the river, and when I came home, you were already in bed. Also, I think I would've heard if someone had fallen into the river-seeing as I was in Gregory's most of the evening after you disappeared."

Who put the fucking bee in her arse? Keyara thought, irritation flaring. Aura never pressed her like this.

Keyara began pacing. "Don't act like our mother, Aura. I don't have to tell you everything."

Aura let out an exasperated sigh, closing her eyes before speaking again. "Do you really think I haven't noticed the bruises all over your body? Or how you rarely come home before the early hours of the morning anymore? And when you do, you reek of wyne, and gods knows what else."

Keyara crossed her arms and flicked her dark hair over her shoulder.

The defensiveness in her posture didn't deter Aura.

Whatever she wanted to know, she would get out of Keyara eventually.

"If there's something you need to tell me, Keyara, now's the time," Aura said, her voice softening. "I saw you and Mother at the table last night-you both looked like you'd seen a ghost. You were whispering all evening, then you left with such a look on your face, I felt like I needed to warn anyone who got in your way."

She wasn't exaggerating.

Keyara had felt like she might burn the very ground she walked on, the soil and grass beneath her turning to steam and mud.

"Aura, I-" Keyara hesitated, taking a long pause. If there was ever a time to tell her, it was now.

Fuck it.

She would have to swallow her stubbornness.

She knew she wasn't being fair to Aura. The fear of the unknown was, in truth, eating Keyara alive.

"Keyara, what's going on?" Aura urged, her eyes pleading.

"Do you know why you were brought to us that night? The night we took you in?"

"Of course," Aura began, her tone thoughtful. "Berran knew Mother had just lost a baby, so he brought her an orphaned newborn whose parents died at sea. You were no older than two maybe."

Letting her hands fall to her sides, Keyara moved forward, closing the gap between them.

That was the story they'd always told her every time Aura had asked. Berran, heir to the throne of Silvanh, had found Aura adrift in a wicker basket, floating on the open ocean.

Mother would kill her for revealing the truth without her being there.

But too damned bad. She'd deal with Mother later.

"No…I mean, yes, that's true, but there's more to it than that." Aura's wide eyes searched Keyara's face, confusion flickering within them.

Keyara took a deep breath and continued.

"You were brought to us because Mother owed a favour to Lord and Lady Corall. Yes, Berran found you, but he didn't bring you here right away. He took you to them first, and they decided what to do with you."

Berran had gone over the story with Keyara many times, ever since he began training her.

The Reothadh syren had taught her everything from swordplay to combat tactics, how to throw a wicked punch, and how to wield her daggers with precision.

Along with everything she needed to know if she ever wanted to become the heir of Eira.

She had gone looking for him last night, as she always did for their evening training, but he was nowhere to be found.

Thinking back, it had been days since she last saw him…

"I don't understand," Aura finally replied, confusion deepening in her voice. "Why didn't either of you ever mention any of this before?"

Keyara gave a sad smile. "Because we never felt the need to. Until now."

"Why?"

Keyara's heart pounded as she prepared herself. "When I was born, the Mother's Maid tested my blood like everyone else, but what they found was unlike anything they'd ever seen in Eldorhaven before-maybe even in all Eira. I'm strong, Aura. I can *feel* how powerful I am."

She paused, watching her sister's face as the weight of her words sank in.

"When my name and blood were to be written in the book, Mother begged the Mother's Maid not to document the full extent of my power, though what they wrote down in truth, we will never know. Regardless, Mother was so hysterical that Lord and Lady Corall were summoned. They struck a deal-my power would be written down as nothing more than anyone else's, and in return, Mother would owe them a debt. The Mother's Maid was paid for her silence, and that was that. Two years later, you arrived at our door, and the debt was repaid."

Keyara watched as Aura chewed the inside of her cheek, fingers absentmindedly twirling the ends of her hair.

"There's something else, Aura."

Aura let her hair drop. "What is it? Don't tell me you've eloped with Gregory."

Keyara wrinkled her nose. "Gods, no." She sighed. "Someone must've revealed the truth about me."

The look on Aura's face made it clear that the coin had finally dropped.

"Aura, the letter-it was for me."

In a blur of white and purple, Aura shot toward her, her cup clattering onto the scratched table, spilling tea everywhere.

"Keyara, this is madness! What business do you have entering the Heir's Rite, for gods' sake? It's for Lords, Ladies, and fools with dreams of grandeur and too much power, and it's dangerous. What are you thinking?"

Keyara took a step back, hands on her slender hips. "You can't tell me, Aura, that you don't dream of a better life for us. Do you really look around at this place-our rotting, miserable home-and feel satisfied? The constant fear of not having enough food, these disgusting rags we wear, the never-ending worry about how we're going to take care of Mother when she's too old to manage?"

Her long legs began pacing, a familiar routine to Keyara, a way release the pent-up anger threatening to explode.

"Of course I dream of more," Aura said, her voice soft but firm. "But I'm realistic, Keyara."

Keyara's head whipped up so fast she nearly gave herself whiplash. "Realistic? I'm more powerful than anyone in Eldorhaven, probably more powerful than most humans in all of Eira! Where do you think I've been getting these bruises? I've been preparing for this-training for the Heir's Rite since I learned of it."

"Training?" Aura echoed, confusion flickering in her voice.

"Yes, training. With Berran and his warriors." Keyara smiled, a small curve of her lips. "They've been teaching me everything-how to fight, how to win. I've had lessons on history, politics, and swordplay-things no human could even dream of being taught by syren warriors. And by the Reothadh heir himself, for ten years."

The uncertainty remained etched in Aura's expression. "And has he taught you how to properly control your magic?"

Keyara hesitated. "Well... no, not really." She quickly added, "But my magic is the strongest it's ever been, Aura. You should see it."

They had tried, many-many times.

But being a male whose very essence was ice, Berran struggled to teach her anything other than how *not* to use it.

She had apologised to his burnt warriors, one too many times.

"And if you win? You expect us to just leave this life behind, for you to become Queen of Eira? Keyara, listen to yourself. And what about Mother? Does she know about any of this?"

Her mouth dropped, and Keyara stuttered slightly, "Not officially. But she can't be that ignorant to have not considered that one day, maybe the letter would come for me. After she told me the circumstances of my birth, she would be stupid to think that I wouldn't be curious and explore my magic. Who wouldn't want to be Queen? Aura, please…"

She grabbed her sister's hands again. "Imagine, us, living in Oridae palace. Never having to want for anything again. You could have the most beautiful things. Mother could have a home that wasn't falling apart around her. No more praying to the gods for a scrap of food,"

"…and you would be Queen," Aura interrupted, finishing the sentence for her.

The tone in which Aura responded took Keyara by surprise. "Well yes, I will be Queen. But I may not even want it Aura, I'm not sure I want to get married and have children of my own. So I'll call an Heir's Rite sooner than is required, and once the victor is found, I'll give up my crown and we can live out our days in a home by the sea, with more money than we will ever need."

Not knowing what else to say or do, Keyara turned and ran to their room.

She grabbed the daggers from under her bed and ran back downstairs. "These are what I have been training with." They felt so comfortable in her hands, like they were an extension of her body.

The weapons were extremely intricate; the pommels were a matte black, with raised carvings engraved around them.

What looked like an emerald, a shade of darkest green, was inlaid at the bottom, just above the lethal blades.

The daggers had blades of darkest obsidian. The metal constantly shifted colour and shone brightly, even in the dim light of the cottage.

"Keyara, where did you get those? Are they even human-made?"

A smirk twitched at Keyara's mouth. *They're not,* she thought.

She knew Aura must be wondering how she acquired them. Keyara replied at last. "No, and you should have seen the look on the prick's face when he realised they were gone".

3
Selsie

The whims of the Maolin Sea were ever-changing, its currents
strong and temperamental. *A reflection of its inhabitants*
thought Selsie, as she swam in the shallows around Cildraethe.
Her pod of newly matured Laeths flanked her, their sleek forms
gliding effortlessly through the water.

"The time is approaching, Selsie. You will be the first of the
newlings to surface and show them how the first song is done.
What better example than the daughter of their ruler?"

The Laeth matriarch spoke with her usual steely authority. Her
dark grey hair, adorned with trinkets stolen from drowned
sailors, floated around her stern face, catching dappled sunlight
in its strands. Hundreds of tiny treasures gleamed among her
locks, each a reminder of her power and age.

As the pod neared the entrance to the castle, the ever-present
mist surrounding Cildraethe began to dissipate. The massive
structure, seamlessly melded into the smoky bedrock of the
island, loomed ahead. Its entrance, hidden beneath the waves,
was often difficult to locate-even for Selsie's sharp syren
eyesight, and she was sure it moved with the tides.

Glancing around, Selsie noticed the judgmental stares of the
others. Their displeasure was clear-they resented being told to
follow the lead of a smaller, physically weaker syren, even if
she was the heir. One of the males nudged her golden tail with
his own muted bronze fins, perfectly camouflaged for the
Maolin Sea's sandy depths.

Selsie snarled at him, refusing to let the larger male think he could assert dominance over her. She was a female, the future matriarch-his superior in every way.

Her bright golden tail and smaller stature might have been disadvantages in these unforgiving waters, but her beauty and intelligence outshone them all-qualities she knew she had in abundance and frequently used against them. That's mostly why the other newlings hated her, she thought. She slowed them down-and against the wishes of the other females-always held the attention of the males.

By Alysee, they would soon respect her. When it came time to surface and ensnare her first victim, she would prove her worth. As she was the second most powerful Laeth in the sea, her syren song was expected to be legendary, destined to join the ranks of her mother and the goddess Alysee in the histories and songs of the Akoaàns.

"We leave for the shipping routes tomorrow," the matriarch announced with a sly grin. "Spring has ended, and within the moon-tide, we'll reach Noran, just in time for the season's shift. The ships will try to avoid the autumn storms," she added with a cackle through her thin lips. "But they won't be expecting the storm of a dozen Laeths, all singing their first song."

Her laughter rippled through the water, and the others joined in, some nearly boiling the water around them in their excitement. Selsie's soul whispered to her with possibility. A human would never resist her first song-not through willpower, not through magic. Those tricks might work any other time, but not against the power of a Laeth's first song. The humans would be helpless. The pod would have its first taste of human flesh within the week, and the thrill of it coursed through them.

But Selsie's thoughts lingered on another possibility. A choice all Laeths could make. Would she keep her victim captive, as her mother had once done? It was rare in Cildraethe now, though not unheard of. She had heard the stories-how her mother had kept a man whose eyes burned with mania, his body withered and frail, so fragile a breeze could knock him over. Her mother had fed his obsession, letting it drive him into madness before disposing of him after a year.

That memory had stirred something in Selsie as a youngling. She liked the idea of someone being so hopelessly devoted to her that they would descend into the depths of insanity itself. They swam toward the castle's submerged sanctuary; the place they called home. The matriarch ascended to the upper levels above the water, a world none of them could enter yet. Not until they made their first kill and took their first breath of air.

Selsie couldn't shake her nerves as she wrung her hands, swimming into the deeper caves at the heart of the castle, biting her lip. Her chamber was simple, with a bed of the softest kelp at its centre. Scattered treasures she had gathered during her solitary swims lay haphazardly across the floor.

Above her, a small hole in the ceiling allowed sunlight to filter down into the chamber. Selsie sank onto her bed, staring as she often did at that narrow beam of light. It called to her, like a distant syren's song, urging her to follow it-to rise and embrace the light that beckoned from above.

Selsie yearned to surface so intensely it physically ached. She longed to witness the vastness of the sky, feel the wind tangling in her curls, and bask in the sun's warmth on her bronzed skin. The elders had shared countless stories of life above the water, and her mother's tales painted vivid images in her mind. Most were about helpless sailors who died in the arms of the females, or the males who had called a lonely widow into the waves before quickly dispatching of the human with their razor-sharp teeth.

The matriarch, however, had little regard for the males of their own species. They lacked the ruthlessness she admired and didn't revel in the violence of a kill the way her prized females did. The matriarch's females were vicious, lethal, and proud of their ability to cause suffering. The longer and more agonizing the suffering, the better the story. More kills meant greater power, and a higher place in their deadly hierarchy.

Selsie could only hope to live up to the towering expectation placed on her. Her mother's subtle displays of disappointment over the years had only heightened her nervousness. The matriarch had earned her status as their leader through two hundred and sixty years of carnage-so many human men had fallen to her that there was no longer any room in her silver hair for more trinkets. Renowned for her cunning and her ability to seduce even the strongest men, her mother's legend loomed large.

Though Selsie's heart twisted with anxiety, she clung to the belief that her first song would be legendary. It had to be. All she needed to do was avoid the deadly weapons the humans wielded, summon every drop of knowledge she'd gained, and wield the magic that coursed through her veins. Yet the nerves persisted, making her first glimpse of the surface world feel even more daunting. She had waited for this moment for nearly fourty years, and her Laeth maturity had finally arrived.

Surrounded by the treasures she had gathered from the sea, Selsie watched the shaft of light in her chamber shift from the warm white of day to the silvery blue of night. Dreamless and restless, sleep found her hours later, leaving her anxious thoughts to churn beneath the waves.

"Selsie, are you awake?" came a voice she recognized instantly, washing away the last remnants of her sleep. A shadow lingered outside her chamber door.

"Yes, Neesh, I'm awake. What's going on? What time is it?" she asked, her voice groggy.

The young guard took the reply as permission to enter. "They're leaving-your mother and the newlings. They're departing for Noran this morning. Your mother's given the orders."

Selsie swam toward her friend, pulling her hands through her tangled hair as a sense of urgency gnawed at her. "I thought we weren't leaving for a few more days! By Alysee, what's the rush?"

There was a hint of unease in her eyes as Neesh glanced toward her, motioning for Selsie to follow. They swam through the castle's winding corridors, bubbles trailing behind Neesh's silver tail as she spoke.

"Rumours have surfaced about a ship that left port ahead of schedule. It's said to be setting sail from Noran sooner than expected-possibly within the season tide."

"That's in four days," Selsie said, disbelief creeping in. "Do they really think we can make it to Noran in time? It's a six-day swim, even with little rest."

Surely her mother knew the pod couldn't reach Noran in time to intercept. Selsie didn't understand the urgency; the tide for the sailing season wouldn't peak for another week. After that, the Maolin Sea would be flooded with sailors, ripe for the Laeths' hunt.

Neesh hesitated, her expression troubled. "I don't know all the details. Your mother's kept quiet, but she insists we leave at first light." The guard wouldn't meet her gaze, and Selsie's unease grew. Something was amiss.

Grabbing Neesh's arm lightly, Selsie pressed, "Do we know where this ship is headed?"

Dark green eyes met her own again, a clear sign that the situation was far more complicated than it appeared.

"Neesh, what's going on?" It wasn't a question; it was a demand.

Though Selsie was not physically imposing, she was still her mother's daughter-the heir to the Laethian kingdom of Cildraethe. The weight of that authority pressed down on Neesh, who finally relented, her voice barely above a whisper.

"It's a Saynt ship, Selsie. Carrying the Damned back to Oblitus."

The water seemed to still around them, the usual swirling currents freezing in the wake of those words.

"Are you certain?" Selsie asked, her voice tight with disbelief.

"By Alysee, I am. A white ship with silver sails-there is no mistaking it. They say it's *The Brendann*."

Every syren knew *The Brendann*. It was the fastest ship in the world, and it bore the one unbreakable rule of the sea.

"No syren would dare attack a Saynt ship," Selsie murmured, her mind racing. "It would spark an all-out war with the humans. No one is that reckless."

Neesh pulled her into a small alcove along the castle walls, where glittering jewels embedded in the stone cast soft reflections around them. "You don't have to tell me. I was just as shocked when I heard. But even so, it doesn't make sense. Saynt ships only ever carry a skeleton crew."

Selsie's thoughts whirled. Her mother wouldn't be so foolish as to attack a Saynt ship, especially not one carrying defenceless newborn humans.

The matriarch couldn't after giving their Laethian cloth to the humans. The enchanted coat of her species was woven into the silver sails, a calling card ensuring the ship was a real Saynt and not an imitation used to deter syren attacks.

Three ships had been granted these enchanted offerings: *The Brendann, The Nikolas,* and *The Christofer.*

"This can't be true," Selsie whispered. "Attacking a Saynt ship goes against every vow we've made. It's madness."

Neesh's gaze said it all. Whatever the truth was, it wasn't good. Panic rising, Selsie left Neesh in the alcove and swam with urgency toward the newlings' chambers. She found her mother outside, overseeing the guards as they prepared for departure.

"Mother!" Selsie nearly collided with the matriarch, her voice trembling with barely contained emotion. "We are sworn not to attack a Saynt ship. This is madness!"

The female turned on her, fury blazing in her ancient eyes. Before Selsie could react, the matriarch's sharp nails raked across her cheek with a speed that left her reeling.

Her mother's 'Other' form occasionally bled through. A part of their physical makeup that was used only in times of killing for other Laeths. Not her mother, however.

"How dare you question me, girl!" Her mother hissed through a mouth deeply lined with age and fury. The lively preparations fell silent, every syren in the chamber frozen in place.

"If you were anyone else, my dear daughter, I'd have torn your throat out with my teeth before you could even flick those fins. You're fortunate I haven't ordered the Domhianns to drag you to Abyssal for the sheer audacity of questioning me." Even the ocean seemed to hold its breath, the currents still, as if afraid to intrude on their moment.

The menace was unmistakable in her mother's voice, "However," she continued, "since you are my blood and the only heir we have, I've chosen to spare you. But the next time, it will not end well."

Selsie felt her breath freeze in her chest. Her mother didn't make idle threats. Desperate to avoid further wrath, she began to lower her head, her pride in tatters but her neck still intact.

Just as she turned to swim away, her mother's hand shot out, wrapping around her throat in a vice-like grip. The dominance in her voice was chilling, making Selsie feel like nothing more than a helpless anchovy caught in a predator's snare.

"I owe you no explanation," her mother sneered, squeezing tighter, "but understand this: we are doing this because I said so."

The pod left with the next tide.

4

Jonn

The seagulls were out in vengeance this clear spring morning, flapping in their hundreds. Their shrill cries blended with the rhythmic crescendo of waves crashing against *The Brendann*, docked in port. The ship's enormous silver sails fluttered in the breeze, embroidered emblems glowing in the early sunlight. Oblitus was bathed in an unusual warmth. Jonn raised an eyebrow at the bright sky. Spring on the island was typically wet and miserable, with the sun not making its grand entrance until mid-summer.

"Must be a good omen!" Symon called up from the gangway, his wiry frame busy loading supplies into the cargo hold. Jonn glanced down at his friend's gleaming, shaved head and couldn't believe this was the same damned man he had grown up with. The childhood spent together, chasing girls and helping their ageing adoptive parents with the farms, now seemed hundreds of years ago.

Both of their parents, forbidden from having children of their own, had passed away before Jonn even turned eighteen. Scraped knees from wrestling in the fields had been replaced by rope-burned hands and wicked splinters. And though they had joined *The Brendann* together at the age of eight, twenty years at sea hadn't matured Symon one bit.

A stiff, salty breeze swept a strand of hair into Jonn's face, and he tucked the dark wave back into his topknot. He had meant to cut it months ago during their stopover in Halè, but if he was honest with himself, Jonn had grown to like it-at the behest of

Sy who took the piss out of it every five minutes. And truth be told, the Akoaàns on Halè knew how to fucking party. Haircuts were forgotten the moment the wyne began to flow.

Sounds of the crew bustling on deck were like a familiar hum to Jonn, his hands busy guiding ropes, securing cargo, and inspecting the rigging with his practiced eye. Every detail mattered. The rigid, pre-sail routine had been drilled into him over countless journeys across Myrantis. Striding across the weathered deck, Jonn mentally ticked off his checklist, ensuring the ship was ready for open waters. *Shit,* he thought, there was still so much to do before they set sail that afternoon. They were going to be cutting it damned close.

Jonn made his way toward the captain, who was berating a young deckhand. The boy had apparently failed to scrub the deck to a standard expected of a Saynt ship, and Captain Lane had earned himself a nasty splinter because of it.

"Captain, a word?" Jonn called out, stepping closer.

Without taking his beady eyes off the trembling boy, Captain Lane grumbled, his rotund belly moving up and down. "What is it, Cayson?"

Jonn suppressed a flinch at the formal use of his surname. The tradition of addressing sailors this way was a mainland custom that had never quite fit on Oblitus, where many shared the same last names. Jonn remembered his own confusion when he first joined the crew. Captain Lane was notoriously short-tempered, and no one wanted to be on the receiving end of his fiery anger. Whips left nasty scars and were fuckers to heal.

Not that Jonn would know.

"The last of the cargo is loaded, Captain. If we keep to the schedule-and that's a big 'if'-we can depart with the tide this afternoon."

The captain's eyes stayed fixed on the boy, unblinking in the morning glare. Jonn felt a pang of sympathy for the lad, no older than eight or nine, all bones and matted mousy hair.

"Hm. See that the port master is informed of our intended departure," Captain Lane grunted.

"Yes, sir," Jonn replied. He gave the boy one last glance. The child, head bowed and trembling, clutched an empty bucket with white-knuckled hands. He clearly needed a decent meal, likely an orphan from one of the island's children's homes. It was a harsh reality in their small, isolated world-some years, more Damned children arrived on Oblitus than there were families to take them in. Jonn wondered how many newborns from this pickup would end up in those orphanages. His thoughts were interrupted by the sound of familiar footsteps and a voice shouting from a few meters away.

"Hold on, Jonn!" Sy jogged up to him, grinning. "Wherever you're going, I'm coming."

Jonn didn't slow his pace, heading toward the narrow buildings at the far end of the port. His undone, cream-colored muslin shirt billowed in the wind, which had picked up noticeably.

"Don't you have something more important to be doing, Symon? Your duties, for example?"

"Na, all done," Symon replied, unbothered. "I need one last taste of a woman before we're stuck at sea for gods know how long."

Jonn let out a sigh. "I doubt even your favourite at Annie's will take your money this time."

"Ah yes, Loren," Symon said wistfully.

"They all know you've fucked every woman who will take your money on this island."

"What you on about?"

Jonn turned slightly, nearly laughing at his friend's wide-eyed expression. "Annie bought all the brothels, mate. No more secrets, I'm afraid."

"Shit," Symon hissed.

"Time to settle down, Sy. Find a wife, adopt a Damned kid, maybe buy yourself a farm with the retirement coin…"

"I will-when you do," Symon shot back, grinning.

Sy had him there. Jonn was fully committed to the sea. A wife and kids were not on the cards for him in this life.

"Alright, go if you must," Jonn relented. "But the wind's shifting, and we need to leave by the next tide. Lane's in a particularly shitty mood today, so I can't afford any delays. If you're not back by three, we'll leave without you. Lady Rast won't wait around for us."

A few hours later, Jonn stood anxiously aboard the ship, waiting for his friend. It was well past three, and there was no doubt Captain Lane would sail without him. Abandoning his post would land Symon straight in the damned gaol.

"Fuck it," Jonn muttered, deciding to hunt the prick down himself. But just as he lifted the gate of the gangplank, he spotted Symon stumbling toward the ship, beer bottle in hand, sloshing and spilling all over the port.

Jonn crossed his arms, eyes narrowed. "Where the fuck have you been?" He rarely pulled rank on Symon, but after hours of waiting, it was hard to hold back his frustration.

Symon jogged casually up the gangplank, finishing the last of the bottle before tossing it over his shoulder. "You know me, Jonn. Once I start, I can go for hours," he said with a wink, clearly drunk. Jonn gave him not even a hint of amusement.

"Don't worry, we'll get you a woman someday who'll love every miserable bit of you. Some of them even have a thing for long hair and small cocks," Symon teased.

Jonn turned to walk away. There was no point trying to reason with him when he was this drunk. He loved Sy like a brother, but he could be godsdamned intolerable at times.

"Alright, alright," Symon slurred, stumbling after him. "But listen, I've got something to tell you. You'll wanna hear this, Jonny boy."

Jonn grunted. Oblitus was small and unexciting-a reflection of the people that inhabited it. Resulting in the same four variations of a story, circulating the island time and time again-it bored Jonn to tears. "Let me guess, old watcher Harris was found hanging out the back of the captain's wife again?"

Symon scoffed. "In the captain's *own house* this time. They fuck more than me, and that's saying something."

Those two were frequently caught in compromising positions-a fact not unmissed by the captain. Probably his reasoning for being in a constant foul rage. Last time, they were caught behind one of the fishmongers on the seafront.

Crude comments on the smell were chucked around for days. Jonn shook his head. "I'm sure she'll invite you to join next time we're back. Harris probably doesn't have much left in him."

Symon laughed, trailing after Jonn like a lost puppy as they descended into the belly of the ship. "As tempting as that is, I'll pass. But that aint what I was gonna tell you."

With a large hand, Jonn fished out his cabin keys from the chain clipped to his belt. "What is it, Sy?"

As he unlocked the door to his fair-sized cabin, Jonn nearly tripped into it at Sy's next words. "They've only gone and called an Heir's Rite."

Shit, that *was* interesting, he thought.

He turned to Symon, brow raised. "An Heir's Rite hasn't been called in hundreds of years."

"Would be a laugh to go watch, right?" Symon grinned, poking Jonn in the back as he opened the porthole on the left-hand side of the cabin.

"Too bad we can't," Jonn replied, stepping into his cabin. Only sailors were allowed to leave the soil of Oblitus, and only on official duties.

"I know that" Symon said, clicking his tongue. "But still, would be a crack."

Jonn sat down at his ancient, worn desk, legs spread, and eyed Symon. "If it's even true. Where'd you hear this? One of your brothel wives?" He pushed up the salt-stained sleeves of his shirt, idly picking up one of the charts scattered across his cluttered desk.

He was a master map reader and one of the damned best sailors they had, if Jonn admitted to himself. If it weren't for the fact that captaincy was passed down through family, Jonn knew he'd be leading a crew by now. He had the skills, the knowledge, the respect of his peers and a natural inclination for leadership.

And he quite liked the hat.

Sy continued, "No, it was one of their regulars actually." Picking up a green apple from his desk and taking a bite, Jonn rolled his eyes. "And you believe it, do you?" he said, his voice dripping with scepticism.

Symon perched himself on the desk, his skinny arse flattening the map of Coral Quey. "Yeah, I do, and you will as well when I tell you who the source was." Jonn raised a thick black eyebrow as if to say, *go on*.

"It was the head scholar himself. Father Dafyd," Symon said with dramatic flair, clearly hoping for a bigger reaction than he got. "Chatting away to Annie he was, going on about how Eira has been left with no heir and the King's only option was an Heir's Rite. He said there's been whispers about it being different this year, but who knows. All I know is, he's leaving on the next ship to Eira to represent Oblitus in the upcoming celebrations and political shit in the next month. Says it will be occurring at the end of the summer, even asking Annie to come with him. I'll give him respect for the confidence I'll tell you that." Symon snatched the apple from Jonn's hand, finishing it in a few quick bites.

Jonn scratched at the dark stubble coating his jaw, inclined to believe his drunk friend. Although he was reeling from the revelation that the all-knowing, peaceful leaders of their island had a preference for women of the coin.

"I do believe it, Jonn, the scholars never lie. If they've gone to represent us on the mainland it must be for something important. They wouldn't leave the Library of Souls for a piss up and a bit of cake."

A low grunt left Jonns chest, "To be honest, Sy, I don't give a shit. The only thing I care about is reaching Noran on time and getting the Damned back safely. That's my duty, and that's what I get paid for. The politics of Myrantis mean nothing to me."

Symon narrowed his eyes. "Do you know how boring you are sometimes Jonn?"

A rare smile tugged at the corner of Jonn's lips. "At least I'm consistent."

Symon barked a laugh and shoved his broad shoulder, just as the cabin door burst open. Captain Lane stormed in, hollering, "Get those men to their posts, Cayson. We're ready to sail, and I want this ship on the open ocean in half an hour."

The captain's breath, reeking of rotten teeth and cigar smoke, hit Jonn square in the face as he shot up from his chair to stand at attention. Jonn, towering over the captain, always made an effort to seem smaller in the old man's presence, careful not to offend him with his height.

"Aye, Captain," Jonn replied.

Captain Lane's beady eyes shifted from Jonn to Symon. "Are you drunk, Hedge?"

"No, Captain," Symon replied smoothly.

Bullshit, Jonn thought.

"Well not enough to impact my work sir. Had a little party with some special ladies you see."

Huffing, the captain squared his jaw before turning back through the door. Slamming it shut as he went.

Symon smirked, mimicking a salute behind the captain's back.

"Well, I'm off to pretend I'm doing something useful on deck, whilst doing absolutely fuck all. See you up there, Cayson."

As he watched Symon go, he couldn't help but wonder how his friend got away with so much, including his insolence. Both he and Symon seemed to be exceptions to the captain's ire, though Jonn wouldn't go as far as to say they were treated kindly. The more Jonn thought about it, Sy was a terrible deckhand, frequently getting knots wrong or leaving loose lines laying on deck for men to trip over.

How his oldest friend got the job, Jonn will never know.

5
Selsie

The undercurrents were exceptionally strong, and Selsie struggled to navigate such turbulent waters. The sea surrounding Noran was in a perpetual fury, its churning waves a dull, frothy teal, reflecting the stormy mood of the ocean. At the head of the pod, her mother led them with unrelenting force, her kelp-green tail whipping through the water. For days, they had been driven forward, exhaustion not allowed to slow them, and rest given only in the briefest of moments.

Not a single word had been muttered between herself and her mother since they had left Cildraethe. The fierce determination on her mother's face was enough to warn her not to even try. There was a dangerous glint in the matriarch's eye, like that of a Maolin Shark poised for a kill, and Selsie had no desire to provoke her.

They must be nearing their destination now. Shattered shipwrecks began to litter the seafloor, their broken masts reaching toward the surface like skeletal fingers. Torn hulls, split in two by battles long past, stood as silent witnesses to Laeth conquests. Normally, Selsie would have loved to explore these ghostly remnants of lost ships. She loved the thrill of discovering hidden treasures among the wreckage. Her greatest joys were the necklaces, especially lockets, with their tiny portraits of handsome men and the occasional love letters tucked inside. Those moments of quiet, personal history were what she treasured most.

The writing was always faded but she tried to decipher them anyway, searching for answers to her unspoken questions. Did a love so powerful truly exist that one would feel the need to carry a reminder of it always? Was there a span of time in which living without seeing one's beloved was too unbearable to endure? These were not questions a Laeth like her could answer…

Ahead, the pod came to a halt, and Selsie slowed her fins. She spotted her mother's raised fist, held high in the distance, a signal to the pod.

"I'm going up. Wait for my signal," the matriarch called. They watched in silence as their ruler ascended to the surface, an impressive journey given the depth at which they lingered.

From what Selsie knew, if *The Brendann* was nearby, the Laeths would use their magic to conjure a thick, disorienting fog, blinding the sailors. This would allow the pod to approach unnoticed, increasing the likelihood of a successful attack. Yet, something still felt off. This was a Saynt ship, crewed by the barest of men, with far too few humans for the number of syrens in their group.

The thought of attacking a ship filled with newborns caused a maelstrom of nausea in her stomach. She was no stranger to death and had never felt any pity for humans, but now a strange unease gnawed at her. It felt…unnecessary. They were Laeths, capable of downing a fully manned naval ship without hesitation, their reputation already cemented as ruthless killers. This, however, felt wrong.

But it wasn't her place to question her mother again. She could not risk undermining the matriarch's authority, not now. Selsie was forced to go along with the plan. She was helpless against the whims of her mother, and it was not yet her decision or authority to lead this pod.

Soon, the signal was given from above. At the front of the pod, five newlings smirked as they released a thick white liquid from their fingertips. The magic spilled out of them, rising toward the surface and no doubt spreading in a dense fog.

Why her mother did not ask her to do this, she was unsure. When the newlings stopped their flow of magic, the matriarch descended once more, rejoining the pod as they prepared for what came next.

"It is time. You five shall be the first to make a kill and surface. Myself, Neesh and you-" she said, pointing to one of her male guards, "-will go up and begin the attack. As soon as you five have made your first kill, you may go up and sing first song, then the rest of you may follow," the matriarch instructed, her cold, steely eyes locking onto Selsie's. "Selsie, you are to follow me and wait just below the surface for my return."

"Yes, Mother," Selsie said and bowed her head, her golden tail swishing in long, deliberate strokes. As she followed her mother to the surface, she drew on her courage.

"Mother, may I ask a question?"

Her mother's tail continued its steady push, and Selsie took her silence as consent.

"I do not understand what we gain from this endeavour."

Her mother's voice was flat, as though she were speaking to a particularly tiresome child. "Get on with it, Selsie. We do not have all tide."

"*The Brendann* will not have enough men to feed us all."

Without a flicker of emotion, the matriarch reached the surface and replied, "There are not only men aboard."

A torrent of dread surged through Selsie as she replayed her mother's words in her mind, grasping their meaning.

"Mother, consuming children is not our way. We kill for survival, not for cruelty."

She knew that by attacking this ship the infants would be unfortunate casualties, and she was fully prepared to try her best and discreetly save each one, if her instincts allowed.

Though the revelation was chilling, it was not entirely surprising. It only confirmed what she had sensed about her mother's capabilities, and what the sea had been whispering to her for years.

Her mother was different.

As Neesh, along with the matriarch and a large male guard, ascended to the surface, Selsie caught a sympathetic glance from her friend, who had overheard their one-sided exchange. Under the water, a heavy silence settled in their absence, broken only by the curious eyes of fish and other sea creatures observing them with wary interest.

Laeths were not as one with the sea creatures as the Akoaàns were.

With a promise of violence in their eyes, the others in her pod matched the silence. She imagined that, like her, they could not wait to breach the waves. Even as her soul writhed with uneasiness, her fingertips were twitching with anticipation, her tongue salivating for the taste of a man.

The muffled sounds of human shouting sent the pod into a melody of tentative voices. Then came the screaming, breaking them into a feverish harmony.

The syrens below her began whooping, their voices overlapping in a chaotic symphony. Driven by bloodlust, some swam urgently toward the surface.

Selsie hissed at one of them. "No! Wait here for my mother's signal!" The blood-driven syren bared her teeth but complied. Selsie may not have the total respect of her pod or kingdom just yet, but she was still the matriarch's daughter, which meant she had the power in the female's absence.

A sudden splash drew Selsie's attention to her mother and Neesh, who had returned to the water in their Other forms. Dug deep into soft flesh, sharp claws penetrated the shoulders of four men. Neesh and her mother each held a man in one hand, dragging them underwater. The men's frantic eye movements revealed they were still alive-but not for long, Selsie surmised.

Her mother signalled to the male guard, who had re-entered the water moments later. Crossing his hands in front of his face twice, he gave the signal to attack. Without hesitation, the five syrens who had been waiting sprang into action, fighting over the four men. One syren, clearly weaker than the others, was pushed out of the fray and swam a few feet away, seething with anger. The remaining four transformed into their Other forms and tore into the men.

The males went straight for the throats, dispatching their victims swiftly. The females, however, embraced a more brutal violence. Blood stained the churning sea crimson as their wickedly sharp teeth shredded faces, while bellies were torn and punctured by those hell carved claws. Four humans were transformed into flotsam and jetsam in a matter of seconds-by Alysee, it was a thing to witness.

Now full of human meat and fully transformed back into their Laeth form, one by one the group of syrens began making their way up to the surface.

Selsie had never heard a first song before and she was excited to hear them sing before they could partake in furthering the attack and get the next victims, for the rest of the syrens waiting down below.

From across the depths, she could feel her mother's eyes upon her, Selsie stared right back.

"Your turn," her mother's gnarled, pointed finger directed at Selsie alone.

All around Selsie, the pod was making their first kills. By Alysee she hoped there were enough men to satiate them all.

In a blur of bubbles, blood and fins, a man with mousy hair and big brown eyes wild with fear was in her mother's claws. His face-too old for the dreams of youth, yet too young to have seen the possibilities of life-was thrust before Selsie.

He looked no older than she would be in human years.
The raw scent of blood ignited a primal hunger within her
Other form, stirring a bubbling intensity that demanded release.
Embracing the transformation without hesitation, Selsie
surrendered to her Laeth nature. As the heir and a syren, this
was her destiny.
Her toasted honey skin shifted to a sickly gray, lethally sharp
claws pulled through her short nails, and she knew her face now
looked like a demon from the deep. A reflection of what she
now was. The transformation was swift, and as her senses
adapted to the ocean's embrace, she was momentarily
disoriented by the tunnel vision that accompanied her new
form. She remained herself, yet altered, like the sea under a
starless night.
Taking one look at the man brought before her, it took Selsie
less than a heartbeat to decide she did not need to make this
man suffer any more than he already was. The terror etched on
his face assured her that she would taste the essence of fear in
his blood. That was enough to satiate her body's intrinsic
craving.
Feeling her mother's presence beside her, Selsie couldn't delay
any longer. Without hesitation or thought, she slashed a sharp
claw across the man's throat in a single, fluid motion. Blood
flowed from the wound, mingling with the dancing currents
around her.
As she inhaled a drop of his blood, a subtle change rippled
through her, not remarkable but enough to make her shiver.
Though tradition demanded she consume the man's flesh, her
overwhelming desire to breach the surface eclipsed her
appetite. Her longing to escape the depths was far greater.
Turning her gaze to her mother, Selsie saw no hint of emotion
as the man sank beneath them. As the guards began to devour
his body, she turned away.

The matriarch's voice broke through the underwater silence. "You need to sing, Selsie. Change back. We're going up." She did not need to be told twice.

6

Aura

Anger was not an emotion Aura was used to, though after what happened yesterday with her sister, it bubbled underneath the surface. She felt betrayed, hurt that her mother and sister had hidden the truth about her past. Did they think she was too fragile to handle it? The idea that they saw her as weak only deepened her fury. She understood why they kept Keyara's true power a secret, but they had no right to withhold her own story from her.

Keyara had tried to make light of the situation last night, but Aura couldn't shake the fear for her sister's safety in the upcoming Heir's Rite. It was dangerous-Keyara could get hurt, or worse, killed by the calibre of competitors.

Strolling beside the Aetha River that flowed quietly through their sleepy village, the three of them walked home from the greengrocers in town. Under a blanket of clouds, her mother and Keyara chatted away.

Aura, however, remained silent. The tension between them was palpable, and while she was still angry, she hated the rift between them. Her power was feeding off the negative energy, causing a roiling, sickly feeling to take over her stomach.

It was late Monday afternoon and they had bought what little groceries they could afford. Her family could desperately do with growing their own food, all of them no stranger to the scratching and gnawing of hunger.

She had tried to grow vegetables and herbs once, to stave off starvation from a particularly feeble harvest one year. It was to no avail-the whole lot had withered and died. Aura suspected the poor saplings were innocent victims of her desperation and anger, absorbing the emotions through her magic, subsequently failing to grow.

Creating life through her hands had always ended the same way, so she gave up, letting the garden go wild, picking only what naturally grew.

Her power, for all its uniqueness, came with flaws. Like Keyara's constant chill, Aura was always weighed down by an undercurrent of sadness. The gift she could give to others, always stole a little of her own spark, her own joy. Her darkness to bear.

No one ever knew how she felt, though. She kept a smile on her face, never complained, never let her mother or sister know that sometimes, she felt like flinging herself into the icy sea-despite her fear of it.

As their cottage came into view, Aura spotted the lone apple tree in their garden. Its branches were not yet heavy with autumn's fruit, but the thought of its sweet, tart apples made her mouth water. Walking ahead, she opened the creaky door for her family, wincing at the groan. Aura feared it might fall apart one day-like everything else they owned. Broken, old, and disintegrating seemed to be the theme of her life.

Her mother brushed past her. "I'll get supper started, girls." If she noticed the tension between Aura and Keyara, she didn't show it.

"Can we talk?" Keyara whispered. Aura hesitated, then nodded, gesturing for her sister to follow her outside. They made their way to the edge of the garden, near the bubbling river.

Crossing her legs underneath her, Aura sat on the plush grass underneath a willow tree, Keyara joined her, stretching her legs out in front of her. They sat in silence for a few moments, the soft sounds of the river and birds filling the air. Aura absentmindedly twirled a daisy between her fingers.

Keyara finally spoke. "Aura, I know you're upset, but you don't have to ignore me. I thought I was protecting you by not telling you. What difference would it have made? It would've just made you worry all these years, wondering if I'd be called upon one day."

Aura faced her sister, "I had a right to know the truth Keyara, this isn't just about you."

Those hazel eyes looked away, Aura knew her sister wouldn't keep it from her if she didn't think it was for the best, but that did not take away the betrayal she felt at being kept in the dark about her own history, and the potential danger her sister could one day face. A day that had now come to fruition.

"Fuck, I know that, Aura. But it wasn't just my choice. It was Mother's too. She tried to keep the truth of who I was from everyone-not just you. I'm sorry I didn't tell you everything sooner."

Aura would have fallen in the river if she was on two feet. Her sister rarely said sorry to anyone-her stubbornness and pride always prevented her. Aura would have been less shocked if a giant Skuidd swum past them.

"I'm worried, Keyara. I don't think you've fully thought this through," Aura said, her voice heavy with concern. "The competitors you'll be facing-they're the most powerful in all of Eira, and they have far more experience than you. I don't doubt that you believe you can do this, but I think you're overestimating yourself. Berran can only teach you so much, and even he doesn't know what the challenges will be. These people are fighting for the throne-for the right to rule. They've spent their entire lives preparing for this: noblemen, warriors, people who have been trained for years. And you? You're just a woman from Eldorhaven with a bit more power behind her magic than most."

Hurt swept over Keyara's sharp face. *Maybe that was a bit harsh,* Aura thought, regretting her choice of words. But it was the truth.

Keyara shot up from where they were sitting, towering over Aura. "Thank you for having such confidence in me Aura. That will most certainly help me win the Rite. Or maybe not, and I will get eliminated, or even killed, in the first challenge, being so fucking weak and all."

Aura's mouth opened and closed, words failing her as she tried to backtrack, to fix what she'd said. But before she could respond, Keyara turned on her heel and stormed away, leaving Aura sitting in stunned silence beside the chattering river

7

Aura

Gregory's Tavern was always packed with thirsty patrons, eager for cheap honey mead and Akoaàn wyne.

It was late evening, and the warm glow of candlelight bathed the tavern's thick oak walls, illuminating the intricate carvings of dolphins, whales, and other sea creatures that decorated the space. Aura knew exactly where to find her sister after their heated exchange by the river. She just hoped it wouldn't involve searching through all three levels of the bustling tavern. Having grown to like the taste of honey mead and the way it made her feel, Aura liked to come here now and again. Dancing on a belly full of alcohol to the enchanted instruments that played on the lowest floor, the lilting music permeating every inch of the place through some magic. Akoaàn ancestors could often be heard singing along, their ethereal voices retelling tales of old wars, drawing the patrons into their haunting melody.

Pushing her way through the boisterous crowd, Aura ducked under the low wooden beams and winced at the noise coming from behind the bar.

"Come on then, you prick!" There was no mistaking Keyara's husky voice.

Aura weaved through the mass of bodies, earning herself a few trodden toes, a dress stained with spilt alcohol and gods knows what else. By the time she reached her sister, she was met with an unexpected sight-a full-blown brawl.

Keyara, blood trickling from her nose, was squaring off against a fae male. His presence seemed out of place in the rowdy tavern, with his pointed ears and effortless grace. He must be here from the fort at One Bridge crossing. Though what he was doing here she had no idea. They were months away from market day on Athvar, and no one would need a fae escort to the mythical land until the new year.

"Keyara, what are you doing?" Aura yelled through the rabble, her voice barely carrying over the din. Her sister, blood smeared across her pale hand, had a look of pure determination etched across her face as she glared at the fae.

There was no lingering smell of cinnamon in the air, indicating the fae had not used any magic against her. The place had not melted to the ground yet either and Aura could see no scorch marks, so Keyara was holding her power in check. This was going to be a fistfight, plain and simple. Not a good idea when fae could reach impossible speeds, and their strength rivalled that of the vampyres.

"You're not going to win this fight, girl," the fae male said, his voice smooth but laced with amusement. "Walk away now, and I'll leave you with only a broken nose."

All eyes were turned toward her sister. Keyara's response was a sneer. "Not going to happen, shithead." She threw a right hook, narrowly missing his face as he easily sidestepped the punch. With a feral grin, the fae squared up. "Okay, bitch. Let's go." The crowd roared in excitement as the fight escalated, the two circling each other like predators. Keyara swung again and again, her punches landing on nothing but air. The fae moved with fluid grace, his speed far beyond anything Keyara could match. Each of his strikes hit its mark, the sharp sound of his fists meeting her cheekbone ringing out like a series of thunderclaps.

Aura winced at each blow-the realisation that he was holding back the overwhelming majority of his strength unnerved her. Leaning against a column by the bar, Aura watched helplessly as Keyara stubbornly refused to back down, her punches wild but with purpose. Though she managed to land a couple of solid hits, leaving the fae momentarily stunned, it was clear that he had the upper hand. The jeers and cheers from the crowd grew louder with each passing second.

As fatigue crept into Keyara's movements, Aura couldn't take it anymore. The realisation that Keyara was going to hit the deck soon, hard.

Shuffling forward to jump in between them, she was stopped in her tracks by the scent of fresh fallen rain and green moss filling the air around her.

"Twenty gold coins on her losing," a deep voice murmured from her left. Aura turned to see a tall, fair-haired male leaning against the bar. Facing the fight in front of them, with a jug of honey mead in one hand and the other propped up next to him, he wasn't looking at her.

His long, pointed ears and the conceited tone of his voice immediately marked him as another fae.

"Twenty gold coins on her winning," Aura heard herself reply, her voice filled with conviction. She didn't have a single coin to her name, but in that moment, she needed to believe in her sister.

Deep brown eyes finally turned to look at her, travelling slowly from her shoeless feet up to her eyes. The scent of rain and moss bloomed around her when he shifted closer to her, so close that their bodies were inches from one another. "It's a bet," he said with a smirk.

A fae had never been so up close to her before and Aura was slightly taken aback. They rarely came to Eldorhaven, and she had never been among those selected to visit the elusive market in his home kingdom.

"She won't give up, you know. She hates losing more than anything."

The fae's smirk deepened, but he didn't respond, his gaze returning to the fight. Aura watched, heart pounding, hoping

Keyara's sheer stubbornness would somehow carry her through.

He took a swig from his jug, leaning even closer into Aura's space. "Hmm, fair enough, but so does he," he said, nodding toward his companion.

She looked away from the male and back to her sister -just in time to see Keyara staring at them both. In that split second of distraction, the fae male landed a punch so hard it sent Keyara flying backward in a tumble of dark hair and blood. She crashed to the floor, the tavern erupting into a mix of gasps and applause.

The victory was undeniable.

"Shit," Aura muttered under her breath as she rushed over to her sister's sprawled figure on the floor. Brown eyes continued staring into her back-the feel of them on her was like the sun on a warm day.

"Keyara, are you alright? Can you get up?" Aura asked, crouching beside her.

With a groan, Keyara managed to sit up. "Fuck me, that hurt," she muttered. The crowd had already lost interest, turning back to their drinks and card games. Aura held out a hand, pulling Keyara up as she grasped her outstretched palm.

Once she was upright, Aura searched for something to clean her sister's now-broken nose, noticing bruises beginning to bloom, like the wildflowers outside their home, across her face.

A young waitress handed Aura a rag, and she couldn't help but smile slightly as she passed the tattered cloth to her sister. The filthy thing looked like it might give Keyara an infection, but it was better than nothing.

"As much as I hate to admit it, Keyara, you held your own against him," Keyara's eyebrows shot up in surprise, the rag pressed against her nose. Aura guessed she was too bruised and breathless to respond.

"Not that I'm saying you should go out and do it again," Aura continued, "but the fact that you lasted that long against a fae male? Without magic? That's impressive."

Placing a gentle hand at the small of her sister's back, Aura led them to a quiet corner of the tavern.

Once they were seated, she asked Keyara. "I don't think it's me that needs to worry over you in the Rite. The other entrants won't know what's hit them once you're in there. What did that male even do? He must've really pissed you off."

Removing the rag, Keyara's voice came out in a nasally grumble, her nasal passages clogged with blood. "Thanks, but honestly, I was just in the mood for a fight and he happened to irritate me."

Aura cocked her head, "Why what happened?"

"Nothing. His pretty face annoyed me."

They both chuckled quietly, not wanting to attract attention in case the fae overheard and decided to start round two.

Keyara tossed the rag onto the table, then glanced over toward the bar. "Who was that, the one talking to you? He wasn't rude, was he?"

Aura realized she didn't even know his name. "I don't know. He didn't say." She decided to leave it at that-Keyara didn't need to know they'd bet on her.

With Keyara's glass of wyne finished in a record three sips, to *'take away the sting'*, they decided to leave. Thankfully, there was no sign of the fae males, which Aura took as a good thing. "I don't have any money to pay for this, Keyara."

"It's fine, I'll put it on my tab."

"You have a tab? How much is on there? "Aura asked, anxiety beginning to curl inside her.

Keyara half-smiled. "A lot. But Cal's working tonight, and he hasn't taken his eyes off you. I'm sure he will let me off, especially if I say you want another night alone" she said, walking unsteadily in the direction of the bar.

Aura shook her head, calling after her. "Not a chance." She wasn't the slightest bit interested in Cal. Sure, they'd shared a nice evening once, and Aura appreciated his kindness, but that was it-they were just friends. She'd have to insist they repay the tab some other way, maybe by offering to clean the tavern, in repayment for the tab Keyara had recklessly run up.

"Someone already paid it."

Aura blinked as Keyara returned. "What? Who?"

"They didn't say, just that someone with too much money covered the whole tab and left these as, in their words, *a consolation prize*." A few gold coins clattered on the table towards her, thrown from Keyara's hand. The money clattered down, and Aura stared at it. This could really help them, at least for a little while.

A suspicion of who that someone was tugged at the back of her mind, but she said nothing.

"A fixed roof better be worth the black eye I'm going to wake up with tomorrow."

Huffing a laugh as she got up, Aura linked her arm with Keyara's as she handed the money back for her to pocket.

"Come on, let's go. Mother's probably wondering where we've been all night. You know she'll blame you for being a bad influence on me."

Keyara feigned innocence. "Excuse me, but it was you who kept us out for two days during the last winter festival."

She forgot about that.

As they stepped out of the stuffy tavern air, they nearly tripped over an enormous dog. The animal had long white fur with black markings on its head and lifted its dark brown eyes to them. It was alert, sniffing the air, its enormous paws sprawled out on the dusty ground. The creature had such an otherworldly presence that a few people nearby were staring, some pointing and calling it a wolf.

Keyara noticed and proclaimed loudly that people were idiots. "Wolves only live in Derryn. Get a grip, it's just a puppy." Though Aura had never seen a *puppy* quite like that before. Stumbling along the cobblestone streets, giggling like little girls, they made their way home. Once inside their ramshackle cottage, they quietly sneaked upstairs and slipped into their cramped beds, their whispered drunken laughter filling the still air.

"Goodnight, Aura."

"Sweet dreams, Kiki-cat."

8

Jonn

A few days had passed since their arrival on the heavy, mist-laden shores of Noran, and it was time to depart with the tide. A familiar sadness tugged at Jonn. He never wanted to depart from this place that, deep in his bones, felt like home. He loved the brash, take-no-shit attitude of its people; it resonated with him deeply.

That said, Noran was undeniably a mess-a complete shithole. Derelict houses lined every narrow, winding avenue of the city, which clung precariously to the cliff tops and sprawled out like mould into the boggy Derryn landscape beyond. The first time he had wandered along the moss lined streets with Sy, his best friend had suggested that Jonn was without doubt, from this place. Honestly, he couldn't disagree. Details of the Damned were never shared with adoptive families, so his origins were a mystery.

But as a few feral orphans darted between them-on legs no thicker than broom handles-Jonn was inclined to agree. Their dark hair and taller stature were reminiscent of his own haggard appearance as a child.

The children threw their magic at each other, laughing at the muttered curses of people dodging to get out of the way.

The Kingdom of Derryn as a whole was poor, relying mostly on trade with the Reothadh who swam upriver and its dwindling fishing industry. A terrible outcome of the King Harolld's ruling choices. How he had let his kingdom get into such a state of poverty was a travesty.

A fair and progressive ruler would make sure orphans were a thing of the past. In no world would Jonn let children go without food in their bellies, destined for a future belied by the harshness of life, shackled to the streets.

Yet here, orphans were a common sight. The King's open hatred of other species made trade with other nations nearly impossible, leaving Derryn isolated, vulnerable, and poor.

The Lost Kingdom people called this land, which Jonn thought fit well.

As their ship pulled away from the sorry excuse for a port, the cries of newborns from below deck summoned Jonn from his thoughts. Sy was already complaining. "It is too early in the day to be crying already" he said, rubbing at his temples.

"They're babies, Sy. I don't think they care what time it is," Jonn replied, checking the rigging lines as Sy continued to whine.

"You'd think the Mother's Maids would keep them quiet. Shove a tit into their mouths or something." Jonn ignored his friend's crassness. He was too busy to listen to Symon's bullshit today.

"Bit foggy as well for this time of year aint it?" He heard Symon say to the captain.

"You will address me as 'Captain' boy," Lane snapped.

Still, Sy wasn't wrong. While thick fog was common in the passage away from Noran, something about it felt off today. A fleeting anxiety gripped Jonn as he looked back at the crumbling city, now hidden completely by the blanket of grey mist that covered *The Brendann.*

There was no real danger of a Laeth attack-the ship's silver sails and the enchanted emblem, a golden seal of a shipwreck, offered protection from the creatures they feared most. But the oppressive fog gnawed at his nerves.

For reassurance, he took a glimpse at the shimmering cloth.

Releasing a sigh, Jonn made his way below deck to the infants' quarters. The ship would sail fine without him for a few minutes.

Like the womb in which they recently departed, it was warm and inviting down here. Glancing around he could see all the bassinets were full. They had more Damned than usual from Derryn this year, eleven in total. The average for any given year was only around four or five.

Jonn reached into a basket, where a small hand gripped his calloused fingers. The baby's blue eyes stared up at him, wide and curious.

"Can I help you, sir?" one of the Mother's Maids asked, cradling a sleeping infant.

Pulling his hand free of the grip of the babe, Jonn spoke softly. "No, no you can't, I was just making sure you were all settled in and comfortable down here." He placed his hands behind his back.

Before she could respond, Symon burst into the room, his eyes wild. "Syrens, Jonn! They're attacking the ship!"

The world around them lived and died in the silence that preceded the Mother's Maid's scream, her wail awakening the slumbering infant in her shaking arms. Panic swept through the room as the others scrambled to gather the children, fear uncontained.

Hate for the creatures that killed his baby sister burnt inside Jonn's chest. Years of murderous dreams had haunted him, calling him to the syrens whose songs were transcending reality.

With a moment's hesitation, Jonn narrowed his focus, letting the hate consume him.

"Get these women and children to safety-now!"

Symon nodded and brushed past Jonn, giving instructions to the women and picking up the Damned as he went.

Jonn's boots thudded heavily against the stairs as he sprinted back on deck, the cries of the newborns echoing in his ears, driving him forward. As he ascended, the clamour grew louder with each step.

Flinging open the door to the deck, Jonn was met with utter chaos. Not that he could see much-thick fog coiled around the ship, obscuring everything. But the sounds were unmistakable: the haunting melodies of syrens.

Men were stumbling toward the sea, completely entranced by the phantom songs, helpless against the magic invading their minds.

What chance did those men have? Jonn thought grimly. *The Brendann* wasn't equipped for this. No catapults, no crossbows loaded with poisoned bolts-nothing to defend them. Deterrents that all other vessels had upon them.

They were completely fucked.

Amidst the pandemonium, Jonn spotted the ship's young orange-haired navigator, already caught in the lure of an older syren. She was close, her grey hair glistening with hundreds of trinkets, a terrible power radiating from her.

With his heart racing, he sprinted over to the man, going as fast as he could through the fray.

"Move!" he shouted, shoving men aside as they hurled whatever they could into the water.

Lurching forward, Jonn attempted to grab the navigator by the collar of his shirt with all his strength, but by the time he reached him, it was too late.

With hundreds, if not thousands, of shining trinkets in her grey hair, a terrible, haunting power rolled off her. A shiver flooded through Jonn as the Laeth looked at him with steely malice, a menacing smile plastered on her sharp face.

Shit, he was too late.

"No!" Jonn shouted as the syren's strength outweighed his own. The young man went tumbling into the frothing sea below, a lover's grin still imprinted on a mouth that would soon be filled with ocean water.

"Fuck!" Jonn cursed, his eyes scanning the waves as the fog lifted slightly.

He could still see the fiery glow of the navigator's hair just beneath the surface. There was no way in hell he'd let this man die. Desperately, he searched for something-anything-he could use as a weapon.

His eyes landed on a pickaxe-like tool near a broken deck board, one side sharp and pointed, the other flat and heavy. Heavy and lethal-good enough for a weapon, Jonn decided, flipping it in his hand. It was designed for hammering nails into the ship's planks, but it would do.

Grabbing the tool, Jonn ran back to the rail, searching the waves for any sign of the navigator. But the man was gone. Disappeared under the waves to meet a certain, agonising death.

Just then, Symon appeared, his face pale. "Jonn, I've hidden the Mother's Maids and the babies in the storage hold. Told them to sing as loud as they can to drown out the syrens. But what the hell are we supposed to do? If we die, they'll come for them next."

Jonn didn't need Symon to spell out the fate awaiting the women and children.

"You go down there with them, Sy. Take this." He gave Symon the tool without a second thought, locking eyes with him.

"Those syrens will not hesitate to kill you and them, Sy, so don't think twice about doing the same. And for god's sake, don't listen to your cock this time."

Despite the grim situation, Symon cracked a laugh before disappearing below deck.

Jonn, meanwhile, grabbed another tool and hiked his way up to the helm, searching for Captain Lane. Glancing around, he saw their numbers dwindling fast.

Shit, he uttered aloud. No sign of their leader.

An attack this swift meant only one thing: these syrens were using the First Songs, the most ancient and powerful of their melodies. Normally, men had some resistance to Laeths, but today, they were falling like moths to a flame.

Tossing the tool in between his palms, Jonn nearly impaled a man as he pulled him back from diving overboard, straight towards the old syren who took his shipmate. She rose from the waves in a show of power and water, a look of recognition flashed upon her face as she gazed at Jonn. His breath caught, he knew she would sing at any moment and surely dispatch of him.

Not today you witch he thought, throwing the weapon overarm as hard as he could at her head. It whistled as it went through the air before it slammed into the syren.

But she was too quick, diving out of the way before it killed her. Though from the burst of slightly translucent blood that had spurted from her head and shoulders, it had hit.

Her scream pierced the air, freezing everyone-human and Laeth alike-for a moment.

He wanted to take the moment to get away, but once more, fate had other plans. Before he had a chance to leave the rail, something caught his eye.

A syren, different from the others, emerged from the water. Her piercing emerald eyes locked onto him, and he froze. Her dark, golden-brown hair gleamed in the dim light, her skin a radiant golden tan with the iridescent shimmer unique to her kind. She was breathtaking, more beautiful than anything Jonn had ever seen in his damned years.

He couldn't move.

His mind screamed at him to run, but his body wouldn't obey. Gravity itself seemed to anchor him to his spot against the rail. The whispers started then, quiet and seductive, not one voice, but many, weaving through his thoughts.

Was this the syren song? Was this the beautiful end he'd been destined for?

The older syren had returned, and Jonn could hear her shouting in their language at the other, spindly fingers pointing straight at Jonn. If he was not mistaken, he could have sworn the syren with the piercing green eyes hesitated for a split second, her eyes darting around the ship before she opened her mouth and started to sing.

Her song was unlike anything Jonn had ever heard-full of promises, desire, and love. The whispers retreated, only leaving her wordless voice behind to lift and lower in a unique melody, the crystal-clear notes perfectly balanced. But the song was not enchanting and something was off-Jonn did not feel the magic trying to pull him in. The whispers and music had not been the song of his destiny. As her voice seemed to transcend the air, Jonn realized something.

The song wasn't working.

Bewildered, his eyes swivelled around, taking in the sight of the ship. It was nearly empty, save for the boy hiding behind the mast, hands clamped over his ears. He looked godsdamned helpless as he sat against the chalk white of the beam.

Jonn slowly met the piercing eyes of the syren, who was deep into her song, and he laughed. Not from humour, but from relief and a revelation he could not quite believe.

"It doesn't work," he said to no one in particular.

He would have continued laughing if a crashing, blinding pain didn't explode in his side, sending him flying over the railing. Oblivion welcomed him into the arms of the waiting creatures below.

9

Berran

Amidst the swirl of expensive gowns and the clinking of wyne-filled crystal glasses, Berran was deep in conversation with Mileya, whose wit-as always-matched his own.

Her jet-black skin, smooth and silky, shimmered with the iridescence of her Domhiann heritage, shifting like liquid in the candlelight. She looked damned pretty tonight, and if Berran saw her as anything more than his best friend, he would have married her. Her long, pin-straight hair, as black as her skin, hung loose and free of any restraint or adornments. The briny, citrus scent of her was strong in his nose.

Their conversation flowed like a river, as they discussed their lives above the waves. "Tell me, Berran," Mileya inquired, a teasing tone in her thick accent, "how is your sister faring? Still fucking your father's guard, or have her standards improved?" Those giant pitch eyes were darting around, as though they could see.

Berran chuckled, a fond smile tugging at his lips. "Oh, she's still with him. Word is he's going to propose any day now-head over fins, that one. Keeps bringing her the rarest furs every week."

Her deceivingly slender arms crossed over the front of her tight, deep-blue gown, the fabric skimmed down her tall lithe body, ending in a puddle at the bottom of her feet like an oil spill. Berran couldn't help but notice the other men and males in the room were admiring Mileya in that gown as much as he was.

"Your father must be overjoyed that his daughter is sleeping with a guard," she said, dripping with sarcasm. "I'm sure he's rejoicing at the thought of that union."

Sipping his wyne, Berran huffed a laugh. "My father has more important things to worry about."

She snorted. "Of course he does."

Berran raised a white eyebrow. "You don't think the King of Silvanh has better things to do than worry about his daughter?" His tone carried a playful disbelief, though he knew how much his father cared over his youngest child. Cass was the apple of their father's icy eye, commanding their father's kingly ear from the moment she first sat on his lap in the Silvanh throne room.

Mileya sniffed the air, her heightened Domhiann senses always alert. "I hate this place."

His hands wove through his snow-white hair, scratching at his scalp. "You hate everywhere that isn't the depths of Maya."

"That is true."

"Why the Domhianns chose you to be their emissary on land, I'll never know." He nudged her elbow with his own, grateful to see her after so long. He had not left Eldorhaven in months- his post with his warriors there had been a long one, and Berran was relieved to finally have a break.

Months ago, his summoning to the capital had arrived. As the Reothadh representative and heir to the Silvanh throne, he'd come as soon as he could. Emissaries from every kingdom and province were gathering for the ball, celebrating the announcement of the Heir's Rite.

Not that Berran was complaining. A few weeks of drinking, partying, and bedding sounded godsdamned great.

Yet a pang of guilt twisted in his chest. He regretted not telling Keyara about the Rite when the letter first arrived. But things had moved too quickly, and he hadn't had the chance. If he was being honest, he was still in shock. He had trained Keyara for years, keeping the magnitude of her power a secret. But now that the possibility of her competing was real, he didn't know how to feel.

Berran had to admit, he did feel uneasy about his disappearing act. He loved Keyara and her sister like his own, looking out for them as best he could. After all, he was the one who saved Aura's life when she was just a newborn. He would one day tell her the truth of what exactly happened that stormy night-if she didn't know already.

As the conversation shifted naturally between him and Mileya, it turned toward more serious matters. Her curiosity led them into discussions of politics, currents far beyond the palace's walls. They spoke of the shifting alliances among the syren species and the turbulent tides of their underwater society.

"How many drinks will it take before you tell me what's really on your mind, Berran?" Mileya asked, her voice low and knowing. "I can smell you're hiding something from me, and don't insult me by pretending otherwise."

Damn her Domhiann senses. Mileya supposedly had not been gifted with the power to read minds like some of her kind, but she could read him so well that sometimes he questioned whether it was in fact a ruse.

"I've heard some dangerous rumours on my way here from Eldorhaven, and if they're true..." He glanced around, frosty blue eyes scanning the room, making sure no one was listening in. Berran lowered his voice. "Damned Laeths took down a ship off the coast of Noran. Barely any survivors."

Mileya cut in, unimpressed. "So? That's what they do. I don't waste sympathy on humans that are stupid enough to sail into Laeth waters. Even if the rest of my kind do."

Shaking his head, Berran's white hair came loose from its frozen style.

"That's not it, Mileya. If these rumours are true…" He paused, taking a deep breath. "It was *The Brendann*."

Mileya froze mid-sip, her entire body going unnaturally still. The Domhiann were unworldly even at the best of times, but when they stilled like this, it was like gazing upon a carving from something not of this realm.

"Who told you this?" Mileya asked, finishing her wyne in one swift gulp and handing the empty glass to a passing servant.

"No one. I overheard it from a few humans sailing up the Aetha on my way here."

She barked a laugh. "You're listening to human rumours now, Berran? How unlike you. No, wait-come to think of it, it's exactly like you." She teased, but Berran ignored her jesting.

"We mustn't speak of this again, Mileya. Not a word to anyone."

"Trust me, I will not. All my respect as a syren would cease to exist if anyone found out I was speaking of such human *chatter.*"

That caused Berran to smirk. "Shut up and drink your Mycillium. I think your fins are starting to show."

He knew it would be time to drink his own dose of the stuff soon. It had been a few days, and that familiar dry, tightening feeling was creeping in. The thought of the horrendous concoction nearly made him gag. He prayed the alchemists in Valhir would someday figure out how to make it taste like anything other than filth. Chugging another glass of wyne to erase the memory of its flavour, he watched as Mileya downed hers. Being a Domhiann who mostly lived out of the water, she needed to drink it twice a day or risk death-unless, of course, she made contact with the sea, where she would shift back into her syren form.

As the evening wore on, the melodic tones of Akoaàn voices drifted toward them. A group of them approached, dressed in bright tunics with gemstone buttons that ran down the right side of their garments, matching the vibrant jewel tones of their hair.

The females, voluptuous and effortlessly radiant, had sunny dispositions that seemed effortless.

Among them, Berran recognized Nahese, his purple hair bright and his orange eyes sparkling with an almost predatory gleam. The fruity, overpowering scent of him stung Berran's throat.

"Berran Winfell of the Silvanh clan," Nahese said, his tone cool and measured. "How delightful to meet again. And always a pleasure to see you too, Mileyakhan."

Mileya barely acknowledged Nahese, her disdain for him apparent but never explained to Berran. Nevertheless, he was enjoying her cold response. Nahese was crass, power-hungry, and, truth be told, a bit of a dick.

Nahese kept his gaze on Mileya as he spoke to Berran. "It's a long swim from Silvanh, isn't it? You must be exhausted."

"Not me, Nahese. Barely dulled a scale." Berran's spine stiffened slightly, his gaze unyielding. There was no need to tell him he had come from Eldorhaven, not his home.

"Of course," Nahese said, his tone laced with false humility. "The Reothadh heir is the strongest among us syrens. We lowly Akoaàns could never compare to the mighty warriors. Though, I notice…" he added with a theatrical glance around, "…they aren't here with you?"

Berran clenched his jaw. "They stayed behind. My father didn't permit them to leave their posts. We can't all live lives of frivolity, Nahese."

Nahese raised a hand in mock surrender. "Ah, you're right, of course. Speaking of which, will you be joining us for cards later this evening, Berran? It would be an honour to play with you again, given your many...*superior* talents."

"Yes, he will." Berran was surprised to hear Mileyas strong voice from his side.

Nahese smiled broadly. "Fantastic," he nodded, exchanging smug glances with his companions before moving on.

"Asshole," Mileya muttered as they walked away, not quite out of earshot.

Berran ran a hand through his straight hair. "Agreed."

The moon hung high in the sky as the guests gathered around a lavish table, illuminated by the soft glow of flickering lanterns. Every inch of it was adorned with delicacies: fish from the Longh River, exotic fruits from Valhir, potent honey mead from Derryn, and a special platter of deep-sea molluscs and Moscht reserved exclusively for Mileya.

"Enjoy your lovely meal, Mileya," Berran quipped, eyeing the slimy, green sea plants that only her kind found edible.

The gentle clink of silverware was interrupted by the rise of King Farhand's voice, commanding the attention of the room. His words were slow and a faint stutter betrayed his age-reminding everyone that beneath the glittering splendour of Oridae's exquisite palace, the fate of the realm hung in a delicate balance. He wouldn't live much longer-unlike syrens, vampyres, or fae, humans aged quickly.

King Farhand's kind brown eyes looked at them all, worn with the stress that only years of rule could bring.

"Tonight," he began, his tone still holding the weight of authority, "we gather not only in celebration, but in contemplation. I am dying, with no one to take my place on the throne. Your beloved queen and I have not successfully produced an heir..." His voice wavered for a brief moment, a flash of sorrow crossing his lined face. It was no secret how the royal couple had struggled for years, their hopes dashed by stillborns and miscarriages.

"And so, the Heir's Rite approaches, a ceremony that marks the path to a new era." His tired expression scanned the assembly in the purple-tiled room, pausing briefly as if searching for a successor in the faces before him. His queen, equally aged, sat quietly by his side, her hands folded in her lap.

"This year, history shall witness something unprecedented. For the first time, it is not just humans who will compete, but those from other species as well."

A murmur of surprise and speculation fluttered through the sparkling room like the wings of a bird.

"You may wonder why. As you all know, this has never been done before but the past few years have not yielded enough humans of significant power to fill the Rite's required twenty participants. Therefore, we have broadened the field."

Soft whispers travelled up and down the long marble table.

"Trust in your king," he continued, raising an azure gloved hand to still the conversations. "This was the only decision to be made. Now, enjoy the feast, and we shall reconvene at Shadowfern."

Berran's eyes bored into Mileya's with a mixture of anticipation and uncertainty. He knew she would appreciate this, her lust for violence was well known. As was her love for the dramatics. Whilst the king's words hung in the air, the airy room grew louder and louder with a mixture of voices and scraping chairs. Noblemen and women sent their servants away to write letters that would reach far and wide across Myrantis.

Berran chuckled softly to himself. *Here we go.*

10

Berran

Around a finely carved table in the palace's conservatory, the salt-filled air from the ocean below was awash with tension and smoke. The white glowing light, conjured from magic, danced upon the features of Berran, Nahese, Mileya and other syren's, their expressions ranging from focused to amused.

Cards shuffled and hands were dealt, marking the start of a high-stakes game that extended far beyond the realms of chance. Berran couldn't fucking wait to win.

Mileya had convinced him to play tonight. If Berran has his way, he would have happily left them to their game to go to bed with one of the females in Nahese's posse, who had looked so damned tempting this evening. But she had insisted he join.

Berran's pale fingers moved deftly over his cards, his eyes narrowing slightly as his gaze flickered toward Nahese. The male exuded an air of cocky confidence that grated on Berran so much he could knock that stupid smile right off his preening face. He tried to prevent his lip from curling ever so slightly-he'd played hundreds like Nahese before, and the male relied on more than luck to secure victory.

Mileya observed the scene from behind a curtain of inky hair. Even though she could not see the cards, the enchantment woven into them translated the hand perfectly in her mind. She ever calm and played her hand with the cool detachment of a predator lurking beneath still waters.

As the game progressed into the night, Nahese's smirks and sly glances grew more blatant, rousing Berran's simmering disdain for the prick.

Amidst the shuffling of cards, Nahese's hand would disappear beneath the table for fleeting moments. Berran's fingers twitched with suppressed frustration-the signs were damned unmistakable.

However, it was Mileya, calm as the depths of an untouched sea, who emerged-as always-the true contender. Her expressions never betrayed her. As the rounds unfolded, Mileya's stack of gold coins grew, casting a shadow over Nahese's smug grin and his quickly depleting supply of gold.

"Are you sure you're not cheating, Mileyakhan? How do we know you're not reading our minds?" Nahese jabbed, his voice dripping with false humour.

Berran's growl was low and dangerous. "Watch your tongue, Nahese, or you'll find yourself thrown through that glass."

Before Nahese could clap back with a retort of his own, with a final, calculated move, Mileya revealed her hand-a triumph that left Nahese's face blanched of its usual rich colour.

The table erupted in gasps and curses, Berran meeting Mileya's gaze with an unspoken acknowledgment of her skill and his respect. Her face was laced with her arrogance, that-for once-he loved to see.

Nahese's protests were swallowed by the realisation that his deceit had been stripped bare. His arse fully on show.

Mileya's voice cut through his floundering, cool and emotionless. "Perhaps next time, Nahese, you'll consider playing by the rules. Or is decency a concept beyond your understanding?"

A not-so-humble victory and a resounding lesson for the shithead, thought Berran. As the coins changed hands, the table's tension gave way to a shared want of more wyne.

With a lighter pocket and more than his fair share of wyne in his belly, Berran made his way to his quarters on the lowest floor of the palace. With access to the calm sea below, the room was perfect. Though the night had ended on a high, he could not help but feel slightly unsettled by the news of the evening-it was all anyone could talk about.

He prayed Keyara would be prepared when she was called upon. He had been training her for so many years and had to give credit where it was due. She was good, possessing such strong magic for a human. But the fact remained-she would be no match for a fully grown 81ampire with access to blood magic, or a syren of his species. He could not even think about a fae putting themselves forward. They did not concern themselves with the politics of humans, seeing them as nothing but a weaker animal.

Concerns aside, Berran had to admit one thing to himself-this would be one hell of a competition.

11
Keyara

Beneath the starlit sky the forest stirred with untold stories, its rustling leaves weaving a symphony of secrets and a forewarning of a wickedly dry summer for Eldorhaven. Keyara walked alongside her sister, the weight of the impending Rite pressing down on her like a sodden wool cloak. Her trudging footsteps were silent, absorbed by the cushion of the green moss that carpeted the forest floor. Beside her, Aura matched her pace.

Breaking the comfortable silence, Aura's voice rang out. "I've decided I'm coming with you."

Keyara halted and turned to face her sister, "Aura, don't be ridiculous, you can't. You have to stay here and look after Mother; she won't be able to cope with the both of us gone." Their mother had become increasingly fragile, flitting around the house with a constant air of exhaustion that had begun to grate on Keyara. The two sisters often found their mother's strands of long brown hair in clumps around the cottage-a subtle sign of her weakening health.

With strong blue eyes that were surprisingly iron, Aura's lips curved into a gentle smile. "Keyara, you've never been alone in anything, and you won't start now. My power, it might be able to help in some way. I've spoken with Mother and she understands. She doesn't want you to go through this alone either. Maybe with both of us gone, she can finally afford to look after herself now the house is at last being repaired. Also,

I've been researching the Rite, reading about past trials and winners--what they did differently, their powers, everything."
Keyara's gaze softened, gratitude and concern swirling within her. "Really?"
A spark of determination jumped from her sister as she nodded, and Keyara could have sworn she felt more relaxed.
Fucking Aura and her magic.
"I've studied every account I could find," Aura continued, her voice gaining momentum. "Even from the scholars on Oblitus, and you know how those hermits are."
She had a point, Keyara silently agreed. Those moles who lived on top of a hill inside the Library of Souls rarely left the small spit of land they called home.
Aura continued as they padded along the mossy ground. "And yes, I know, me reading something other than stories about men on white horses with open hearts, deep pockets, and big..."
Keyara playfully shoved her, laughing.
Aura's love of romantic tales was no secret, and Keyara remembered every sordid passage Aura had read aloud during their few stolen moments of privacy. She pretended to be uninterested, but there were a few...memorable scenes that lingered in her mind.
Reluctance tugged at Keyara's heart, but the thought of facing the trials alongside her sister did not sound so terrible.
She knew she could be a miserable bitch at times, and she might need allies in Shadowfern. Aura would be perfect for that.
With a sigh, Keyara relented.
"Alright, Aura."
With a firm nod Aura embraced her, their sisterly bond transcending words.
"But promise me you'll be careful," Keyara muttered into her sister's hair. "There'll be plenty of shitty people looking to take

advantage of you, and I won't be able to protect you all the time."

Muffled by Keyara's long chocolate hair, Aura's voice was filled with mischief.

"Don't worry about me. I'll find Berran and make him my knight on a white horse. Maybe he can help us with the challenges too. He'd never say no to us."

Pulling away, Keyara smirked. "Doesn't Berran actually have a white horse?"

The next evening found them in Gregory's.

Again.

The tavern was alive with conversation and the clinking of mugs. Keyara and Aura claimed a table at the Orca corner, their laughter mingling with the tavern's hubbub.

In her peripheral vision, Keyara noticed the two fae from the previous brawl sitting at the bar, watching like vultures.

With an air of superiority sludging off them, they looked as out of place in here as a vampyre in a vegetable patch.

The male with eyes the colour of tree bark had his gaze fixed solely on Aura, with an intensity that made Keyara's heart quicken with unease. Leaning towards her sister, Keyara kept her voice low. "That male from the other day...he's staring at you. What did he say last time?"

Aura's expression remained composed; not acknowledging the stare.

"I noticed. Let him look."

Keyara glanced over her shoulder at the fae.

Aura was easily the most beautiful person here, but the way he was staring made Keyara's hand itch to add another fae to the list of those who'd felt her fist at Gregory's.

Without hesitation, she flipped them off. The smaller fae, the one she had fought with before, shook his head and turned his back on them.

Coward.

The fair-haired fae smirked, throwing the gesture back at her before turning back to his mead

12
Selsie

The clash of elements and the desperate cries of drowning men filled every inch of the air as Selsie's pod fought fiercely around her. Their bodies twisted and contorted with the fluidity of water itself, circling the ghostly ship that loomed atop the waves. Its stark white hull stood in defiance against the dark sea, a beacon of challenge to the syren's domain.

Blood stained the waters a deep crimson-a mix of human and syren lifeblood-making it nearly impossible to see under the surface, even for Selsie's sharp vision.

Amidst the clash, Selsie's eyes finally locked on a man standing tall on the ship's deck. His hair was as dark as the deepest ocean depths, and despite the pandemonium around him, he was laughing, shouting something she couldn't make out over her own song.

The shipwreck seal of her species billowed on the sails above him, an ominous display.

He was unlike any human she had been told of-nothing like the weak, pitiful, and unfortunate creatures she had come to expect. She sensed a strength in him, and something else. Something she could not quite put her fin on, and that tugged at her curiosity.

Confused as to why he was not in her grip yet, she continued with her song. It was a melody meant for him, one that should have ensnared him. Yet it was failing.

Just then, in a blur of movement, a large rock, hurled from the seabed, struck the man from behind. His body crumpled, unconscious, tumbling toward the water. A syren in her Other form, her ash-grey eyes gleaming with triumph, darted through the waves toward him, teeth bared, ready to claim his throat.

A surge of possessiveness swept through Selsie. *He's mine.* Without thinking, she acted. With a powerful flick of her golden tail and a burst of strength, she reached the man first, clutching him tightly. The other syren snarled, and with a hiss, Selsie spat.

"He's mine!" Her bared teeth shone in the blood-tinged water. Gripping the man by the piece of torn clothing by his neck, Selsie's knuckles were white with the strength of her grasp. Behind her, she sensed her mother approaching, her scent thick and overpowering. The wounded matriarch loomed, and the other syren immediately backed off. The Laeth in her whimpered at the thought of her matriarch coming to harm. Though her mother would heal quickly, the wound looked serious enough to need a healer's attention.

That whimper disappeared as swiftly as it came, her immediate attention was on the man in her arms. He was bleeding too, profusely from his head. Her Other form was begging to come out, the ripples on her skin sending animalistic urges through her, screaming for Selsie to kill him. She would never do that. *He was hers.*

Her syren mind wanted him, *needed* him.

Her thoughts were a typhoon, swirling in all directions-not knowing where it would land. Diving into her mind for a spell to put him to sleep and to keep him warm in this cold water, she was interrupted by the man as he stirred whilst coughing and spluttering.

His eyes opened wide with panic as he realized where he was. A frantic struggle ensued as he tried to break free, but the waves were against him, churning unnaturally at Selsie's will. She held him tight, their bodies swaying amid the screams and splashes of the battle around them.

He was strong-stronger than she expected-and it took all of her power to finally pull him beneath the water. Her magic simmered beneath her skin, a spell forming in her mind, ready to be unleashed. She murmured the incantation, weaving it like a net around him, and slowly, his eyes fluttered shut. A protective bubble of air formed around him, keeping him alive in the depths in a frozen, timeless state where his wound would not get any worse. For a moment, she simply watched him, unable to fully comprehend what had just happened.

"The Queen is wounded! Retreat!" Neesh called out, her mother in tow. Relief washed over Selsie as she scanned the waters-no tiny bodies floating in the water, no wretched smell of newly-formed human blood.

Retreating, they made south to Cildraethe-to home. The journey passed in a blur, the water still brimming with unspent aggression.

Selsie had to wince at the tension as a few hushed, spiteful whispers sounded in her ears. It was clear they soured at her decision to keep the human. Keeping one alive was rare, and the venom in their voices stung, but she paid them no mind.

It was this venom towards her, and the man she had captured that forced Selsie to order Neesh to watch over him whilst she slept, simultaneously promising death to anyone who put a fin in the wrong direction or looked at him in a way Selsie or Neesh took any offence to.

The human floated silently beside her, his unconscious form never leaving her sight. If she trusted anyone to watch over him, it was Neesh. Her mother, too wounded to intervene, stayed silent.

The matriarch's injury was a topic no one dared broach-suggesting a human had almost killed her was dangerous territory. The Queen and Matriarch of the Laeths was meant to be the most fearsome among them, invincible.

As they entered Cildraethe under the moonlight, an awkward hush settled over the pod. The moment they passed through the effigy of Alysee that guarded the underwater kingdom, her mother was whisked away to the healers.

"Do you want me to take him up into the castle?" Neesh asked, breaking the silence as they hovered outside Selsie's chambers. "He'll need to wake soon."

Selsie glanced from the human in her phantom grasp to Neesh, who was holding out her arms in wait.

They hovered like slumbering whales outside Selsie's chambers, the gentle rocking of the currents swaying the human back and forth in his suspended state. Selsie flicked her tail fins in thought-she had not quite figured out what she was to do with him once they had returned home.

Her song hadn't worked, and she knew he'd fight to escape the moment he awoke. By Alysee, the reality was harsh-he couldn't stay. Only those under the syren's spell could remain in Cildraethe, the threat of being killed and eaten negated by the protection of the spell, safe from being hunted by their kind. This man was more like a prisoner.

"Yes," she finally said, handing him over. It would give her time to think, without the distraction of him nearby. Otherwise, she would spend her days and nights staring at his features. A stab of pressure haunted her as she handed him over, and a shiver ran over her body as Neesh took him, casting a spell of her own to control his suspended state.

"You should surface, Selsie," Neesh suggested softly. "You've sung your first song. You're ready." Neesh was right. With the release of her first song's magic, Selsie should be able to surface now. Her body free to make the change, no longer shackled by the chains of underwater life.

Bowing her head, the guard took her leave.

The thought had consumed Selsie for as long as she could remember. Th-e light that pierced her room had been her countdown, her timepiece, each shift signalling the approach of her ascent.

But she would need rest first. A syren needed to be in good health to transform, and Selsie hadn't slept or eaten properly in days.

Exhaustion pulled at her as she flopped onto her bed. She knew sleep would evade her, the dreams of her surfacing a promise that prevented a deep sleep from reaching her.

13
Keyara

Two small bags held what little they owned.
Keyara noted how lightly they were travelling as she stood
beside Aura on the threshold of their cottage. The breaking
dawn painted the sky with hues of gold and rose.
Their mother stood in the doorway to say goodbye, her grey
eyes teary.
Every emotion was written all over her small-featured face-a
face that looked so much like Keyara's own.
"My strong, beautiful girls, I love you so very much. I wish this
day had never come, but here we are. We must carry on, as we
always do."
Aura clasped her tiny hands in her own.
Their mother took a deep breath. "I have so much faith in you
both. I've always known my girls would have an adventure of
their own someday."
Keyara noted a wistful look pass over her face, as though their
mother was recalling a forgotten memory.
"Now then, off you go. Look after each other-and please,
Keyara, don't be too hard on yourself. Whatever happens, I'm
still so, so very proud of you."
Keyara rolled her eyes as her mother winked and hugged them
both.
They had said their real goodbyes late last night, sharing
memories of their childhood-laughter filling them with love and
hope.

They also spoke of what really happened all those years ago on the night Aura was brought to them.

It had been a hard conversation for their mother, but it was long overdue.

Even after all was said and done, Keyara couldn't shake the feeling that there was something else her mother wanted to say-though maybe that was the anxiety creeping in, throwing her off.

Wanting to make the most of the morning weather, they left, leaving their mother behind and waving from the door. Her small frame remained there until they were out of sight.

On Aura's insistence, they walked hand in hand down the main street through the village.

It was very early, and not a soul was awake-apart from their mother to send them off.

Keyara wondered if anyone even knew that one of their own was going to be a competitor in one of the most ancient and important traditions in all of Myrantis.

Probably not.

The quietness was unusual to Keyara, who rarely left the house before noon. She didn't know if it was her unfamiliarity with the time of day or something else, but she could swear the air felt heavy with a sense of gravity.

Keyara nearly shed a tear as they strolled past Gregory's.

Damned it, she'd miss that place.

She couldn't think about that now though. They were about to embark on their journey to Shadowfern, and it was a long damned trek to the city, high in the Vaelorn Mountains at the very centre of Myrantis.

At the edge of the village, they paused where the cobblestone path ended and the forest began. The dense woods ahead threatened to swallow them whole.

Neither had ever crossed this boundary-they never had to.

Shit, maybe I should have, Keyara thought. *A queen would want to see her kingdom.*

"Not too late to turn around, Aura," Keyara said.

"This is about to be the most exciting thing I've ever done, Keyara. Not a chance I'm missing it," Aura replied.

"More exciting than watching Gregory fix the leak for the thousandth time?" Keyara teased.

Aura knitted her eyebrows together. "I wouldn't go that far."

They chuckled together as Aura led them into the forest, the trail worn and barely visible beneath their feet.

As they walked, Keyara shifted her bag from one shoulder to the other, praying to the gods they wouldn't get lost.

That would be godsdamned humiliating.

The silence accompanying them spoke volumes as they walked. The uncertainty of their future laying like a dead body between them.

Hard to ignore.

Shadows played together among the tall trees-a reminder that darkness and light were two sides of the same coin, much like themselves.

Oaks, elms and ash trees towered over them, their immense height a testament to how old, untouched and wild this part of the country was.

Aura spoke, her voice as gentle as a whisper. "Whatever happens, Keyara, no matter what we face, remember that we do it together, alright?"

Taken aback by her serious tone, all Keyara could say was, "Yes, I know."

The sounds of the forest were amplified by their continued silence.

Though it was a comfortable, sisterly quiet, Keyara wished Aura would start her usual rambling-if only to make this place less intimidating.

Berran had told her that he and his warriors frequently hunted here: deer, elk, rabbits, and other animals were all on the menu. He had also told her stories-when she was barely older than fifteen-of other, larger creatures that lived and hunted in these woods.

Though he had promised her, he had never seen them.

Berran had never told her a lie so far.

Keyara pulled out the map she had purchased with the last of their gold coins. "According to this, there should be a small hunting lodge about five miles from here."

Aura propped a foot on a fallen tree stump, one hand resting on her plush hip. "Five miles? How do you know?"

Keyara sat on the stump, swinging her bag off her shoulder. "Didn't you know? I'm the best map reader this side of the Vaelorn Mountains."

Aura playfully snatched the map from her hands. "Give it here."

Biting her lip, Aura scanned the freshly inked pages, shimmering with magic from the man who printed its images straight from his mind.

"Keyara," Aura said, exasperated.

Keyara tilted her head back, closing her eyes. "I've read the map wrong, haven't I?"

"The lodge is ten miles from here."

Keyara kicked at the foliage beneath her feet. "Godsdamn it."

"It's going to get dark soon. We need to get moving."

Groaning, Keyara pushed herself up from the stump and followed Aura's lead. "We should've gotten horses."

"Oh yes, with all the money we have."

Keyara shrugged. "Who said anything about *buying* horses?"

Eventually, after what felt like a lifetime, they finally stumbled upon the hunter's lodge, just as the last sliver of sun dipped below the horizon.

Signs of Berran and his warriors were scattered everywhere-animal bones, empty bottles of Akoaàn wyne, and-of course-the ever-present snowmen with huge cocks standing guard outside the wooden hut.

Despite it being nearly the hottest time of the year, the frozen sculptures remained intact.

Keyara inhaled deeply, catching the faint, familiar scent of Berran's fresh, aquatic scent lingering in the room.

Sleeping with one eye open, Keyara had tried to rest.

The occasional howl of wolves and the scurrying of unseen creatures jolted her awake whenever her heavy lids begged to close

Aura's fear stifled the cabin-whether she was aware of her power leaching out around them, Keyara wasn't sure.

The eerie caws and screeches echoing in the night made Keyara uneasy.

It was fucking scary Keyara had to admit.

Worse, Aura had hinted she might face such creatures during the Rite, especially given past competitions. One of the previous heirs had even battled a recently hatched Dune Dragen from Valhir.

She would worry about that on the night she thought, chucking it towards the back of her mind.

They had left the cabin at sunrise, knowing their journey through the forest would likely end tomorrow, late in the day. After that, the long, gruelling trek across the open countryside would begin.

With Aura now reading the map, they aimed to sleep at another lodge later tonight, one that mirrored their path through the woods.

Sitting for a momentary rest, her sister groaned. "We should have stolen those horses."

Keyara huffed. "The lodge should only be an hour from here."

Aura tied her strawberry hair back with a ribbon and rose from the ground. Keyara looped her arm through her sister's, hoping the lodge really was just an hour away.

When it finally came into view *many* hours later-a squat wooden building with another icy companion keeping guard by the door-Aura sighed in relief.

"I hope this one's better company. Oh, look-it's bigger than the last," Aura remarked, eyeing a familiar area on the sculpture.

"I wonder if it's a self-portrait," Keyara muttered, rolling her eyes as she pushed open the door.

It was surprisingly tidy compared to the last lodge. Berran and his males must have grown bored of their partying at this point of their hunt.

The trees thinned out in this area of the forest, so there were few options regarding animals to hunt.

From the quiet of the night around them, and the few hours of sleep she managed to grab, Keyara was sure the creatures were confined to the depths of the forest behind them.

Thank the damned gods.

The Longh Road was only a few miles away now-the vital artery that connected Myrantis and all her kingdoms.

Once they cleared the forest, the horizon stretched out before them-it was a bronze landscape of pale yellows, dusty olive greens and rolling hills, bathed in the warm glow of dusk.

A gentle breeze carried faint memories of laughter from Gregory's, their wisteria-covered cottage, and the countless nights Keyara spent preparing for this very moment.

Eldorhaven was miles behind them now. As Keyara looked ahead, she tried to grasp the feeling that welled inside her.

It was waiting, just out of reach.

Waiting for her to take the plunge, dive in, and drown in it.

EBONY WILKINS

14
Berran

Berran awoke to a palace alive with anticipation, as first light pierced through the cream-coloured drapes. Leaving behind his pastel green room-adorned with ornate marble furniture and the damned comfortable bed-he headed to meet Mileya, who waited beside a giant potted fern in the bustling inner courtyard. Today marked the beginning of their journey to Shadowfern. Berran, Mileya, and the entourage his father insisted on sending from Silvanh, would all depart at noon.

Berran would have preferred his own warriors, but his father didn't want them to "embarrass" the royal heir at such an important event.

Not that they would. -Berran had trained them well the courtly manners of their own kingdom and others. -But whether they followed those teachings was beyond his control.

Around him, the royal court gleamed like living pearls under the morning sun, excitement swirling in the sea-salted air of the palace. Among the scattered vampyres, humans, and the occasional syren moving through the crowd, a familiar shock of black hair caught his eye.

His long strides quickly closed the distance between him and Mileya. Even though the mosaic ceiling above their heads was enormously high, Mileya still managed to seem crushed by the enclosure.

He wondered how long it had been since she had returned to her home in the impossibly dark depths of Maya. His worry for her lingered, especially with how much Mycillium she had been consuming lately. The thought of her early death, brought on by the overconsumption of the drink, haunted him.

Before he could speak, she sensed him approaching. "Your steps are as heavy and loud as a marsh hog, Berran."

"Good morning to you too, Mileya. I trust you slept well," he said, clasping his hands behind his back.

She turned to face him, wearing nothing but a strip of cloth to cover her lower body. Berran wished Reothadh culture was as free as the Domhianns, who cared little for modesty. Their bare-chested ways were simply part of who they were.

He tugged at his silver vest, already feeling overheated. The light fabric clung to him uncomfortably in the unfamiliar warmth, his high body temperature exacerbating the heat.

"Stop fussing," Mileya hissed.

"It's too damned hot," he muttered, hitching up his embroidered trousers that matched the vest.

She sighed, her patience seemingly waning. "You're such a grown Reothadh male, yet you act like a youngling."

"I'm built for ice Mileya, not the sun of Oridae."

"And what if you're called down to Valhir or Halè. What then, hm? Will you melt into a puddle and drip away into the dirt?"

Berran coolly channelled ice into his veins, bringing his body temperature down, not caring if those around him felt the chill. If anything, they should be grateful.

"When that day comes, I'll send Cass. I think she'd love to see the pink sands of Halè."

Mileya moved beside him with liquid grace. "Are you ready? I want to leave. This court is dull." He chuckled, guiding her away from the crowd. "Let's go."

They quickly penned a letter to the King, explaining their departure and sending a servant girl to deliver the message. The Heir's Rite was only a week away and they were already cutting it close by leaving so late.

"Are your little cubs meeting you there, Berran?" she asked.

His fins ruffled slightly at her pet name for his warriors. He asked her why she called them that once, and Mileya delighted in telling him how they were always by his side, following him everywhere and taking orders from him no matter their own opinions.

Though he hated that she called them that, he let it slide. His warriors were like brothers, having fought alongside him for nearly ninety years, and they paid no mind what Mileya thought. She was, after all, the apex predator of them all.

"No they are not," he replied. "They don't fare well in court, especially Tal. Unlike you, Mileya-always a hit."

She tutted as they passed a group of women in fine gowns, flocked around an Oridaen nobleman flaunting his charm, their giggles echoing through the hall.

"Tal is a brute, with gills too large for his body."

Berran barked a laugh, "That male is obsessed with you, Mileya, cut him some rope. Come to think of it, as is our favourite Akoaàn. I'm pretty sure he fell more in love with you every time you took his gold."

Mileya shot him a glare. Despite her protests, he knew she enjoyed court life as much as he did-the wyne, the parties, the constant battle of intrigue. It suited her perfectly. Much to her protests otherwise.

They exited the palace through the grand gates, the white marble adorned with intricate mosaics that glinted in the daylight.

Ahead stretched the Longh Road, its ancient stones worn smooth by centuries of travellers. It wound down from the palace, past the bustling Stalls Corner Market and the vibrant Pink Quarter, through the packed city and out into the distant hills of Eira.

Descending from the palace's high perch, they approached the Veridwyn River, which flowed parallel to the Longh Road. Shielded by high birch trees, in a corner of the city reserved for noblemen and women, Mileya stood by his side at the riverbank as they prepared for the long, arduous swim upstream.

He dipped his hand into the saltwater river, nearly passing out from the pleasure it gave him to feel the moving water against his parched skin.

"We should have gone with the others," Mileya said, her words barely audible over the rushing current. Their syren companions had left on foot, transporting Berran's cargo in the large white carriages reserved for Reothadh royalty.

Berran peeled off his court clothes, folding them neatly into a waterproof pack that he slung over his broad shoulders. "Fuck that. I'm dying to feel the water."

Tearing the strip of cloth off her obsidian body and onto the grassy bank, Mileya dived with feline grace into the water-crystal splashes of water staining the high rainbow walls of the houses around them.

Within seconds, her long legs transformed into an ebony tail, matte scales shimmering faintly, translucent fins running down its spine.

He followed her not long after, his legs dissolving into the deep blue tail he hadn't seen in far too long. It was thick, powerful, and as he flexed the fins at its end, he felt the freedom that came with the water's embrace.

The stifling humidity of Oridae fell away, replaced by the soothing balm of the river. The climate in the capital was always slightly warm, but their spring and summers were so humid it made Berran wish for the familiarity of the frost and waves of home.

He missed it, but not enough to return just yet.

The current was strong and pushing them back, but Mileya swam ahead-her bioluminescence flickering to life in the darkening waters. She thrived here, a creature perfectly at home in the depths-her species the living embodiment of the ocean.

Small carp darted through the swaying reeds below them, seemingly waving as they passed by. The Veridwyn River was deep, and Berran watched as Mileya sank gracefully into its depths, answering the silent call of the abyss.

Gods, I'm tired, Berran thought, as fatigue tugged at his muscles.

He squinted through the dim water, trying to spot her. It was nearly impossible to see anything-not even a river carp-save for the faint blue glow surrounding his friend.

"Gods, Mileya, how do you navigate down here?" Her soft, bioluminescent light was the only thing that betrayed her position. Without it she'd be a ghost, unseen until her sharp teeth and claws struck-a fate reserved for the unfortunate fish they hunted. Though, he still didn't know what the hell they did with them.

They didn't eat them themselves, that's for damned sure. Berran suspected it was for their pets...

"Let's surface. We've been swimming for two days and need to rest," Berran called out.

She ignored him.

"And I need to eat, Mileya. I'm starving."

Her voice echoed faintly through the water, distant but firm. "No, you need rest. I can keep going through the night. If you can't keep up, I'll meet you there."

He growled under his breath. "Mileyakhan, we both need sleep. Come on."

She swam past him, the razor-sharp fins on her tail narrowly missing his face. "Tsk, such a youngling."

As they broke through the rushing water, Berran scanned the area for a place to rest. They must have covered at least a hundred miles today, and his tail throbbed from the exertion. Reothadhs were built for strength and speed, not the endurance of the Domhianns and Laeths. He knew Mileya could go on for hours longer than he could.

With no signs of civilisation in sight, sleeping under the stars would have to do. Not that it bothered him-his nights spent on the glaciers of Silvanh, and hunting parties spent in the forest around Eldorhaven, had prepared him for uncomfortable beds. Besides, Berran hadn't liked the thought of sleeping down at the very dredges of the Veridwyn.

"We'll rest under that alder," he said, pointing to a large tree by the riverbank, its green leaves a stark contrast to the dry farmland beyond.

Mileya clicked her teeth in annoyance but didn't argue. Her shadowy form glided toward the river's edge, and Berran followed closely behind.

Once they emerged from the water, their tails transformed back into legs, and they settled under the sheltering branches of the alder.

"I'll catch you something to eat," Mileya offered, her tone unusually generous. "What do you want?"

Berran raised a brow. "You're going to catch me something?"

She shook out her wet hair. "Yes, I'm better at it than you. Besides, I've already got my meal." She pulled a few dried strips of Moscht from her pack, taking a bite.

With a grin, Berran snatched the half-eaten piece from her hands and ripped off a chunk with his sharp canines. "You don't even like it." He grunted in agreement, chewing the tough Moscht. Though he'd rather eat it than send Mileya back into the river to catch something.

They finished the Moscht in silence, watching the stars emerge in the night sky. Their conversation ebbed and flowed between banter and quiet contemplation until, eventually, the moon climbed high, casting a silver glow over the river.

The cooler night air nudged Mileya closer to Berran for warmth, her slender frame seeking the heat of his body.

He drifted to sleep with the lingering thoughts of the coming days, and what the future would hold for them all.

15
Selsie

With sun-gilded fins tingling with anticipation, Selsie swam away from the sharp words of her mother, heading for the castles exit. She replayed the conversation in her mind, cursing herself for everything she should have said.

Their voices had clashed like opposing tides.

"Why didn't you kill him, Selsie? He fell right into your arms!" Her mother's voice was cold and unyielding. "And why, pray tell, did your song fail? I should kill you myself for the disgrace."

Desperation had welled up within her as she met her mother's stern gaze. "I do not know why it failed. I...I tried." Her stumbling words were not helping her case, and neither were her glances at her mother's wound, which was now almost fully healed.

"I *want* him, Mother," she had finally confessed, trembling with a newfound resolve. "Not to kill him-I want him to be mine." Her mother's eyes remained cold and stiff. "Very well," she said. "Prove your power. Ensnare him with your syren song before the next new moon, or you will kill him yourself. If you do not...well, I have no need for a weak daughter."

The matriarch swam away, leaving a storm of bubbles in her wake and her daughter frozen in the throne room.

Selsie never understood the hatred her mother held for her. She was her only daughter and still, she felt no love between them. Never a *kind* word or a loving touch.

Pushing those immature, youngling thoughts to the darkest corners of her mind, she let excitement replace them. Today, she would finally ascend to the surface. She had made her first kill- now the law of her nature demanded that she let her tail transform into human legs, lest she never would, *could*.
The ancient goddess and great matriarch Iara, made it so. Rendering her life meaningless.
Returning to her room, she discarded her gemstone tiara and let the morning rays flood the space. The ocean seemed to sing for her.
Skipping her usual routine of rubbing coral oil on her deep ochre skin and running coconut milk through her long curls, Selsie hurried to the castle's surfacing chamber; a wing she had never been permitted to enter.
The chamber was completely unguarded, and as Selsie reached the bottom of the grand staircase within, she paused. She had waited for this moment her entire life. These wide stairs led to the surface and her future-her destiny.
She gazed upward. Instead of the usual rocky ceiling or the filtered ocean light, the chamber was bathed in an unnatural glow that cast long, wavering shadows.
A male swam through those shadows, his form massive with talons protruding from his arms, gleaming in the dim light.
"Excuse me," he said, dipping his head in deference before swiftly ascending with his jade-green tail.
He followed the steps as they swept from the very bedrock on the ocean floor up into the castle. They shimmered slightly from the many crystals that were embedded into the rock itself.
Leaning against the enormously tall lanterns at the base of the staircase, Selsie brushed her fingers through the enchanted lights that spiralled around the lanterns, watching the male as he disappeared from view.

She could wait no longer. With a deep breath she held onto the rail running parallel to the stairs and slowly swam towards the lapping water's edge above.

The transformation, she had been told as a youngling, would be as simple as changing into her Other form-as easy as navigating a current.

As her head broke through the water, the change began. Magic tingled inside her, slowly at first, then in a crashing wave as she fully embraced the ancient melody.

Through the shimmering substance, long legs stood firm on the steps where her tail had floated moments ago. Gills were replaced with lungs that expanded and contracted, adapting to breathe down gulps of damp air. Blinking rapidly, her eyes were tender, screaming with sensitivity as they took in her immediate surroundings.

A great hall rose around her, its green walls and towering ceiling mirroring the depths below. Selsie concentrated on her steps, pausing as the staircase below her feet ended on a balcony, leading away in two different directions into the depths of the castle.

She wobbled slightly, not taking her hand off the rail. Hushed gasps escaped the few syrens atop the stairs who were staring at her.

Selsie made sure her back was steel straight, composure intact for her future subjects. Yet an unfamiliar sensation crept over her-something akin to shame, though she couldn't pinpoint why.

A passing servant did a double-take, clearly shocked to see her. The news of her ascent would reach her mother within the hour, she was sure.

Walking felt strange at first, her unused muscles weak and unsteady. Then, an intrinsic instinct bloomed inside her, the new appendages below her waist not taking long to feel as natural to her as a tail. The sensation of walking became smoother second by second.

She reached the top of the staircase-the Laeth's first true test of strength on land-and paused, victorious. The long, wide steps were a mountain for newly matured Laeths to conquer.

Scent alone alerted her to Neesh's arrival. The sound of her friend's footsteps, foreign to her ears, echoed down the hall.

"By Alysee, you did it! You made the ascent!" Neesh beamed. Selsie couldn't help but return the smile.

"This feels very strange Neesh." Her third eyelid had gone, Selsie realised as she looked down at her new body, admiring the strength of muscle she found in her toned legs, and a dark, unfamiliar mound of curly hair between them. "Though, I think I like it already."

The female beside her laughed. "It takes time, but you'll get used to it. Now, let's find you something to wear and take you to your human. By the way, he's still asleep. That spell you used on him must've been strong."

Neesh led Selsie to her chambers, ordering a servant to fetch clothes on the way.

As the Laeth General, Selsie fully expected Neesh's room to be orderly, tidy and everything to be in its place. She couldn't hide the shock on her face when the door opened up into a messy, cluttered chamber, littered with armour and various weapons. Strewn across the floor were old dishes, dirty scale brushes and empty cups, the rim of the latter stained purple by the liquid it had held. This was not what she expected from Neesh, Selsie thought to herself as she stumbled over a sharp sword.

Neesh shrugged. "I've been busy." Selsie grinned, trying not to judge, as she carefully sat on a chair Neesh had cleared of thick, ancient tomes.

"I'm sure you have more important things to do," Selsie said to her only friend, hoping to reassure her.

A timid knock at the door announced the servant's return, bearing bundles of bronze and jade fabric in her arms.

"Ah, thank you Marwain." Neesh took the clothes and shut the door.

"In the castle," Neesh explained, "we wear clothes. As the heir, we had some pieces made for you, ready for this day."

Selsie was surprised. She looked down once again at her new bare form, feeling a twinge of disappointment at the prospect of now having to hide it away.

She held out her arms as Neesh handed her the gown. It took them a few minutes to dress her, Neesh showing her how to fasten buttons and tie knots, with a material she had never felt in her hands before.

Flowing against her skin like moonlight on water, Selsie marvelled at the gown, how it was a cascade of emerald silk that skimmed every curve on her body. Intricate patterns of bronze thread adorned the lining edge of the bodice, separating into two along the skirt, which was a waterfall of fabric, crashing to the floor in a pool of green.

Selsie glided over to the wall-length mirror. Staring at her reflection, she noticed how much clearer the female looking back at her was when not marred by water.

She admired how the slit up the front of the gown allowed one of her strong legs to peek through as she walked.

Her fingers lightly touched her collarbones, exposed by the neckline as it dipped in a gentle V, threatening to expose her breasts.

Sleeves billowed to her elbows and the same bronze thread that danced through the bodice- caught the light at the hem. Her small waist was cinched with a silken ribbon, adorned with iridescent beads and a metallic badge with the Laethian shipwreck crest, which took its place in the centre.

With every step, the gown seemed to stir with a life of its own, it was a garment fit for a Laethian heir, and it must have taken the seamstresses-even with their magic-months to make.

Neesh gently tightened the ribbon at her waist. "There you are," she said to Selsie. Something flittered through her eyes, an emotion that Selsie could not place.

Then with a steady breath, she allowed herself to feel like the powerful syren she was.

"Take me to him now, Neesh. Please."

Neesh bowed her head. "Of course."

16

Selsie

Leading the way, Neesh strode through the long corridors, and Selsie followed close behind. The dim passageways seemed to breathe with a life of their own, whispering echoes of forgotten melodies that tugged at the edges of her mind.

As Selsie moved gracefully in her gown through her ancestral home, the sea-crystal chandeliers hanging from the stone ceilings cast prismatic light across the walls, reflecting on her skin like rainbowed ripples.

The castle was a twin to the one below, but here, everything felt lighter, as though the very air carried a sense of freedom absent in the depths beneath.

Tall, scattered windows allowed the sunlit day to spill into the pale halls, illuminating the sea stone walls and offering glimpses of the world outside.

Each step they took brought her closer to the surface, and Selsie's heart quickened. She struggled to contain her excitement for the outside, her yearning clawing to break free from within.

As they descended deeper into the castle, the atmosphere changed.

The light from above dimmed into an oppressive gloom, and the surroundings down on Selsie's chest. Her thoughts darkened. The dungeons-she knew it.

The weight of her choice pressed upon her like she was too deep in the ocean, a place where a Laeth did not belong. The

decision to spare the one who should have met a different fate-
a rash and ill-thought-out impulse on her part.

"Not long now," Neesh called back to her as they ventured
through increasingly dim walkways. The vibrant halls of earlier
now flickered ominously with torchlight, casting eerie
silhouettes upon the cold walls.

Selsie swore the shadows were alive, writhing in the thick air,
drenched with the lingering power of centuries-old spells and
carrying the salty tang of the sea.

What threat could he pose to us, she thought. A human man
with no magic, had they truly brought him into such a place. A
dungeon whose sole purpose was to hold those of immense
power; Laeths who had committed acts of serious magnitude or
enemies of the Kingdom.

"Neesh, you promised to take care of him..." Selsie's voice took
on a sharper edge, droplets of her rising temper peppering her
tone.

"And I have kept that promise," Neesh replied, a flicker of
unease crossing her face. "It was your mother who ordered him
down here, Selsie. I cannot disobey her. But I assure you, he is
comfortable. You'll see."

They arrived at the iron gate of the dungeons, its shadow
looming large in the echoing darkness. Two guards stood on
either side; their faces etched with solemn duty. Bowing to
Neesh, they lowered their swords, granting her passage.

"Selsie commands to see her prisoner," Neesh declared,
stepping aside so the guards could catch a proper look at the
heir to the kingdom.

With a nod, the gate groaned open, and torches along the walls
flared to life, casting flickering light into the depths beyond.

Inside, the silence was absolute. No screams of torment or cries
of agony. Just a quiet, oppressive stillness.

The whispering in Selsie's veins grew quiet.

Few prisoners had graced these halls in centuries-there hadn't been a war since the fall of Emerglade, and her mother's rule was firm.

No one dared defy the Matriarch.

Neesh led them to the first door on the left. "Open it," she ordered one of the guards. Selsie stepped back as the guard muttered a spell, the low whistle of magic filling the air. The door opened with a slow creak, and Neesh gestured for the guard to return to his post.

Whether the guard had left them or not, Selsie did not know. For her whole focus was on the man before her.

On a small bed beneath the window, he lay asleep, atop simple blankets and shackled by a single hand to the wall. Selsie heard the sea lapping beneath the window ledge, telling her it had been keeping him company down here; it had been watching. Her eyes drifted to his large wounds, expecting them to be festered and rotten, waiting for the stench of inevitable death to fill her nostrils. But to her astonishment, they were healed. Magic must have been at work.

"He needs to wake up," Neesh softly whispered. If he slept too long, the magic binding him would consume him. Selsie had not realised the strength of her spell upon him. She looked to the syrens around her. "Leave us."

Neesh bowed, shutting the door behind her. The lack of echoing steps away from the door confirmed what Selsie knew; they would not leave her down here alone with him. She could feel them just outside the door.

With tentative steps, Selsie approached the bed, pulling her skirts up as she sat on its edge.

Silently, she brushed a dark curl away from his face, his skin warm beneath her fingertips. His scent-fresh, clean, but tinged with something she had never smelt before and the unpleasantness of days without a wash-filled the air.

She rested her hand on his large chest, feeling the steady rise and fall of his breath. She could end it here, kill him with a simple motion.

To consume his blood and flesh made the Other within her swim with excitement. It quickly bristled once she told it the thought disgusted her. A large wave crashed against the windowpane behind them, a wordless agreement from the sea. She had spared him, and now, they were bound by a choice she could not fully understand.

Placing her hands on his temples, she whispered the spell to wake him. A storm raged beneath her touch, lightning crashed beneath her palms, and she had never encountered anything like this male...man, before.

Whereas Laeth males were calm with an underlying peace to their demeanour, she could practically hear the howling wind that blew in his soul.

His eyes snapped open, eyes engorged with a cyclone of horror and anger met hers, the force of his gaze piercing her.

In the silence that stretched between them, the weight of their intertwined destinies hung heavy in the air, like the echoes of a song sung long ago, waiting to be completed. She had set them on a path of uncertainty, and in his eyes, she saw the consequences of that decision.

Suddenly, he sat up, dislodging her from the bed. "What the fuck do you want?" he spat at her, pulling up his once creamy white shirt, now ripped and bloodstained.

There was such venom in his deep voice that it shocked her. She knew humans feared Laeths, but there wasn't fear in his words, it was hatred.

Pure unfiltered hate.

Racking her brain for the right words in the limited human language she knew, she cleared her throat, clasping to the most non-threatening thing she could say.

"My name is Selsie." He gave her nothing, so she continued.
"What is yours?"

He ignored her question, gripping the metallic lampshade
beside the bed with such force she could see his knuckles
whiten. She remained calm, knowing full well that no human
weapon could truly harm her, and her movements far too quick
against his own.

"There is no need to fear me. I mean you no harm," she said
gently, forcing a smile. "On the contrary, you are mine now. I
will take care of you."

His blue eyes flared with defiance. "The fuck I am". He pointed
at her with the makeshift weapon, "I know you, you're the
syren that tried to sing to me and as I remember, it didn't work.
You have no claim to me".

He was right of course, but she had yet to explain to him the
deal between herself and her mother. "Details that are of no
concern. I have until the new moon to sing again, until then you
will stay here in Cildraethe, as mine."

The look on his beautiful face was etched with such horror, the
gravity of his situation falling as he realised he was a prisoner
here. His shoulders squared, his lips pursed into a thin line.
"Say I'm yours one more time bitch."

Her temper raged and Selsie struggled to contain the flood of it,
how dare he insult her. She was the Heir to the Laethian
kingdom, a kingdom in which he now resided. She deserved
respect from him, a man she could have killed without a second
thought when her song failed to enchant him. Others of her kind
would have done it with no hesitation, but instead, for reasons
she did not fully understand herself, she had chosen to keep him
alive.

He would need reminding of the power she held. "You are
mine," she repeated softly.

A hurricane lunged toward her, but the chain on his wrist yanked him back just inches from her face. She didn't flinch. She simply smiled.

"I'll arrange for food," she said smoothly. "You must be hungry."

"Get out," he growled, his tone cold as ice.

No one, save her mother, had ever commanded Selsie. Yet something deep inside urged her to leave, to comply with his demand.

Gritting her teeth, she stood, but not without a final word. "Tell me your name, and I will go."

His nostrils flared with anger or frustration, maybe both, she couldn't tell. He turned his back to her and walked away towards the window.

The silence went on for what seemed like three turns of the moon, before he finally spoke, his voice flat. "Jonn."

He did not move from his place by the window, did not even notice, as she quietly left the room.

"I will see you tomorrow then, Jonn."

17

Berran

The swim became more strenuous with every mile as the river climbed gradually uphill, whilst the days wore on.

Catching carp to fill their near-empty bellies, the two of them only paused when absolutely necessary, surviving on the occasional carp to fill their empty stomachs. The inns and taverns along the way would hinder their progress if they sought food from anywhere other than the river.

In hindsight, they should've taken the carriages. After weeks of indulgence in wyne and little exercise, Berran was out of his depth. Swimming this journey in half the usual time was pure idiocy.

On the later end of dusk and way behind schedule, they emerged from the water of one of the two lakes, droplets glistening like stardust upon their skin.

Cassidae's familiar voice echoed across the lakes shore, her silhouette mirrored with the towering peaks above. "Well, well, what do we have here? My two favourite syrens in a scandalous rendezvous?"

He turned to see Cass approaching them along the stones of the lapping shore, her playful smile aglow in the sun's waning warmth. Her flowing white hair, shimmering with undertones of turquoise blue, bounced around her lower back.

"You never could resist an opportunity for drama," he teased as they embraced. "Hey Cass" His sister's feminine laughter danced like sunlight over water. "And you, dear brother, never could escape my watchful eye."

Cassidae's glacier-blue eyes then softened as she looked at Mileya. "Mills, I've missed you so much," she whispered. Mileya's smile, rare and warm, was one she reserved only for Cass. They shared a quiet moment before Cass turned the conversation to the road ahead, her tone more serious. The Vaelorn Mountains loomed silently above them, ever watchful. "I was beginning to think you two would never arrive. You're awfully late. Everyone else ascended to Shadowfern yesterday."

Berran scrubbed a hand through his damp hair. " We would've arrived sooner, but someone couldn't get their fins away from Nahese and his card table."

If looks could kill, he would be dead and floating in the lake with his bare arse towards the Vaelorns. "Asshole," Mileya hissed under her breath.

Cass laughed uneasily, slipping her arms through theirs, lining the three of them up like penguins on ice. "Well, you're here now, and I've got good news. The queen left one of the royal carriages for us. You both need to rest." She led them along the shore, toward the bustling town of Heim, nestled at the base of the tallest peak, Vaelorn itself.

The town was busy and bustling with people, animals and every species of Myrantis, all eagerly awaiting their turn to ascend the mountains.

Tall, wooden framed buildings, filled with laughter and noise echoed behind them as the three of them left the throng of the crowd to the outskirts of Heim, along a cobblestone path lined with early summer flowers-to the huge, enclosed carriage bay, that was hidden away along the base of the towering monolith above.

Berran let out a low whistle.

It beat the small, ancient carriage of Silvanh. The grand vessel, large enough to comfortably accommodate eight individuals, floated a mere inch above the ground, suspended by an invisible force. The frame was an intricate dance of curves and arches, each meticulously carved. Gilded accents adorned every corner, catching the light in a mesmerising display of shimmering gold and silver.

Precious gemstones of every blue were nestled within the ornate patterns. Inside, cascading curtains of rich, velvety fabric, the hue of deepest azure, adorned the sides.

A stout man was lounging against the side of it, presumably the coachman. He wore the same midnight blue, silver and gold that encased the carriage, the colours of Oridae.

"Fuck me," Mileya muttered as she stepped inside, clearly taken aback. For a woman of practicality, unused to such extravagance, this was overwhelming. For her, if something didn't bring value or usefulness, it was discarded.

He couldn't relate to that sentiment.

Berran followed, settling his large frame onto one of the plush seats next to Mileya. Cass took the seat opposite, a wise choice given how much space he occupied.

The coachman peeked his head in. "Ready to depart, Your Highness?" he asked, addressing Cassidae with formality.

She smiled and shook her head. "Yes, and there's no need for such titles with us."

As the carriage began its hours-long ascent up the steep mountain, Berran let the females chatter amongst themselves. Mileya was unusually talkative around Cass, never pausing between sentences, a rare sight for him.

Berran was content to look at the remarkable landscape around him from the window. Heim was disappearing from view minute by minute, the world below falling from his sharp sight the further they ascended up the mountain.

After several hours, the distant murmur of thousands of voices reached their ears, accompanied by the sounds of turning wheels, clashing metals, and the whinnies of horses.

They were close.

The sun had long since set, and the early hours of morning quietly shepherded their arrival. Up ahead, the towering gates of the city loomed, misted and ghostly in the dim light. Perched like a crown upon the mountain's craggy brow, the city of Shadowfern blended into the storm-grey mist that perpetually clung to it. It was not a place Berran would have chosen to visit. Rugged and unforgiving, with weather as miserable as its towering, jagged landscape, it felt like a punishment just to be there.

He had no business in Shadowfern. He wasn't in the trade of weapons, and this was the first Heir's Rite in many, many years. A city he had no reason to visit, until now.

Even in summer's whispers, the air carried a faint chill. Stone stairs and bridges crisscrossed the steep slopes, their surfaces worn smooth by countless journeys over time. Buildings, four to five storeys high, leaned against the rocks that were the bones of the mountains, their glowing lamps casting small pools of light across the narrow streets below. With a roar born of ancient power, a waterfall surged through Shadowfern's stony heart. Its rush was untamed, a torrent of raw force that carved its own path amidst the stone. Like a wild animal, it cascaded with ferocity, casting droplets like diamonds into the air. Its roar was a constant companion, a heartbeat that echoed through the village's veins. One wrong move here, one foot placed out of step, and you will fall down the sheer drop below.

Shadowfern was rough, rugged, and ancient, a place that seemed to peer down at the world from its lofty heights as if it had existed forever.

They made their way toward the residence of the ruling family, the Trewiths, who lived in a small castle on the far side of the waterfall.

"Do the guards know we're here?" Berran asked his sister,

unsure of how they were meant to cross.

Cass unlocked the golden carriage door and stepped out, her silver-slippered feet landing on the mossy street. "They know, but let's not bother them at this hour."

He followed her to the wall that ran along the water. The spray from the waterfall pelted them like shards of glass, and Berran raised a hand to shield his eyes.

Cass extended her hands toward the raging water, and the freezing wind of her power began to flow outwards. Berran mirrored her, his own power a darker, wilder twin of hers.

"This won't hold for long, Cass. The water's too strong."

Together, their powers wove a blizzard of ice and wind, freezing the torrent in place as it climbed higher up the mountain.

Cass let her hands drop, the icy flow stopping. "It'll be fine," she assured, lifting her skirts and flashing a smile to Mileya, who watched from the carriage.

They had frozen the water that usually flooded 121amp the bridge that led to the castle, leaving just enough space for them to cross. As Berran returned to his seat, he ran a cold hand through his hair. The ice creaked and groaned ominously around them, as if the waterfall resented their interference.

The crossing was thankfully short, though Berran could feel Mileya tensing beside him while Cass sat back, utterly unbothered.

They might be syrens, built for enduring raging currents, but they had fins, not wings. If the ice gave way, there would be no surviving the crushing fall over the mountain.

Just as their carriage floated over the bridge's threshold, the ice shattered behind them, the Reothadh power succumbing to nature's strength.

Their arrival at the squat, sturdy castle was swift. The night watch was already there to guide Berran to his room after he bade goodnight to the females.

Damn, he couldn't wait for sleep. Every step was shadowed by weariness, the last few days of travel stretching on endlessly, and the large bed waiting for him called like a Laeth's song. "Busy night?" he asked the guards as they led him through the castle's dark corridors. On one side, thin windows offered glimpses of the world outside, small breaks in the mist revealing the awakening sky.

The guards muttered a gruff response. Miserable bastards, Berran thought

Turning a sharp corner, two male voices he recognised- one very deep, the other in the throes of laughter -echoed from further down inside the castle.

Fuck, he could do without laying eyes on the two males tonight. He hoped they would reach his rooms before Berran had to have a confrontation right after his arrival. It wasn't ideal, especially when he was supposed to make a good impression as both the Silvanh Heir and Reothadh prince.

But seconds later through the flickering darkness, the owners of those voices came into view.

Clad in Valhir red and black, two vampyres strode toward him. The taller one flashed a brilliant smile, his sharp, needle-like 122ampire canines gleaming even in the dim light. They locked eyes, and Berran instinctively bared his own thicker, more animalistic canines, akin to a lion or sand tiger.

"Your Highness, may I ask what brings you out at this late hour?" one of the guards inquired. "Lord and Lady Trewith have forbidden anyone, even royalty, from leaving their rooms after midnight."

Berran had to respect the guard's nerve for confronting two fully grown vampyres capable of tearing him apart.

"My apologies young man, we were just on our way back from another room." Deep, burgundy red eyes looked down at the guard, whilst contempt laced his every word. "However, if I recall correctly, the curfew only applies during the Rite, which doesn't begin for a fortnight. So, unless you wish to argue otherwise, we'll be on our way."

The falseness of his tone grated on Berran's "instincts.

"Care to join us, Berran?" the 123ampire asked, his eyes locking with Berran's again. A muscle ticked in Berran's jaw.

"Taris." Berran gave him a curt nod before turning to his companion. "Kadeen."

Without another glance, Berran followed the song of sleep toward his room.

18
Keyara

Eldorhaven was now a few weeks behind them-weeks of stifling, sun-drenched walking-and Keyara winced at the rising heat, cursing herself for not stealing those horses.
She fucking *hated* this journey.
The walk had been hard enough on her, but she knew it must have been pure torture for Aura, who had barely broken a sweat a day in her life.
They had hitched on passing carts when they could, but the Longh road had continued to stretch on for miles ahead of them.
It had been a gruelling hike, with only brief stops in tiny hamlets to sleep, eat, and shit.
Olive trees lined the way, their silver-green leaves shimmering in the lazy wind, while vibrant wildflowers painted the fields in hues as rich as a painter's palette.
Aura had frequently gasped at the sight of them-Mottel blooms, roses, and other flowers Keyara had never seen before.
Spring had now finally given way to the sun and the sweet scent of day-blooming blossoms, mingled with the earthy aroma of the road.
The rain had stayed behind in Eldorhaven, leaving the terrain dusty and dry, a fine layer of grit coating their sun-kissed skin.
Not that Keyara was complaining; her usual creamy complexion had darkened into a healthier glow, while Aura's skin had turned a light honey colour, highlighting the blue of her eyes.
Keyara glanced up at the sky. It was past noon, and they would

reach the base of the Vaelorns today. The landscape was already shifting as they approached the mountains.

Finally, she muttered to her sister.

The air grew crisper here, as the terrain grew gradually steeper and the sky stretched into an endless expanse of blue, set against the rugged peaks that loomed ahead.

Those peaks, growing larger and more imposing with every step, staggered upward like sentinels.

"Oh gods," Keyara heard Aura whisper in awe. "How beautiful."

"Shit," Keyara exclaimed.

The Vaelorns were *high*, and steep.

She had known the climb would be tough, but seeing the mountains up close sent a stab of doubt through her stomach. Craning her neck to see its summit, snow-capped and majestic- the mountain's peak pierced the sky as if daring the heavens themselves.

Mist clung to the slopes, and from their vantage, at least two miles away, Keyara could have sworn she could hear the faint roar of a waterfall cascading down the mountainside, its journey ending in the twin lakes nestled at the mountain's base, fringed by the town of Heim below.

Following the grassy banks of the Aetha river, where Reothadh were jumping in and out the shimmering water, Heim became less of a spit of brown in the distance and more of a largely populated town around them.

Heim, which had once been just a speck of brown in the distance, was now a bustling town around them as they finally reached the end of the dusty road.

Keyara looked over the heads of the crowds, looking for a face she knew. There was no sign of Berran and his warriors.

"I wonder if Berran's here yet, or if he's already made the climb?" Aura mused, as if reading her mind.

They had concluded on the journey, that their friend must be on his way to Shadowfern. There was no other explanation for his sudden departure.

Keyara huffed, pulling her sister toward the town square. "No idea, but he'd better hope I don't see him right now. I'm still pissed he left without telling me-leaving me to find out about the Rite through some *fucking letter*."

The three-story houses around them clattered with activity as shutters swung open and doors burst wide. Voices filled the air, a mix of languages and accents as diverse as the world itself.

Anxiety gnawed at Keyara as they weaved through the crowd. The ascent up to Shadowfern began tomorrow, but for now, all Keyara wanted to do was bathe and sip on a damned strong drink.

The journey had taken it out of her, and she wanted a moment to breathe.

Just a moment.

Not that Aura had been anything but good company-far from it. Keyara had expected her sister to complain the entire way, but Aura hadn't. She had quietly kept pace, only showing discomfort when she had to pull on her dusty, road-worn clothes.

A blessing, as Keyara wasn't sure how her sister would cope. That small moment of respite, though, seemed further away with every step. Every inn and tavern they approached was full.

"I'm *not* sleeping in the damned street" she grumbled, as Aura came out of another establishment, shaking her head.

Aura chewed the inside of her cheek. "I'll find us something. Don't worry."

At their final option-a run-down hellhole on the outskirts of town-Aura used a little... persuasion to secure a room for the night.

Knowing how much Aura hated using her power for such purposes, Keyara promised herself she'd make it up to her later. Walking into their room, Keyara could not help but grumble.

"Great, another shitty room. You would think with the amount of money these places charge it would be palatial inside. But no-a bucket for a toilet and a bed so small it must've been made for a mouse." She lifted the bucket, grimacing. "And it's got a hole in it. Fantastic."

Aura laughed at her, "Don't be so negative Keyara, it could be worse. You're just lucky you have an extremely powerful sister, otherwise we'd be sleeping out there in the dirt with the drunks and donkeys."

She had a point. The whole journey had been a gamble-there was always the threat of sleeping outside, unprotected, if they couldn't find shelter.

Not that Keyara couldn't have handled it.

Hopes for a bath quickly evaporated when it became clear the inn offered nothing more than a small basin for washing.

Not even a fresh cloth.

Aura pulled one of the pillowcases off the bed and handed it to Keyara as a makeshift washcloth.

With a bit of warmth from her magic, Keyara heated the water, and they silently scrubbed away the grime of the day.

They opted to have their evening meal brought up, rather than go down to the bar and be forced to make conversation with others. Keyara knew that when she won the Rite and became queen, she'd have to engage in conversations she didn't want to have, do things she couldn't be bothered with. But today, she could avoid all that.

Today, she could avoid meaningless conversations.

As the moon watched over them and after finishing a meal of fragrant summer fish stew with crusty bread, washed down with a few small jugs of honey mead to fill their stomachs, they went to sleep, top and tail like children in their mouse bed.

19

Aura

Inside the innermost walls of Shadowfern, Aura finally felt comfortable in the spacious bedroom they shared. Yesterday had passed in a blur.

After entering through the towering city gates-massive structures carved from the very stone of the surrounding peaks-Aura had noticed the sharp spikes that crowned their tops; a silent warning to any who might dare trespass.

Or leave, she had thought.

A dozen guards stood by the open doors, clad in thick black armour, checking names as crowds entered. The same guards quickly ushered them into the castle, where they were shown to their room. Servants had promptly brought them an evening meal on trays, leaving little time to explore or get a sense of their surroundings.

It was frustrating, as Aura was eager to see the castle and the city beyond.

This morning, however, brought a moment of calm. Scooping a spoonful of Greenberry jam into her warm oats, Aura leaned back into the crisp white linens of their bed, grateful it was which was, at last, big enough for the two of them.

Accompanying their breakfast was a note for Keyara-her training would begin today.

Aura noticed Keyara's gaze fixed on the window, where the mist swirled outside in a slow, rhythmic dance. The intricate tapestries adorning the walls of the room framed her figure, their patterns rich with the colours drawn from the surrounding mountains.

Keyara clutched her daggers, one in each hand, relaxing visibly as soon as they were in her grip.

With a voice that carried a mixture of awe and disbelief, she said, "Is this real? Are we really here? I can't...shit, I can't quite believe it, can you?"

Swinging her legs out the warm bed, Aura padded over the soft, shaggy rug that sprawled across the floor. She joined her sister at the window, placing an arm around Keyara's slender shoulders.

"No, not really," she whispered. "But I believe in *you*, and I believe with everything I have that you can do this."

Together, they stared down at the bustling courtyard below, where people scurried like ants, moving from door to door with arms full, preparing the castle for the upcoming revelry.

A weighty knock at the door pulled Aura from her thoughts. "One minute," she called, hastily wrapping her dirty cloak around herself.

She opened the door, already knowing who would be there from the scent alone.

His presence both commanding and gentle, embodying the sea's tranquil strength, Berran stood tall in the wooden frame.

"Welcome to Shadowfern, ladies, I hope I'm not too early," he greeted with a smile.

Warmth swelled in Aura's chest, the ever-present darkness within her lifting a little at seeing his friendly face. She hugged him in welcome.

"Berran, how did you know we were here?"

Berran glanced over her shoulder at Keyara, now standing straight as a steel rod on the other side of the room.

"I knew Keyara would be here, and I asked the guards where to find you. We didn't arrive until the early hours this morning"

As he spoke, he let go of Aura and cautiously, walked over to her sister.

Keyara spoke with an icy edge to her voice. "You should have told me Berran. I deserved at least a warning. You left and didn't even tell me why. I was summoned through a fucking letter."

Fizzing in her blood, Aura's magic could feel the tension in the room escalate. An uncomfortable, cloying feeling.

Hanging his head, Berran hesitated at the edge of the sheepskin rug, his posture stiff as he clasped his hands behind his back, dressed in silver velvet.

His voice was soft, apologetic. "I know, and I'm sorry. You should've heard it from me. I should've made time to tell you, but in the rush of leaving..." he scratched at his scalp, "...I didn't think. I was an idiot."

Keyara's hazel-gold eyes were sharp, unyielding. She wasn't one to back down from confrontation, especially when she felt wronged.

A few moments passed, and Aura couldn't predict her sister's next move. The tension in the room was thick, and she didn't want the awkwardness to stretch on any longer.

Slowly, she approached Keyara and placed a gentle hand on her arm, letting a small thread of her magic flow through-a subtle nudge, urging Keyara to be reasonable and forgiving.

It seemed to work, softening Keyara's temper ever so slightly. "Fine. Apology accepted," Keyara muttered, waving her hand dismissively as she pulled away from Aura's touch.

She sat on the edge of the bed, pretending to pick at her nails with the sharp tip of one of her daggers. Without looking up, Keyara said, "Are you here to tell me we'll be carrying on our lessons, or am I to train with the others."

Before Berran could respond, the door swung open again, revealing a towering figure, as dark and still as the night.

Aura's breath caught.

Mileyakhan.

Aura recognised her from Berrans' descriptions alone. She had only ever seen rough sketches of her enigmatic species in textbooks, but they paled in comparison to seeing them in the flesh. Unable to capture their otherworldly grace, those sketches couldn't quite capture her amethyst-hued skin and hair that radiated an ethereal glow in the morning light.

Almost as tall as the Reothadh warrior himself, Mileyakhan's mere presence seemed to steal the air from the room.

"Didn't take you long to find the women, Berran," she said, her deep voice cutting through the room with authority. "Pull your trousers up. We're going down for breakfast."

Berran turned to Aura and Keyara, his eyes twinkling with a familiar warmth.

"Keyara, Aura-this is Mileyakhan, my oldest friend and the Domhiann emissary here on land. Mileya, this is Keyara, who I've told you about before, and her sister, Aura."

Even though Aura knew Mileyakhan's vision was extremely limited, the female's black gaze felt unnervingly sharp as she stood in the shadows of the doorway.

The female inhaled deeply, remaining in the shadows of the doorway.

"Berran has told me of your unusual gifts, Keyara. How blessed you are to hold such power for just a human."

Keyara met the syren's gaze without flinching.

"Yes, how blessed I am, for a human such as myself." Her tone was cold, and Aura bit the inside of her cheek, sensing the tension rise.

Her sister wasn't done. "Funny, though-I can't seem to recall Berran ever mentioning you before." Aura cringed at the blatant lie.

She knew the *human* comment had stung, but antagonizing a Domhiann emissary?

Brash.

This female was the one and only representative of her species, the only connection they all had to the secretive ocean dwellers. If Keyara hoped to one day be queen, she needed to act like one.

Coming across to others as a petulant child would only serve her ill in the future.

Berran, sensing the shift, smoothly interjected.

"Aura, Keyara, I'll see you soon. Make yourselves comfortable here. Lord and Lady Trewith are generous and have provided maids to assist with anything you need."

He turned to leave, then paused, casting a glance at Keyara, who was flipping her daggers idly from hand to hand. "And please... try to make alliances and not piss anyone off."

His last words were clearly directed at Keyara. He hesitated for just a moment before stepping out, leaving Aura with the daunting task of keeping her sister in check over the coming weeks.

It was going to be like trying to keep a fly away from shit.

20
Aura

Keyara left early that morning for her first day of official Rite training, leaving Aura to explore the castle on her own. By late afternoon, she had wandered through nearly every corner, with only the library left untouched.

Aura stepped into the low-ceilinged room, her hands brushing over a large, jade-green book she'd selected from the towering shelves. Dust rose into the air as she set it down on one of the stone pews lined down the centre of the room.

From the corner of her eye, she could have sworn she saw a large white dog run past the open doorway. Dismissing the thought, she refocused on the book in front of her.

Embossed in pure gold, Aura read the title again: *The Maolin Wars: A Syren Song.* Aura traced the lettering with her fingers before opening it, her mind only half-engaged as she began to skim the pages.

War had never been a subject she cared for, but she knew its intricacies would be essential for her sister's future. A day might come when circumstances demanded it, as awful as the thought was.

Her attention sharpened as she reached a chapter on Alysee, the ancient Laeth martyr of the syren species, who's sacrifice had brought an end to the short, brutal war.

Just as she was about to read further, a familiar scent drifted into the room, filling her senses. It was the smell of rain-soaked forests and fresh spring grass-of moss-lined oaks and sunlight over dewy leaves. She stood abruptly, searching for the source.

But it couldn't be. "It's just the altitude, Aura," she muttered to herself, trying to shake off the absurd notion that *he* was near. Tucking a stray curl behind her ear, she sat back down and returned to the tome. Alysee's story pulled her in again, the vivid description of her selflessness brought a lump to her throat. The mere thought of those hundreds, thousands of Laeth younglings and their mothers being slaughtered by hordes of Reothadh's had sent a few tears down Aura's cheeks.

The matriarch turned goddess had sacrificed herself to prevent the annihilation of her species. She knew the basic history, but the detailed account of Alysee's heartbreak and ultimate betrayal made her stomach turn.

The last passage in the chapter on the ill-fated female compelled Aura to close the book.

'The identity of Queen Alysee's true Bonded has, to this day, never been revealed. Some speculate it was a low-ranking female from her pod. Name unknown.

Alysee's lover, Hescatus of Silvanh, was rumoured to be the one who disclosed the location of the Laeth mothers and younglings seeking refuge in neutral territory-a cove four miles off the coast of Zerithia.

Consumed by jealousy over Alysee's bond with the unknown female, Hescatus betrayed her. In the aftermath of Cildraethe's destruction by the Domhiann Skuidd, the war's inevitable loss, and Hescatus's treachery, Alysee gave herself to the Reothadhs, ending the war.

The accounts of her fate are murky, with no two witnesses recounting the same events of that day. All anyone could agree on was that the ocean and her many seas had left this world. Alysee's great power was gone, and her bloodline, which could be traced back to the great matriarch Iara, was lost with her. Now she joins the great matriarch goddess in the eternal sea.'

Aura's chest tightened as she read those final lines. The weight of history felt overwhelming-the blood, the loss, the betrayal.

She closed the book, feeling as though she'd absorbed all the pain she could bear for one day.
. The rest of the Maolin story would always be there, waiting for her to return. But for now, the blood that had been spilt remained in the past, while the stars above continued to bear witness to what had been written long ago and that same blood-had stained.

She slid the book back into its place on the dusty shelf, among its companions: *The Blood Rebellion, Dance of the Tides,* and countless other tomes chronicling the wars and skirmishes of Myrantis's long history.

They would have to wait, as it was time to return to her room. Keyara should be back from training by now and Aura was eager to hear all about her first day.

Quietly closing the heavy oak doors behind her, Aura left the empty library, silently promising Alysee that she would return to finish her story tomorrow, even if she did terrify Aura slightly. Being that she was a Laeth, Alysee would most likely have eaten her alive without a second thought.

As she walked down one of the narrow, dimly lit corridors, a strange sensation crept over her-she felt as though she were being watched. From what direction, she could not say, but it weighed on her.

Throwing out a spark of her power, Aura tried to clasp onto a thread of emotion, but there was none to hum along the golden vines of her magic. No read of anything other than the background vibration of a bustling castle.

Those unseen eyes followed her through the grey corridors all the way to their room. Outside the door, Berran stood waiting, his smile warm as she approached.

"Anyone would think you're courting one of us, Berran, with how often you stop by," Aura teased, slipping the key into the lock and giving him a wide grin. "Is Keyara inside?"

"I'm not sure I could handle either of you two if I'm honest

Aura." Berran chuckled. "But the men who do will have a lifetime of entertainment, that's for certain." He followed her into the room, his footsteps echoing in the stillness.

There was no sign of Keyara.

"When will she be back?" Aura asked.

"I don't know. I'm not permitted to observe the training or be informed of its progress. No one is," Berran replied.

She raised an eyebrow. "Not even a prince?"

He smirked, sitting on the window ledge. "No, Aura, not even a prince-not that I am one, technically."

Aura loosened the bow in her hair, shaking out her strawberry-tinted curls. She threw the ribbon from her hair onto the bed, before perching on the small stool beside the mirror that hung on the far wall as Berran continued talking. His deep voice was a soothing backdrop as she massaged her scalp, letting the tension of the day melt away.

"I need to tell Keyara something important," Berran began, his voice turning more serious as he pushed a strand of white hair from his piercingly blue eyes. "I tried this morning, but..."

He trailed off, clearly remembering the awkwardness of their earlier encounter. Aura sighed, knowing where his thoughts were.

"You should have told her as soon as you knew about the Rite," Aura said gently. "But she'll get over it. She just needs time. You know how she is."

Berran huffed in agreement, running a hand through his silver-white hair.

"Yes, I do. Which is why I'm going to make it up to her by telling her something no one else is supposed to know." His large frame filled the window, his fine Reothadh clothes shimmering in the afternoon light. Aura took in his appearance-the silver and white jacket with icy blue threads woven through the fabric like rivers over a glacier. The Reothadh royal crest, an ice dragen, was proudly displayed on his chest.

136

She looked down at herself and was embarrassed. How ridiculous must she and Keyara appear to the numerous nobility that occupied the castle? She brushed those shallow thoughts aside. In the scheme of things, clothing was not important right now.

The sound of approaching footsteps caught their attention.

Keyara entered, looking flustered and dishevelled from her day of training. Aura immediately rushed over to help her unload the various items she was carrying onto the bed.

Mud-stained bandages, torn up pieces of paper, a leather hood, all found themselves chucked without acknowledgement or ceremony down together.

Her sister glanced at Berran, her eyes dark beneath the cascade of her hair.

"Two visits in one day. Aren't we lucky?" she muttered, her tone flat.

He stood up from the window ledge. "Very."

Keyara rolled those slightly upturned eyes.

"Even luckier for you, Keyara, because I have information you'll want to hear." Aura could hear the strained lightness in his tone. He placed those large arms behind his back, ever the portrait of syren royalty.

Berran continued. "Before I came here, King Farhand made an announcement in Oridae-something none of the other competitors know yet. Well, something they shouldn't know yet, if the other nobility have kept their silence. But I couldn't keep it from you."

Keyara's brows furrowed. "What is it?"

Berran sighed, the gravity of the moment heavy in his voice.

"It's not just humans competing in the Heir's Rite."

The room seemed to still, the air leaving the room on swift feet. With her hands trembling as they gripped the fabric of her dress, Aura looked to Keyara, who stood frozen, absorbing the words.

"You can't share this information with anyone else, Keyara, I mean it. I would be in serious shit if anyone knew I told you. It will give you an edge against the others if we keep this between ourselves." Berrans' feet shifted on the rug, his stare now fully resting on Keyara.

"I will try to help you however I can. I saved your sister all those years ago, and I will do whatever I can to help you now".

Aura struggled to process the enormity of what Berran had just revealed to them. Vampyres, syrens, fae-how could Keyara stand a chance against them?

Panic tightened in her chest. This was madness, and it brought the Rite to a whole other level.

Keyara's magic is strong, Aura thought. *But is it strong enough?*

Aura tried to keep her voice steady as she spoke. "Thank you for telling us, Berran. Could you give us a moment alone?"

Berran and Aura exchanged a knowing look, their love for Keyara evident in each other's eyes. Reluctantly, he stepped back towards the door.

"Yes of course," he said, his voice heavy with conviction as he quietly left the room, taking the Reothadh strength with him.

Aura looked to Keyara, trying to blink away the tears glistening in her vision. Her words came out in a rush, tumbling over each other.

"Listen, it will be fine. I can't lie to you Keyara, I'm terrified for your sake, but you won't be facing this alone remember? I'm sure I can use my magic to make them trust you, support you, influence them to, I don't know. I'll do something."

"Aura…"

"We'll do this together," Aura rushed on, her words tumbling out. "Berran will keep training you, and your power is probably stronger than theirs anyway-"

"Aura, for fuck's sake, stop!" Keyara's shout echoed in the room, cutting her off. "I appreciate it, but I have to do this on my own."

A flinch escaped Aura, the sudden silence deafening. "You'd let Berran help, but not me?" she asked, her voice cracking.

Keyara sighed, pacing the room. "Berran's been training me for years. He knows what he's doing. And if I win on my own merit, without anyone's help... it'll mean more."

Aura shook her head. "But you promised we'd do this together."

"I need to think," Keyara snapped, her agitation clear. "This is a lot to take in."

Keyara sat on the edge of the large bed, her usual confident demeanour, now replaced by worry etched deep into her eyes. This was going to be a long road for them both.

As the week progressed, anticipation rained down upon the castle. Keyara's training consumed her with each passing day. While Aura admired her sister's strength from afar, couldn't help but wince every so often at the various cuts and bruises Keyara had acquired each day when she eventually returned to their room.

The evenings found them immersed in the books Aura had taken from the library. The history of Eira, Myrantis and its species, was unveiled before them both, as though it were on of the tapestries in the castle, woven with triumphs and betrayals. The two of them had never had access to such a wealth of information before.

The Shadowfern library was extensive and at least four times the size of the one inside the Corall's mansion back home. Aura devoured the pages of old tomes, delighting in each new bite of knowledge. Though she could sense the weight of past events settling on her sisters' sharp shoulders.

As Keyara's understanding deepened like Aura's own, so did her connection to the land she was destined to protect. Aura would make sure her sister was just as educated as her rivals, who had no doubt grown up far more privileged than they, with such information at their fingertips.

Five days had passed since they first arrived and after Berran had told them about the inclusivity of the Heir's Rite. Aura's worry never left and the darkness inside her was all-consuming. Even though her faith in her sister was getting stronger by the day, knowing that Keyara faced such a hard journey ahead of her made Aura want to throw up.

So much so, that the words in the book on her lap began to jumble into an unknown language. She shut the tome's pages together and threw it across the sheets of the bed. Getting up from the mattress, she muttered to Keyara that she needed a walk.

She knew that her magic was influencing her sister when they were close. Aura caught glimpses of her frequently not finishing her meals, looking quite green in the face. The familiar palor of anxiety and fear.

In the heart of the castle's courtyard, Aura walked alone. After skipping breakfast and pulling on the same dress she had worn for weeks, she wanted to explore more of the city.

The pale morning sun warmed her bare skin. Lifting her skirts over the three steps towards the bridge, she felt a presence behind her, a sense of quiet familiarity. Glancing around, Aura's heart raced; her fingers twitching with the need to hold onto something. The same feeling she had felt in the corridors days before, found her now. Someone, or something, was watching her again.

Whenever she left her room, in courtyards, in the library, even now as she wandered through the castle grounds, that feeling never left.

Aura decided to ignore it. She had nothing to hide; whoever it was, she could feel no threat from them.

So let them look.

21
Keyara

The clang of steel against steel echoed sharply through the training yard, reverberating in the draughty arena.

Keyara's sword sliced through the air with a scream, each strike fuelled by her will to beat her competition.

She tapped her foot impatiently, having effortlessly defeated yet another opponent in swordplay-another useless man who could hardly hold his own against her.

The sword masters of Shadowfern were… fine. But not a patch on Berran and his warriors. They'd piss all over this rabble of amateurs.

She would have much rather trained with the Falkrans of the Vaelorns, whose arrows have supposedly never missed a target. Now *that* would've been a better use of her time, rather than wasting it with this damned group of incompetents.

"Will we meet the Falkrans anytime soon?" she'd asked one of the overseers during archery practice.

"No," he'd said, handing her another arrow. "They never leave their perch in the peaks."

"Not even for the Heir's Rite?" she'd pressed, pulling her bowstring taut.

Her arrow went wide. *"Fuck it,"* she muttered under her breath.

The overseer, retrieving another arrow, merely replied, "The Falkrans only come down when the mountain falls."

She'd asked what he meant, but he had said nothing more, urging her to take another shot.

In the weeks since training began, Keyara and the other

competitors had been pushed to their limits, preparing for the trials ahead.

Keyara had noticed from passing a few in the corridors and training grounds, that some were doing far better than others. Not that they were permitted to train together, for fear of alliances in the competition was rife. She had no clue of their numbers or even who she would be competing against.

As expected, she excelled in sword fighting.

Her years with Berran clearly gave her some advantage against men and women who fought with polished court manners rather than practical skill.

She didn't do well, however, in the cryptic puzzles, and treacherous obstacle courses that had all been part of the regimen.

As were the hours she spent with Aura every damned evening, poring over dusty old tomes borrowed from the castle library, attempting to cram the political history of Myrantis into her tired brain.

The mental exhaustion, combined with the physical toll of her daily training, left Keyara longing for sleep; the only respite she had from the gruelling demands.

It would damned well kill her before the Rite even began.

It was so fucking hard, she thought every night as her head hit the pillow, fresh bruises painted along her shins and thighs from yet another day of climbing tall walls or falling off dizzying heights.

Obstacle courses sprawled across the ground and Keyara blocked out the sun from her vision with one hand, as the evening light cast long shadows across the large, stony surface of her walled off section of the arena training ground.

Her limbs ached, but she pressed on navigating the treacherous paths, scaling walls, and leaping over hurdles with muttered curses and heat in her determined veins.

Godsdamned it, she thought, her lurching steps confirming that she was not very nimble or graceful. The overseers watched impassively as she swore under her breath, sweat mixing with dust as she fought to stay on her feet.

Another false step crumbled away behind her as she eventually reached the top of a dizzyingly tall platform.

Her quick footedness was the only thing that had saved her from tumbling down towards the earth. Day after day she had been doing this, and it was getting tiresome.

After a particularly brutal, shitty day of fist fighting, Keyara returned to her room, bloodied and bruised.

Learning how to fight with honour they said. Keyara had rolled her eyes at the word the overseers loved to use.

Not that she needed to learn how to fight with her fists, but the man she had been paired with was huge, and once he began out manoeuvring her, she decided that maybe she did need to learn the technical side of fighting.

Then again, he had also cheated by kicking up dust into her face.

Prick, she had spat after the match, not quite managing to keep the insult to herself.

Aura had nearly wept at the sight of Keyara's swollen face that evening. Keyara had brushed it off, lying about having been in worse shape after a night at Gregory's.

But that was a bare-faced lie and they both knew it.

"I'm doing this for us," Keyara pleaded, her gaze locked with her sister's. "For Mother."

She knew Aura saw the fire in her eyes, the unbreakable fire that burned like a beacon, for she finally gave in, wiping away those salty tears.

And so, the nights carried their whispered conversations into the wind, the room a haven where sisters shared their dreams and fears. Keyara's roaring mind calmed as they cuddled up like two young girls again.

When the sun rose each day and as Keyara returned to her

training alone, she felt the love from her sister radiate around her bruised body, healing her anxieties.

As did the golden light from Aura's power.

Their mother would have such pride if she could see them now, how strong Keyara had become. The experience and confidence she had gained over the weeks.

She reminded herself to write a letter home as soon as she had completed her first trial of the Rite, which began tomorrow.

The contents of which would include questions over the trustworthiness of Lord and Lady Corall and how they had betrayed her mother...

The thought made her stomach flip as she wobbled atop one of the towering platforms in the obstacle course.

Shit, the realisation that the Rite began tomorrow was finally sinking in.

Now that the false steps had broken away, the journey down was notably quicker than the ascent and her training ended with a shaky descent and the handoff of a ribbon from the summit.

No words of encouragement from the overseers-just the same cold indifference, with not even a *'good luck, don't die, have a long and fulfilled life'*.

Unlacing her hair from the braid atop her head, she walked into the castle, its atmosphere abuzz with energy.

The Lord and Lady of Shadowfern were hosting a ball tha' evening, marking the start of the event.

A letter accompanying their breakfast this morning had informed them so and it had sent Aura into a panic as they had nothing to wear.

Keyara could not give less of a shit if she tried.

It made no difference to the competition outcome if she ate with the nobles or not.

Keyara's footsteps echoed through the draughty halls. She was quite relieved they had an excuse not to go tonight. Honestly, she was exhausted and could do with a hot bath and a warm bed.

Though no sooner had Keyara's aching feet crossed the threshold, the look on Aura's face told her they were, in fact, going to the ball after all.

"Keyara, look! Look what Berran gave us," Aura said excitedly, holding up something red.

With a yawn, Keyara replied, "What is it?"

"Gowns for tonight, here's yours." Aura held up a gown in a deep shade of summer

cherries, its silhouette flowing and elegant.

Keyara raised an eyebrow, fingering the delicate layers of sheer fabric between her calloused fingers. "Who would've thought Berran had such a feminine taste. Red certainly isn't his colour," she quipped.

Aura giggled, spreading the gown across the bed. "He said they were from his sister. He came by earlier today, knowing we wouldn't have much to wear. I guess he asked her to help. I didn't even know he had a sister."

"I did," Keyara said, reflecting on the rare times Berran mentioned his sister, Cassidae. He spoke fondly of her, but not often.

"I told him your favourite colour and gave him a rough idea of what you might like. Is it okay? I've never seen you in a dress before," Aura asked tentatively.

"Yes, it's fine," she said with genuine thanks, her sister didn't have much to work with and she had done her best.

Keyara looked at the gown again. It was simple but pretty-billowing sleeves ending at cuffed wrists and a soft off-shoulder neckline that would reveal her sharp shoulders and milky collarbones.

The gown's ethereal design, like the mist circling the castle grounds, added a touch of elegance she rarely felt in herself.

It wasn't something Keyara would have chosen for herself, but the colour was lovely, and it was a gift.

She wasn't that damned rude to turn it down.

Aura gave her a tentative grin, picking up her own gown.

"I'm going to put mine on. Tell me what you think," she called, disappearing into the bathroom and leaving Keyara to wrangle her dress on alone.

A few stubborn tendrils of dark hair came loose as she re-pinned her hair into a quick updo.

"For fuck's sake," she muttered, struggling to lace up the black velvet corset that cinched the waist of her gown. "Aura, when you're done, can you help m-"

Her words faltered as aura appeared in the doorway.

On any given day, Aura's innocent beauty caught the eye of everyone, but this was the most beautiful she had ever seen her.

Which was saying something as the woman looked stunning in a potato sack.

The soft meadow green of the dress complemented her sister's braided strawberry hair perfectly, as it lay gently on one side of her head, hanging over her shoulder.

Small, puffed sleeves framed her petite shoulders, while the neckline gently skimmed across her chest, modestly covering but still enhancing her figure.

Adorned with intricate lace appliques of pure ivory, each petal-like detail meticulously crafted to create an ethereal garden on the bodice. The lace extended gently down the flowing skirt, gradually fading into the satin as if nature itself were weaving it.

"How is it?" Aura asked, her voice uncertain-a tone Keyara had never heard from her before.

It saddened her to see Aura doubt herself when she looked nothing short of perfect.

"Aura, gods, you look beautiful. You know I would tell you if you didn't."

Her sister nodded, the train of her gown billowing behind as she came over to Keyara and laced the corset that was hanging off around Keyara's hips.

Keyara pulled at the tight corset with one hand, the other clung on to her sister's arm and together they left the safety of their room, down to the viper's den.

22
Keyara

Keyara didn't quite know what she was expecting from the
ballroom of this castle, but it certainly wasn't this.
She inadvertently rolled her eyes, taking in the simple,
practical, room around them.
The colourful, shimmering ballroom of the Coralls' manor was
a dream compared to this.
The hall was a space that was so obviously rarely used, the lord
and lady of the castle appeared as strangers in their own home,
like ghosts wandering the halls of a castle that was once theirs.
The coffers of Shadowfern were quite clearly dedicated to
things of higher priority.
Looking at her sister, Keyara could see Aura was trying to hide
her disappointment. Aura had always wanted to go to a ball,
they had practised dancing together their whole lives.
Even Keyara had secretly, diligently remembered the steps.
After all, if she were to be Queen one day, she would need to
know dancing etiquette.
Gowns of silk and satin billowed like storm clouds on the grey
dance floor, whilst noblemen gleamed like polished shits
against the smooth stone walls.
An enormous glass door, leading out into the night beyond was
going to be her first port of call. She needed the tonic of fresh
air before the performance began.
Sipping on white goblets aside the glass doors, Keyara spotted
Berran with the dark-skinned syren.
"Look there's Berran," Keyara led her sister over to the syrens,

"we better go thank him for the gowns."

Berrans' double take on their approach didn't go unnoticed. Keyara couldn't blame him. The drastic change in her appearance must have given him a heart attack.

"Evening ladies, you look… different."

"Better I hope." Aura nudged him with her elbow. "Please say thank you to your sister for us."

Berran took a sip from his goblet. "I will, and that reminds me, I must introduce you both to her."

Keyara was too busy trying not to stare at the syren standing next to him. Clad in a sheer gown that hugged every ripple of her body, the Domhiann was mesmerising. The deep purple of the material would not be particularly noteworthy on others, but on her, it brought out the iridescent undertones to her skin in such a way that made it hard to look anywhere else.

He saw her looking at his friend, "You remember Mileya. " He gave Keyara a wary look as he gestured to his friend.

Keyara must admit, Mileyakhan intimidated her.

Slightly.

She gave off such an otherworldly feel that it made Keyara want to turn away and run in the other direction.

Or that could be the shitty look the syren was giving her.

"Yes, of course we remember her," Keyara heard her sister say. "Hello Mileya, you look beautiful."

Accepting the compliment, the syren angled her head down to Aura, giving her a tight-lipped smile.

Shit, she supposed she better say something now to not look like a rude bitch.

Putting on her best grin, even though she knew the syren was pretty much blind, and with the insult from their first meeting at the forefront of her mind, Keyara said, "I agree."

Filling the silence she quickly followed up with the first thing she could think of.

"I like your gown Mileya."

A vicious hiss whipped from Mileyakhan, "If you want to live to see the sunrise, *Keyara*, I advise you to address me by my full name."

Sensing the threat, Keyara's hands instinctively went around one of her daggers, strapped to the inside of her arm beneath the sleeve of her dress.

Though why her sister got away with the informal address, Keyara had no clue.

Aura put her arm around her. "Excuse my sister, it has been a tiring few months for us both, what with the journey and the training. Court etiquette is not natural to us just yet."

An awkward chuckle left Berrans throat, his side eye to Keyara a desperate signal of peace.

Taking a deep inhale, she let the calming effect of Aura's power work its way through her, giving it a moment before she walked through the glass doors of the balcony, mumbling her excuse to the others, leaving her sister with them.

She could feel all eyes on her back, following her out into the darkness.

"Fucking Domhianns," she muttered under her breath, grabbing a drink from a passing waiter and downing it in one gulp. Snatching another, she did it again.

Keyara winced, the fruity, tropical tang coating her tongue.

Akoaàn wyne she realised. The taste was certainly not unknown to her and was usually the last thing she remembered before the wild ride that followed.

Never mind she thought, placing the empty goblet onto a tray that floated past.

Leaning over the edge of the balcony, she gazed out over the waterfall that tumbled through Shadowfern down the mountains below.

Obscuring the view, the mist of water and clouds disrupted the moon's glow, its light casting flashes through the night sky.

It was silent out here, save for the crashing of water and faint music emanating from the closed glass doors that led into the ballroom behind her. Keyara relaxed as she realised for the first time in months, she was finally alone.

Under her rough hands, Keyara could feel the night-blooming flowers intertwined with the balustrade. Embracing the soft feel of them, she closed her eyes, trying to gather her rapidly scattering thoughts as her face grew hotter with every passing moment.

She would kill for a cool breeze, Keyara thought as she watched the shimmer of magic surrounding the castle disappear and reappear with every illumination from the silvery light above.

Inhaling the fragrance of the flowers to ground herself, another...*intoxicating* scent found its way to her senses. Leather with an undertone of warm spices. It ricocheted through her.

She also felt it scarring her brain, marking its place there, daring her to try and remove it.

"Careful, someone might push you over that."

A voice with a velvet cadence sent shivers down her spine, and Keyara snapped her eyes open.

Her hazy gaze was drawn to a large figure a few feet behind her. A man shrouded in shadows, and like a predator, he stalked towards her.

She couldn't quite make out his features from this distance, though she could see he was dressed in purest maroon with deep skin.

Not quite the pitch blackness of a Domhiann, but rich and warm.

As he drew closer, she pulled out her dagger, gripping it behind her back.

His nearing presence revealed striking, angular features that caught the scattered moonlight. Full lips that held a wicked smile and cropped, shaven dark hair.

His eyes held a depth that seemed bottomless, and they were red. An endless, full-bodied red.

Vampyre red.

She held the dagger out to him. "Stay the fuck away from me." The prick walked straight up the point of it, his side grin showcasing deadly sharp canines, whilst the black blade threatened to pierce his chest.

Keyara was tall for a human woman, but this vampyre towered over her.

Taller than Berran too; he must be close to seven feet.

Not that he scared her. She had dealt with Reothadh warriors far more frightening than him. He was just an arrogant vampyre like the rest of his kind. All compensating for something she would wager.

The leathery, spicy scent radiated off him, drawing her in.

He looked down at the dagger on his chest, then back up to her face. Raising a thick eyebrow he said, "If I wanted to harm you, do you not think I'd have thrown you over that balcony whilst your eyes were shut."

He had a point.

But she didn't know this male, and he was a vampyre. Not to be trusted on either account.

"Why didn't you?" She challenged him, not removing her weapon from his red jacket, which would now most definitely have a hole in it.

Bending at the waist, he leaned in closer, viciousness gleaming in his eyes.

"Where's the fun in eliminating the competition when they have their back turned".

With the swiftness of a snake, he grabbed her weapon and nicked her wrist with it, surprisingly gentle as he did so.

"Fucking hell!" Keyara exclaimed, forcing heat into her hands and singeing his fine jacket as she pushed him away.

The sly grin didn't leave his handsome face as he stumbled

back. With slow movements, the vampyre placed his thumb with a few drops of her blood smudged on it into his mouth. Through the darkness, she could see his pupils dilating in an instant.

Keyara was so sure he would be dead from the look she was throwing at him. She was about to put all her power into her dagger and shove it straight in his arsehole's face when the grand doors of the castle flew open.

From over his shoulder, she could see Aura standing with Berran by her side. The fragrant aroma of the banquet filled the surrounding air.

"Keyara, come inside, the banquet is ready."

With one last glare at the male, Keyara shoved past him, knocking into his shoulder as she went.

The tension in the atmosphere seemed to crackle and Keyara could feel an icy blast breeze past as she got closer to Berran, his glacial eyes staring hard at the vampyre beyond.

"Everything ok?" Aura asked her tentatively.

"Yes, fine, just some arsehole. Let's go to eat, I'm starving."

23
Jonn

Anytime he opened his eyes, Jonn immediately regretted it. With every lifting of his eyelids and closing with each passing moment, he couldn't escape the four godsforsaken walls that were his prison. Trapped by the whims of a Laeth – who by his fucking luck, was the heir – his life hung in the balance. He knew time inexorably counted down to the moment when his fate would be sealed.

His options were limited. The choice between a vicious death that ended in his consumption, or to be put under her syren spell. Not brilliant options, though if he dared to admit, he would much rather die than be under *her* spell.

He didn't give a shit if it was the coward's way out. A heart and mind not belonging to oneself was a cruel and twisted existence and not one he would choose in any lifetime.

Selsie had kept to her word, visiting him the very next day after his imprisonment and every day since. The moment she had walked through the door, he had recognised her as the very same syren that he saw in the water before he was thrown from the ship.

Though he had no access to the time and his meals were scattered in their deliverance, he knew when she was minutes from his door.

He could sense her nearby from the way his breath caught in his throat and his heart quickened, despite his better judgement and many curses to himself. The deep-seated hatred for her, along with her kind, was his excuse for his body's reaction to her. Laeths disgusted him and he made sure she knew it every day.

Her frequent attempts to engage him in conversation had irked him at first. Her blatant ignorance of his situation, a twisted game or genuine naivety, made him question his sanity at times. However, as time wore on, he let her. Each night as he lay in his shitty excuse for a bed, he could feel his guard dropping ever so slightly, day by day. A dangerous game to play when your liver could be served alongside cod by sundown.

The precious time away from his prison was spent on excursions around Cildraethe with her, with hours of conversation on various topics. Mysteries of the sea beyond Myrantis, the legends of Cildraethe and the Laeths and stories that had shaped her world.

Jonn soon got the impression that Selsie was both captor and captive, caught between her loyalty to the Laeths and her growing fascination with the world above. He had rarely given her his opinion on the matter, letting her speak on whatever she wanted.

Weeks had passed since he had been taken captive, and the days began blurring together. It was a monotonous cycle of solitude, punctuated only by Selsie and their daily walks around the city.

The next full moon was due any day now and he would remain a rat, caught in a trap until his future would be decided by the creatures that held him. Decided by the… *success* or failure of a certain syren princess and her voice. Though that is not how the Laeths addressed her, he noticed. They called her simply by her name; a strange custom that other syren species followed. It had taken him a while to figure out who she was, the truth only being revealed to him by the young guard who had brought him his food one night.

He had asked Neesh who Selsie was, due to the looks the population gave her as they walked through the labyrinth streets. Moving akin to shadows within the chambers carved deep into the rocky heart of the city, wide-eyed stares followed the figure of pure grace that passed by them. Those same syrens gave him a very different stare; one of pure hunger that matched the unforgiving tides that surrounded this land of ruthless beauty. The salt-laden air hung heavy with the scent of brine and the whispers of spells yet to be cast.

He thought about her eyes and how they shimmered like the depths of the sea. Jonn was not so oblivious as to disregard her otherworldly beauty. The perfect line of her jaw and the way her golden bronze curls skimmed her perfect arse, which begged to be touched.

He scolded himself. *Get a fucking grip. Less than two months without the touch of a woman and you are pining after a creature of death*, he thought, as he waited for the knock that would inevitably come in the next few minutes.

A gentle storm was rumbling outside, the waves lashing over his window creating the feeling of being underwater. Sighing, Jonn grabbed the blanket on his bed, the thin material a useless piece of crap that did very little in keeping him dry on the walks that Selsie insisted they took, even in downpours.

"It's rain Jonn, it won't kill you," she had said to him last time they ventured out in the summer rain, drudging along a path that ran adjacent to the city's towering and impenetrable walls, built from the bedrock that hunkered down underneath the island.

He had raised one eyebrow at her. The irony was missed by the female, even with the cruel hieroglyphs that told the tales of the syrens' power and cruelty etched along the walls they followed. That cruelty was reflected everywhere he turned in Cildraethe, a place where the very architecture echoed the viciousness of its inhabitants. It stood as a testament to the power of the Laeths, a realm shrouded in darkness and enigma, a fortress guarding the secrets of the deep, and a symbol of the relentless might of the sea.

A place where he now realised humans would be fools to ever

attempt an attack. Land or sea, they would be overpowered. Not only that, but this kingdom was also extremely wealthy. Jonn couldn't believe it at first. The multicoloured gemstones embedded within the walls of the castle would be worth more than what some kingdoms made in a lifetime. Here, the syrens use them for mere decoration; precious stones reflecting the sunlight in all spaces within the castle, perfectly matching the exterior.

"Years ago, they were used as our currency," Selsie had explained one afternoon whilst they sat on a pebble beach. *"But they grew too rare, too valuable to part with. Now we have to go deeper and deeper into the ground under the island to find them."*

She had told him it was dangerous, sometimes fatal, work and that millennia ago, the gems were scattered everywhere on Cildraethe as common as daisies. Now, they were still plentiful, just not as they used to be.

Jonn had tried to pocket one of them when she wasn't looking, planning to stash it inside one of his boots. But the diamond had refused to budge, and the whispers that so often filled his ears began to laugh at him.

As he looked out at the storm, as with any time he gazed out to the sea, Jonn often thought of his shipmates; of Symon and his loyal comrades who had been with him through thick and thin. Jonn wondered if they had met a watery grave beneath the unforgiving waves. The memories of their camaraderie, the laughter shared around a bottle of mead in a tavern somewhere on the continent, and the songs sung under a starlit sky haunted his thoughts. He knew Sy would have given his life for those women and infants if given the chance; the righteous fucker. But he knew that he would have done the same if it was he who had been left on the ship.

The passing of time had made that fateful day of the Laeth attack feel a lifetime ago. And though his wounds were healed, the scars on the inside…not so much. His mind ached with unanswered questions, and he longed for news of their fate. Were they still alive, drifting out at sea with no wind in their tattered sails? Or had the syren's claimed them, as they had almost claimed him? He would ask Selsie today if she had heard or knew anything about the fate of his ship.

The unending nights also brought on reflections of his sister, all those nights ago. How fucking poetic, he thought, that what had killed her now loomed over his life, threatening to do the same with each passing day.

Though there had been no efforts on Selsie's part to sing her song at him again, neither had she given him the impression of her intent to kill him either. Even with the many chances she had at her disposal. Fuck, she could just come in here one night, put that sleeping spell on him again and be done with it.

Amidst the suffocating solitude of his room, a soft knock sounded at the door. Even though she was the very reason he was even here, Selsie's visits turned out to be a welcomed respite from the torment of his thoughts and the loneliness of captivity.

Not waiting for his response, she pushed open the door. He took in her appearance, swallowing down her ethereal presence as she stood with syren grace, in a gown of emerald green that brought out the vivid hues of her eyes.

That damned captivating voice of hers was impossible to resist, as she bid him good morning. Jonn could not stop himself from giving her a tight smile and a good morning in return.

"There is to be no walk today; the lightning is fierce and hitting the ground. We wouldn't want you to be hit and burnt to a pile of cinders now would we," she said to him lightly. Raising an eyebrow, he moved towards her, keeping a few paces behind her lead as always.

Close enough, however, to be downwind of her musky scent. She smelt like the most expensive oud, and it reminded Jonn of sex.

Heady and delicious.

"If we're not walking, where are we going?" He kept his words short and brief with her, holding himself back from completely letting go. There was little point; the deer does not converse with the tiger.

That was what he kept telling himself anyway, to keep his mind out of…places it shouldn't be. His cock, on the other hand, would not let him ignore her. Another thing he told himself was the consequence of 'Laeth magic'.

"Well, it will be the new moon in the next few days, and I thought that you might want to do something for yourself before that day."

She led them up into the castle, to the grand hallway entrance that led out to the city surrounding it. No door or gate, just a large, cavernous mouth guarded by a dozen syrens. Enriched with an enchantment that would kill anyone not permitted entry.

"Great, thank you." He replied dryly, the unspoken words from her lips not needing verbalisation.

Talking over him, as if he had not uttered a word, Selsie continued.

"…and if it is death that awaits you, then I will not feel the weight of denying you free will in your last hours, on my fins." Raising her hands, she cast a spell over the entrance, extending the magic over him, giving Jonn access to the outside and he shivered as it passed over him, goosebumps rising over his arms.

He asked her in disbelief, "Why did you do that?" He could now escape, find a boat and leave this damned place for freedom.

Selsie cocked her head, "We are friends, aren't we? Are humans not…*nice* towards their friends?" She stumbled over the word nice, like it wasn't natural on her tongue.

No matter the case, Jonn could not let her think they were anything but enemies.

"We are not friends, Selsie. You are my captor, a *Laeth*. I am your prisoner under the threat of death or enchantment, do not make the mistake of confusing our small talk over these last few weeks for friendship."

Jonn felt nastiness permeate his words, as he let it settle between them. Silence thickened the humid air in the space between their bodies, the thunder and rain outside the only sound echoing around the castle.

What felt like twenty years crawled by before she finally spoke, "Friends or not, I am allowing you the chance to go and do whatever you want in Cildraethe. Sword masters are waiting in the armoury, ready for your arrival if you so please. Or a drink, perhaps, down at the loveliest tavern in the city square, which I have ordered to be for your use only; no one shall bother you. Reading maybe? Our library may be small, but it is well stocked, and the Laeths who assist there are most helpful..."

He butted in before she could finish, his large strides taking him towards the exit.

"I'll be back for supper."

Turning away, he embraced the storm outside.

24
Jonn

Casting a silvery glow over the city, the evening descended. The storm had finally passed, and Jonn found himself back in the confines of his room, savouring a humble evening meal of codfish and boiled potatoes. No apple lay on his tray tonight; he must have pissed the syrens off.

After he had left her and the castle behind, he had gone immediately in search of a boat. By logic, they would be at a dock. But being Cildraethe, there was no dock. The syrens had no need for one and no ship would ever moor here.

His hopes of escape had dwindled with each fruitless hour spent scouring the island for any sign of a vessel, and ultimately finding none.

By mid-afternoon, he conceded defeat, coming to terms with the undeniable fact that Selsie had anticipated his every move. Her preparations were meticulous and her intentions clear; escape was a privilege he would not be granted. As for the remainder of the afternoon, Jonn begrudgingly accepted the offer extended by the sword masters, engaging in rigorous training and sparring sessions beneath one of the taller spires that towered above the castle.

Laeth swordplay, he quickly realised, was wildly different from his own, or anything like he had encountered before.

Characterised by fluidity and grace, the masters of swords wielded their blades with a featherlight touch. Transitioning effortlessly from one hand to the other, almost gentle with it, they kept their swords so fucking light in their fingers, changing hands so often that it had Jonn questioning that they were syrens at all. They moved like fae, dancing with each other with such lethal finesse and wicked precision, that he took more than one look at the barbs on their arms to confirm who the males were.

Not being used to it at all, he was fucking useless with his left hand. As his dominant right hand had mastered the art of swordplay, its twin was an awkward partner, neglected in his prior training. Life at sea on *The Brendann* had rendered swords almost obsolete for its crew. Fists were the weapon of choice when conflicts arose. Which being men, was often.

This must have been obvious, as the sword master's assessment did not spare Jonn's ego. "You must place your trust in your weapon, Crow, feel its rhythm. At present, you resemble a bog troll wielding a stick, thrusting and grunting."

Remembering the insult and the...*pet* name he had been given mere minutes after their meeting, Jonn scowled, making a mental note to tell that guy to go fuck himself if he ever saw him again.

Startling Jonn from his brooding, a familiar knock tapped against the wood of the door. He knew who it would be; he could sense her presence through the ten-inch thick, rocky walls.

Still pissed off from this morning, his voice was gruff as he said, "The hour is late, what do you want."

Harboured feelings of anger soon dissipated, and his whirring mind went blank for a fraction of a second, as he looked upon the female in the doorway. Selsie stood before him in a nightgown of bronze, so sheer and with such a close resemblance to her skin tone, that she might as well have been wearing nothing at all.

"I'm sorry to interrupt your evening Jonn, but I was wondering if I may come in."

A skipped heartbeat later, he opened the door wider to let her through, the scent of her filling the room as she breezed in. He

closed the door behind them, leaving her guards outside.
He wondered for an instant what Sy would do if he was in a
room with the most beautiful creature he had ever laid eyes on,
even if it was a syren. Though it didn't take much thought to
bring him to the likely answer, and Jonn shook his head to
himself at the notion, knowing exactly what his friend would
do.
Then he remembered and quickly baulked at his casual inner
tone. He didn't even know if his friend was alive.
"So, what is it?" Jonn asked her, rubbing a hand across his
beard, which was now longer than he had ever known it.
Chucking something at him, she said, "I brought you this." He
caught the object mid-air, and surprise filled him once he
realised what it was.
"An apple?"
"I see what the servants bring you for your meal each night, and
I see what you have eaten from your plate on its return. No
matter what you eat for supper, you always finish this right to
its core. I noticed that tonight they did not provide this for you,
so I took it upon myself to bring you one as soon as I could."
Jonn couldn't contain his bemusement; a syren princess
slumming it in the kitchens, caring whether he had an apple or
not. What game was she playing he wondered, inspecting the
apple, looking for signs of...
"You think it's poisoned, or enchanted?" she said with slight
amusement in her melodic voice.
"Is it not? It would be one way to worm yourself into my mind
in the absence of a song."
Selsie furrowed her brows. "Laeths do not need to lower
themselves to such trickery."
"No, you would enchant them instead. Eat them alive, or keep
them as your prisoner for years, until you get bored and throw
them away, like a dog that you can't be bothered to keep alive
anymore." He threw the apple onto the bed and crossed his

arms upon his large chest. "Your kind are evil, bloodthirsty animals."

"That is not true!" Selsie hissed at him. He knew he had struck a nerve, but he didn't fucking care.

"Oh, it's not? So, the men aboard my ship just willingly jumped into the water, did they? My crew just fancied themselves a leisurely swim?" He could feel himself growing heated

"I suppose I came here just for a holiday. And those newborn infants were damned anyway, so who gives a shit that they were innocent and most likely killed."

He knew there was no point in this argument. She was a syren, he was a human; predator and prey. To her, it was natural, it was life. But he couldn't stand for their disregard for human souls, as though they were shit floating in Cildraethe waters.

"I had a sister," he began, his harsh voice now tinged with the bitterness of melancholy. "She was just a newborn when our ship was attacked by Laeths. I was five years old at the time, and I still remember the chaos, the terror. She... she didn't survive the attack."

In sombre silence, Selsie listened. She took a visible deep breath before whispering softly.

"I'm sorry about your sister," she inched forward, "and your men, it wasn't my idea. I made my feelings known to my mother about attacking a Saynt, though if it eases your conscience, we did not kill any infants. The attack ended when you fell into the water."

A black weight that had been pressing upon his shoulders lifted at that. Knowing that the infants made it away safely gave him hope that Symon may have escaped harm himself. The look on Selsie's face told him that she was being sincere.

"Look, I cannot undo the past, but I promise you, Jonn, that I will do everything in my power to make amends. I do not want our time together to be filled with such anger and hate."

Jonn scoffed, almost laughing at the notion. The female was

extremely misguided if she thought he would feel anything but resentment for her. But with this promise, maybe he could take advantage of her current eagerness for friendship.

Jonn had no option but to take a leap of faith. Shit, he had nothing to lose by asking.

"Then there's something you can do for me. I need you to deliver a message to my shipmate, Symon, if the prick didn't die in your attack. He was like a brother to me, and I need him to know that I'm not dead. That I'm here… and I'm alive."

Selsie bit her full lips, and he couldn't help but look at her mouth. How long had it been since he lay with the vampyre in Oridae? Too long for his liking. Even then he was too drunk to fully remember and appreciate the moment.

She finally nodded. "I will find him Jonn. Though I'm not sure my mother will like it, as the full moon is upon us."

She did not need to explain what that meant, for either of them. He nodded, the closest to a thank you he would give her.

"In the meantime, may I stay with you a while? For all our time together, I still feel like I do not know you, and as you are mine…"

Jonn shot her a warning glare. She knew he abhorred her claiming him as his own; he was not her property.

"You cannot own a person, Selsie."

She raised her sharp chin. "I disagree."

"Humans are not property to be owned and it's fucking abhorrent you think otherwise."

"Do the vampyres not *own* their humans, to feed upon their blood? We may live below the shores of Myrantis, Jonn, but we are not ignorant to the world above."

He shook his head. "Then you should already know that it is entirely different. The humans have a choice, a life that is completely their own. The slave and master relationship ended with the human rebellion seven hundred years ago."

A knowing smirk graced her features. "Fine, then what about

you?"

"What about me?" He didn't want to hear where this was going. "I know all about Oblitus, the way humans from the continent are sent there as newlings if they are devoid of any magic. You talk of how Laeths treat our enchanted, as though humans are any different, better. Your ruling masters send children away as though they are chattel, disposable. Banished to an island with no hope of leaving. Unless they become like you… destined to traverse waters with the threat of my kind haunting your every journey across the western seas, the unknown of the east. Does that make you any freer than you are now?"

Jonn audibly gulped. The female standing before him had her words around his throat and they both knew it. He had nothing to say. The truth of her words were a harsh reality he could not deny.

Her squared shoulders relaxed as he lowered his head; the whispering in his ears that was moments ago fervent and hurried had quieted back to its usual hum.

"If you do not want to be called certain things, then fine. You are my…*guest*, and I want to know more about you. We have walked for hours together, and I feel like you have barely spoken more than a few words."

She was searching him, trying to pry something out of him, he could feel it. He decided to humour her if it meant she would leave him alone to his brooding sooner.

Sitting his arse on the window ledge, he watched as she sat on his small bed. Jonn couldn't help but think how intimate it felt; her on his bed.

Beginning from where he could remember, he shared stories of his childhood, the adventures of his youth, his time at sea and the circumstances that had led him to the life of a first mate. He told her about the selection process of the future crew of a Saynt ship. When disclosed details about how they learnt the anatomy of a Laeth, Selsie's eyes grew wide. The gruesome image of one of her own lying dead on an autopsy table must have been a hard stone to swallow for the Heir of the Laeth kingdom.

He skipped over some of the more…*need to know* details. Letting him speak further of his life, Selsie listened in comfortable silence, her gaze never once leaving his face. When he had finished, she had left the room with a formal goodbye and a smile. Jonn didn't know why, maybe something had shifted, but the innermost part of him wished she had stayed, if only for a moment longer.

25
Keyara

Adjoining the ballroom, Keyara and Aura took their seats with the other competitors at the far end of the banqueting table. The anticipation of the Heir's Rite vibrating through the room like a lightning charge.

There was so much magic gathered here and of such strength, it gave the room a tangible heaviness, tinged with the taste of sparks.

Keyara could feel it rub against her skin, pulling at her power, the magic wanting to come out to play.

She wondered if Berran felt it too. His fidgeting among his fellow nobles and lords at the opposing end of the table indicated to her that he did.

Keyara knew her staring was rude as she looked around the banqueting hall, but the different species around her took all of her attention; visions of fascination she had never before encountered.

Resembling the colourful artwork of a children's book, the vibrancy of the Akoaàns that lined the rectangular table far outshone the clan in Eldorhaven.

She could hear their giggles and jokes, a tinkling crescendo of lilting voices.

Honestly, in her drunken state, she longed to join them.

Not too far down from her, she spotted – or rather heard – the vampyres.

There were not many of them, maybe three or four. But they were as loud and as pissed as she was. Blood sloshed in golden goblets, splashing crimson droplets over the white tablecloth.

Rolling her eyes at them, she wondered what the other competitors thought of the syrens and vampyres being here. Surely her competition in the Rite did not look at them and think they were solely here to watch?

If they didn't suspect a thing, they were fucking idiots.

She looked over to Berran and the others. From the glistening silver crown atop her white hair, Berran's sister was the female that sat between him and Mileyakhan.

Cassidae had been the subject of the many stories Berran had told her, and Keyara couldn't wait to meet her.

"Are you not eating?" Aura gently asked her, glancing towards the vegetarian meal that sat half-eaten on Keyara's plate.

"I'm not that hungry," she lied.

Truth was, the people of Shadowfern predominantly ate goat, sheep, and heavy grains, so preparing a *vegetarian* meal for her was clearly beyond their capabilities.

Night after night she was presented with the same two dishes: cabbage and potato soup, which was the consistency of loose shit, or turnip and swede stew with cream. The latter was slightly better.

With a heavy emphasis on the *slightly*, she thought.

Tonight, she had been given a new meal for the occasion. A gift of leek rice with mushrooms, smothered in butter.

If she hadn't been so unnerved by that vampyre earlier this evening, she would have eaten it all, but her stomach was in knots, like a thread of yarn caught in a spindle.

Aura had asked who the male was, and Keyara had told her the truth.

She didn't know.

Looking around for a servant, Aura suggested, "Shall we ask for something else?"

"No no, seriously it's fine, I'm just nervous for tomorrow," she lied again.

As the feast wore on, plates were cleared, courses were brought out and drinks were consumed, the room alive with laughter and conversation.

Right until the king of Eira stood up from his chair.

"Ladies and gentlemen, females and males of my kingdom, it is with great honour and pride that I join you all here for this historic occasion. It is also my joy to announce that this Heir's Rite will be slightly...*different*, than the others that have occurred before."

Knowing what the king's revelation would be, Keyara knew she would have to feign her shock to the other competitors around her, who all of a sudden were restless in their seats, as though ants were crawling along their skin under their fine clothes.

"For the first time in the long history of Myrantis, not only will our fellow humans be competing for the title of Heir to the throne, but those not of our species as well."

The revelation sent shockwaves through the room, like a thunderclap on a silent night. Keyara exchanged a secret knowing glance with Aura.

He continued through the hushed, hurried whispers. "Let us celebrate this moment, where unity and diversity shall shine in the Rite, proving that strength and nobility come in many forms."

Amidst the applause that eventually erupted and murmurs of the assembled guests, Keyara overheard the other competitors talking amongst themselves.

"I thought the vampyres and syren's were only here to watch, not compete. I'm such a fool..."

"I could have sworn on the gods that I saw a fae male drinking in town..."

"Impossible, they would never lower their lofty selves to compete with us humans..."

Those long nights spent with her bruised head in a book would surely pay off when she had an edge against these idiots, Keyara thought, smirking to herself.

The weaknesses and history of every species known to
Myrantis lay in the palm of her calloused hands.

Sometimes, knowledge was power, and she sure as hell had a
wealth of it under her skin.

The satisfaction she would get from humiliating these types of
men, who love to think of themselves as superior to regular
humans. Their inferiority complex against other species, a
badge of dishonour they frequently wore.

Leaning over towards a young, low-ranking aristocrat to her
left, and wearing her most innocent voice, she decided to jest
with them, to get under their skin and stay there.

Just for a while...

"Frightening isn't it, the thought of competing against a fully-
grown syren, especially if they have completed the Stelthe. I
heard that a Reothadh male can crush a man's skull with one
hand. That one, the Reothadh prince, Heir, I'm not sure what
they call him…" she said, pointing over towards Berran,
"…apparently can absorb magic, drain it whilst the person is
alive. The most horrific death I've ever heard of. You know
what brutes his species can be."

Berran noticed them looking over at him, he smiled over at
Keyara baring his large teeth. The man next to her paled.

Keyara flinched in a false sense of alarm, lightly grabbing the
lord's knee underneath the table. The thought of Berran's
inevitable confusion made her want to laugh out loud, but she
kept it in, giving the lord beside her the impression of a scared,
meek young woman.

He brushed off her touch.

Sneering, he said to her "He may be a syren, but that doesn't
make him the only powerful one here." Lifting one hand, the
lord commanded his power to move the frothy gold liquid from
his tankard into the air. It wobbled slightly, moments later
turning into solid metal and thumping onto the table, smashing
into her goblet of wyne.

He's Derynian, she thought, the dark hair and aquiline nose a dead giveaway if the variant of water magic wasn't telling enough.

Her shoulders relaxed at the disappointment. If that was one of the most powerful lords that the secretive boggy kingdom in the north had to offer, then she was in for an easy yet boring ride. What a letdown.

"Impressive my lord!" She gasped in mock amazement, picking up the hardened heavy mass in her hand.

She let the silence between them get comfortable, let no other words come from her lips as he watched her.

In her palm, the metal warped from yellow to orange, red, then finally settling on a blazing white. The heat from her hands was slowly melting the ball down into liquid, which began dripping off her hands, down to the floor between them.

Gasping like river fish, the lord's mouth opened and closed, plainly too stunned to speak.

Bored, she rearranged herself back into her chair, flicking the now-cooled shards of metal from her dress.

A servant witnessing the exchange hurriedly stepped over, using what little magic he possessed, to summon a refilled goblet from the ether. Politely she took it off him, taking a small sip and saying her thanks.

The liquid went down her gullet as though it was a tumbleweed through a marsh. She'd had enough of drinking now and was itching to leave the table. Anymore wyne would sit in her belly like stagnant water.

To her right, the conversation between Aura and a noblewoman had paused, so Keyara took the moment to whisper in her sister's ear. "Can we go dancing now? This is boring me to tears."

Her sister whispered her hushed reply. "Okay, shall we ask Berran to join us?"

Keyara pulled a face, she didn't want Mileyakhan to join them and ruin her night.

"No, let's not. It looks better for him if he stays in the company of the king and he's too nice to turn us down."

Aura nodded in agreement.

In the ballroom, which was as visually uninteresting as its sister banqueting hall, they danced together for hours, neither daring to acknowledge what could be their last night together if past Rites were anything to go by.

For fear that uttering those words would bring that very fear to life.

Retreating to the privacy of their shared chambers around midnight, Keyara locked the door behind them.

Joining her sister, they settled into the chairs by the fireplace. The dancing shadows cast onto their faces by the flickering flames, mirror images of their revelry minutes before.

Haunting her thoughts, the vampyre she met earlier in the evening was not only annoying in person, but now he was taking up space in her mind.

Arrogant arsehole, she whispered to herself.

She hoped that the blood he stole from her scalded his mouth. Keyara quietly smiled to herself at the thought.

When they had left the table, she hadn't seen him again. Many had retreated to their rooms early, with the intention of a good night's sleep before tomorrow, although she knew most would be too anxious for rest.

Maybe they would ask a slumber maid to send them to sleep. For once, Keyara was in mind to ask too, but the grogginess of spell-induced sleep would impede on her magic tomorrow and she wouldn't, couldn't, let that happen.

"Keyara," Aura said, her voice soft but resolute, words slightly slurred. "What's going to happen tomorrow?"

With her gaze focused on the flames, Keyara sighed.

"I'm not sure. But if something happens to me, you must go straight to Berran. He will look after you. Promise me?"

Aura did not look up from the flames, "If I were to agree, you must make me this promise Keyara. Do not let your stubbornness cloud your judgement. Do not allow arrogance to prevent you from making smart choices."

She had a point, Keyara admitted to herself, when a knock sounded at the door. They exchanged a quick glance before Keyara crossed the room to answer it.

Both wearing easy expressions, Berran stood at the threshold with Cassidae at his side.

"I am sorry for disturbing you so late ladies, but I wanted to introduce my sister to you. She's been like a shark at a fish all night, pestering me to say hello."

Aura jogged over from the fireplace with a huge grin slapped on her face and Berran moved back an inch, letting his sister take the spotlight.

"Come in! Oh I'm so happy to finally meet you at last, and to be able to thank you for the gifts."

Aura proceeded to ramble on at the syrens, kicking the mess out of the way, as she went around the room trying to find them somewhere to sit, eventually leading them to the chairs by the fire.

For a split second, Keyara thought that the ice-white gown the striking female was wearing would melt against the heat of the small fire.

It seemed to be crafted from the glaciers themselves, the ethereal material gathering to a halter neck, before trailing down her back in a cape.

A keyhole design fringed with blue gemstones sat at the front, giving a small glimpse of the cleavage underneath.

Cassidae's blue eyes danced as she regarded Aura, her movements easy and fluid. The female was striking, the resemblance to her brother uncanny. Both held that air of royal grace that Keyara knew she would never possess herself, no matter if she won twelve Heir's Rites.

Though that may be where the resemblance ended, she thought as the two syren's settled down.

Berran was a calming, solid influence on his surroundings, Cassidae on the other hand, exuded charm and a playfulness that could almost be touched.

The female was the first to speak. "Berran has told me so much about you both over these years, that I feel like you are almost part of our family now." Cassidae's silver iridescence glowed starkly against the light of the flames.

"I have told Berran I want to help you."

Lowering her head and wishing she could pace, Keyara said, "Thank you, Cassidae, but I cannot accept your help. I already have my sister and your brother covering me. What kind of champion would I be if I relied on everyone else's help to win?"

Cassidae laughed, a melody that filled the room. "A smart one! A future queen and Heir needs to know when to rely on others, especially powerful ones who would make great future allies."

Keyara gave in to her urge and began to pace. Cassidae was right. She knew they had much to discuss, and the hour was late, so fuck it, she had nothing to lose by accepting the help. Apart from her dignity and pride.

With newfound allies by their side, her odds of winning only became stronger.

"Okay. If I ever need the help, then I accept."

Cassidae squealed, a mischievous glint in her eyes. "How exciting!"

"But only if the need is dire, or I'm on death's fucking door."

26

Keyara

The dim light of dawn painted the skies with a palette of muted greys and powdery blues. Keyara gazed in silence out of the window, her composure unwavering as she rose from the bed, stealing a glance toward Aura lying beside her.

The strawberry curls framed her serene face as she slept soundly, the weight of the day yet to bear down upon them both.

An air of quiet enveloped the castle. Surprising, considering the day to come.

Fixing her eyes on the sky, where a canvas of clouds obscured the sun, Keyara approached the open window, deeply inhaling the early summer air.

Her thoughts were as still as the morning.

Keyara had spent years preparing for this very day, mastering the arts of governance, diplomacy and combat; she wouldn't let her emotions steal that iron composure from her.

Turning away from the morning, she crossed the room to Aura's side, her steps falling softly on the plush rug.

Gently, she reached out and touched her sister's shoulder, rousing her from sleep.

Aura stirred, her eyes blinking open, "Gods, is it time already?"

Keyara nodded, keeping any evidence of nervousness to herself.

Iron composure.

"They will come for me soon; they love an early start around here and I can't imagine today will be any different. These people seem to be allergic to any kind of rest."

Aura stifled a small smile.

"I've told Mother all about the early starts, and how much you hate them, in the letters I've sent to her."

Keyara smirked, "What did she say?"

A faded emotion passed over Aura, "Nothing yet, I've had no reply."

Keyara had to be honest, she had been so wrapped up in her own head that she had not thought about their mother too much.

She knew that made her incredibly selfish, but it was like her head was so full of other – more important – things, that she could leave home and mother to Aura.

"Shadowfern probably gets its letters thirty years after everyone else. I doubt the lettermaids can be bothered to scale the mountain every day," Keyara replied, trying to keep the tone light.

Picking up the competitor's uniform she was brought this morning, Keyara frowned at the dark charcoal slacks with a matching tunic.

It scratched at her skin as she pulled it on, and she commented on how ugly it was to Aura, who wordlessly agreed whilst pulling on her pretty clothes.

A guard announced himself at the door as Aura finished braiding Keyera's hair down her back.

They exchanged a final, knowing look. Aura's eyes held a faultless belief in her, silently acknowledging the challenge they were about to face.

She knew Aura would have her back no matter what. She also knew her sister, Berran and maybe even Cassidae, would do whatever they could to help her win.

"Good luck Keyara, I love you."

Leaning forward, she placed a sisterly kiss on Aura's forehead, before she was led away by the palace guards.

Keyara held her head high. She was prepared for the challenges that lay ahead. Fuck, was she ready.

She was led through corridors and down many stairs, past the training grounds and deep into the Vaelorns surrounding the castle.
Keyara had underestimated the size of the place, feeling almost disorientated from the sameness of it all.
The day was heavy with clouds, plunging the mountain into darkness, the vivid green of the moss-coated stones, washed of their usual colour.
She remembered the drawing she had seen of the arena, situated under the peaks. An enormous underground chasm inside the mountain, just a shell of a space. The contents and appearance within altered with each competition.
Walking beside the guard through a huge iron gate, eerily similar to those protecting the city, Keyara was brought to what looked like a stable. Crafted from heavy oak, rows of tall fences were lined up side by side.

However, instead of horses grazing inside the wooden structure, throngs of people wove between the tall stands.
The arena entrance with its iron gates grew further and further away as she was led to her pen.
"Wait here," the guard instructed, shutting the large door behind himself.
Her eyes were immediately drawn upwards, to the vast expanse above her head that had seemingly no end.
Instead, she cast her gaze over an expansive stage, wherein the king and queen sat upon thrones of purest gold, flecked with multicoloured marble veins.
Sitting on either side of the greying royals, with hungry looks plastered across their faces, the nobles sat with lofty arrogance.
Beside the stage, Keyara had to physically move her head side

to side, to get a full view of the rows upon rows of benches that were rapidly filling as the spectators took to their seats.

Craning her neck, Keyara searched for three familiar faces. None were visible.

"*Tight bastards*," she thought, plopping down into a splintered wooden chair whilst the commotion around her grew louder, as other contestants filled the pens on either side of her own.

A selection of meat and bread was chucked at her after a short while. Although Berran would nag her to gratefully take the sustenance to keep her energy up, it would remain uneaten.

She was too jittery and anxious, her stomach ash.

Keyara jumped up from the chair, as a flash of blue and silver caught her eye in the audience.

Her sister was with Berran and, oh great, Mileyakhan. Wanting to snag Aura's attention, Keyara waved anyway.

Her sister looked straight at her, blue eyes meeting her own and still, nothing. No wave, no smile.

Fuck, maybe Aura couldn't recognise her from this far away. Come to think of it, Keyara thought, no one was looking into the stables.

Chattering amongst themselves, many in the crowd were pointing to an area behind the competitor pens, unseen to Keyara.

The lord of Shadowfern, cloaked in resplendent robes in the colours of his kingdom, stood to address the assembled crowd, hushing it to near silence. His voice carried the weight of hundreds of years' worth of excitement.

"Welcome, your Highnesses and my honoured guests. Today marks the first trial of the Heir's Rite."

The arena erupted into claps and cheers. Keyara could hear a few whoops and hollers around her in the stables.

Lord Trewith used his hands to settle the crowd.

"I will keep this brief, as I know we are all anxious to get this historic day underway. The first trial will be a test of knowledge for our potential Heirs."

The rules were laid out with precision and Keyara listened with a determined focus, aiming to absorb as much as possible.

Each contestant would be placed alone into a chamber; a room filled with enchanted scrolls and ancient texts that held the various histories of Eira. Each competitor was required to read the scrolls and arrange them in the correct historical order.

Any errors, or not completing the trial within the allocated time, would result in elimination.

Gods she hoped those nightly reading marathons with Aura was enough. Keyara would remind herself to thank her sister; if not for her, she would never have bothered to spend her nights with books in the library or their room, and right now Keyara would be royally fucked.

From the look on her sister's face in the crowd, she knew Aura was thinking the same as her.

Berran was giving away nothing, while Mileyakhan just looked uninterested and stoic.

Lord and Lady Trewith, along with the King and Queen, took their place around a large cauldron, which Keyara recognised as part of a family of crucibles used to test newborn blood for magic.

A handful of mother's maids were brought out onto the stage, carrying vials of what Keyara knew was the competitor's blood, taken and stored on the day of their births.

The women gave the vials to the King and Queen, and the enormous book they carried everywhere was given to Lady Trewith.

No one save for them knew of its contents.

A hush fell over the audience; history was once again being made. Even the rowdy stables went still.

One by one, King Farhand began pouring their blood into the cauldron.

Magic sparked, with power fizzing out of the cauldron rim in all colours. Light and dark danced together in flashes, water splashed over the floor as the varying magic of each contestant played together.

It was a sight to see, far more exquisite and exciting than the books had made this moment out to be.

A huge burst of power came from one vial that was seemingly newer than the rest. After which the scent of leaves and forest floor rolled like a green wave through the room, leaving a trail of leaves and rumbling earth in its wake.

After counting eighteen vials, there were two vials left, with the King and Queen holding one each. Keyara had to wonder if her sample had been poured in yet.

She couldn't fucking wait to see what would happen when the moment came.

One of the two vials went in and as it did, the air above the cauldron began to hum, giving off such a powerful energy, that Keyara could feel it vibrate through her from down in the pen. This was not human power; she could feel it in her bones.

Hundreds of eyes grew wide, as the audience seemed to sense it too. The royals looked at each other in amusement, clearly impressed.

Taking in a collective breath, the audience froze in time as the last vial went in. Everyone – including Keyara – expected something brilliant.

But nothing.

Not even a bubble or small puff of smoke.

She almost laughed at the anticlimax, the audience gormlessly staring at the cauldron on stage. Quite honestly, she was waiting for the heckles.

Keyara didn't know if the rattling from the stage came first, or the vibrations below her feet. Quiet at first, then in the space of a few seconds, deafeningly loud.

Originating from the cauldron, which was trembling ferociously, Keyara could have sworn she smelt burning leather and hot spices, tinged with something else.

"*Was that coffee?*" she questioned, sniffing the charged air. Then like nothing ever happened, the cauldron grew quiet and still once more. Not a trace of magic stirred from its depths. Lord Trewith and the royals turned their backs to the crowd to face the stables below.

"Let us begin!"

With her face nearly touching the immense perimeter of a circular stone wall, Keyara scanned the ring of contestants to her right and left side.

"We meet again." She recognised the haughty, 'stick up the arse' voice that came from her left.

"Unfortunately," she muttered under her breath, just loud enough for him to hear.

The nobleman from Deryn looked like shit, the heavy bags under his eyes and pasty complexion; evidence of his overindulgence from last night's banquet.

He narrowed his already swine-like eyes. "You know, just because you have… unusual power, does not mean you can win this."

She turned to face him fully. "Is that right?"

"Who even are you? I've never seen you at any ball, tournament, or any gathering of nobility in all my time at court."

Keyara ignored the condescending nature of his tone. He was trying to goad her, unsettle her, and there was no chance in hell she would let him.

Trying to convey boredom she just rolled her eyes and looked away.

Behind them all, a flourish of magic signalled the trials to commence. Lord Trewith up on the stage, sent a flash of light shooting up to the cavernous ceiling, ending in a deafening bang.

The crowd began to cheer as chamber doors that were invisible just seconds before, swung open before her, into the stone. Giving herself no time for hesitation, Keyara jogged through the doors, leaving he prior self behind, only slightly acknowledging the fact that everything in her life would depend on this very moment.

Her heart was steady with a rhythmic beat in her chest as she entered the room, enveloped in the scent of aged parchment. A soft golden light revealed the chamber to be small and nondescript.

Keyara approached the source of the light, emanating from scrolls that lay scattered across an enormous circular table mirroring the chamber itself.

Scanning them briefly, she noticed a few of the parchments looked impossibly old, while others were brand new, the ink barely dry.

A huge ticking clock took the place of a ceiling above her, showing only the hours of twelve and one.

If she had to guess, they had an hour to finish.

Pulling out the wooden chair beside the table, Keyara sat down and picked up the closest scroll to her. An electric shock shot up her hand like needles piercing the skin as she did.

"Fuck!" she shouted, throwing it back down onto the table.

What in God's names was that, she thought, inspecting her hand for damage.

Nothing, not a mark or scratch on her.

Gingerly, she reached for the scroll again. The pain once more ran up her arm, but she hung on until the pain disappeared a few moments later.

Keyara felt strangely invaded by another magic, deep in her brain. The scrolls were enchanted, though for what purpose? Shaking off the invasive feeling, she began to read the scrolls with all the scholar's precision she could muster.

The first few were straightforward, detailing the earliest epochs of Eira's history and the origin of all species, the pages crackling under her swift fingers.

Shoving another scroll into the wall behind her, Keyara did her best to assemble the scrolls in the correct order inside the holes. The clock was ticking.

The initial scrolls were easy, a history that anyone with half a brain would know, though as she progressed further into the parchments the texts became increasingly vampyre-focused.

Her forehead creased in concentration as she began to pace.

Keyara knew barely anything about them, a little at best.

It was like her mind refused to listen to anything about the desert dwellers, it rejected anything to do with them like opposing ends of a magnet.

Nevertheless, Keyara was certain she had got it right.

That damned clock seemed to mock her.

It had been forty-five minutes, and she didn't have much time left.

The crowd's cheers sounded so far away in the distance, obviously others had made it out and finished already.

"Fuck!" she shouted.

Her confidence, once unwavering, began to dissipate.

She could not fail at the first trial. She would rather die than endure the humiliation.

Keyara had arranged all but the last few scrolls, with the remaining empty holes in the wall glaring at her.

Not bothering to sit in the chair, she unrolled the last few scrolls and placed her palms flat against the table.

Leaning over them, her heart raced, the weight of the moment bearing down upon her.

The remaining texts were like elusive shadows, refusing to reveal their place in history to her. Taunting her like they knew she couldn't do it.

The human rebellion against the vampyres was one of the most important periods in history, and yet she struggled to recall any of the events she had been taught in her schooling.

There were three scrolls left all about that war, and she could not for the life of her place the events in order inside her mind.
Did the humans leave Zerithia to establish a new capital city of Oridae, before electing a king?
Or did they elect a king, leave Zerithia then establish Oridae?
Eurgh, she was confused.
With each passing moment, she became more frustrated. Her thoughts couldn't be pieced together and time was slipping away.
She was going to lose on day one.

27
Aura

Aura could see down into the sprawling, circular arena below. A huge maze-like circle, the occupants inside resembling bees in a hive, some sitting down at their tables, others spreading the scrolls out on the floor before them.

Around her, the space echoed with hushed whispers and expectant murmurs as the crowd speculated on the winners and losers. Aura's magic was alive from the emotions in the room. It was intoxicating being around so many people and her power thrived on it.

Within ten minutes of the trial beginning. A triumphant cheer came from the opposite side of the arena; someone had completed the task already.

From her vantage point on the benches, Aura smiled to herself as Keyara made good progress. The glow from each shelf was a beacon of hope, as it lit up every time she placed a correct scroll inside.

A red glow burst from the room beside Keyara's, the man inside hung his head in failure. Another one bites the dust Aura thought, as he was eliminated.

After a while, Aura noticed a subtle shift in Keyara's demeanour. It was a flicker of doubt that passed through her sister's eyes as she delved into the remaining three scrolls.

A pang of concern flipped inside her as Aura watched Keyara struggle. Seated next to her, leaning over his knees with his hands interlaced, Berran sat with an air of intent observation. Aura shifted her head towards his. "Why can't she figure it out?

We must have gone through that entire library, what is it that she doesn't know?"

Mileya's hushed, husky voice came from Aura's other side. "She has the history of vampyres."

Aura whipped her head to the left, "How do you know that?"

Berran smirked and tapped his ears. Of course, Domhianns have exceptional hearing.

Mileya pointed down to the stage, where Lord Trewith was talking into the King's ear.

"Those two talk so *loud,* no secret of the Rite could possibly remain just so"

Aura's thoughts raced as she considered how to help her sister. Keyara knew little of the vampyres, her journey to the crown was going to end before it had even begun.

The Heir's Rite may be a trial to reveal who was worthy of the throne, but that didn't mean that Keyara had to face it alone, without others to guide and assist her.

Well, officially she may be prohibited and some would even call it cheating, but unofficially, Aura didn't care.

"She's running out of time," Berran tutted, as the clocks showed fifteen minutes left.

Aura couldn't let her sister fail in the first trial. She knew Keyara would never live it down and the thought of returning to Eldorhaven empty-handed made Aura want to be sick.

"What can we do?" she asked those around her.

"Nothing. You cannot help a competitor, and if you do, she will be eliminated," Mileya replied dryly.

"I can't just watch her lose. There must be something." Aura sighed, not being able to think with the noise coming from further up the benches above them, where Akoaàn's were laughing loudly and singing crude poems to themselves.

"Godsdamned Akoaàns," Mileya hissed, "always chirping their ridiculous songs. Why can't they sing about anything other than fucking and drinking for a change."

Berran laughed and in that moment, Aura knew how to help. Casting anxiety and embarrassment behind her, Aura's racing heart surged with strength as she began to sing. Her voice wasn't exquisite and nowhere near as beautiful as any syren, but it rang out in the enormous room.

Her voice strained, as it tried to catch up with her memory as it rang out a melody of every Akoaàn song she knew, that held the history of the vampyres. Each note and word she took from the songs she had heard the ancestors sing in Eldorhaven, all day every day.

Berran must have realised what she was doing and joined in with her. Being that he was a Reothadh, with the power of syren song reserved only for war, she knew there would be no magic in his voice, but it was just as strong.

The crowd around her went quiet in confusion, at the two of them sitting there singing. The Akoaàns behind seemed surprised but couldn't resist joining in.

Keyara had not shown any indication she could hear them. It wasn't loud enough, Aura thought, quieting her voice momentarily. She would need more voices to join the harmony, to make the singing as loud as she possibly could.

Drawing upon her power, Aura knew what she had to do but she would need to be subtle, and she wasn't entirely sure it was possible.

It was a rare ability to influence the emotions of those around her, and it had never really proved useful for her practical life. Only ever curing Keyara's emotional hangovers and draining Aura of her own happiness in the meantime.

Fuck it, as Keyara would say.

She directed her power through her feet and into the very benches. It felt harsh against her magic like it was alien to enter the wood and metal, not the flesh and soul of others, but she ploughed through the feeling and eventually, it was a steady stream exiting through her body.

Emotions of those around her began to shift, Aura had to mask
her surprise with a high note as she witnessed the change in the
audience, from confusion to camaraderie. Her aim had hit its
mark, the audience felt as one, a part of something bigger than
themselves and revelry was enjoyed best with song.

As the arena was a circle, the conjoined efforts of the singing
crowd barely reached the opposing side in a disjointed
cacophony, but that didn't matter. Keyara was this side, where
the singing was the loudest and by the time the voices all
mingled the song was clear enough.

As slow as a blooming flower, a sense of clarity descended
upon the competitors surrounding Keyara, as if the knowledge
they sought was being imprinted upon their minds.

Aura could see the pieces fall into place for Keyara as she too,
had a wave of understanding pass over her features, as she
stopped pacing to listen to the crowd. The details must have
aligned in her brain as she began to arrange the scrolls with
newfound confidence and with such speed, she became a blur
of movement.

The trial was nearing its end, and the tension was palpable in
the crowd as the choir of singing voices drifted into murmurs.
Aura's intervention had not only helped her sister but had also
ensured that a few others had completed the task correctly too,
but she decided that was a necessary sacrifice.

With a wickedly triumphant cheer, Keyara slumped into the
chair as the final moments of the trial passed. She met Aura's
gaze from across the room, eyes shimmering with pride and
peeking out below the edges of the clock.

Berran put his fingers in his mouth and whistled as Aura stood
up and clapped harder than those around her.

"She did it, Mileya, I thought for a second that she was sure to
be eliminated."

But Mileya wasn't there, she had disappeared.

She let out a relieved sigh as she watched Keyara be led away from the room by the guards, and Aura didn't stop clapping, even as the audience was led away from the arena.

Keyara's sharp face was glowing with appreciation, as she regarded Aura in the sanctuary of their room. Her sister's ramped up emotions and adrenaline fizzed through the room and skittered along Aura's power like sour, sugared raspberries.

"Aura, you saved my fucking arse in there. How did you even think to do that?"

Aura explained how she had grasped onto the only thread of inspiration she had been woven, the Akoaàns singing and Mileya's comment on the nature of their songs.

An uncontrollable smile radiated from her lips.

"I told you, we're in this bloody thing together, Keyara. Not only me, but you have Berran, Cassidae, and even Mileya to help you win."

Keyara rolled her eyes and scoffed. "Eurgh Mileyakhan, she can't stand me. I doubt she had a little singsong with the rest of you."

"Well, you aren't the easiest person to get along with Keyara, let's be honest and… she *did* sing."

The last bit was a lie. Aura didn't know whether Mileya sang or not, as the syren wasn't there to ask when they had left the stands.

Their conversation was soon interrupted by the Reothadh royal siblings and two of their servants, who were bearing a huge chest between them.

"A gift for passing your first trial Keyara. And for you Aura, for the lovely song you sang for us all," Cassidae said with a wink, her servant placing the chest, crafted from purest glacial ice and engraved with the heaviest silver, in the middle of the room.

"What is it?" Keyara asked, hesitating to open the lid.

A wave of dainty power kissed with snowflakes, breezed over

the chest, which groaned open to reveal yards of material. Aura gasped, padding over to what she hoped would be inside.

As they perused the gowns, each more enchanting than the last, Aura couldn't believe her eyes; there were not only gowns, but new tunics, trousers, and jackets for Keyara.

She looked over at Berran and his sister, who looked so alike as they stood together that it was almost startling.

"Thank you, I don't know what to say."

Moving a stray lock from his face, Berran jerked his head to Cassidae.

"It was her idea"

As they stood together, Aura felt an odd sensation that she was once again being watched, whispers of eyes in the shadows haunted her.

Glancing over Berran's shoulder into the hallway, just outside of the open door and standing with a regal air in the silver moonlight, was the white dog she had seen in Eldorhaven. Its deep brown eyes held recognition, just for a moment, and Aura felt a connection that she could not grasp. Before she could even open her mouth to say something, the dog was gone.

"What's wrong Aura, are you okay?" Keyara called to her.

"I thought I heard someone out there, but I was mistaken."

A puzzled look passed over Keyara for a second whilst she quietly put the new clothes away in various drawers and cupboards.

"What do you think the next trial will be?" Aura asked the room.

Keyara shrugged her narrow shoulders.

"Only the gods know. Something physical this time, I hope. Maybe then I won't finish near dead last."

Cassidae gave her Keyara a sympathetic look,

"It's better than not finishing at all."

"Exactly," Aura agreed with Cassidae. "Besides, all anyone wants is a show, for someone to root for, to really make them feel like they *know* you."

"She's right," Cassidae chimed in. "This is all about the spectacle as well as finding a new heir. You need to be memorable."

An easy feat, she thought. Aura didn't know much about the world, but she knew this much: Keyara was unforgettable.

28

Berran

Shadowfern had witnessed the conclusion of the first Heir's Rite trial, and the atmosphere around the castle and the surrounding town was humming with excitement and whispers about the competitors' performances. The feel of it against his senses was addicting and Berran revelled in the thrum of it. Keyara had made it through the trial, thank the gods. It was a testament to her knowledge and steely determination; determination that could be confused with unending stubbornness if he was honest. But if the truth continued to be told, it was also through Aura's help.

They could not be certain that Keyara would have made it to the next round without her sister's ingenious idea to sing her through it. He had to give it to Aura, she surprised him. He didn't know as much about the younger sister, but he was impressed by her so far and was enjoying her company.

Berran knew Keyara had next to no knowledge about the history of the vampyres or Valhir; whether through ignorance or hatred, he hadn't quite figured out yet. Either way, it was the one trait in his long-time friend that he disliked. To write off a whole species for a culture you do not understand was not an admirable quality to have in a potential ruler. He had asked her about it, but she always gave a non-answer, putting it down to them drinking blood. Being a vegetarian, it disgusted her. That, and she said she had tried and failed to take interest in them. Not a good enough reason, in his mind, to hold such wilful ignorance.

Mingling amongst the crowd in the steep streets of Shadowfern and up atop the criss-cross bridges over their heads, Berran was enjoying a rare night outside the castle walls. The tension in his soul and body subsided, though his sharp eyes were forever scanning the scene. A habit the warrior inside him would never break.

When Berran arrived back to his chambers after the trial, a letter awaited him from Lord and Lady Trewith.

The King has chosen to retire back to the Palace of Dawn and will not be present to watch over the remainder of the Heir's Rite.

His Majesty's health is the kingdom's utmost priority, and our King requires the power and expertise of the royal physicians in Oridae.

There will be no banquet this evening as we reflect and pray to the gods for his Majesty's good health.

With a furrowed brow, Berran had read the letter. The King's withdrawal from the Rite was a bad omen, a signal of the kingdom's uncertain future. Not to mention, it did not inspire confidence in the competitors, even so much as giving a rude impression.

Berrans' father would rather drop dead than have the subjects of Silvanh bear witness to their King's weakness. Whether that was a fault of the Reothadhs, Berran couldn't quite say, though he did agree with the sentiment: strength was everything.

His mother and father would look down upon the King of Eira once they heard the news. He had known the King was getting older and frailer – humans tended to suffer from illness and disease more than other species – but the news of his decline cast a shadow in his thoughts.

Folding the letter back into the envelope, he decided he would go into the town rather than sit miserably on his own tonight.

On his way out of the castle, he grabbed Mileya from her room, convincing her to join him for dinner.

She had insisted on inviting Cass, but he noted her neglect to invite Keyara and Aura. Berran did not protest, as the three of them rarely had a chance to spend time together alone.

They had made their way across the expansive bridge, into town away from the castle, laughing and joking on the short walk.

A large tavern squatted on the very edge of the mountain, leaning over the cliff precariously and without fear.

Berran steered the females towards it, recognising a few of the nobles who were sat out the front, sipping on jugs of mead and scoffing down plates of steaming stew.

From the street, the heaping throngs of people inside created a rhythmic hum of noise, which only grew louder as they passed under the threshold. It was outrageously busy, with not one spare table from what he could see.

"You are sitting at our table," Berran heard Mileya say to a table of half-drunk men behind him.

Berran held in a chuckle. The look upon the faces of men who had never encountered her kind before never ceased to amuse him. From the long beards, weathered skin and gnarled hands, they had probably never even left the mountains they called home, let alone come face to face with a Domhiann.

"Move…*please*," she hissed.

They did as they were told, the empty jugs clinking loudly as the men swiftly vacated the table.

Berran smiled as he shuffled down to the table. "You know you could have just asked them nicely."

"And why would I do that?"

"Because it makes us look rude and entitled. You might not care about appearances, Mileya, but I *have* to. As an emissary to the Domhianns, you should care about these things. We don't all live in the dark."

He was half serious. As the Silvanh heir, certain things were expected of him. His mother would send him to the iceberg of Lonely Isle to be forgotten if she found out he abused his power, or came across as a prick.

Mileya waved a hand at him in dismissal. Cass did not join them, and he watched as his sister was deep in conversation with the same Akoaàns who were seated behind them at the trial today.

Berran noticed how intensely Mileya was watching her, even though those eyes could barely distinguish the light and shadows of the world. Cassidae's laughter and flirtatious banter with the male Syrens sent ripples of both amusement and exasperation through the packed room.

Mileya's fingers brushed against his own calloused hands across the table, a shared glance conveying the unspoken understanding between them. Cass's charms were undeniable, but amidst the sometimes seriousness of life, her antics were like playful gusts of wind, at times refreshing, but at other times unsettling.

Her beauty and gentle grace were, more often than not, taken for weakness. Those unfamiliar with his sister would get a shock if they ever knew what she was capable of, deep down. They would be equally shocked and probably piss themselves from fear, if they were ever unfortunate enough to discover a certain secret of hers; one that Berran wasn't even sure his parents knew.

"Must she always seek the attention of males? I'm tired of coming up with shit excuses as to why she cannot marry every poor fucker that asks for her hand."

If his words registered with Mileya, she didn't register them. But it was true. Every other day he was refusing syrens, vampyres and humans alike, asking – even pleading – for his sister's hand in marriage.

A fool's errand, as everyone knew marriage outside the Reothadh species was unheard of.

"She cannot in any reality enjoy the company of those idiots," Mileya said, her habit of protectiveness over Cass seeping into her voice.

He would occasionally hear the two of them bickering about it, with Cass complaining to Mileya that it was her choice who she entertains and takes to her bed, but Berran knew it was just Mileyas way. Domhianns saw the threat in everything.

He put his hand up, signalling to one of the serving girls to take their order. His jaw tightened as he took another glance at his sister, noticing a new face had joined the group.

Taris.

A low snarl started in his chest, which Mileya picked up on in seconds. "What is it?"

"He's talking to Cass."

Berran did not even have to specify who *he* was. With one directed sniff of the air, Mileya mirrored his snarl. The memories they shared of Taris were far from pleasant. Their last encounter with the Valhirian prince was a fateful card game in Oridae, where Berran had suffered a bitter loss to the vampyre.

The resentment he held for Taris was as vivid and tangible as the day they had crossed paths. Not only for the card game, but for the other events that transpired that night.

The sight of him mingling with his sister only intensified his dislike for the prick. His instincts and experience told him that Taris was not to be trusted around her. The prince was a notorious womaniser, who kept a harem of women at his beck and call back in the Valhirian capital; not a custom Reothadhs were partial too.

A jingle of the bell over the tavern door sounded, the faint smell of chocolate and freshly brewed coffee following the opening of the door. Berran recognised the scent immediately, as did Mileya.

"It seems we must suffer her company as well this evening," she muttered, scooting down the bench.

He waved to Keyara, beckoning her over to sit with them. She smiled in return, gently pushing her way through the intoxicated patrons.

Moments before reaching their table, Berran saw Taris had left the company of Cass and was striding over to Keyara, a predatory glint in his blood-red eyes.

His long legs itched to stand up, aiming to stop the interaction. As much as he wanted to hide her away from him, he knew his sister could handle herself with the male. She had experience with vampyres and their superficial charms. They were much like the bludhounds that roamed the Ary Ynarth and its red dunes; beautiful to look at, but deadly when close.

Keyara however, had no experience with the species and Berran did not like her vulnerability.

Mileyas stern voice rippled through him.

"Sit down you fool, she's fine."

The order in her deep voice unsettled him slightly, like the very darkness of the ocean was behind her tone.

"It's Taris, Mileya. You know as well as I do what he's like. I can't sit here and watch him take advantage of her."

"Your concern over that woman is beginning to wear thin. I am getting tired of it and I know she would be too. Does Keyara know how much you underestimate her, or is that something you keep to yourself, Berran?"

He gave his friend an exasperated look as he warily sat back down, peering over at the two figures on the other side of the room as they finally collided with each other. By the look on Keyara's face, she was just as displeased to see the vampyre as he was.

"Smile brother, people will think you terribly miserable," Cassidae said, as she gracefully parked herself next to Mileya, picking up her long glacial skirts so as not to dirty them on the tavern floor.

"He's pissed because Taris dared talk to his human pet."

Berran threw Mileya a warning stare. "Don't call her that."

"Well, she is. She follows you around just as much as those warriors of yours. Speaking of, where are the brutes? I thought they would be here, pining after their leader."

"They're better off in Eldorhaven. I told them to keep an eye on the village whilst I'm gone."

Cassidae shuffled in her seat, seeming to try and prevent herself from saying something she shouldn't.

"What is it, Cass?" he asked her pointedly.

"I might have sent them home."

"Cass!" He nearly shouted, not believing that his sister would go against his orders to his clan.

"Mother and father have departed for the Utuu ceremony in Halè, and with our absence, you cannot leave Silvanh unguarded."

He rolled his eyes. "That was not your call to make. Godsdamn it Cass."

Berran knew that as loyal as his warriors were to him, they were too susceptible to his sister's allure. A Reothadh syren in nature, they would always follow the whims of a female.

Fucking males, he thought, they cannot control themselves.

His sister continued, an air of sarcasm not missed in her tone.

"As… *heir*, Berran, I would have thought you would come to the very same conclusion as I did."

Berran ignored it and allowed himself to glance back over to where Keyara has been, except now, she wasn't there. Neither was Taris.

"Where..." He began, but Mileya cut him off.

"He left before she did, I heard them both walk out, one after the other. Just forget about them and let's enjoy the rest of the evening."

Mileya gulped down her vial of Mycillium. It reminded him that it was high time he took his own; it had been at least a week since he last drank the stuff and leaving it this long was cutting it fine.

Ordering himself and Cass a bowl of mutton stew, they delved into their bowls with numerous jugs of honey mead, over hours of non-consequential small talk. Mileya made do with her dried Moscht.

With bellies full and lungs well laughed, the three syrens strolled back towards the castle.

"You two go on, I'll be back soon," he said to them as they reached the waterfall, gesturing to one of the guards to let the two females through.

Cass let go of his arm. "Where are you going?"

Mileya did not face them, she just stood Domhiann still whilst lifting her head to the now full moon.

"For a walk," he answered lightly. "Go on, it's getting late."

His sister nodded reluctantly, kissed him on the cheek and walked arm-in-arm with Mileya into the parting torrent.

Berran turned around, seeking a way higher up the mountain. He found it behind the guard's stone tower, built into a shallow space just beside the roaring water. A narrow path wound its way up into the darkness above, illuminated by the silver lunar light.

It was extremely steep, his syren feet not as steady as a fae, vampyre or even human would be navigating this terrain.

"Shit," he grumbled, stumbling over another small rock that wedged itself under his feet. Higher and higher he went, ascending without any further incident. Eventually, he reached a small natural ledge, just wide enough for him to stand on without fear of tripping over the edge. That would be an awful way to go, he thought, peering over the precipice. Falling down into the endless black below, flying without wings straight down for gods knows how long.

The height began to make him feel dizzy, his eyes wobbled as he pulled himself from the boundary of the ledge. Berran came up here solely for the view and he would enjoy it from the safety of the mountain's spine.

But fuck, even from here, along the natural stone wall, did it meet his expectations. In the pale light he could see for hundreds of miles, right into the horizon.

Towards Oridae in the west, was an expanse of rolling hills and wheat farms, so small from this height, they resembled ant hills. The heated spring and early summer sun had bleached the grass and wheat below, a golden brown.

To the north, Deryn beckoned, with its swampy marshland sweeping over the green kingdom. Silvanh lay a few hundred miles off the coast of that lost kingdom, which Berran had visited a fair few times. King Harolld was far from one of his favourite humans, and his nature resembled that of his wet castle; miserable and harsh.

Finally, his gaze turned southwards, towards a kingdom Berran had never ventured; only a few sirens ever had. The world of sand and desert was a hostile environment for a water being, and Valhir could be an unkind mistress to those who didn't accept its hostility with a familial embrace.

He tried to get a glimpse of the Szaro, its glowing water legendary and sacred. A sight he would like to see one day, but it seemed that would not be from here, not tonight. He tutted, the vast expanse of red stone that was the Kilamaj mountains stood firmly in the way, spanning the width of the continent. Though he could stare at the various directions of the horizons all night, and the glowing banks of a sacred river be damned, Berran only really wanted to see one thing…

Water.

His blue eyes ventured downwards, as did he. He sat softly on the rough ground, not letting the sight of the two lakes below, leave his eyeline.

As much as he liked being on solid ground, he could not escape his pull to large bodies of water. If looking at it relieved the itch he could not scratch then he would seek it out.

No larger than the palm of his hand, they shone like mirrors, reflecting the Vaelorns above. He felt the lakes were reflecting his own emotions back towards him. The calm, cool world below a twin to his inner self.

As soon as the Rite was over, he would make his way back to Silvanh. To home, his family, and to Berran's reluctance, his duty.

29

Selsie

The salty, early morning breeze gently ruffled Selsie's walnut hair, which glowed with golden light under the full moon, hanging low in the predawn sky. Her jade skirts billowed as she stood on the precipice of her rocky island home, her gaze focused on the vast expanse of the open sea that surrounded Cildraethe.

The decision to leave had weighed on her mind since making the promise to Jonn hours before.

She had to be discreet. If anyone were to discover her activities, there was no doubt in Selsie's mind that her mother would kill her. Despite the very real threat to her future soul, something other than a promise to her captive compelled her to take this daring step. It whispered to her, urged her on, ordering her to follow this uncertain path.

The city had not yet awoken or swapped fins for feet. Cildraethe was quiet, only the crescendo of waves and occasional bird song drifted on the morning wind. She had planned her departure just so, timing it perfectly for the night in which Neesh was on guard duty, for if she was caught, Selsie could maybe rely on her friend to not betray her to the matriarch.

Taking one last deep breath, Selsie discarded her skirts in one smooth movement and dived into the water.

With her tail propelling her through the dark depths, Selsie purred in the familiar embrace of the water. It flowed through her veins like lifeblood, uniting her with the sea. Once again accustomed to the depths, her vision adjusted to the murkiness beneath as she went deeper towards the ocean floor, trying to stay away from prying eyes that would no doubt spot her if she swam near the surface.

She could not deny the sense of home that surged within her when she was beneath the waves. The Maolin Sea welcomed her, its currents wrapping around her body like a lover's arms as she swam further from Cildraethe and northeast toward Oblitus, where Jonn had instructed her to begin the search for his friend. If Symon was still alive, that was where he would be.

She reflected on their hushed conversation earlier this evening, the private tales of his life that he told her and how privileged she felt hearing them. They were his stories to tell, he owed her nothing but told her anyway. She liked hearing him speak, the way every syllable was laced with passion and such soul when he spoke, though it was when he spoke of his family that the weight of his heartache became palpable.

Her heart was filled with a mix of empathy and sorrow. She had never heard Jonn speak of his past in such detail before, the pain in his words tugged at her inside, and a connection Selsie felt unlike any other had started to grow between them.

Her magic continued to awaken, growing stronger as it absorbed the energy of the Maolin sea. Immersed in the water, her power thrived. The dampener that was the open air, now fully shaken off. She would need her full strength and capabilities for the journey ahead, Oblitus was a few thousand miles from here by sea, it would take her at least a month to swim there, and Selsie was not so sure Jonn had that time to spare back in her mother's castle.

Once she knew her daughter had left without killing Jonn or capturing him in her syren spell, the matriarch would no doubt dispatch of him herself.

Selsie had ordered Neesh to tell her mother that she had gone to the sea, to live in her Other form for a while, to envelop herself in the violence and nature of the form. If that excuse did not work, Selsie fully entrusted Neesh to act in a manner she thought best. Her friend was clever and quick and Selsie would support her judgement more than any other syren in the castle. As the current began to push her along, a niggling thought had her mind casting a net of doubt. Maybe she had made a rash decision, a frivolous venture based on pleasing her human. One could not disregard the possibility that this man had set her on a course of ruin and death, that maybe he had plunged her into a trap.

Though as quick as that thought entered her brain, the water around her ordered it to leave, whispering reassurances to her that this was where she was meant to be.

Though once she arrived at Jonns homeland, Selsie had no discernible idea of how to find this man. She couldn't simply walk onto shore, hollering for a man with the name Symon. Her throat would be harpooned before she could even put two toes in the sand and Selsie did not want to meet her end in such a careless manner.

Alysee would be thoroughly displeased when her soul arrived in the Eternis Nerinium, Selsie's place in the Eternal Sea marred with disappointment.

Unless…she did not follow Jonns advice. He may know his friend, but Selsie knew the sea. The man may not be back on his home soil just yet. If the ship was attacked off the coast of Noran, they could not have gotten too far around the continent in the time that had passed since.

Besides, the ship had been torn into tatters, barely afloat from what she remembered. The survivors would need a new vessel to take them home, and there would be no journey across the sea for those sailors just yet.

If luck was on her side, they would have been picked up by *The Nikolas* or *The Christofer*, rendering Selsies search that much easier if she focused her gaze on visions of white and silver.

EBONY WILKINS

30
Selsie

Her underestimation of the journey was taking its toll. Days had passed since Selsie had left Cildraethe and the weight of exhaustion pressed down upon her weary body. She had not paused for any kind of respite. Instead, she had simply snatched fish when she could with a lightning-fast snap of her hand, using spells to keep sleep at bay more often than not.

But now her magic was waning, begging her to stop, rest and close her red-rimmed eyes.

The only thing keeping her moving was the sea's natural currents. They had guided her tired body with gentle hands towards the choppy waters of Noran.

It was not too long ago she had been heading this very way with her pod. The familiar shipwrecks that had caught her attention before were much closer now, as she swam along the seabed.

In amongst the mud and silt surrounding one of the wrecks that haunted the seafloor, a glint of silver and gold shone in the filtered sunlight. Her pulse quickened as the temptation of long-forgotten treasure reached out to her as it did before.

Its call would not go unanswered this time.

Brushing off prickling shivers along her arms and squashing down her Other form that was suddenly thrashing beneath her skin, she propelled herself towards the broken ship, the treasure beckoning her forward.

Selsie was not even a tail fin away from the glinting prize when a flash of movement behind her took away all the wind in her body. Moving too quickly for Selsie to react, a thick sharp thread had woven itself tightly around her tail, winding around her scales with a force of its own.

One glimpse confirmed to her what she feared. A syren net. Selsie had been so distracted by the treasure she had let her guard down just enough to be captured by the very thing a newling syren is taught to avoid from the moment they are born.

The net ensnared her in its embrace, and panic clawed at her chest as she fought against the enchanted threads, her movements restricted by the powerful magic.

Stupid, reckless, weak newling!

Her mother's voice screamed in her ears, words that echoed Selsie's own fears.

She had been reckless. Though to hear that confirmed in her mother's voice ripped through her like a spear hook.

Selsie started to tear at the threads with her hands, her teeth, but to no use, the fae woven threads were too strong.

The sharp claws and enhanced strength of her Other form would have no doubt gotten her out, but her magic was paralyzed. The creature within, trapped in the cage that was her syren body.

With her desperation rising, Selsie gritted her teeth as she shouted.

"No, no, no!"

The surface was getting closer now and a shadow loomed over her from above, promising death and darkness.

"By Alysee, not like this."

There was no more she could physically do and Selsie gave in against the net, calming herself as best she could. Even if the storm inside her raged to be let free, she would not meet her captors screaming and wailing like a youngling.

Breaking the surface with a splash, she did her best to take in as much as she could with her syren eyes. The shock from the quiet underneath, the waves to the furore and excitement above jolted her resolve slightly, bringing forth slight apprehension in her gills.

Through the two-inch wide holes in the net, she saw a small, rickety boat with brown sails, crewed by what she counted as five men.

What were fishermen doing out here, so far from the fishing grounds? Did these fools have a death wish?

"We got one!" someone cried out. "Shit we got one! Quick fellas, get the harpoon."

By Alysee, she was going to be killed, she thought, as they pulled her ever closer, the net's woven threads dragging her over the edge and into the boat.

"Jonn, Symon,"

Shouting the only human names she knew, Selsie prayed to Alysee that the men aboard would recognise the words flooding from her mouth.

"Symon, Jonn!"

Nothing but bewilderment met her fervent stare. Until a man's voice came through, louder than the others, so she repeated it.

"What the fuck..."

A man with a closely shaved head pushed his way through the others as Selsie thumped to the deck inside the net, which was now snaking its way tightly around her recently formed legs. Now she was out of the water her body instinctively adapted and changed on its own.

"Hearing my name come out of a Laeth's mouth, now that's something I didn't know would turn me on."

"Symon?" she sputtered out, looking into the human's blue eyes, not quite believing the luck Alysee was granting her. Not quite believing that this truly was Jonn's friend who had caught her.

Keeping his distance, the man squatted down to her with a puzzled expression.

"Now then, who the fuck are you, and how do you know me?"

"Jonn," the name fell out of her mouth.

The man rolled his eyes. "And Jonn."

"Is this it Symon? Have we caught the right one?" a male said.
He looked her over, up and down, eventually shouting back to
them, "Na, she aint."

Hushed voices began murmuring like sea kelp over the boat.

"Answer me syren, you've got five seconds before I shove this
straight through that pretty neck of yours." A harpoon, once
lying on the ground, was now in the man's hands.

"Jonn sent me."

Her keen eyes picked up his loosened grip on the weapon.

"He's alive?"

Selsie took an intake of breath, growing impatient with him.

"Yes, he's alive, he sent me to find you, to tell you."

After a moment, where Selsie was sure the sea grew still, a
flicker of realisation passed between them and Symon reached
out cautiously with a finger, as recognition dawned in his eyes.

"You're the one who took him when he fell in the water?"

"Yes, he's mine, I have him," Selsie stated loud enough so
every human on this boat could hear, without hesitation.
She knew Jonn hated being called hers, but she knew he
wouldn't mind this time.

"Godsdamn," Symon laughed, but not with any humour. He
stood back up and told the men to take him back to Noran, with
the syren.

"Fuck off, you can't keep her alive! She'll kill ya the moment
she gets free!" Selsie heard one of the men protest.

It was her turn to laugh. "If I wanted to kill any of you, I would
have done it by now."

Not necessarily true, inside the enchantment of the net, her
power was near non-existent, though the moment she got free…
Besides, she was here for Symon. Even so, they all looked
down at her with flashes of fear marring their faces. Good, by

Alysee they should fear her.

"I ain't gonna take her out the net, you silly pricks. She's got Jonn and she's gonna take me to him."

Silence overtook the boat, only the gentle lapping of the waves against the sides permeated the tense air.

"Your funeral pyre." One of them said, and the boat began to move.

Symon, clearly torn between scepticism and hope, listened as Selsie recounted the events – from inside her net prison – that had transpired since the syren attack on *The Brendann*.

They had pulled up to a small cove somewhere off the shores of Deryn. The other men had departed some hours before, leaving Selsie and Symon alone in the darkness.

Not before they had all made their feelings towards her clearly known. The threat of a slit throat and ripped open belly being hissed her way. She had bore her teeth back at them, hoping her own threat of death was visible in her eyes.

Softening herself for Jonn's friend, and with her voice tinged with a mixture of urgency and authority, she spoke of Jonn, alive in the dungeons of her home.

The mention of Jonn, alive and seemingly well, seemed to make him happy, a sense of ease radiated off him, but also surprise.

"I thought he was dead. We all did. We were out here trying to catch one of you lot."

"Why?" she asked.

"Aside from the obvious…" He gave her a side eye from across the boat before continuing, "…we were out for revenge I suppose."

Selsie could not help but ask, a touch of anger in her steady voice, "How many of my syrens have you caught"

He scratched the back of his neck. "Three."

Three of her kind, caught and killed by this man she was meant to be civil too, for Jonn.

212

The taste of salty iron bloomed in her mouth, as her sharp teeth bit her tongue, the effort to not let violence consume her overwhelming.

Symon snorted a laugh, rubbing his shaved head.

"I can't believe I am sitting here talking to a bloody Laeth. I'll be eating tea and biscuits with the fucking gods tomorrow."

Selsie quietly agreed. She was the next in line to take over the Laethian throne, and he was just a human, avenging his friend. The two of them together without the presence of bloodshed or song, gave way to a highly unusual situation.

"Are you going to let me go?"

More of a statement than a question, it was her time to go home, her duty done and there was no need for any more interaction between them.

Symon looked at her body, sprawled naked in the binds of the net.

"I meant what I said to them earlier, I'm coming with you. You're gonna take me to him."

"Have you lost your mind to the sea?!" she barked back. "You will die as soon as you come within five miles of Cildraethe." After a moment of contemplation, he got up.

"You ain't taking me to Cildraethe," he grinned. "We'll go to Alboste, you can bring him there. I wanna be sure he's alive and that you aint fucking with me."

She had no idea why he would want to go to that small spit of land that was dirty, riddled with poverty and had been neglected by her mother for years.

Did he need to trade with the Laeths in neutral territory? She doubted it. He carried on his person no more than a wrinkled map and a pathetically empty purse.

"I am not fucking with you, and I am not taking you to Alboste."

"Oh, I think you'll find you are…" He got up to unleash the sails, letting the boat drift out into the night sea. "…or I'll just kill ya."

Pulling this ridiculous plan off without alerting her mother would be nearly impossible. As soon as her scales reached the waters surrounding Alboste, the matriarch would be alerted and Selsie would be dragged by her fins back to Cildraethe. Where she would be promptly murdered or put in the dungeons for disobedience.

Alysee knows what fate would await Jonn if that were to happen.

However, her own possible demise could not distract Selsie from the weight of the task at hand – reuniting the two men. Not long into their journey, the sun began creeping into the pink horizon. Selsie's mind clung to desperately needed sleep, not releasing her from slumber's firm grip as she awoke with a start.

"Woah easy, no need for dramatics."

She scrunched her nose in discomfort. "Let me out of this net, I would rather swim alongside the vessel if you don't mind".

Symon gave her a pointed look. "So, you can swim away and alert others of your kind to come along and attack my ship? I don't think so."

She raised a brow.

"It's a boat, not a ship."

"Yeah alright it's a boat, but the point still stands."

Selsie shook her head.

"There is a binding spell I can cast, it will prevent me from breaking any promise I make to you."

Humans can be very slow sometimes. Laeths never needed to distrust one another, there were spells for everything, including making a deal. Breaking the spell would reap dire consequences for anyone stupid enough to go against it.

He hesitated. "Yes, I know all about your spells. I ain't stupid."

Debatable, she thought.

"You need to let me out of this net so I have access to my

power. I also need something of yours to bind you to the spell."

"No bloody way!"

She let out a loud sigh. "What purpose would it serve to lie to you? We are evenly matched on the deck of this boat, and it will not work without you."

After a heartbeat, he nodded, "Okay, but I won't hesitate to beat the shit out of you just because you're a woma…female,"

She had told him they would be evenly matched to ease his fear, a small lie that would serve them both.

"And I want you to put in that spell that you won't hurt me either," Symon continued.

Rolling her eyes, she agreed.

Shuffling into a compartment beneath, Symon loudly rooted around before coming back out with what looked like a knife, but it was glowing and was only the size of a pinkie finger. She had never seen anything like it.

"What are you doing with that?"

"Relax, I'm Damned so don't have access to magic, do I. This thing is enchanted, it will cut the net and release you."

Moving towards her as he spoke, Symon flicked his wrist in a swift movement, using the knife to cut a single thread of the net. It dissolved away in seconds, and Selsie couldn't believe that so many of her kind had been trapped and killed by something as simple as this.

If she was her mother, she would have taken this fleeting opportunity to kill him, take his knife and deliver it back to their own in Cildraethe. The most intelligent of their kind would then work on the tool and replicate its magic. Giving them all a weapon in the future against those deadly nets.

But she was not her mother, a fact she had to remind herself as she stood up straight, shaking out her hair.

"Now, give me something, hurry," Selsie ordered, holding her hands out towards him.

He sniggered and pursed his lips.

"Stupid man, quickly or I will not be able to do the spell."

"Well like what? I don't know what to give you."

"Anything, a piece of clothing, a lock of hair?"

He spat in his own palm and held it out to her.

Disgusting, but it will do, she thought as she shook his hand and began to recite the spell.

Sea-foam green light lit up her palms and soft syren voices whispered around the glow.

Symon's eyes widened. "Fuck me," he gasped.

Selsie realised a human would have never seen a syren spell before, let alone be part of one. Unless it was a song of course. She smiled slightly. "I will not hurt this man, or deceive him in any way," were the final words of the spell.

"Or eat him," he called out.

The bonds of loyalty and promise stirred in the air as the magic was cast into the water below.

"There, it is done."

Symon gave a wide smile, "Then let's go."

It was said that the sea held echoes of every story, and Selsie was determined to unravel the threads that bound her fate to the man she had left behind.

31
Selsie

Selsie had delivered Symon to Alboste in good time, and credit to the human, his sailing was true and strong.

She instructed him to wait on the fringes of the shore for her, as she was to go back to Cildraethe alone to retrieve Jonn.

Symon's mistrust for her was evident, as he asked for another spell to ensure her return.

Slipping back unnoticed into Cildraethe, Selsie was very surprised to discover that her access to the castle was unchanged. She was expecting her mother to banish her from the fortress, to deal with her daughter herself.

On the contrary and to Selsie's relief, no such enchantment was in place, and it had been incredibly easy to walk in and gather what she had needed.

The rest of her afternoon had been spent locating Neesh. After hours of searching, Selsie finally resorted to theft, stealing the castle guard logbook to find the young guard. Neesh had in fact, been at the first place Selsie began her search.

As it turned out, Neesh had to hide Jonn from her mother, claiming he had died from human ailments. The matriarch had seemed unbothered, only instructing Neesh to find her daughter and bring her back.

The two young females spoke about it now, in Neesh's family home on the outskirts of the city underneath the waves. It was a tiny cave-dwelling, not much bigger than Selsie's own submerged room, with stairs that led out of the water to a dry area upstairs. It was quiet, the home surprisingly empty of other syrens.

Selsie had never asked about Neesh's family, which made her feel like a terrible friend and a selfish leader.

"I had to bring him here, Selsie. I didn't know what else to do. I had no idea if you would return."

Selsie swam inside as Neesh closed the rolling cave door behind them. She laid a hand on Neesh's mesh cladded arm.

"You did the right thing, Neesh, thank you. But how did you get him here alive in one piece, without him being eaten?"

Neesh smirked. "I have ways."

Selsie was about to ask her to elaborate, when she heard a noise from the upper level, her head whipping in the direction of the stairs.

"He's upstairs," Neesh softly said.

Her fins took on a mind of their own, propelling her to the steps and rushing her up the stairs, transforming into limbs as she did. Her legs could not release quick enough, she half stumbled, half fell onto the hard floor at the top, barely two feet away from Jonn.

He looked the same as he did when she left him, however many weeks or months ago that was, except his hair was longer and his stubbled face was now framed with a thicker beard.

The smell of him she could now place as freshly washed linen and ripe green apples. The same smell that would greet her every evening as she went to sleep in her bed, inside the dry castle. It was a smell she would wrap herself up in every night. He froze as he watched her rise from the floor, trying to reclaim her dignity as she began brushing off her naked form.

His blue eyes were as wide as the horizon as he stared. Not filled with amusement as Symon's were when he saw her bare body, but consumed with something else entirely. For the briefest of moments, she thought he was more Laethian than human.

Selsie's heart swelled with anticipation and anxiety at seeing the man who stood before her.

"Jonn."

32

Jonn

He knew the second she had entered this damned cave. It was as if his body sensed the danger and went immediately into fight or flight, his senses heightened, the blood in his veins became slightly too warm and his mind only focused on the female.

She stood on long bare legs before him now, naked as her day of birth. He was accustomed to seeing Laeths with next to nothing on their upper halves, and he never took notice of them. But with her, he couldn't look away.

"Jonn."

His name whispered off her tongue, the first time in weeks he had heard the voice that haunted his dreams every night.

Jonn's mind had been in a constant battle ever since she had left. He half hoped she would never return, the threat of being enchanted no longer bearing down upon his shoulders and he could somehow escape to freedom.

The other side of him, buried way down deep, longed to see her, smell her and just feel her presence nearby.

It was seriously fucked up.

Clearing his throat, Jonn tried to think of something appropriate to say.

"You came back then," was all he managed.

She blinked a few times, her large green eyes measuring him up and down.

"Of course I did."

He scratched his temple. "Hm."

Selsie began to take a few steps closer to him, but he could not allow it whilst she was bare. He held his arm out in protest, "Woah, put this on."

Neesh had given him Laethian clothes to wear while he had been in her care. He had begrudgingly taken them, not wanting anything from these syrens, but he had no choice in the end. His cream sailing shirt and black pants he arrived in months ago had been torn to shreds and were beyond repair.

He undid the tiny emerald buttons that ran up the length of the collarless chocolate shirt. It was a fucking nice garment; he would give them that. The whorls of bronze and gold that traced the arms were more intricate and well-made than anything he had ever seen. It was a near-perfect fit to his body and was as soft as shit.

Shrugging it off, he threw it to her. Not taking her eyes from his own, she caught it in deft hands.

The soft cave light bounced around the room in the silence that accompanied them.

"Does my body offend you?" her soft, yet commanding voice asked him.

He wanted to tell her that, no, it most certainly bloody did not. The opposite in fact, and he needed her to cover up before he grabbed her and did something he would regret. That line would not be crossed whilst he had free will and a mind of his own.

Jonn settled on avoiding the truth, for both their sakes. "Yes."

If he offended her she didn't show it, as she put the shirt on and Godsdamn, seeing his shirt on her did something to him. He desperately needed to alter the direction of his thoughts, so he asked the question he had been waiting for the answer to, for weeks. "Did you find Symon, is he alive?"

She smiled. "Yes, and he knows about you and where you are."

Jonn didn't think as he grabbed Selsie's arms that were resting at her sides.

"Thank you," he said with full honesty this time, letting go of her as soon as he realised what he was doing.

"He is a strange one, that human."

Jonn huffed a laugh. "That he is."

What he would fucking give, to have been a witness to their first encounter.

"Where is he now? Where did you find him?" He wanted to know everything. Did the newborns survive? the rest of the crew? What of *The Brendann*? He had a thousand questions, but space on his tongue for only a few.

Selsie opened her mouth to speak, just as a loud crash reverberated through the cave, its origin the waves below.

On some instinct he didn't know he had, Jonn went to throw himself in front of Selsie, though not before she had pushed him with syren strength behind her own lithe body in a flash of speed.

Her teeth were bared, her beautiful face contorted into pure Laethian lethality. He supposed he was hers as she saw it, and syrens were extremely territorial.

"Well, well," came an old female's voice from the stairs.

Standing firm at her side, Jonn had removed himself from behind Selsie. There was no chance he was cowering behind a female.

He could feel the tension roll off her, the power in the room became palpable, the whispers chattering heatedly.

Shit, he thought, there was a new, powerful energy joining their little gathering.

"Who is that?" he asked Selsie.

"My Mother."

"Dear *daughter*, what do we have here? A human and a syren together, alone, hidden away from prying eyes. Whatever could you be keeping from me?"

Fuck, it was the syren that pulled his shipmate in the water, the one who Selsie was communicating with that day. She must be the matriarch, the queen of the Laeths.

With a naked form covered only by her white grey hair, the old witch of a female strode in on still glowing legs.

"Oh godsdamn it," he uttered. He was in trouble here.

Neesh had squirrelled him away one night, telling him nonchalantly that he must be hidden from the queen before she ate him. Jonn had no objections; he didn't want to be eaten, such a shit way to go.

Performing a spell that created a tunnel to this place, Neesh brought them to her home.

He had never heard or read about such magic. Powerful Laeths could create storms, control the waves to some extent, perform basic spells, but this? Being able to appear anywhere in the world in a second, simply by walking through the magic, it was dangerous, Jonn made a mental note to tell the right people, warn them of this new, unknown magic the syrens possessed.

Selsie's golden brown curls fell in front of her face as she bowed her head.

"Mother, how…happy I am, to finally be back home."

Jonn noted the lack of fear or timidness in her voice. He saw no inclination that she would back down from the old queen, whose many, many stolen trinkets of all kinds twinkled in her greying hair.

The speed at which a clawed, veiny hand smacked across Selsie's face took Jonn by surprise. It was as though there had been a crack of lightning in the cave. The force of it was so strong, it would have taken any man down, but not Selsie. She stood her ground, as solid as the castle around her.

"What the fuck?!" he shouted.

Completely ignoring Jonn with a storm of fury brewing in her eyes, the old bitch drawled in a bored tone.

"What have I told you about lying to me?"

The shadows of the cave enveloped him as Jonn watched the confrontation unfold between the two. The air was charged with tension, and the echoes of the sea's disapproval seemed to resonate around them.

Jonn could have sworn he heard thunder crack in the sky above him, muffled by the tonnes of water that lay heavy between himself and dry ground.

The matriarch's voice was steady. "You thought you could deceive me? Your naivety betrays you, my daughter. I placed wards to track your every move, I then came to find this, *human*, is not dead or yet enchanted."

Jonn felt a shiver of dread run down his spine, as the queen's eyes shifted towards him. The weight of her scrutiny felt slimy on his skin, and he knew she saw his lack of enchantment that had thankfully eluded him thus far.

The matriarch continued with her scathing remarks.

"How careless can you be, Selsie. Or is it deliberate? A defiance against your own kind?" Low and threatening, her words slicing.

Selsie hesitated. Jonn could see the internal struggle within her, the conflicting currents of loyalty and the clear desire to protect him, to protect what she thought was *hers*.

She wasn't fucking around here. Jon could feel his short unfulfilled life was about to fall from a cliff's edge.

The queen was unfazed by the hesitation, her gaze bore into Selsie with an intensity that could drown a thousand ships.

"I gave you until the full moon and that has been and passed. If your song does not work here, now, in my presence, then you will kill him, or I will kill you right here. A traitor deserves no mercy."

Jonn was too stunned to speak, to breathe.

This was it.

Selsie's big almond eyes met his, her conflicting emotions swirling within them. Then, as if surrendering to the inevitable, she began to sing.

It was the same song as before, haunting, and ethereal, devastating even.

Jonn's heart quickened, not from the enchantment, but from the realisation that this was Selsie's sacrifice to spare him. She would rather try this futile attempt at enchantment than kill him, which was the easier option for her.

For if she failed, she gave her life for him, rather than just spill his blood outright.

Jonn may not be as smart as the scholars on Oblitus, or as good of a performer as the Akoaàns, but he would try his best at the most stupid, brilliant idea his sailor brain could think of.

Letting his eyes droop, he began to feign the effects of the song as it wrapped around him like a gentle current. Though in reality, he felt no magic.

Dropping to his knees, he began to crawl to Selsie. Looking up at her with eyes he hoped, bore complete admiration and love, obsession even.

Symon would be in fucking hysterics if he saw him now, at how pathetic he must appear. Gods this was humiliating.

Selsie's song had come to its end, the melody tapering off in a single note as Jonn made it to her feet.

The Queen laughed, a harsh sound that echoed off the cave walls.

"I've heard enough." The old Laeth snapped her fingers. "This human is beneath you Selsie, dispose of him, or keep him, I do not care. We shall discuss your transgressions later."

With a dismissive gesture, the Queen left the cave, her personal guards shifting shadows beneath the water at the bottom of the stairs, left with her.

Jonn kept the ridiculous act going until he was sure they had all left Neesh's home.

"Jonn?" Selsie softly said down to him, the questioning tone of her voice told him she didn't even know herself if it had worked or not.

He should go lump in with the Akoaàns if his little act was so convincing, that a Laeth herself could not differentiate reality from fiction.

Jonn slowly got to his feet, rising to meet her gaze, before reaching his full height to tower over her.

"Well, I can safely say I won't be doing that again," he said with a scratch of his beard.

Selsie's mouth was opening and closing like a fish out of water. "It didn't work?"

Jonn cocked his head down to her.

"Don't sound too disappointed, my performance wasn't that good."

"I... I thought it had worked..." she trailed off.

He felt a hand on his arm, and he turned to see Neesh who had emerged from the water below. She gave him a subtle nod of approval.

"Well played. Selsie we must go, he has to leave before she figures out the truth."

Selsie ignored her, mumbling to herself.

"I'm so stupid, of course, she had wards".

"Selsie?" Neesh said louder this time.

With her chin thrust forward, Selsie finally acknowledged the guard.

"Let's go"

"Where are we going?" Jonn asked.

"Alboste."

Jonn and Neesh both looked at Selsie.

"By Alysee, why?" Neesh asked.

"Because my mother never sets fin on that island, also it is close, and.." Selsie trailed off.

"And what?" Jonn urged her.

"And Symon is there."

"What?" Neesh said.

"He's in Alboste?!" Jonn exclaimed.

"I took him there. He wants to see you alive; he didn't believe me when I told him you were here alive and unharmed."

"Godsdamned." Jonn rubbed at his face, which was now framed by an ever-increasing halo of dark hair. He desperately wanted to trim his beard down, the fucking thing made him look like a castaway at the moment.

"This…*Symon*…trusted you enough to think you would return to him, with Jonn?" Neesh questioned. It must have sounded unbelievable to her, a Laeth warrior through and through. Her mistrust for humans ran as much through her as the fear of the Laeth species spread through Jonn's kin.

"He made me cast an oath spell," Selsie's tone sounded almost like exasperation.

The syrens looked up at him, expecting Jonn to say something.

"Come on then, and let's hurry up, I do not trust that man to keep his cock in his pants. Even if it is on an island full of Laeths."

Neesh gave a curt nod of her tightly braided head and put a long arm out before them.

She closed her deep brown eyes, the wrist at the end of her arms creating small circles in the air.

When she began to chant a song under her breath, a portal emerged from the end of her arm. A shimmering gateway that pulsed with magic. Its power felt old, even to his Damned self. The language of the spell was unlike any he had heard before. It was the same portal she had created in the dungeons.

Jonn couldn't help but look over to Selsie, whose eyes were wide with a look of wonder on her face. It was extraordinary. He wondered if she had ever seen this before. A fleeting thought passed through him: why would the Laethian heir not have any knowledge about this powerful magic? It seemed like the best weapon they could have in their arsenal.

But there was no more time for thinking. Neesh had finished

her chanting and was now gesturing for them to go through. "Come Selsie, there is no time."

Without looking back Selsie confidently strode through, the shirt he had given her billowing in a phantom wind. He went moments after, not for one moment letting her out his sight. The transition through the portal was swift, and Jonn found himself standing on the shores of Alboste, the air carrying a different kind of magic.

On Cildraethe, such a concentration of one species created an atmosphere thick with the weight of all their power. To Jonn, the moment he stepped foot on Alboste soil, it was like ten tonnes had been lifted off his shoulders. The whispers that had haunted him from the moment he had met Selsie remained, however.

From their place on the shore, the echoes of laughter and bartering voices originating in the busy town reverberated across the water.

Externally, it resembled Cildraethe, but it had none of its luxury. Jonn couldn't help but notice the dirt and sea moss coating the land buildings. Laethian young emerged in and out of the water, looked slightly malnourished and not unlike the street urchins that ran through the mists of Noran.

The Laeths were wealthy, far more so than some of their cousins, but Jonn didn't know of the extreme disparity between the two islands. Human poverty levels were worse of course, but this wasn't far from it.

"Where can we find this man?" Neesh asked Selsie, as she closed the portal behind them.

Jonn walked up the shoreline, scanning the low-level cave dwellings.

"Where's the nearest tavern?"

33
Keyara

Keyara's long legs made quick work of getting her across the castle courtyard. The damp air carried the scent of an approaching trial as she meandered through the stone archways with no particular hurry.

It was the stink of body odour, perfume, and anxiety.

Amplified by the clanging of swords in the distance, horse hooves against cobblestones and loud calls of workers within the castle.

She turned in the direction of the heavy doors that led back inside, stopping in her tracks when she saw two familiar males engaged in an animated conversation.

Their large silhouettes danced in the shadows of the courtyard and from the raised voices coming from their direction, it wasn't a friendly conversation between old friends.

Skirting along a larger stone archway, she tried to be as quiet as she could as she neared, doing her best to remain hidden as she watched Berran – one of her oldest friends – engaging with one of her newest enemies.

Aura would tell her to stop being such a busybody, but she couldn't help it. The pang of curiosity was getting the better of her.

Her gaze found itself lingering on the male clad in red; a male who seemed to embody both mystery and pure fucking arrogance.

She still didn't know his name, the vampyre she first met on the terrace and then again in a Shadowfern tavern a few days ago.

Keyara reflected on their encounter.

"It's interesting, a lowborn entering the Rite."

She had given him a look that would have sent someone with any ounce of self-preservation running. But he didn't, he stood next to her, so close to her that anyone near would have thought them intimate.

"Yes, isn't it interesting, how they let just *anyone* enter nowadays."

He had sketched an eyebrow at her retort.

"Come to think of it, I'm pretty sure you're the first vampyre to ever enter, they must be desperate for competitors."

The vampyre had only smirked at her, not giving away anything. He just simply popped a bar nut into his mouth, edging closer.

"I would advise against making enemies so soon if you want to become heir, Keyara."

Damn it, he must have overheard Aura call her name on the terrace.

"And why would I take your advice?"

His stubble-coated throat bobbed as he swallowed the nut he was chewing on.

She had flinched at his proximity whilst a spark had stirred in her lower belly.

"Do you fear me, Keyara."

It was not a question.

Not satisfying him with an answer, she had asked instead, "who even are you?"

He had paused. "Someone you want to know."

This male was pissing her off and she was no longer in the mood to drink with her friends.

Not once breaking eye contact, Keyara said through gritted teeth, "I doubt it."

Now at this moment, speaking to Berran, this arsehole had her attention once again.

One hand was in his trouser pocket, the other swatting the air and occasionally pointing at the syren.

These males were fire and ice alive, each trying to douse the other. Opposites in every possible way.

"They're going to kill each other before the week's out."

Keyara pulled her daggers out from their sheaths inside her jacket, nearly taking out the eye of a vampyre right behind her. He put his hands up in mock surrender.

"Woah careful, It wasn't my intention to startle you."

Liar, why would he sneak up on her?

She had seen him before; he was always in the company of the other one. They both dressed the same, with the same dark colouring to their rich skin. Only this male's complexion was a few shades deeper and his hair was worn longer than his companion's closely cropped curls.

He also had softer eyes that matched his skin and a tangible kindness that radiated from him, if that was fucking possible for a vampyre. She put her daggers down slowly, not taking him out of her view.

He cocked his head to her. "Berran and Taris have never got along, it's hard to keep the peace between them sometimes. You're Keyara Allis, if I have that right?"

Taris. Why did that name ring a bell? And an acquaintance of Berran? She reminded herself to ask him about that.

She nodded.

"Kadeen," he offered his wrist out to her, and she looked down at his outstretched arm. He must have sensed her confusion.

"In Valhir, vampyres offer their wrist to a human in greeting, as a sign of respect."

"And Humans bite you back?" she said with genuine curiosity.

He laughed softly. "No, if the human wants to offer the same sentiment, they would tap their neck, here."

He put two fingers to the base of his neck, just above the crook of his shoulder.

"And if neither respects the other?"

He pulled a half frown. "A human would show and do nothing. A vampyre? Well, it wouldn't end too well for the human, but that is rare. A fairly new custom in our ancient culture, a relic from the human rebellion."

Keyara tapped her throat where he showed her.

"If you truly want to know what they were talking about, you could just go up and ask, instead of eavesdropping around the corner."

Keyara blushed slightly, she wasn't usually the type to be sneaky and hide.

"I wasn't eavesdropping. I was looking out for Berran, just in case."

Kadeen smiled. "In case of what?"

"Well, it's clear they don't like each other, and I know what vampyres are like. *Taris* has also not given the impression that he is the most trustworthy of males."

"And what do you think you could do to help in a brawl between the two? One a seasoned Reothadh warrior, who has the power of a thousand blizzards behind him, the other the most powerful Valhirian prince my home has seen since Luluah left us all, for her bed in the sky."

Keyara was taken aback; that was why she recognised that name.

She may not know much about their species, but she wasn't that ignorant of the world around her.

A strange thing for the prince of Valhir to be in this place. Why would he want to compete for another throne when he already had one waiting for him?

Stupid question, she knew why.

Male arrogance.

A slimy, intangible trait that most of them shared, it lurked in the shadows of every man's mind, seeking a way out either through stupidity or dominance.

With Taris, she would take a guess and say it was the latter.
Why settle for one throne when you could have two?

"Is it a common custom in Valhir to question a woman's power to her face?" Keyara could feel her temperature rising.

Kadeen looked taken aback, almost as though she had insulted his mother.

"On the contrary, females and human women are sacred in our kingdom. I'm sorry, I didn't mean to offend you. I was honestly curious at what you thought you would do."

She let out a low huff, acknowledging she may have bit at his comment without need.

Keyara didn't want to make an enemy of Kadeen, the male seemed sincere enough. His soft eyes betraying his kind nature. She was about to speak, to soften her tone and tell him exactly what she would do when the large doors to the castle began to open and one of the servants called out into the courtyard, their evening meal would soon be served.

The promise of food beckoned the remaining competitors inside, drawing them in like moths to a flame.

"If you will excuse me."

She left Kadeen outside, not looking behind her as she felt three pairs of eyes on her back.

34

Jonn

It didn't take them long to find the nuisance they were searching for.

The first place they had walked into had been near enough empty. Jonn watched as Selsie took in her surroundings. What he took for sadness, chipped away at her beautiful features. Each run-down street after the other, creating clouds in her eyes. The care for her subjects became increasingly evident. Going from the palace of Cildraethe to a place like this must be jarring to her. No crystals were adorning these walls, no bronze and jade engravings along the pavings of these streets.

No one recognised her and if they did, they didn't show it, as the three of them tried their best to blend into the crowds as much as possible. Tricky, when one was a syren princess in a man's shirt, a queen's guard whose gilded armour gave away her station, and a human.

When they reached a shit hole of a tavern, they found him. Symon was, as expected, wasted. Shouting, laughing, drinking and just being a drunken arsehole.

When they walked through the rolling door, Jonn took one look at his friend bravely pawing all over a female Laeth and smiled. Fuck he had missed the degenerate, even if the man was sometimes more trouble than he was worth.

"It's a bad day when a syren doesn't even want you."

Symon's shaved head whipped towards him in the doorway. His friend threw down his tankard, unable to contain his clear excitement and ran straight into Jonn's arms. The bear hug ended with each man clapping the other on the back.

"Still a cockblock, Jonn," Symon laughed as the men released each other. Sy pulled at Jonn's hair.

"Fuck me, you've seen better days."

The reunion that followed was charged with raw emotion, the realisation of their time apart hitting them both.

As Selsie and Neesh engaged in a hurried conversation, Jonn found an empty booth for them to sit in, carved out from the cave stone into the tavern wall.

"Neesh and I must leave you two for a time. Can I trust you to not do anything...*reckless?*" Selsie stared at Symon, her words meant for him.

He feigned offence, making the sign of the gods star over his heart.

"On my honour my lady. Which I don't have much of, but we'll make do."

Selsie rolled her eyes.

"We will be fine, trust me," Jonn tried to reassure her. He really would try his best to keep his friend under control. There were no ideas of an attempted escape today, not here anyhow.

Accepting Jonn's words, Selsie withdrew gracefully with Neesh, giving the men the space they needed.

The moment they were alone, Jonn had asked about the fate of the newborns on the doomed ship and to his relief, they had all made it out alive. Sy had told him that he, the remaining crew and even the Mother's Maids had made a joint effort in manning the ship to keep it afloat until they were rescued by a passing merchant on his way to Silvanh.

When Jonn had asked about their captain, Sy recounted that he had found Captain Lane hidden with the newborns in storage during the attack, with pissed-through trousers.

Fucking coward.

As the two friends caught up on the months they had lost, the echoes of their laughter and shared memories drifted through the tiny booth; a reminder that even in the depths of Laeth territory, bonds forged in time at sea, travelling the world, held a strength that transcended time and distance.

"So, are you fucking her?"

The question Jonn knew his friend would be dying to ask, was finally out. Even though he expected it from the moment he walked in with Selsie, those words spoken aloud still made him choke on his mead a little.

Jonn had told Sy everything that had transpired during his time in Cildraethe. No secret was ever kept between them, no reality too dark for each other's hearts. But with Selsie… some part of Jonn wanted to keep her a secret, to shield whatever stirring of a *bond* was growing, just for them.

Another part of him didn't like the way he phrased that question either. He wanted to tell him to have some fucking respect.

But there were too many unanswered questions in that statement itself, too many things to unpack for this moment. He just simply said, "No."

Sy clasped Jonn's bare shoulder "Damn."

"What?"

"I know she's a Laeth but come on Jonn, your eyes work, don't they? Don't tell me you ain't thought about it."

Jonn took a big swig out of his tankard, before continuing in a gruff tone.

"What I've been thinking about is the memory of her trying to cast her song on me. I've also had a long time to think about her agreeing with her mother – the fucking Matriarch of the Laeths – to kill me if I'm not syren struck by the new moon."

"Well the moon's been and gone mate, and she ain't killed you yet, has she? And she could have, quite easily."

"Of that, I have no doubt," he replied, shrugging Sy's hands off his shoulder.

"All I'm trying to say is, don't be too harsh on her now, she got herself caught in a net for you. She didn't have to come find me either did she?"

His words rang true, for once. Selsie did put her life at risk to find Symon, with the added threat of the wrath of her mother, which Jonn knew too well about; his own life hanging by the thread of an amateur performance.

"Hm," was all he would let himself say.

"I'd love to know what a Laeth tasted like."

He knew his friend didn't mean grilled over a plate of potatoes and veg. Jonn simply shook his head, not lowering himself to the tavern etiquette his friend held and not wanting to talk so intimately about a female, especially Selsie. Instead, he offered up an overdue truth.

"She will kill me one day, Sy."

Symon sighed, his reliable humour somewhat muted.

"Yeah, maybe. Why don't you try and get rid of her first? Finish the game before it starts, because I tell you something: I may be Damned, but I can feel a storm on the horizon. Something in my bones ain't sitting right and I can feel *her* in the eye of it."

Jonn had no answer for his friend and in the following silence, both men drank from their tankards until Symon gulped down the last of his honey mead and ordered them another.

While the two of them had been discussing strategy and the unpredictable currents of their circumstances, the sun had made its way across the sky, casting long shadows across the shoreline they now walked along. The females had finally returned, and Jonn strolled with Sy at his side, a silent understanding passing between them. The two men found a secluded spot on the shore, the rhythm of the waves playing a backdrop to their hushed conversation.

With his eyes reflecting the glint of the low sun on the water, Sy gave his friend another hug. "You better survive this, Jonn. Don't let yourself drown, you hear me? Find your way back to the surface."

"What do you mean?" Jonn asked him, but the two syrens approached, halting any further conversation.

"Ladies, my beautiful syrens, I must leave you. Now don't be sad, I'm sure I will see you again."

Selsie gave him a small grin. "By Alysee, not too soon I hope."

The Merchant ship bound for Oridae awaited Symon offshore, its deep blue sails billowing in the strong breeze. Neesh had somehow guaranteed passage for Sy, and they were to deliver him to the nearest port on the mainland, for his journey back home on the next departing Saynt. It would be *The Nikolas,* if Jonn's calculation were correct and if his brain had been right in its keeping of the passing of time.

The glint of the ship's gold embellishments caught his eye, calling for him to come aboard.

Unfortunately for Jonn, if he attempted to escape now, he would be caught in minutes and that would be that; death for fucking certain.

No, he would have to wait.

"See you Sy, keep yourself out of trouble on that ship for fucks sake."

The familiar melody of a spell pricked in his ears, as Neesh created the portal to take them back to Cildraethe.

Sy gave him a mock salute as the females made their way inside the shifting mass of magic.

"Ey ey, Captain."

Jonn threw him a middle finger and went to leave, but not before Sy uttered something that would halt him in his tracks.

"See ya later, Cayson."

Jonn winced through the glowing light to grab one last look at his friend, but the walls of the portal were enclosed around him and with neither flourish nor fanfare, he was gone.

35
Keyara

The two of them had taken their evening meal with Cassidae in the syren's chambers.

Keyara couldn't help but notice how her sister and the Reothadh princess were so similar in many ways, and she loved to see her Aura make new friends for them both, just as it had always been back home.

They had been given sentiments of good luck for the next day, which had now arrived, heralded by the echo of footsteps running up and down the hall outside their room, first thing this morning.

Keyara had shouted shut the fuck up under her pillow to any of those who could hear.

Aura laughed, telling her to shush. But even she shouted for them to keep it down when there was no respite from the noise at five hours past midnight.

Keyara had been instructed to put on a deep grey, leather outfit that was given to her shortly after breakfast. It clung to her body and was uncomfortably revealing.

Shadowfern grey washed her out completely, but Aura had tried her best to reassure her she looked fine.

She was a godsdamned terrible liar.

Along with the leathers, she had been given a letter. The contents held details of today's trial.

It was a test of strength; a show of power, to impress the world with magic. It was an examination of the very essence that coursed through their veins.

They would be scored on their ability to wield their magic, the strength of the power and its potential.

Godsdamn it, Keyara rarely used her magic for anything other than drawing a hot fucking bath. A few party tricks here and there didn't inspire awe from anyone.

In her training here, it was wise to keep one's true strength of their power under wraps, to not reveal oneself too quickly. Godsforbid a weakness came to light. A quick way to get yourself eliminated by the vultures.

She didn't know how she was going to pull this off, doubt crept up on Keyara's racing mind like a bludhound.

Aura was quiet as the two of them made their way down to the entrance of the arena.

Her sister had read the letter, but if she had anything to say about it she had kept it to herself. Only throwing wary glances at Keyara when her legs took her for a pace around the room.

All the competitors were waiting in the holding areas behind closed doors already, the laughs and shouts of excitement clouding Keyara's hearing.

Steeling herself for the watchful gaze of the audience, nobility and the Trewiths themselves, Keyara baulked slightly at the emptiness of the grounds surrounding the arena.

"Shit, Aura, I'm not sure about this trial. I've never done anything more than warm up a wash basin," Keyara confessed, as the shadows of uncertainty lingered in her like spectres waiting to be unveiled, ready to take the unoccupied benches and haunt her.

A deep chuckle came from behind them, the resonance hummed along her bones.

Pushing himself from the wall his large frame was leaning on, walking towards her, Taris gave her a descending whistle as he looked her up and down, seeming to drink in every inch of her in this ridiculous outfit.

Keyara noticed a flicker of amusement in Taris' eyes as he must have overheard her conversation with Aura.

The damned vampyre had heard everything she had just said.

Her self-doubt laid bare for him to witness.

Great.

Wearing the very same clothing as her, Keyara couldn't lie and say she wasn't a little satisfied to see it wash his complexion out too.

She pointed to him now, "They didn't have it in black? Or red?"

He smirked. "No they did not."

Keyara tutted, grimacing slightly. "That's a shame."

A small giggle escaped Aura, who was a few feet away from them both.

Keyara's hands immediately went to her daggers as he moved closer. But they weren't in their usual place, the weapons were not clipped to her as there had been nowhere to put them in this outfit.

He was so close, the spices of him filled her flaring nostrils. Once again, his proximity caused her to flinch.

"Nervous?" he asked, as he finally came to a stop mere inches from her.

"Not at all," she said, way too quickly, her lie evident to even the dead.

Shit.

A second passed, though it could have been longer. She couldn't tell, it was so fucking loud in here.

"You know what's good for the nerves, Keyara?" She wasn't sure she liked the way he seemed to purr her name on his lips. She was so close to smacking that grin off his face.

"A glass of wyne, a walk in the forest, being anywhere away from you?" Shit, she planned to never give him the satisfaction of knowing how much he got under her skin.

He leant down to her. "A good fuck."

"Do you know a male who could give her one?" Keyara and

Taris whipped their heads to Aura, who was looking so innocent with that smile on her pretty face.

"Come on Keyara, you need to get ready," Aura pulled her to one side, sliding her arm in hers as they walked away.

"What an arsehole," Keyara said, loud enough for him to hear.

"I wonder if his large ego is compensating for the lack of…other, *smaller* attributes," her sister replied, the volume of her gentle voice the same as her own.

Their laughs followed them into Keyara's pen in the holding area.

One of the guards stepped in Aura's way.

"She cannot be here."

Aura touched his arm. "I won't take more than a few minutes." The guard blinked a few times before he nodded and shuffled away, shaking his head in bewilderment, not having any clue that his decision had not been his own.

Damned fool.

Keyara spoke as she sat down hard on the bench, "I can feel the power in me, Aura, it's *there*. I know it's there and I know I can do it. But…"

Aura sat next to her, rearranging her skirts. "But what?"

Keyara leant her head against the wall behind her.

"These competitors have all been trained by the best in Myrantis, their whole lives they have lived a life of nobility, every available resource and privilege handed to them on a golden plate. That arsehole is the godsdamned Valhirian prince." A sigh escaped her. "Berran trained me in hand-to-hand combat and how to use my daggers, not how to use my magic. He kept saying 'it's different to mine' and 'it would be like the fae teaching a syren how to fly.'"

Her sister's blue eyes narrowed. "Did he not at least try to show you how to use it, to wield it?"

A ripple of unease coursed through her "No, well a little, but my magic didn't want to cooperate around his ice, it was too incompatible. Even his warriors tried with their weaker magic, but they were the same".

"Well, let's do the best we can with what you do know," Aura held her hands out. "Don't doubt yourself Keyara."

Keyara hesitantly took them. She felt the comforting, familiar embrace of Aura's power flow gently through her. Until it wasn't familiar at all.

No, this was different.

"What are you doing Aura?" If they were found cheating, Keyara would be thrown out of the competition, or shit, chucked in the dungeons.

Also, winning by underhanded tactics was not her way, she wanted to win because she was capable of it by herself.

A new, white light was emanating from Aura's dainty hands along with its golden partner. Keyara could feel it within her, melting into her magic.

They liked each other, like two old friends meeting again for the first time in forever. Her self-doubt was being replaced by hope, confidence and something else.

With a tentative look on her face, Aura finally removed her hands from her own.

"What was that Aura, what did you do?" The new light settled within her, into the simmering lava within, ready to be awoken.

"Whilst you've been training every day, I've been in the library. The locked away, under supervision, section actually."

No doubts about how she got in there, Keyara thought.

"There were such old books in there, some predating even a united Myrantis itself. Anyway, I found one that was about all the different magic that exists and has ever been discovered and recorded in Myrantis. It turns out, mine never has. Not that's been written down anyway."

Keyara's eyes went wide, letting her sister speak.

"I know, it's so strange, I carried on reading, and I came across another book, well actually it kind of just appeared one day on the shelf the other came from, I found it as I was putting it back…"

Confusion passed over Aura's face, she was piecing together some information inside her own head that Keyara wasn't privy to.

"That book, I, I think it was from Athvar. It had a feel to it you know, like it was written by the fae, like their magic had bound the pages together. It felt so different in my hands, but so familiar at the same time."

"Aura…"

"Okay sorry, I know I'm rambling, but listen. If I'm right in what I think I read, my power originates in Athvar. It has only ever been recorded there once, a long time ago."

"Aura, there's no way, you were found at sea, you're as human as I am."

"I know, I know, I thought that, so I tested a theory. The fae recorded that the one with this power could create light, a blinding light that could be gifted to others, for a short while. I focused on it, every second of every day, that light was in my mind. I could feel it, wanting to come out, it was just waiting, for what I don't know. But one day it just appeared."

She made the light again in her cupped palms.

"Somewhere in me, in my lineage, is fae. Not enough to matter, but it's in there."

Keyara couldn't believe it. Actually, the more she thought about it, in a way she could.

Aura had this something about her. No one could place it, not even their mother. Her beauty, the way she held herself, her grace. It made sense that there was a drop of fae in her somewhere.

A shame about the winglessness though, she knew how much Aura admired them.

"I don't know what it does, this light, the book wasn't translated all the way. But you can have it, it may help."

Keyara hugged her and kissed the top of her strawberry head.
"Thank you, Aura,"
"It's fine. Keyara, you'll do fine"
Keyara nodded to her sister, and as they withdrew from their embrace the guard finally returned for Aura.

36
Keyara

Silence echoed through the arena as Keyara stepped into it; the lack of an audience jarring.

Gone was the structure from before, the ceilinged chamber rooms were transformed into one large circular arena with high wooden walls.

She was clearly not the first one here, the air thrummed with leftover magic, the crumbs of power teasing hers to come out. She could swear a cinnamon taste coated her tongue, though she doubted her senses. No fae would bother with the Rite, and they would never waste their precious magic for a human kingdom.

They had done that before, aiding in the destruction of many towns in the human rebellion.

Many still hated them for it, their motivations still unclear, but the fae ruler's obvious preference for a divided Myrantis was clear to anyone with half a brain.

Following the instructions from the guards, she stood inside the red square in the centre of the dusty floor.

The beige dust settled at her feet as she stilled, the floor seeming to pulsate with the anticipation of what lay ahead. The arena was hungry for more power, it had been given a taste, and now it wanted it all.

Taking a deep breath and centring herself as the whispers of unseen spectators niggled in her ears, her power simmered beneath her skin, ready to be unleashed.

In that bubbling broil of heat inside her, the flickering glow of white light added an element of unpredictability to her arsenal and Keyara was fucking glad for it.

The radiant energy surged within her, a double-edged sword of dazzling brilliance and unbridled intensity. Keyara's fingers tingled with the raw power at her disposal, and it wanted out.

She was given no time to ready herself when a vision was projected a few metres before her. It was Lord Trewith raising his hand, signalling the commencement of Keyara's trial.

In the quiet before the storm, she closed her eyes, focusing on the wellspring of heat within her.

The space around her seemed to respond, crackling underneath her leather-clad feet.

Her power coiled, begging to be unleashed. With a graceful motion, she lifted her hand, fingers outstretched, and a wave of scorching warmth emanated from her, casting a radiant glow across the arena.

There were no flames, her magic never came through as fire. No, it was pure sun-scorching heat, a visible shimmer in the dust-speckled air.

Given no clear instructions about what she was meant *to do* with her power, she just let it loose.

The temperature rose, the wooden walls around her began to scorch with the intensity of her magic.

Shit, she needed to let off a little or they would all boil away. Keyara's dark brow furrowed as she grappled with the formidable force she wielded. The heat, while magnificent, seemed to have a will of its own, resisting her attempts at control.

Beads of perspiration formed on her forehead, not only from the physical strain but from the sheer challenge of mastering a power that danced between her fingertips like a fleeting flame. Not only that, but her sister's gift of the blinding light was also awaiting its turn, and she could feel it getting impatient.

A passing thought sent shivers down her wet spine; this light is alive, the magic gifted to her felt *alive*.

Just as alive as her power now felt for the first time in her life, let go from the chains of her caution.

With a hesitant breath, Keyara summoned the radiance, the arena bathing in an intensity that would rival the noonday sun in Valhir. The brilliance of it blurring the boundaries between dreams and reality.

"Fucking hell," she shouted in frustration, as she voiced the struggle within her.

The radiant power surged forth, and its trajectory proved elusive, casting erratic beams across the arena. It was a sight to witness, a vision of untamed luminosity, a testament to the dual nature of her abilities.

And a big fuck you to anyone watching who ever questioned her place in the Rite.

As the light intermingled with the residual heat, the arena transformed into a celestial canvas, a mesmerising dance of warmth and radiance.

Yet Keyara couldn't enjoy the view – the pressing need to harness the dual forces and bring them under the sway of her command was getting critical.

She pressed on, control be damned.

With power ringing in her ears, she fought to merge the energies, to mould them into a harmony that would impress even the most experienced and hardened nobles.

The circular arena became a battleground, a symphony of heat and light vying for supremacy, and amid the war that was raging, Keyara began to rein her power back in.

A comfortable temperature finally settled back into the arena – the light no longer blinding anyone who would look at it – when across from her the blackened walls turned into a dance of shifting shadows.

Slowly, a ghostly army materialised from the fringing walls around her.

Figures of warriors, ephemeral yet just as fucking formidable, emerged with weapons drawn. Images of syrens, vampyres and even fae advanced towards her.

She was surprised they didn't include animals and beasts in the mix.

Keyara made quick work of assessing the illusory onslaught whilst a bead of sweat trailed down her temple, her exhaustion getting the better of her.

She had never used this much magic in such an enormous quantity before. That along with this new power she was harnessing meant Keyara was getting shit tired.

"Tired, Keyara?"

The smooth mocking from Taris whispered in her ears. There was no way she would let anyone bear witness to her weakness.

With a focused breath, she summoned the latent magic within her, the residue of her boiling heat still humming beneath her pale skin.

She extended her leather-clad arms, using her fingers to beckon the visions closer, daring them.

Come on then fuckers, let's get on with it.

The first wave of illusory warriors lunged forward, weapons glinting in the spotlight overhead.

She spun around on the spot, the world around her becoming a blur. Spinning and spinning as quickly as she could.

Then she stopped and stood tall, marvelling at what she had done.

The ghostly army began to fall, wave after wave into the circular valley she had created around her.

A deep pit ran around her and the dusty red marker in the middle of the arena. Her power had melted away the floor and she looked at what she had done like it was a fucking prize.

Roiling red heat awaited the army as they tumbled into it, boiling away before they even reached the bottom.

Keyara let herself relax a little, enjoying her victory.

Short-lived, however, as not even two seconds of Keyara
celebrating her cleverness passed before the next wave of
illusions, more cunning and elusive, materialised with silent
lethality.

"Oh, Godsdamn it," she uttered to herself. Berran would scold
her for being smug and celebrating a victory too early.

This time, the illusory warriors were different, their movements
unpredictable and they had magic of their own.

She had to duck from the ice, wind and sharp objects being
thrown her way, whilst also making sure, not to fall into the
ravine she had created.

Once or twice a shard of deadly sharp ice skimmed across her
arms and legs. Thank fuck she was wearing leathers she
thought, or the slash on her skin could have been an arm gone
and that would end not only her journey here, but probably any
other dream she had of bettering their lives.

With barely any time to think, she once again had to duck and
roll, the strain of using her power to such an extent causing her
body to use up more of its energy than she was used to. Though
her power never waned, her energy to wield it could and the
visions were closing in.

As if from nowhere, a spectral Laeth grabbed her.

She braced herself for the puncturing pain of his barbed
forearms and wicked talons, but it never came.

The illusions could not physically touch her, but there was a
force around them that held her in place as if mimicking
capture.

Shit, shit, shit she cursed. Everything Berran had taught her in
all the years had left her brain like piss in the wind.

For an illusion created by some human working for Lord
Trewith, everything felt as real as the heat in her veins, as did
the pressure that was running up along her arms.

Keyara summoned the radiant light that was waiting patiently
to be used again. The brilliance emanated from her, bringing

the Laeth to let out a deafening scream as he dissolved away and the illusory warriors hesitated in their advance, disoriented by the radiant onslaught.

Seizing the opportunity, Keyara unleashed a torrent of scorching heat with all the energy she had left, a concentrated beam that cut through the illusory ranks like one of her blades through the mist.

As the last echoes of the illusory warriors faded, Keyara stood at the centre of the arena, her breaths measured. She was alone again, eerie quiet accompanying her loud breathing.

In the same place as before, Lord Trewiths form was projected into the arena, he acknowledged her with a nod and a raised grey eyebrow.

He then told her a number that she would remember for the rest of her life.

"Eight hundred and fifty."

With a triumphant smile, Keyara bowed to an invisible crowd and left the arena.

37
Jonn

They emerged not in Neesh's cave as Jonn had expected, but in another, grander room. If it could be called a room; it was damned fucking huge, and even that wording didn't do it justice.

Jonn let out a low whistle. He imagined this was where kings and queens slept, fucked and – in this lot's case – dreamt of devouring humans.

The walls were adorned with that same crystal as the rest of the castle, except here they were all of one stone. A glistening green emerald that matched perfectly with Selsie's own eyes. He winced as his dirty boots left marks on the floor, which was a swirl of bronze and gold marble.

Large stained-glass windows, taller than his own six-foot-four self, framed the far wall opposite the bed. Built up from the shimmering floor, it could easily fit five people in its temptingly clean sheets.

"Thank you Neesh, you may leave us," Selsie said, turning to Neesh who then left quietly, shutting the door behind her.

The soft silence that followed was deafening.

Selsie was the first to break it. "My mother has left Cildraethe for a hunt."

That explains why she felt safe enough to bring him inside the castle.

Her feet quietly padded over to the two middle windows which were bigger than the others, and smoothly swung open, revealing themselves to be doors.

A chilly, early evening breeze whispered through the room, raising goosebumps on Jonn's bare chest. Selsie didn't seem to notice as she slipped through the doors onto the balcony beyond. He followed a few steps behind, tracing her scent trail that he was getting more and more addicted to the longer he spent in her company.

He watched as she leant over the marble wall, her long curly hair billowing down her back.

The sun was beginning to tiptoe over the horizon and sunbeams shone through the pink and white clouds that streaked across the orange sky. Luluah and her sister star Iara could just about be seen in the pastel expanse.

Mirroring their glow, twinkling lights danced under the surface of the churning sea below, the city beneath the waves just as alive as the world above. Evening songs could be heard from the starlings that flew overhead and Selsie was watching them intensely.

Trying to relax a little, Jonn mirrored her stance beside her, though every fibre of his being was as tense as a coiled sea snake, ready to strike.

Her gaze left the birds and found Jonn's own. There was a vulnerability in her eyes, a flicker of something that went beyond the politics of the sea, beyond the nature of syren and man.

Jonn knew the danger that lingered around them, the unspoken truth that their paths were diverging.

He would be a fool to deny it. To be so naive as to think he was the master of his fate and not the many gods, though he couldn't quite put his faith in just one.

The weight of unspoken words hung between the two like a delicate current, and Jonn felt the pull of something deep tugging at the edges of his heart.

Fuck, he could not let this happen. He could not want her as much as he was starting to, but he didn't know how to stop it.

As the days of his captivity had turned into weeks and months, Jonn's bond with Selsie had, to his own resistance, deepened. They had laughed, shared stories, and it seemed they found solace in each other's company. But amidst the ever-present threat to his life and the secrets that lurked in the depths of her mind, Jonn's feelings began to shift.

He had to finally fucking admit it.

The sun bathed them in its lazy molten glow, the golden iridescence of her skin and hair casting a halo of radiance around her. Gods, if Jonn had to die in the hands of anyone, he supposed he would rather it was a female as breathtaking as her.

He smiled, thinking of something to say, he wasn't always the best with words. "This is my favourite time of day."

"Oh?"

"On the ship, sunset meant we had lived to see another day."

Was that a look of guilt that swept over her features, or did he imagine it, Jonn thought quietly.

"Out at sea, there are more than just Laeths that want to kill us. Pirates off the coast of Valhir, poaching and scavenging for the coral they so desperately crave. Ice dragens in the north, the giant Skuidd in the east – which may I add, the Domhianns can barely control. Not to mention the monstrous shit that lives in the sea around Athvar."

"You have been to Athvar?"

Selsie's wonder was evident, and he was in the mood to indulge her curiosity.

"Of course. Not too close though, the fae would kill us before we even saw the shore."

A pointed side-eye in her direction earned him a playful shove.

"When you sail through the passage past Silvanh and under Onebridge crossing, there have been creatures in that water that I or other sailors have seen, that I can say with full confidence we wish to never see again. The fae are keeping more than a few secrets from the rest of us, let me tell you."

Selsie looked out over the water, as though Athvar was just beyond the horizon. In reality, it could not be further away.

"I have not been further than Noran," she uttered. "My whole existence has been only Laeth territory."

"Why?" Jonn was genuinely curious, as all species of syrens were free to roam wherever they wished. The relationship between Reothadhs and Laeths could be slightly…*tense*, sometimes, but not enough to have any consequence.

She sighed, "Because I am a Newling. I rarely even left the castle. I had never even been to Alboste, to see our subjects there." She shook her head. "Mother... she also rarely let me out of her sight. You are not the only prisoner here Jonn."

He didn't agree, but he understood. The silence returned briefly but this time, he was the one to break it.

"Alright… what do you like to do?"

"What do I like to do?" The puzzled look on her features nearly made him chuckle.

"Yeah, what do you like to do, for *fun*?" he said, giving her a small smile.

She bit her lip, thinking for a few moments. Fuck, the urge to bite that lip was overwhelming and surprising.

"Well, I like to collect things from the shipwrecks on the seafloor. My room in the castle below is full of treasures I have found."

"Stolen you mean?"

She pouted and began to protest, it was his turn to give her a playful push. "I'm jesting, Selsie."

The look she gave him as she leant back over the balcony, was nothing short of evil.

"Truth joke," he said blankly, still teasing her. But she was no longer joining him in the game, her attention firmly on the sky, which was finally letting the world below have a glimpse of the other stars breaking through the dimness.

"I have to go whilst my mother is away. I have things that I need to attend to under the water."

She turned to leave but Jonn stepped in her way. He didn't know if it was the influence of Cildraethe, or the constant whispering secrets playing in his ear since the day he arrived on this island messing with his head, or maybe it was simply just the sunset making him do crazy shit, but fuck it, he was going to roll with it.

"Jonn," she began as his large hand moved slowly to a strand of hair fluttering in her face, his fingers lightly putting it behind her twitching ear.

He had never touched or been near her like this. It was always either playful or threatening, but this was both.

God's scent of her, he wanted it to envelop him. Jonn hadn't slept with many women, but this one, this female, he knew would be his last. He wanted to be as near and as far from her, all at once.

With an intake of breath, he moved down to her, his large, cupped hands hovering mere fractions away from the sides of her heart-shaped face.

It was a stolen moment, a fragment of time where the currents of destiny and nature allowed a brief respite. It must have only lasted a few seconds, no more than a fleeting connection amidst the chaos of their worlds. But to Jonn, it felt like forever.

For weeks it had circled his brain, what it would feel like to kiss her. It had been whispered to him in the night. He had told himself – and those fucking voices – that it was tough shit, it can't happen.

Though right now, he let himself indulge the fantasy just for a heartbeat more before he began to pull away.

The conflict of disappointment and want in Selsie's eyes was a cold deluge over his burning desire.

"Selsie..."

Her voice, soft like the murmur of waves, muttered, "I have to go."

The last slither of shining sunlight went with her.

38
Keyara

Having proven her strength, Keyara was directed to a small viewing platform. There was only one other competitor there, a small mousy haired girl who could not have been older than sixteen. Freckles were scattered across her nose, her skin a deep tan; the metallic grey of her eyes gave away her Oridae heritage.

Keyara sat down next to her. "First one through, eh?"

The girl took her eyes off the arena before them. Keyara could now see for herself, the next competitor in the very same arena she was just in.

On the other side, the audience in steep, horizontal lines of benches watched in their droves.

"Yes...well no... There was one before me but he was eliminated. I was the first through I suppose. That was amazing what you did down there, I'm impressed," the girl gushed to Keyara with full sincerity in her metallic eyes.

Keyara gave her a small grin. "Thank you."

"You're welcome, I'm Jenney by the way." The girl held out her hand and Keyara shook it, giving her name in return.

The man in the arena below was doing a lousy job at impressing her, his water magic barely more than a drizzling cloud and completely unremarkable.

From up here, Keyara could see there was in fact, a mirroring arena to the one she had occupied. The woman on the other side was doing much better, her power enabling her to fly wingless off the ground. The arena was putting her through an assault course, objects of all sizes flying straight towards her, trying everything to knock her to the ground below.

Jenney spoke again. "I heard your score. Eight hundred and fifty; that's one of the highest scores there has ever been."

"I know."

Keyara was surprised at her own cockiness, but she masked her shock by asking Jenney what her score was.

Pride swept across the girl's face as she replied. "Eight hundred."

Keyara raised her eyebrows. "Shit, that's amazing, well done."

Jenney blushed. "Thanks."

Keyara gave her attention back to the crowd, trying to spot her sister and the rest of her friends.

Behind the walls of the arena, in a safe space, Keyara could see many men and women all sitting in perfect uniform ranks, working together to create illusions with their magic, which was directed into the arena before them.

The flying woman had reached the end of her trial. Keyara didn't catch her score, she was too busy watching the other guy get eliminated, his dismissal from the Heir's Rite brief and uneventful.

The other woman left the arena, a few minutes later sitting down behind Keyara and Jenney. She didn't say a word to either of them.

"So, what can you do Jenney?" Keyara asked whilst the next competitors were being prepped.

In answer, Jenney stuck out her tongue and vanished into thin air.

"Woah!" Keyara said as she jumped up. She heard Jenney laugh from all around her.

"Shit, that's damned impressive Jenney," Keyara laughed.

The girl reappeared in the same spot she had left. "I know."

As the next competitors were brought in, Jenney nudged her.

"Oh, we're in for a show now."

Keyara looked down into the arena to where Jenney's gawking gaze was directed.

Waving with one hand to the crowd opposite her – which Keyara knew for a fact he could not see – Taris swaggered through to the red marker.

He held the air of a predator, embodied with a full, wide-toothed grin that drew you in before those same teeth clamped around your neck.

She rolled her eyes at his showmanship. The audience did not share her sentiment, they were clapping and hollering at him, drinking in his allure with desperate gulps.

Did they know they were hidden from view up there, the competitors unable to hear a single clap or whistle in the confines of the arena?

Keyara looked again, to find Aura in amongst them between Berran and Cassidae, silently praying she wasn't one of them, cheering him on.

From here, Keyara could not see her clearly, but something was bothering her sister. Aura looked as though she had seen a ghost.

Aura's whole focus was on the arena before her. Her small shoulders were square, her back rod straight. She was neither clapping nor cheering, just staring at the man on the ground below.

Buttery blonde hair shone in the light. It wasn't a man, it was a male.

It was him, the very same man who was there the night she had fought inside Gregorys.

"I've never seen a fae in the flesh before," Jenney whispered in Keyara's ear, bringing her back to the present.

With his head turned up at an angle, to where her sister sat, the male stood still; timeless.

The trial commenced with a boom and the walls around the fae went higher and higher until they eventually joined, and he was fully encompassed inside.

Above the new roof that had been formed, a projection of the inside was displayed.

An artificial forest had appeared inside, with seemingly no end. Trees, shrubbery and all manner of life sprang from the dusty floor.

I wonder if he will use his wings, she wondered to herself. Keyara had never seen the mythical appendages with her own eyes – only in books – but faes' were supposed to be the most beautiful.

They were large, sheer, and unique to each fae.

Males and females had varying shades of all colours; like rainbows turned to flight. Aura had poured over the sketches when she was little, showing their mother her favourites and wishing she had her own pair.

While she was intrigued to see how the fae fared, Keyara's full focus was on Taris, who had his hands clasped behind his back for lack of pockets.

Beside the red marker, a figure began to emerge from the floor. Dressed in full Valhirian garb, a woman formed, piece by piece akin to a puzzle, right next to the prince. She was followed by another, then another, until Keyara counted five women all lined up, side by side against him.

Taris exuded power, tangible and real – every inch the prince he was – as he stood before them, proceeding to kiss them all softly, one by one.

All the women gave him a coy smile as if he was the most spectacular being they had ever laid eyes upon.

"I've heard about this," Jenney said under a breath. "The strongest vampyres can use blood magic to conjure a near-perfect clone of anyone they have drank from."

"That's invasive…and damned wrong," Keyara replied, leaning forward on the bench.

Pulling his lips away from the final woman, Taris turned away from them. Without even batting an eyelid in acknowledgement, they all dissolved into a heap of bloody, gory mess on the floor.

All around, loud gasps murmured their shock.

Keyara was silent when a new figure came together, again-piece by tiny piece.

"Keyara is that..." Jenney's girlish voice sounded a million miles away.

The figure was naked with lithe, pale limbs and taller than most. Covered by long dark hair were large breasts. It was only when those hazel gold eyes appeared that Keyara suspicions were confirmed. She stood, fists clenched, with the heat of a thousand suns burning in her veins.

Taris brought his hands to the figure, moving the hair over sharp shoulders to reveal the pink nipples underneath.

Keyara could feel hundreds of eyes staring at her, tentative whispers moving through the crowd like a breeze amongst trees.

The fucking audacity of this...*male*. How dare he use her image for his trial.

How dare he even have the image of her naked body in his damned head.

To his discredit though, she thought: her tits aren't that big, and she has far less hair down there than he has imagined.

39

Aura

"A fae in the Heir's Rite?! Now that's a first. Has anyone ever seen this male before? I don't recognise him at all," Mileya asked the group. Her glistening jet hair moved on a phantom breeze, sending wafts of brine-soaked citrus fruit up Aura's nose.

Aura could not quite believe her own eyes when she had seen him enter the arena. The male she had first met in Gregorys, waltzed in with the force of a thousand forests behind his back. From the moment those doors shut behind him, she felt as though he could sense her. These suspicions were confirmed when his brown eyes looked straight at her, even though they were assured by the guards that the audience would be hidden from view.

This fae was unlike anything Aura had come across in her life. His magic commanded the very essence of nature and life like it was given to him by the power of the Myrantis itself.

Green light of every shade sparked from his fingers every time he wielded it, the cinnamon fragrance of fae magic replacing the stench of sweat radiating from the crowd.

"Actually, Mileya, I have," Berran said, giving her a side eye from Aura's other side.

"Really?" Aura asked in surprise, not taking her eyes off the male with golden hair.

Berran nodded. "Years ago, I was sent on my first royal visit by my father's orders. It was to Athvar, the closest kingdom to ours. I met Queen Adne at Skies Rest…"

Aura felt her eyes widen at the mention of Skies Rest, the palace that touched the sky. Legendary, mythical, much like everywhere else in the realm of the fae, and yes before you

"What's it like?" she asked him hurriedly, touching his arm.

His smile told her everything, as did the wary look in his eyes.

"It's…as breathtaking as everyone says it is."

"Tell me, *please*." Aura wanted to know everything: images of a palace suspended in the heavens, with spires that tickled the stars and windows that were misted from the clouds that touched them.

Berran raised a white eyebrow at her.

"You know I can't."

He was right. The fae kept details of their kingdom close to their chests, and they had ways of knowing if anyone spoke of their land. No one knew how – maybe it was a fish tale, spun to scare their few enemies and children – but no one ever risked it. She could use her magic to force him to tell her…but no, that was beneath her.

Berran continued. "Anyway, one night, I was invited to a game of cards, and I'm not so much of a fool to turn down a game with the fae and have a chance of winning a favour. So, I went to the game, and he was there, I'm sure of it."

"Did you win?" Aura asked him.

He cleared his throat and Mileya laughed, a hearty deep sound.

"No, he didn't."

"What happened?"

"A godsdamned cheat is what happened," Berran muttered whilst shifting in his seat, anger flashing through his icy eyes.

"I thought the fae were meant to be honest," Aura replied sincerely.

"It wasn't the fae who cheated," Mileya answered for him.

Berran opened his mouth when Aura suddenly threw herself against the wooden rail along the benches.

"Keyara?!" She called out to the image of her sister, naked, in the arena with the vampyre from the terrace.

"Keyara!" Aura shouted, but Keyara could not hear her.

Berran got up, seeming to assess the view for himself.

"It's not her Aura, he's using blood magic. Mileya, please tell her. They would not let Taris bring Keyara in there."

Mileya too got up, putting both dark hands on the rail, sniffing the air.

"He's right, I would be able to smell her from here."

Berrans hand squeezed hers as they sat back down.

"How does he do that?" she asked them both. Before she got her answer, the image of Keyara dissolved away to nothing at the vampyres feet.

A few seconds passed and no one said a word. Taris leaned against a wall behind him idly, with his arms and ankles crossed.

Berran bent forward on the bench, "What is he..."

In a violent crash of sound, a few of the walls surrounding Taris burst open, with various bodies flying through human-sized holes, pulled violently by a force not seen.

Real flesh and blood. Not the illusions that tormented Keyara in her trial.

Aura shielded her face with her hands, she felt Berran lean over her, and Mileya let out a hiss. No debris hit them of course, they were all hidden from view with an unseen shield around the arena, preventing any wayward magic from reaching the audience.

Peeking from behind her hands, Aura nearly retched when she saw servants of Shadowfern, lying in pieces around the vampyre. One or two were groaning in pain, shards of wood sticking out of all manner of limbs and body parts.

The crowd around her were in shock and no one said a word; even the guards couldn't hide their surprise.

Peeking their heads through the obliterated walls, the surviving servants looked terrified of the male before them. Together, they had fashioned the ghostly illusions for Keyara, the obstacle course for the flying woman and everything else for each competitor before.

The prince of Valhir never gave them the chance to create his opponent.

Unsurprisingly, Lord Trewith was not projected into the arena. Instead, in bold red lettering, the number nine hundred hovered in the air.

Taris smirked to himself, leisurely walked out through a space in the destroyed arena and left the servants to their fate.

Healers ran in, picking up as many mounds of flesh as they could and placing two injured men on stretchers.

"He shouldn't have done that," Berran growled. "Killing innocents in an Heirs' Rite is unjust."

"You're mistaken," Mileya's dark eyes narrowed at Berran. "It is an Heir's Rite, there is no wrong or right."

Their attention was diverted away from the gory scene, when the splinters of wood from the arena walls flew up from the floor, out of the servants' bodies and towards the fae's enclosed space.

Aura watched in awe, as the debris joined a towering redwood tree that smashed through the fae's arena. Its branches reached heights that pierced the roof of the cavern, ploughing through it like it was no thicker than skin.

Shrieks of awe and unease rippled around them, as shards of rock rained down below.

"Hm," Mileya huffed with unexpected approval on her face, whilst Berran was dusting off the fragments of broken wood of his fine jacket.

Aura looked up at the impaled ceiling above, admiring the ethereal essence of the tree and how its bark seemed to move in the light when something caught her eye.

Descending from one of the highest branches of the tree, was a purple flower with many heads. It floated down on an unfelt wind, where lazily it settled into her lap.

Mottel; she would recognise it anywhere. She delicately picked it up, the petals feeling smooth in her hands. She raised her head, to see if anyone else had seen the flower.

Aura's eyes caught sight of the fae, whose name she still did not know. He was sitting at the base of the tree, elbows on his raised knees with his eyes closed.

The number *Nine hundred,* illuminated above the fae's head as his trial ended.

Aura had counted twelve competitors left, including Keyara. Two women, seven men, one vampyre and one fae – all against her one sister.

Back at the castle, the pasty sun had descended, taking the remaining dregs of the end-of-summer heat with it. In the fading light, Aura sashayed down the hall to dinner, the pastel pink of her gown matching the sunset.

Pulling up the strapless bust, she silently cursed the lilac flower appliques adorning the material, as they scratched slightly at her skin.

"Shit, hang on." The clacking of heels came running up behind her, the midnight blue satin of Keyara's dress swishing over the floor in a quiet sweep.

"This fell out of your hair." Her sister had a sprig of Mottel in her hand and she tucked it back into Aura's intricately braided updo.

Her sister's long fingers gently scratched against her scalp and Aura glanced at Keyara with pride.

The dress her sister was wearing clung to her body in all the right places, and Aura thought she resembled the river that ran past their home in the summer. Wild and dangerous, untameable, especially as Keyara had left her hair unbound.

The thread thin straps led down to a v-neck, which only just covered her breasts. Aura knew she wore this deliberately after what Taris had done today. If people were going to see her body, it would be on her own terms.

Keyara had insisted they eat with the others tonight; she wanted to hear what they had to say about her high score and Aura wholeheartedly agreed. Whatever her sister wanted to do she would support her.

"I still can't believe he did that," muttered Keyara. Aura didn't have to ask who the subject of her tirade was.

"What an absolute arsehole. Who does he think he is?!" Keyara stormed ahead, the long train sweeping behind her.

"He's only the prince of Valhir," Aura jested. She knew not to poke at Keyara when she was pissed off, but she had not stopped talking about what had transpired since they had reunited after her trial.

"I couldn't give a shit if he was one of the gods themselves."

"Keyara…" Aura cocked her head toward her sister.

"No Aura, what right does he have to do what he did? Embarrass me like that in front of the entire kingdom. It's humiliating."

"I thought you didn't want everyone to know you cared."

"I don't," she said, crossing her arms.

"Then stop talking about it, because they're all here."

Leading her outside, the two of them walked through tall open doors onto a large terrace. The protective air of magic around the castle shielded them all from the bracing wind that would have otherwise chilled them at this height.

The view was spectacular, providing a perfect backdrop to their evening meal. The clear night sky was obscured only by the enormous stone pillars that were steadfast guardians between the castle and hundreds of feet below.

Aura looked around for their friends, small waves of excitement flowing through her as she took in the crowds around her, the smell of rich perfumes and food on silver trays. She loved the company of others and was looking forward to a night dining with them all.

As much as she loved her home, Eldorhaven was remote and sparsely populated. Aura was alone too often, having no one to talk to besides her mother and sister, so she often resorted to talking to herself half the time.

Walking further into the throng, Aura couldn't help but notice the number of eyes turned their way.

Hungry, judging eyes, all on Keyara.

Aura put her arm through her sisters, throwing filthy looks at anyone she thought deserved it.

"I can feel him."

"Don't be ridiculous Keyara."

"No really, I can. Look over there."

Aura looked and sure enough, the vampyre was drinking wyne from a crystal glass, his large frame leaning against the deep grey marble of the centre table with a cacophony of women surrounding him.

"I don't know why they give him any attention," Keyara uttered aloud.

After what Taris had done, Aura was also surprised to see other women wanting to be in his company.

With a large grin that would melt even the sternest of hearts, Berran came over to them, two glasses of wyne in his hands.

"Evening my girls."

In unison, they took the crystal glasses from him, Aura nearly choking on hers when she saw Keyara swallow the entire pink and gold liquid in one go.

"Cassidae and Mileya not joining us tonight?" Aura asked him. She couldn't spot the two syrens anywhere.

"No, they've gone into the town for some female time, or something, I don't know. I think they've got sick of me," he replied, chuckling as he sipped his wyne.

"Never," Aura winked, glad for the change of tone. Keyara had been as light and merry as a storm cloud all afternoon.

A clinking of glasses from the table told them all it was time to take their seats.

40

Aura

Her name was elegantly etched in silver on the back of the marble chair, alongside the crest of Eldorhaven. The sigil of the Coralls-an artistic depiction of a manta ray, leaping over an oak tree in a field of flowers-was intricately engraved; the encapsulation of her home.

Their family name of Allis did not carry any title, or anything as grand as sigils or crests, so they were left with no choice but to use the one from whence they came.

As they approached their seats, Berran lightly touched Aura's arm.

"I'm sitting with Lord and Lady Trewith again tonight. Enjoy yourselves-and behave," he said, casting a pointed glance at Keyara, who silently flipped him off. They walked in opposite directions, leaving Aura alone at the table.

Aura had barely begun to relax when she heard Keyara's voice, sharp and irritated.

"Is this a bad attempt at a jest?"

Peeking over, Aura saw her sister glaring at Taris, who was pulling out her chair beside his. The vampyre must have said something to simmer down Keyara's fire, as she stiffly sat down into the chair in one swift movement.

Aura sat in her seat, letting them get on with whatever quarrel they had. All the while anxiety gnawed at her insides, completely putting her off the meal that was due to be served. Leaning back in the heavy marble chair, Aura glanced at the name etched on the seat to her right: *Fennin Ashverne*. She didn't recognize it-no crest or sigil offered a clue. Perhaps a new noble house, or maybe a syren from Silvanh? The name didn't sound like it originated from Reothadh, and surely Berran would have introduced them if they were familiar.

"Oh," she sighed softly as the owner of the name sat down; the scent preceding him was all too familiar.

"You're a long way from Eldorhaven, Aura Allis." He gently took her hand and pressed a kiss to the top of it.

His unruly golden hair, with a few tendrils lazily falling over his earthy brown eyes, contrasted sharply with his well-groomed appearance.

Fennin let go of her hand and raised his jug toward her before taking a sip of his honeymead.

"So are you, it seems," Aura replied with a soft, closed-mouth smile. The warmth of his hand and lips lingered on her skin, and she wondered if this was some fae custom. It was certainly a more intimate greeting than she was used to.

Aura cleared her throat. "You did well today."

"Thank you, Aura. I did my best," he replied with a smirk. His 'best' was clearly an understatement. From everything she had learned, fae were the most powerful beings on the planet, aside from the lost gods. What Fennin had shown in the arena was a mere taste of his potential, the power he could hold.

Taking her out of the moment, Aura nearly fell out of her seat as something large and fluffy brushed against her legs under the table.

"Careful," Fenn's hand swiftly steadied her.

"What was that?" she asked, looking down to see what had startled her.

"Aiza," Fennin said as the large dog emerged from beneath the table, placing her head into Fennin's green and gold lap, eye's gleaming. Immediately, Aura recognised it as the same creature she had seen around the castle in the passing weeks.

"He's yours?"

"She is mine, yes." He ruffled the thick fur above her neck. "Though I'm not sure I could call her mine; I think the ownership is quite possibly the other way around. She came to my family home the day I was born and never left. Which didn't go down well with my father, who was violently allergic."

He scratched behind her ears, her tongue lolling out in response. The repetitive thumping of her tail echoed from under the table.

"Your sister scored high today; it seems to be all anyone can talk about."

"I know, I have never seen her use her power like that." They had celebrated in their room after the trial with sparkling wyne and tears. Aura was still in shock at how the magic Keyara had only just begun to figure out was more effective than they both hoped.

Fennin's brow furrowed thoughtfully. "The light she summoned... it was unusual." He looked at her with one finger tapping on his drink, "In all my years, I've never seen anyone with that kind of power. Your sister handled it well."

Aura searched his expression for any hint of mockery or suspicion but found none-just sincerity. She tried to focus her magic to read his emotions, but it was hard to concentrate in such a crowded space.

"She's never had to use it before. Eldorhaven's not exactly a place where you need that kind of power," Aura joked lightly. He cocked his head. "No I guess not".

Keyara had mentioned that she no longer felt the gifted magic inside her after the trial. Aura would have to find out how it worked, this light, as her sister may need it again in the future. Maybe this male would know, but Aura would have to be discreet. If it was known Keyara had been given help, she would be disqualified and thrown out of the competition. "Fennin..." she began, but he winced.

"Please, call me Fenn. Only my mother calls me Fennin."

"Fenn," she corrected with a smile.

"Yes?" he replied, his voice making her momentarily lose her train of thought. The way he said *yes* made Aura struggle to find words for a second.

He made her nervous; whether it was his fae nature or something else, Aura wasn't sure.

But deep down, she knew she needed to be cautious around him, no matter how devastatingly handsome he was. She wasn't even sure "handsome" was a strong enough word for him.

"Since I have been here, I've had the oddest sensation that someone has been watching me, you don't happen to know who that might be, do you? I know the fae have incredible senses."

He gave a half smile. "It is true, our senses are exceptional." He raised his drink to his lips. "As your luck would have it, I'm one of the most elite hunters Athvar has ever seen. Aiza and I have been hunting and tracking together for years, since I was eight."

"Which was… how long ago?" Aura asked, raising her tawny brows.

"One hundred and eighty years."

"Oh, a long time, then," she said, surprised.

"Indeed," he smirked.

She didn't take her eyes off him. "It's you, isn't it."

He grinned. "Truthfully, Miss Allis, it's Aiza who's been watching you, not me."

"What do you mean?"

Fenn didn't get a chance to answer, as a noblewoman sitting next to him grabbed his attention, using her magic to pull his chair towards her. Aiza gave a small whine from beneath the table, landing with a huff as she lay her large body underneath Aura's seat. Whilst she gave her a tentative stroke, feeling her deep breaths rise and fall in her hand, Aura glanced over to her sister down the length of the table.

From here, Aura could feel the tension that rolled off Keyara's porcelain shoulders. Her sister and the vampyre were completely in their own world, an impenetrable bubble seeming to surround them.

Above the chattering clamour, Keyara's chair screeched back on the stone floor, furious anger in her eyes. It brought everyone to a silence around them, the bubble had popped and on instinct, Aura stood up with her.

Keyara shook her head subtly, signalling that she didn't want to be followed and she stormed off without so much as a glance back, her long chocolate hair bouncing as she went.

The interest in the situation had ebbed and everyone returned to their conversations, not wasting any more of their precious time on a human they deemed unworthy of it.

As the evening wore on, the moon watched over the winding-down festivities. Dinner was finished, drinks had flowed, and conversations faded.

Aura couldn't help but notice how much she had enjoyed the flirting between herself and Fenn. When it was time to head to bed, she happily accepted his offer to walk her there.

"I think you've had a touch too much wyne, Miss Allis," Fenn teased, holding his arm out for her. A wise move, considering she wasn't sure she could make it down the steep, winding steps on her own. Aura had tripped over her dress multiple times while dancing, and each time, Fenn had caught her, even when she was in someone else's arms.

"Miss Allis," Aura mimicked the way he said her name.

"You don't like to be called that?"

"No, I don't. That's what they call my mother, and do I look like my mother? No. Well, I mean I wouldn't anyway, because she isn't." Aura could hear herself slurring her words, talking nonsense.

Fenn laughed softly. "Alright."

Their steps echoed off the high walls as they descended, torches lighting the way down, replacing the stars' glow that had illuminated the roofless staircase. Fenn moved with an unworldly grace, like a wolf through a silent forest, a stark contrast to her heavy, drunken gait. Aura suddenly became self-conscious of her dishevelled appearance. Her hair had unravelled from its pins, and the rouge she had painted on her face was smeared. The dark mass that always lingered within her reached out, feeding her anxious thoughts.

"Is something wrong?" he asked, breaking the silence that must have lasted longer than she realised.

She feigned a grin. "I'm okay, just feeling tired, that's all." He didn't press further, and she took his silence as acceptance of her white lie.

"Your sister left early," he said after a short pause, steering them into the familiar grey corridors inside.

"I think that vampyre pissed her off again."

"Taris?"

"Uhm-Hm" she hiccupped.

"He can be difficult, but I'm sure he doesn't mean any ill will towards her."

Aura shook her head vigorously. "He's rude. What he did today at the trial! Disgusting."

"I'm not excusing what he did, but this is the Heir's rite Aura. What happens in the arena is not personal, you know that." They rounded a dark corner, the door to her room finally coming into view.

"Well, I don't like him. Even if he is handsome."

Fenn's eyebrows shot up. "You think he's handsome?"

"Jealous?" she teased, narrowing her hazy eyes. He gently unhooked her arm from his as they reached her door. There was no humour in his voice when he replied. "Not jealous, Aura-curious."

Well, that's humiliating, she thought, as darkness blanketed her with its companion, anxiety-an enemy that threatened to reduce her to a quivering mess every day.

"I'd better go to bed before I embarrass myself any more tonight." Aura tried to reach for the key in her dress pocket, fumbling around as it hid beneath folds of slippery material.

"Where's the shitting thing?" she muttered.

"Can't you knock?" Fenn suggested.

"No, Keyara will boil me alive if I wake her."

Fenn crossed his arms, amused. "We'd all certainly get drunk from the fumes."

Aura avoided looking at him.

"Here, let me help," he offered, but she put her hands up.

"I can do it myself, thank you very much."

"I don't doubt it, but we'll be here all night otherwise, and I need my beauty sleep."

Aura shot Fenn a look as the world started to spin. She didn't have much time before the wyne completely took over and sent her into oblivion. Aura prayed to the gods that she would be in her bed before that happened, she couldn't pass out in the damned doorway.

"Fucking hell, Aura, do you know what time it is?" her sister's voice broke through her thoughts.

Aura felt her body crumple through the door that her sister had whipped open, her dress catching under her heeled feet. She collapsed face-first onto the bed, not even bothering to take off her clothes.

"Goodnight, Fennin," Aura called out, her voice muffled from the soft blankets smothering her face.

"Thanks for bringing her back," Keyara muttered before slamming the door on the male that Aura felt would linger outside for a few moments more.

41

Keyara

She had seen the inside of this damned holding pen more than Gregorys, Keyara grumbled to herself, inspecting her fire-stained hands.

The argument she had with Taris last night was playing through her head like a syren song, the events recurring in her mind like a relentless reel. The lingering anger of the conversation between them, she hoped, would fuel her fire.

No sooner had she read his name on the back of the chair next to hers, he had appeared. Dressed in a suit of deepest black velvet, a crimson sash belting his waist, he had waltzed over to her practically dripping with charm.

He had pulled off the red, white and black chequered scarf of his family house from around the bottom half of his face and tucked it into his back pocket.

"Aren't you lucky, some would kill to be in my company," he had purred at her, his long legs bringing him so close she had been forced to lift her chin to meet his eyes.

"And here I am thinking I'd kill someone to not be within one hundred miles of you, but alas, I left my daggers in my room." Taris had barked a laugh. "Liar."

He was wrong – usually, she would have brought her daggers with her, but the dress had been so godsdamned tight that they would have ripped the material.

Keyara sat down as Taris pushed her chair in. If he thought for a second that she was going to say thanks, he was wildly mistaken.

Smoothing down his jacket, Taris settled down next to her. Turning his claret eyes in her direction, they seemed to shimmer as they danced over her chest. The candelabras placed about the table cast a warm, golden glow on his skin, but the crackling tension between the two of them had painted the atmosphere with a colder hue.

"Well, what a day it has been, wouldn't you say Keyara?"

Not letting him finish his sentence, Keyara pushed in. "If you ever dare do anything like that again, I will rip your fucking balls off with my teeth."

He leant into her space with his arm crooked, elbow on the table.

"Is that a promise?" A goblet of blood he was sipping, left a stain on his thick bottom lip.

She leant further in. "Most definitely."

"Good evening, Keyara," a familiar voice came between them. Kadeen offered her his wrist as he stood inches from Taris. She tapped the base of her neck in return.

His deep ebony skin was complemented by the rich navy of his dinner suit.

She had given him her best smile.

"Evening Kadeen, don't you look handsome. I can't imagine you will be dancing alone tonight."

She could feel burning eyes boring into the side of her head.

He bowed his head slightly. "Thank you, maybe we could have a few turns on the floor later?"

"I would like that."

He offered a small nod before he bent down to whisper something in the other vampyre's ear.

Taris waved his hand and Kadeen sat down in his seat at the table. Keyara had watched as
everyone fervently spoke and grinned at him.

Chittering and nattering like hyenas, all hungry for the vampyre's attention.

The meal commenced, with herself and Taris exchanging a few, curt words. Keyara had tried her best to be the composed, unbothered potential queen she desperately wanted to be. Using all her effort to keep composed in the company of Shadowfern after what he had done to her today.

She played the part well until the prick had to go and ruin it.

"Tell me Keyara, how was the old bastard? Did Lord Trewith show you all of his... talents?"

She froze mid-bite of her goat loin. "What are you talking about?"

Taris cocked his head. "Your trial today, who have you been fucking to score that high?"

Keyara's teeth still hurt from how hard she had gritted them together, marks still visible from her sharp nails biting into her palm from the clenched fist she had hidden on her lap.

How she didn't boil his insides out at that moment, Keyara will never know – but looking back, she fucking should have.

"Fuck you."

"Come on now, Keyara, there is no need to get defensive. No shame in doing whatever it takes to win. You must know that what you performed for us all in the arena today, is not as nearly impressive as what you think it was." Taris had slung an arm over the back of her chair, but she had been too afraid of her potential reaction to move. He took her silence as space to continue.

"Underwhelming at best."

"Must have been good enough for the judges, I received one of the highest scores there has ever been."

Leaning back against the marble he said, "Yes you did. A human with a score of eight hundred and fifty, only beaten by a fae and, well, me."

Keyara narrowed her eyes. "Are we sure you didn't fuck Lord Trewith?"

He gave her a wolfish grin. "A Valhirian prince would never

lower himself to such behaviour."

"That's a first," Keyara had said blankly, her fist still clenched. Taris's lips curled into a disdainful smirk; the condescension evident.

"I wonder then, if it was your sister who visited his chambers last night. She may not be very powerful – weak like you, useless even – but her beauty? I can see why the old git would want to fu..."

That was it, the moment he had sent her over the edge.

Keyara's fist had flown so fast it shocked even her, but Taris had caught the punch before it landed, catching her wrist inches from his face.

He tutted and spoke softer than Keyara thought possible for an arsehole like him.

"So quick-tempered. That fire of yours, the heat that fuels you Keyara, it will take you to hell and back."

"I'll make sure to take you with me," she spat at him.

Taris still had her in his grasp when for a few seconds, their eyes had locked. Keyara remembered searching his face. She recalled how a flicker of…she didn't know what…passed over his chiselled, fine features. Then like an ember in the wind, that something, disappeared.

Afterwards, Keyara had stood up and left, leaving the gawkers to their gawking.

Keyara neglected to tell Aura what had happened between her and Taris at dinner, there was no point. She would only worry and fret over it.

Like she did over everything.

Aura had been told to join the rest of the audience outside today. Gods only knew what trial Keyara would be facing if the arena was to be out on the mountainside.

The leathers she had on suddenly felt too constricting against her skin. Keyara pulled at the neckline as she began to pace back and forth.

She double-checked, then triple-checked, that she hadn't left her daggers behind this time, tracing their outline with her fingertips against her thigh.

"Competitors, this way," called one of the guards as the door to her holding pen swung open.

Most of the others bolted out like Valhirian horses, eager to be the first in line.

Keyara noticed the fae male who had brought Aura home last night-Fenn if she remembered his name right-strolling a few feet away with the fluidity and grounded strength typical of his kind.

He turned his head and gave her a small wave. She returned the gesture.

She couldn't see him, but Keyara knew Taris was not far behind. She could always sense his presence, his scent carrying the unmistakable essence of the wind-blown desert.

Keyara jumped when someone tapped her on the shoulder. Expecting it to be him, she spun around furiously, only to find Jenney grinning from ear to ear.

"Morning!"

The girl was full of nervous energy, her ponytail bobbing up and down with her erratic movements. "How are you feeling?" she asked Keyara, as they shuffled forward.

"Well, a trial outside of the arena is so rare, I'm not sure how to feel."

"The last time a trial was held out in the open was the cliff-top trial, during one of the earliest Rites."

Keyara nodded. "The Falkons picked off every single one of them, bar the winner. Everyone was surprised they came down from the peaks; they haven't since."

"That's right, I can never remember her name…"

"She could control soil, rocks, earth and such, building herself bridges across the cliffs, whilst the rest tumbled down the mountain." Jenney trailed off, lost in thoughts recalling the Queen who in the end, was barely remembered by anyone.

They were lined up in single file behind an enormous stone archway that opened up to the fresh morning air and green mountains.

Keyara followed the line into the morning, scowling at the coldness against her skin.

Leathers were made for protection, not warmth, and summer was coming to an end.

"Oh gods, I hope it's not any further up the mountain. I'm not great with heights," said Jenney.

"Me neither," Keyara replied. That was a lie, heights did not bother her at all, but she wanted to reassure the girl. It took courage to enter the Heir's rite and doing so at such a young age earned Jenney some admiration and respect.

If Keyara won, she would make damned sure to keep Jenney around, to join her court and even perhaps make a friend out of her.

"Good morning everyone." Lord Trewith stood before them all as they entered a valley between two high peaks.

The twelve remaining, arranged themselves side by side on the mossy ground, many of them peering behind the lord towards the wooden fortress that stood at the far end of the valley.

To be honest, Keyara thought it just looked like an overgrown fence.

Lord Trewith's deep booming voice, amplified by magic, reverberated in the confines of the valley around them.

"You have thus far been tested alone, evaluated on your powers, intellect and adaptability-qualities of great importance for any who would aspire to the throne of Eira."

The wind in the valley picked up, the low howling a haunting backdrop to the Lord's booming voice.

"However, as a sovereign, you will find that alliances are essential. The ability to collaborate with others, even those who may rival you in power and strength, is crucial. It is not enough to merely forge these alliances. They must be made strong and dependable, capable of withstanding the trials of hardship and war. This, perhaps above all, is the cornerstone of ruling a prosperous and peaceful kingdom."

Keyara did not like where this going, and from the shuffling of feet to her left and right, she knew the others were coming to the same conclusion she was.

"And so, today, you will face a challenge that mirrors the unforgiving maze of court relationships." Murmurs of confusion and realisation drifted through the valley.

The wooden structure at the end of the valley was a maze.

"You must now arrange yourselves into teams of four. The team that first emerges from the trial will be deemed victorious. The remaining eight will face immediate elimination. I wish you the best of luck.

Lord Trewith turned with a sweep of his charcoal cape, marching towards steep steps that led to the audience up on the side of the mountain, just above the wooden structure.

The soldiers that remained told them all that they had until the sun passed over the tallest peak to get into their teams, which did not give them much time.

"Can I be on your team Keyara? Please?" Jenney touched her arm, a pleading look on her freckled face.

How could she say no? Keyara had made no other friends here – maybe Fennin, but he was more of an acquaintance.

The bird woman could join them maybe, her wings could be a huge advantage.

That idea was swiftly put out, as Keyara saw one team had already been made and she was in it.

"Sure, who else?" Keyara nodded to her. Jenney looked around frantically.

"Shit."

"What is it?" Jenney asked her.

Two large males came sauntering towards them. One with ruffled blonde hair and pointy ears, the other with large fangs and a face that needed to be punched.

"Morning ladies, it looks like you could do with a team?" purred the one with deep red eyes.

"Fuck off Taris, we don't need you."

Jenney jumped, visibly shocked at her outburst, recoiling like Keyara was a marsh snake ready to strike.

With over-exaggerated movements, Taris turned left and right, hands never leaving his pockets.

"Evidently, it appears as though you do."

Godsdamn it, he was right. Fennin and himself were the only options they had left.

"We would love to have you, thank you," came Jenney's high-pitched voice.

"*Jenney*," Keyara hissed.

"Thanks," Fennin said to her, the unmistakable lure of his voice drawing even Keyara in.

Damned fae.

"Jenney, he will slit our throats before we get more than five feet inside," she said, with no need to clarify who she referred to.

"Five? You wouldn't even get that far," Taris replied, and Keyara had no doubt he was telling the truth.

"Join another team. We don't want you, and by that, I just mean you Taris."

Fennin coughed a laugh.

"Well, that's too bad, times up." Taris pointed with his head at the glow emanating from the maze doors that were opening.

Keyara huffed, resigning herself to the fact that this was her team, and like it or not, they had to work together.

She unsheathed one of her daggers, pointing it at the vampyre.

"If I think for one second you are sabotaging us in any way, or I even suspect for a moment you are fucking us over, I will kill you."

Fennin put his palm on the edge, urging it downwards. /

"Let's all calm down. No one is going to fuck you over Keyara, you have my word."

"It's not your word I want." Her eyes could have borne a hole into Taris' own, even if every time she looked into them, her stomach flipped.

"Come on, let's go." Jenney tried to pull her away. Keyara finally let her, hooking the daggers back into their holster strapped around her thigh, the unspoken challenge hanging between them like an invisible thread.

Keyara focused her attention on winning and if she was true to herself, they did have a good shot. A fae, a vampyre, a girl who could turn invisible and herself – together they could be a real threat to the others.

If they didn't kill each other first.

Once the teams were gathered and ready to begin, a woman came over to every one of them, crafting a ball of light no bigger than an apple above their heads.

Each team had a different colour blazing above them. Bird woman's team had purple; the other team had green. Keyara's eyes nearly rolled out of her head when she saw their team's colour.

"Of course, it's red."

Taris looked at her. "It looks good on you, Keyara. You should wear it more often."

Keyara made a mental note to always wear pastels from now on.

The groups were led by guards to three separate entrances within the main door. The walls were so very high, so high Keyara could not even see the audience on the mountainside.

"Ready!" called a guard.

A boom echoed across the valley.

Taris winked at her – she put her middle finger up in return.

42
Selsie

Selsie's heart beat with a chaotic rhythm as she stepped through the corridors of the castle, away from her room and the man on her balcony.

The air felt thicker than usual, laden with unspoken words and the residue of an almost-kiss that lingered on her lips. She could almost feel his skin on hers, the large fingertips grazing her face.

Confusion swirled in her mind; the current of emotions threatened to engulf her.

It was all new to her, and she feared it. Her steps took her down the staircase, towards the inner depths of the castle where she had first surfaced. Maybe the solace of her chambers below would clear her head from the images of Jonn's unreadable expression – a mask that hid his thoughts.

Selsie had only just thrown Jonn's shirt on the bottommost step when Neesh materialised at her side, her face etched with urgency.

"Your mother knows, Selsie."

Selsie shook her head. "What?"

"She knows we lied about Jonn. We must leave, now."

Selsie's eyes widened with disbelief. How could her mother know? She thought they had pulled off the deception perfectly. She almost believed Jonn's performance herself, even praying to Alysee that it was real for a fleeting moment.

Yet, it seemed like they had faltered. The revelation sent a chill down her bare spine as she nodded to Neesh, her thoughts racing.

"She will kill me, Neesh, and Jonn. I need to go to him." Selsie picked up the discarded shirt, shoving it on over her head.

"Selsie, you mustn't go to him; your mother will expect that. We need to get you out safely, now."

"I need to get him out of the castle!" Her heart was racing, there was no droplet of doubt in her mind that her mother wouldn't grant them any more grace. The ruse was up, they had been found out.

"I know Selsie, but not yet. If your mother hasn't taken him already, we will find him. He's a strong man that one, I have no doubt he can handle your mother, but we must move."

"How did you know, Neesh? How did you find out, did my mother tell you?"

She asked her friend as they moved swiftly through the castle, trying to evade curious gazes and silent whispers that seemed to follow them like a haunting melody.

"I overheard. She was giving the order in the barracks. I came to find you as soon as I could."

"She didn't tell you?"

An emotion passed over Neesh's face, so quickly Selsie could have imagined it. If she blinked, she would have missed it.

It was fear.

Neesh created a slight breeze with her power as they scurried along, hoping to blow away their scent to anyone who might be on their trail.

"We cannot go to my home, it's too risky."

Selsie noticed a battered leather satchel slung over her shoulder. They went further and further down into the castle. The walls were no longer adorned with its usual crystals and gems. The sconces on the walls no longer lit.

"Where are we going?"

Neesh didn't reply, just kept them going deeper and deeper until they reached a bolted wooden door at the end of a particularly long and dark corridor.

The large bunch of keys Neesh pulled out from the satchel jingled as they were put in the iron lock.

"This is one of the oldest wings of the castle, built before even the records began. Only a handful of top-ranking guards know of it and are sworn to secrecy by your mother to never utter a word of its existence. It was built as an evacuation route for the matriarch and her family, if the castle is ever under attack."

They emerged from the doorway into a small chamber, no larger than her room under the waves. A river, barely eight feet deep, ran slowly along a shallow ditch.

"How do they know you will not speak of this?"

Neesh lowered her already whispering voice. "There was…leverage."

Selsie once again, discarded the shirt.

"Neesh, what of the magic that brought us to Alboste? Why are we doing this?"

"I have no time to explain now, but here." Neesh gave Selsie the satchel, it was heavy and would hinder her swimming, but she took it with thanks.

"This will answer any questions you have, but do not open it until you are ready."

"Are you not coming?"

"No, you will move quicker without me."

"I'm going to need help finding Jonn."

Neesh's face softened. "He's gone."

Selsie slung the satchel across her bare shoulders violently, her eyes wide in disbelief.

"What do you mean?"

"Before I found you, my guards were alerted to a rowing boat not too far from shore, with two men aboard. One with a shaven head, the other…"

"With long dark curls?"

Neesh nodded. "I'm sorry."

Selsie straightened her shoulders. "You let him go?"

"If I didn't, you would both be dead right now."

Selsie was about to protest when shouting and clangs of armour echoed from further up the corridor.

"Go now, Selsie!"

She didn't need to be told twice. Selsie hopped into the water, her tail emerging the moment the saltwater caressed her skin. She swam to the edge of the chamber, where the water ran under the wall through an opening the size of a small door. Pausing, she peeked her head up just enough to see above the surface.

Neesh had her sword drawn – blessed by the sword master himself, after Neesh had proved herself the best of them all. Selsie knew her friend could take on three or four of her best guards without breaking a scale, but as her mother stepped through the doorway onto the small bank, all Selsie's hope melted away.

"Where are they?" came her mother's cool, calm voice.

They. Her mother thought they left together.

"A million leagues from here I hope," Neesh replied with the same coolness.

Her mother did not change the hard expression on her face.

"You know the price to pay for bringing her here, for revealing this place."

"I do."

The matriarch tutted.

"Such a shame."

What happened next, Selsie would carry with her until the day she died.

A heavy glow took form around Neesh's body as whispering songs filled the chamber. Her mother's palms were raised, grey light emanating from them.

Neesh stood frozen on the spot, her chest failing to rise and fall with breath.

The matriarch bared her teeth and brought up her hands, which together were the only part of her in her Other form. She then began to take chunks out of her friend, with teeth and deadly talons.

Pieces of Neesh fell to the floor in bloody chunks, others were eaten whole by her mother.

Selsie had to stifle a scream and every instinct in her to help Neesh; to jump out of the water and challenge her mother.

Blood began to run into the water, Selsie could taste it. In her shock, something was nagging her, the river calling for her attention. She could feel the water come alive around her as it changed, the current building underneath her.

Neesh was helpless, being eaten alive by her mother without even the option to fight back.

Selsie could not watch anymore. As her eyes closed, she thought she could feel small beads of water dripping from her face into the river as she silently dipped under the water.

43

Keyara

The maze swallowed them, the sun's morning light joining them in the darkness. The red flicker of light over their heads was the only reprieve from the blindness.

Jenney moved closer to Keyara as a few screams in the distance echoed around them.

It didn't take long for the maze to turn on them, as the gravelly, winding path gave way. A gaping hole around twenty feet long – and only the gods knew how deep – replaced the path ahead. Jenney saved Keyara's life when she nearly went tumbling into it, pulling her back just in time.

"Careful," Taris chided.

Keyara had looked to Fenn. "Why don't you just fly over, don't you have wings? I'm not too heavy to carry over, and I doubt Jenney weighs more than me," she had said. "I'm sure Taris can make the jump, so don't worry about him."

The fae hadn't replied, as without even a second thought, Fenn had grown a thick tree, pushed it over and created a bridge for them to cross.

Keyara burnt it when they had made it to the other side. She wasn't taking any chances, if anyone came the same way, they would have to figure it out themselves.

Now they had rounded a corner where the path split in two.

"It doesn't seem fair. The woman that can fly can just look over the walls to see which path to take," moaned Jenney.

Keyara agreed with her, the bird lady did seem to have luck on her side with this trial. Then again, was that not life?

Some had luck, or the gods on their side.

Others, not so much.

Fenn gazed upwards. "Hm." He conjured his magic, a green mist which seemed almost alive, and moved upwards towards the tops of the walls.

It reached the precipice, and as it tried to touch the sky sparks rained down over them.

Landing on uncovered skin, the sparks burned her flesh like acid.

"Fucking hell!" Keyara shouted, covering her head.

A woman's guttural scream pierced the maze.

Bird lady was the only other woman that remained in the trial, besides herself and Jenney.

Not anymore.

"This way," Fenn pointed to the left path.

"Any reason we should take your orders, Ashverne?" Taris put his hands in his pockets.

Fenn barely even acknowledged him, as though Taris was nothing more than a gnat in the wind.

Keyara liked this male.

"I say we go this way," Taris cocked his head right.

Jenney's ponytail bobbed as she looked between the two.

Keyara stood between them. "Woah hold up, what makes you two think that either of you are the leaders here?"

The two males' eyes landed on her. "Neither of you have any more right to lead us than I have," Keyara continued.

"If anyone has the right it's me. Already an heir and the Prince of Valhir, a leader," gloated Taris.

Fenn crossed his arms, a loud scoff leaving his lips.

"I'm sorry, is something amusing?" The humour and smugness that usually laced Taris' words had gone.

"I'm not going down this road, Taris, not now."

"Watch yourself Ashverne, we wouldn't want Adne to know her pet was scampering into places he shouldn't be." Taris pointed at the other male as Fenn moved closer, uncrossing his long arms.

"Running away from something are you? Or is your dick so small you want two kingdoms to compensate?" said Fenn.

Keyara couldn't help the snigger that escaped.

Taris turned to her, venom seeping into his eyes. "Why are you even here? You're nothing, a no one."

Keyara slowly stalked towards him. "To make sure assholes like you don't win."

It came out in a deadly whisper. She surprised even herself, as his cutting remarks pissed her off most of the time, but not enough to warrant the sudden and deep anger brewing inside her.

On her left, Fenn had lost all of his usual calm presence. Since she had met him, he had radiated warmth and familiarity as much as a summer day in the forest that surrounded her home.

Now, he encompassed a shadow that lurked between the trees. The unknown creature that lingered among the trees outside of her window, frightening a five-year-old Keyara in her bed. The monster that darted between the oaks, daring her to come outside before she quickly threw the blankets over her head.

"Someone's going to knock you from your lofty heights one day, Taris, and I can't wait to see it. You know, maybe I'll just do it now, save us all the headache." Even Fenn's voice changed, It was such a stark contrast from his usual unnatural beauty that Keyara was taken out of her simmering rage for a moment.

"You arrogant idiots, just stop, look!" Jenney could have been a wasp buzzing in their ears for all they cared, the fury and aggression in the air was at such strength that they could hear nothing else.

Keyara's heat was screaming to be let out. She could taste the anger in the air.

Then, when a bitter, acrid taste really did hit the back of her throat, Keyara paused her seething for a split second.

Akin to the Berryblues that grew in the fields around her home, the thick coating on her tongue threw her back to the memory of the harsh winters that engulfed Eldorhaven on occasional years.

She hated them, as they had to eat the fruit when food was scarce. Aura did her best to make the Berryblues bearable, turning them into jams and jellies to mask the bitterness.

"What in God's name..." Jenney crouched to the floor where a barely visible, blue smoke, seeped upwards through the ground.

"They're poisoning us," she muttered.

"What?" Keyara asked, crouching beside her, imploring Jenney to repeat herself.

"I think the smoke is turning us against each other."

"How do you know?" Taris called out.

"I was studying Alchemy before I came here. That bitterness you can taste, it's an element that can be turned into a poison. That element, it can make you violent... angry, and it's working, look at you three."

Jenney was right.

The poison in the air had taken effect, even she had a wild look in her eyes.

"Are you sure it's the poison?" said Taris, ignoring the glare Keyara threw his way.

A muscle flickered in Fenn's jaw as his magic scattered along their feet.

"I can feel it but I can't think straight. You seem to be the least affected by it, you decide what path to take Jenney."

They all looked at her and her eyes widened.

A clang of swords accompanied by screams in the distance pierced the momentary silence. It seemed to help Jenney make her choice.

"Left."

Fenn nodded, leading them to the path ahead. A mere few moments later, as they left the poison behind them to fog the crossroads, Keyara's temper calmed down.

The tension between them all – and her fire – immediately simmered to a tolerable level.

The walls along the path began to ascend, reaching over them and knitting together, transforming into a tunnel barely high enough for the tallest of them to pass through.

"Fuck me this is tight," Taris grumbled, his deep voice cutting through the dark.

With Fenn leading the way, Keyara was following the sun-yellow hair of the fae in front with Jenney right behind her.

The vampyre was at the rear of their line formation, at his insistence.

She didn't know if she felt comfortable not keeping him in her sights.

"Shh." Slowing his steps, Fenn brought the group to a glacial pace.

"Somethings coming."

"What is it?" Jenney whispered, hiding her physical self from them.

Fenn shook his head. "I don't know, but it smells familiar to me."

"Fenn, what's going on?" Keyara asked, grasping both daggers at her sides.

Taris suddenly called out with his voice carrying a fervent urgency, his voice growing louder as he ran towards them. "Shit, behind!"

A deathly screech came from further back in the tunnel, sending the dark hairs on Keyara's arms to prick, her pulse quickening with each passing moment.

"What the fuck is it?!" she called out, bringing a heatwave to her fingertips.

"It's a Cray!" shouted Taris, as though they should know what

that was. Fenn narrowed his eyes; he had already drawn his
magic, evident from the smell of cinnamon,.

"Which is what?" Keyara asked him.

"A creature Shadowfern should not have," he replied, pushing
past her.

Keyara looked for Jenney, but she had disappeared. Smart
move, if Keyara was her, she would leave them to it and make a
run for the exit.

The screech came again, ear-splitting and grating.

The three of them huddled closer, their breaths synchronised in
the eerie silence that followed.

Keyara pulled on Fenn's leathers. "Tell me what to do."

"Crays are blind, they are also fucking hard to kill. Don't even
bother trying to take its head off or getting close enough to get
ripped apart. Use your magic if you can."

The thing was getting closer, its screeching calls sending
shivers up her spine.

"If that doesn't work, what in godsname do we do, Fenn?"

"Think fast, Ashverne, I don't want to die just yet," Taris
turned his head just enough for Keyara to catch the wink he
gave her.

Fenn patted just below his left rib, "Here, aim for here."

"Why there?" In the dark Jenney's voice made Keyara jump out
of her leathers.

"Fuck me Jenney, I thought you'd gone."

The girl giggled nervously. "I could never leave you alone with
these two, Keyara. Besides, what kind of future queen would
leave her companions in the face of danger?"

Keyara didn't miss the small hint of a smile that twitched at
Fenn's mouth. She felt the girl's hand on her shoulder, moments
before all chaos broke loose.

At her first sight of the creature, Keyara nearly pissed through
her leathers.

Before them was a massive creature with long spindly limbs

and twisted horns that ran down the length of its rod straight back.

With skin unnaturally smooth, and the shade of a rotting corpse, the hulking great demon loomed in the darkness.

Its eyes glowed with an unsettling luminosity, its elongated claws scraped against the cold, stone floor.

The Cray let out a shrill roar, and the battle commenced, heralded by Taris who was shouting and whooping.

The narrowness of the cramped tunnel was hindering every movement Keyara tried to make. Their line formation prevented any of them from being able to throw any successful blows.

Taking chunks out of the Cray's scaly hide with his bare teeth, Taris was ripping and gnawing into it as best he could.

Fenn shouted into the gloom, "Taris, that's not going to work. Stop, you're just pissing it off!"

She couldn't tell if Taris was listening, there was an animalistic glint in his eyes.

The vampyre remained stubborn, dismissing Fenn's counsel. "I've dealt with creatures like this before. I know what I'm doing Ashverne," he retorted, his fangs bared.

Swiping at them all with impossibly sharp talons, a few of them had scraped along the males' knees and arms. Taris was evidently ignoring the blood pouring from he and Fenn's bodies.

She knew the scent of blood would be distracting for him, enough to get him killed maybe.

She couldn't just stand there and watch them die.

Which they would if no one took control. Despite the urgency of their situation, the clash of personalities within the group threatened to unravel their chances of survival.

Taris was an arrogant arsehole and Fenn had too much patience for his own good.

She exchanged a knowing look with Fenn, who was wielding

his magic, creating sharp shards of wood that would not – try as he might – pierce the scales of the creature.

Stuck behind him with no room for her to even attempt to help kill it, Keyara began poking Fenn with the end of her dagger.

"He's not going to listen to you Fenn, we need to figure something else out. Can't you do anything with your magic?"

"I have to put a damper on my power, the whole tunnel may collapse in on us if I don't. We don't know where Jenney is either and I cannot risk it."

He seemed in thought for a moment.

"I can get to his ribs, if Taris would move out of the way, I would be in a better position."

Both of them looked in exasperation at the vampyre.

"My stakes won't pierce his scales from this angle. We're going to get killed if that damned male doesn't listen".

"He won't, but I have a plan," said Keyara.

The Cray roared, lifting its large talon-ended hands to where his pointed ear used to be.

A deep booming laughter bounced off the blood-stained walls. Taris continued laughing as his chin and mouth dripped with blood, all the while waving something at them.

Fenn crossed his arms. "Damned vampyre bit the thing's ear off."

Keyara took the moment to tell Fenn her plan.

"Make those wooden stakes again and give some to me."

The male nodded.

Keyara didn't know if he was an idiot or naive, but he seemed to trust her word without question.

Fenn raised his hands, wooden stakes forming from the green mist. He created four and placed two in her crimson-stained hands.

She drew her heat out, turning the stakes from a deep brown to a glowing red, then eventually to a pure white.

Keyara was noticing how quickly her power was coming forth

now, how it reached what she thought was full strength in mere seconds.

The Cray advanced, its attention torn between the two of them and the seemingly ineffectual vampyre.

Jenney had not been seen, nor heard in a while.

Keyara prayed the girl was safe.

Taris paused his frenzied attack, and in that moment Keyara and Fenn seized the opportunity.

They lunged forward, their makeshift weapons aimed at the underbelly of the creature.

Together, they weaved magic and agility, their coordination impeccable.

The Cray, caught off guard by the unexpected onslaught, roared in pain as the heated stakes found their mark.

It took several attempts, the creature thrashing and resisting, but eventually, the stakes penetrated the venom gland.

Though not before one of those talons caught her shoulder.

Keyara barked in pain, rolling across the floor right underneath its hulking legs.

She heard a male voice shout her name, but she couldn't respond.

A deathly pain ricocheted its way from the wound site, down to her toes and back again.

The world became blurry, all that Keyara could register was her frantic heartbeat. Then a male voice was in her ear.

"Keyara, Keyara listen to me, listen, you must burn the venom out. It got you with venom, the pain will stop if you get the venom out. Burn it out now, burn it out or you will die. Keyara for fucks sake listen to me!"

Burn it out.

It was burning already.

No, no way.

She needed ice, water, cold.

No more heat.

Someone was smoothing her forehead, soft hands.

But she couldn't see anyone.

No one was there.

"Keyara, do it, do it now."

The world was blurry, was she drunk? She couldn't remember drinking wyne.

"Godsdamned it, Keyara. I will bring you back from the dead and kill you all over again if you let yourself die."

That voice again, she'd like to tell it to go fuck itself, as it didn't know what this pain was like.

Maybe he should try it himself.

Voices, more distant now.

"She's not doing it, Fenn. I'm going to have to force her."

"She will kill you herself if she finds out."

Bastards talking about her.

Fuck that.

Fuck this pain.

She wasn't weak, it would take more than this to kill her.

She concentrated all her effort, all of her remaining strength on the source of the pain.

Her heat enveloped it.

Hearing her own screams echoing around the tunnel was all she remembered before passing out.

44
Selsie

The underground river emptied into the sea a few miles out from Cildraethe. On the west side, she realised, as her body naturally adjusted to the currents she knew so well.

Her mind was reeling from what she had witnessed. Neesh must have known what would happen to her if she broke the secrecy spell woven between herself and the matriarch.

Though she doubted Neesh knew she would be killed in such a way. Laeths were brutal, harsh, sometimes even cruel, but Selsie had never seen such barbaric treatment inflicted on one of their own kind.

Maybe this is how humans felt. Now she could see why Jonn would hate her.

It was a starless night above and the sea was turning. Autumn was on the horizon, the change of season bringing with it an air of uncertainty.

The current was strong, though Selsie needn't fight it as the sea was guiding her. Carrying her along like a youngling in its parent's arms.

Selsie didn't know where to start looking for Jonn. Neesh told her they escaped on a rowing boat so they couldn't have made it far.

The betrayal stung; she had never felt anything like it.

If Selsie was honest to herself, with Jonn she felt a lot of things that she had never experienced before.

These weeks and months she had lain awake at night – either in her kelp bed or the dry one – staring at the ceiling thinking of him.

How he questioned her beliefs, how he was the only other being in the whole world who had partaken in conversation with her other than Neesh. How he had shared intimate, personal stories with her when he didn't have to.

It had taken him a while to open up to her, to even speak to her, but words had found him eventually.

He was so different from the males of her kind, who only saw her as the heir. As the weak newling, the most beautiful syren of their kind.

She also thought about how his hair, so dark; like the sea on a moonless night, longing to be touched. How his skin, sunkissed and freckled from the days they spent walking the length of her city, begged for her to reach out.

Some nights she was so overcome with something she could not place, that in her frustration she asked one of the guards to place a sleeping spell on her. The dreamless sleep the only reprieve from torment,

She wondered if he felt the same; if hours ago on the balcony, he felt the same as she.

Selsie could not think of that right now. However much of a distraction it was to the horror that had just unfolded, she had to find him before her mother and the guards did.

She swam in all directions, asking the waves for even a hint of a clue, but it was useless. The ocean was ignoring her pleas. Fickle as it was.

It was as though the waves had swallowed him whole, leaving behind only the echoes of their shared moments. Though she knew he wasn't far; she could feel it in her bones.

Selsie's frustration mounted, a storm brewing within her as she realised the enormity of the consequences awaiting her at the hands of her mother should she or Jonn be found. The satchel Neesh had given her was cumbersome, and she hadn't even looked inside to see its contents yet.

Days later, Selsie's search was still ongoing. She remained close to the surface, lifting her head above occasionally to check for ships, boats or dead sailors, but there had been nothing for miles.

She needed to spare five minutes on the seafloor to rest, to finally see what was in the bag.

Her eyes scanned the world above one last time. The sun was beginning to climb over the moving horizon, when she spotted the silhouette of a ship. Blinking her third eyelid, she squinted at its sails, finally the silver sails became clear.

There was a one in three chance it was Jonn's ship and Selsie was willing to bet that it was his. The sea urged her on as relief washed over her.

Her will was strong as she approached the vessel. It was brand new; the acrid scent of fresh paint stinging her nostrils.

She could create the dense fog to cover her visibility, but one syren alone was not enough to reach the top deck of the ship. There were only a few men there, and the dark and moonless night worked to Selsie's advantage.

By the time she had reached the ship, she had still not figured out how to find him, or even how to get onboard without being caught and killed.

Making her way around to the bow, Selsie looked for a way in. "She's a dark one tonight boys, keep a keen eye out for rocks won't ya. I don't fancy a late-night swim in Laeth territory." She knew that voice.

Symon stood tall on the deck, his arm slung over another man, quietly laughing together.

To the right, just above her, movement in the shadows at an open porthole caught her eye, stealing her attention from the deck.

Keeping only her eyes visible atop the water she gently swam over to the porthole. The light, powdery scent of a human child kept her from being on the offensive.

Through the orange glow of the porthole, a boy – not yet anywhere close to a man – peeked his own wide eyes over the ledge of the round glass.

They stared at each other in silence for a few moments, neither making a sound.

The sea was whispering to her, but Selsie couldn't make out what it was trying to say. The sea had always been her friend, not her mother's. It had been her saviour many times, her constant companion.

Selsie often attributed her mother's foul nature to the fact that in history, the matriarch controlled the sea. But it must have skipped a generation, as try as she might, her mother had no power over the waves, only manifesting in the clouds above.

Selsie sent a small prayer to Alysee to guide Neesh smoothly to the Eternal Sea and honour her with a star, to make sure the ancient god of the ocean, Iara, would welcome her with grace.

The human boy had not yet alerted the ship to her presence, he was just staring motionless into her eyes, her soul it seemed.

Selsie dipped under the calm water, making quick work of a descent to the ocean floor, where she found the prettiest shell, she could find. A small conch, teal in shade with silver flecks. It came from a crab that never left the ocean floor. A rare shell for a human eye to see.

As she brought it to the surface, the boy was standing up, his whole body leaning against the porthole, his eyes darting, his mouth open, seeming to search for her.

As she broke the water he stepped back slightly, a droplet of fear marking his pale features. She placed the shell on a small column of water and directed it up to the window.

The boy gave her the smallest of side eyes. He was smart to be wary of her, but she nodded her head as if to say *take it*.

The child plucked the shell from the water, admiring the rare item as he turned it in his hands.

"Thank you," he called to her, but before she could reply, loud heavy footsteps could be heard coming from inside.

The porthole shut in a hurry as she dipped under the water. Selsie continued to scan the ship for a way in, or to find any trace of the man she was so desperately looking for.

As she approached the stern once more, a web of magic, unfamiliar and potent, ensnared her.

It was a power that matched the ancient songs of the syrens, entwined with some other, foreign magic. Selsie struggled against the invisible threads, her movements constrained.

No, not again.

Selsie was so sure that she had been thorough in using her magic to feel out for a net this time. Though, this was not like last time. This net was physically burning her skin like poison. Strips of her flesh were searing, melting away like ice in spring. Her tail had given away to her legs as she was dragged out of the water. Selsie thanked Alysee for that at least, her tail was extremely sensitive, and she didn't know if she could take the burning agony it would have inflicted upon her scales.

She clung onto the satchel as close to her chest as she could, trying to not let the net burn it away like it was her skin. Normally, her wounds would have already begun to heal, however, this did not seem normal and her skin was not healing.

"Caught a pretty one, didn't I?" someone chuckled, his voice carrying the arrogance of a conqueror. His breath even from here, through the agony of the net, reeked of rotten teeth.

Selsie's own teeth were clenched together, her pride keeping her from releasing the scream roiling inside her. Many men were laughing, shouting, and talking excitedly amongst themselves.

"Fucking hell Captain!"

"She's put her tail away already for us Captain! Pin her down!"

"Put her back in the water, it's too dangerous!"

Her body was hauled over the railings and dumped upon the

deck. Many of the humans had long wooden sticks and began poking her with them, digging the net deeper into her raw skin. The jabs were harsh and spiteful. She couldn't blame them for their hate. No doubt a few of the crew's shipmates and friends were killed by her kind; maybe even Neesh in the past.

The name brought heaviness to her heart, but she couldn't think of her friend right now.

Selsie's eyes darted between them, realisation dawning that this probably wasn't one of her best ideas.

Panic threatened to consume her, but defiance burned in her gaze. She scanned their faces, searching for two she recognised. Only mean-spirited or wary faces glared back at her, either afraid of her or hated her.

As their laughs and jeers echoed around the ship, more and more men appeared from below deck.

The man who had caught her – the captain, she came to quickly realise – was standing with his stocky arms folded, a proud look on his pock-marked face.

"Jonn," she demanded, looking straight at him, her voice laced with a quiet strength that echoed through the underwater currents. She did the only thing she could think, asking for a man she knew would be on board.

The ocean seemed to hold its breath, awaiting the outcome of the impending clash. A few of the men quieted their jesting, putting down their sticks and looking to their captain.

"What did you just say, bottom feeder?" The captain spat at her, the green phlegm landing on her raw feet.

Selsie ignored the pain searing into her body, using her waning strength to put the power of the ocean behind her words.

"Jonn!" The water around the ship vibrated with the force of her voice, pushing against the magical restraints, to no avail. Selsie had a cache of power, but this net was something beyond her capabilities.

"See, I knew you couldn't resist me."

Selsie rolled her eyes and looked up through her long lashes at the shaven-headed man above her, who was taking wadded tissue out of his ears.
"Hello again, Selsie."

45

Keyara

The ground was hard and cold beneath her bones.
Eurgh, Keyara grumbled. She hated being cold.
She recalled a memory of falling into the river by their home
during an unusually harsh winter one year.
She and Aura were children, herself probably no older than
maybe eleven or twelve.
It was her lifeday and Aura wanted to get her a present. They
were too poor to buy them, but her mother had always managed
to present a cake at every lifeday.
Aura had taken her by the hand and pulled her out into the
snow, so deep it came up to Keyara's skinny ankles.
They got to the river – which had frozen over by this point –
and Aura had begged Keyara to wait by its banks.
Aura ran to the edge of the forest, out of sight.
Looking back on that day, Keyara was an idiot.
An absolute fool.
But at that young age, she didn't know better.
Under the ice, something glinted and sparkled, calling for her to
grab it.
Now, Keyara knew it was just the reflection of the stars but
Keyara had knelt down to the side of the riverbank and placed
her hand on the ice.
During this time of her life, her magic was just finding its
molten place inside her and she had no mastery of it
whatsoever.
It should have been obvious to her then. Of course, the ice

melted way too fast and a hole larger than she intended emerged. Like a bag of shit, Keyara had fallen straight into the freezing river.

Her breath was stolen from her quicker than she thought possible.

She remembered her sister's screams, her tiny frame wrapped up in her flowery pink dress, reserved for special occasions only.

That dress was ruined that day.

A lot of what happened after, remained a mystery to her, even now. Aura and her mother told her that it was Berran who saved her from the ice.

Obviously.

Now though, he wasn't here to save her.

Opening her eyelids, which felt like they had been sewn shut, Keyara took in her surroundings.

Fenn was to her left, staring at her with the intensity only a fae male could possess.

"Paint a portrait, it will last longer."

His mouth quirked up at the corner.

"And she's back."

Keyara ran an internal check over herself. Everything seemed fine, apart from the gods-awful pain shooting through her shoulder.

The Cray.

Keyara jumped up as fast as she could, the memories of before reeling through her brain.

"Here, be careful," whispered Fenn, holding out a steady hand.

"Thanks," she said softly, brushing off the debris from her leathers.

They were still in the tunnel, the near pitch black illuminated only by the lights above their heads.

She looked around.

"Where's Jenney?"

A smooth velvet voice skittered down her spine.

"Took us for a liability and sprinted for the finish line is my guess."

Keyara shot a look to Taris, who somehow looked unruffled despite what had happened with the creature.

He stood beside the Cray who was sprawled out across the tunnel and blocking the way out, dead as a dog in the desert.

"She wouldn't do that. Some of us have integrity, a concept I don't think you've learnt yet."

"And you do?" he asked, with what seemed like sincerity.

She squared her shoulders. "We don't have time for damned petty arguments."

"Says the woman who has been passed out for hours," Taris said under his breath.

"Hours?!" Keyara asked Fenn, panic lacing her voice. If it had been hours, then they for sure had lost the damned trial.

Fenn rolled his brown eyes, which Keyara swore almost glowed with sunrays in the dim light.

"No, not hours, maybe one." He paused. "Or two."

"Shit," she uttered aloud. "Sorry," she apologised to Fenn, and she meant it. It wasn't her intention to jeopardise his potential win.

Well, not accidentally.

He just tapped her arm and shuffled past her, leading the way forward.

Walking further into the gloom, Keyara could feel Taris behind her.

Smell the spices jamming themselves up her nose.

Feel his warmth.

She could almost feel his breath down her neck as he spoke.

"You nearly died, you know."

"Hm."

"The poison from the Cray, if you didn't burn it out as fast as you did…"

A heartbeat of a pause, then he said almost gently, "…you would have died."

"Is that right? I bet you were praying to your priestesses and Luluah for the luck," Keyara said with contempt.

Within a second, Taris grabbed her arm, whipping her around to face him, his eyes ablaze.

"You really think I prayed for your death?! You think I would mock the gods and the fate they have given us, Luluah most of all?"

"Why would you not?"

His nostrils flared. "Do you pray for mine?"

She searched his face. "I pray that I win this rite."

"You didn't answer my question." His grip tightened on her arm. The contact sending scores of heat through her.

Keyara could only think of one thing to say at that moment, one word on her mind and looking back on the moment later, she wouldn't think too hard on why she said it.

"Yes."

His hold on her immediately loosened.

The warmth left her.

As did the fire in Taris' eyes.

Turning round, she strode closer to Fenn, wanting the calming company of the fae right now.

They all walked in silence for a while, letting the occasional scream in the distance fill the void.

"What's with you and with my sister?" Keyara asked Fenn, breaking the stillness.

He did not turn to face her, only the soft glow of her red light illuminating the back of his blonde head.

"What do you mean?"

"Well," she continued, "you've been following her around the castle like a stalker since we got here. Don't deny it, she told me everything. You also look at her like…" Keyara shook her head, looking for the right words. He spoke for her.

"Like she's the sun?"

"Yes"

"Because she is."

She shook her head in the dark. "But you don't even know her."

He did not reply.

Eventually, the tunnel began its end, and the claustrophobic roof that was pressing over their heads opened, tapering out into an enormous square arena.

The mountains framed their return, and along the sides of the monoliths the audience waited. Watching them emerge from one of the many tunnels that lined the arena, like hungry vultures ready for a meal.

"There's the finish line," Fenn pointed across the way, his fae eyesight revealing to him an end which others could not see.

The arena before them appeared empty-no obstacles, no lurking creatures.

At least, none that Keyara could see.

"Do we simply... walk across?" she asked, though no one answered.

Fenn knelt to the ground, brushing his fingers across the earth before tasting it. "No one's been here yet. We're the first."

Taris jerked his head sharply toward him. "Feel it out."

Fenn rose to his feet, letting his magic ripple across the land like a creeping mist. After a moment, he shook his head.

"Nothing. No magic, at least."

Taris clicked his tongue in impatience.

"Then let's move. I'm not waiting here like camel shit in the sand; the others will come soon enough."

Keyara took a few steps and looked over her shoulder at them both.

"Race you."

46

Jonn

The ship creaked and groaned with the rhythmic dance of the waves as his shackles clinked against the chains that held him. A fucking prisoner again. Though for what gods known reason, Jonn couldn't quite say.

'Precaution' were the words of the captain when he and Sy stepped foot aboard the ship. Jonn had never thought he would see those silver sails again until the two of them had organised his escape on Alboste.

Jonn had been shocked at Sy's initiative, his best friend having obtained a concealment spell from a Laeth in the crumbling town to be able to row, undetected, directly below Jonn's window in the castle.

He didn't ask how Sy had managed to get it; frankly, he didn't want to know.

Jonn clenched and relaxed his palms, wincing slightly at the friction burns in his hands from the makeshift rope he had constructed with bed sheets to aid his escape from the castle's balcony.

Holding his nerve had been the hardest part of their escape. If they were to be caught, it would have been moments after leaving the city. But by some gods given miracle they weren't. Jonn had only looked back once, towards the open doors of Selsie's bedroom. He hoped she would find the note he had left for her on the bed and had prayed that she didn't do anything stupid and reckless.

The reunion between himself and his shipmates aboard *The Brendann,* hadn't been what Jonn expected. Jonn stared towards the door that held him captive inside the brig.

Captain Lane could be a fucking arsehole, but this was completely unnecessary even by his standards.

Sy had protested immediately.

"What for captain? Aint he been through enough shit? The man has been in a Laeth dungeon for months. Surely, he needs a nice warm bed and some cheering up. The bastard's bloody miserable at the best of times!"

The warning glare from Lane to Sy had promised punishment if he continued.

"Brig it is."

Jonn had stayed silent during the confrontation, letting Sy go against the captain as much as he wanted, knowing it would make no difference.

They navigated the dimly lit corridor leading to Jonn's new home for the foreseeable future. The scent of sweat and dampness hung heavy in the air.

His muscles protested the confinement, his mind angry at being chained once again.

"Sorry mate," Sy said, as he unlocked the heavy door.

This ship was brand new, the paint barely dry, but the stench of despair permeated the very essence of this place in the belly of the ship; even though it seemed like Jonn was the first poor fucker to be kept in it.

His friend carried on, trying to keep the tone light.

"Gone from one prison to another, how's your luck."

Jonn grunted in response.

Sy cocked his head. "I reckon he's put you in here cos' he's suspicious as to why you're still alive. Paranoid bastard."

Staring from the floor to the one stool kicked over in the corner of the room, Jonn didn't move.

"Syren got your tongue mate?"

"I'm fine."

Sy gave him a look Jonn had rarely seen, wordlessly calling him a liar.

"I'm gonna go speak to the old bastard and see if he'll let you out. I might be damned, but I've got the gods blessing on my side." With a mock salute he had left.

That must have been days ago, maybe even weeks. Jonn couldn't tell, there were no windows down here in the bowels of the beast. His pocket watch was lost to the sea on the day of the Laeth attack.

The day he had met her.

The measure of the passing of time was a growling belly and his piss filling up the mess bucket. He apologised to the young deck boy who came to empty it every few hours, thanking him for doing such a shitty job.

He had learned the boy, Hary, was eleven, born to a poor family in Noran's most destitute district. He was one of five siblings, his adoptive parents had told him; the only one without magic, he had admitted shamefully.

"Don't you ever be ashamed of who you are, boy. A man is not defined by his power or lack of it. It's what's in here." Jonn had pointed to his head, and heart. "That's what matters. That's it. Stay strong, be honourable, be honest."

The words of Derryn: strong, honourable and honest. The boy had nodded his head.

"Protect those who cannot protect themselves."

Hary had given a small nod before leaving Jonn alone once more.

Banging the shackles against the heavy steel bolts welded to the door, Jonn tried once again, using all his strength, to break them.

Nothing.

He sat down with a heavy thump on the stool and leaned his

head against the wall behind him, eyelids so heavy with exhaustion that he could have sworn there was a Derryinian moor giant atop them.

He hoped he didn't fall asleep to miss the Hary coming; he enjoyed their small conversations, as brief as they were.

The last time he had seen the boy, he had said something that had jolted Jonn out of his skin.

"She keeps asking for you."

"Who?" Jonn had asked him.

"The syren, Selsie, she keeps asking for you. Is she the one who captured you? I'm the only one who knows her name, she said to keep it a secret, but I guess now it's not a secret."

Hary's mouth dropped open.

"Oh no, I'm going to get cursed by a syren, I promised I wouldn't tell anyone her name!"

Jonn had grabbed his scrawny arm, too small in his large, calloused hands.

"Where is she?"

His head was spinning. There was no way Selsie was onboard, the gods wouldn't play like that.

Hary winced at his grip, but Jonn didn't let go.

"She's in the captain's quarters. He's kept her tied up in the net." The boy's face took on a sad hue. "It hurts her the net does. I know we are meant to hate Laeths but-"

One of Jonn's shipmates had then come to get the boy before he could finish.

That was yesterday, or maybe the day before, Jonn didn't know. It was longer than usual between mess bucket changes, he knew that much; the liquid nearly overflowing with a disgusting concoction of his piss and shit.

He was tormented by thoughts of Selsie, of what was happening to her if she was on the ship.

It was impossible, the boy must be confused. Maybe the captain had pertained a certain sort of lady on the way and kept her locked in his chambers, telling the child she was a syren to scare him off.

Lane had done it before.

The door creaked open, and Jonn sat up, calling out playfully, pushing thoughts of Selsie to the side for the time being.

"I thought you'd fallen overboard Hary."

To Jonn's surprise and contempt, it was Captain Lane who thudded through the doorway, bringing his stinking breath with him.

"Captain Lane," Jonn bowed his head slightly.

"Your time in the brig is at an end. Come Cayson, time to resume your post."

Doing as he was told, Jonn walked towards the door. All he wanted to do was get out of this fucking brig and see for himself if she was here.

Captain Lane led them up the many steep steps to the heart of the ship, towards the rest area for the crew within the ship.

They arrived at the sweeping stairwell that led to the captain's quarters, nestled within the stern of the ship.

Jonn could not help but stare at the closed door of the room, as if senses alone would confirm her presence.

He could have sworn he smelt her musky, milky scent.

"Captain is there something I need to be made aware of on this ship?"

He was not given an answer.

Captain Lane turned to him, holding up the key to his shackled wrists.

"Any trouble from you, Cayson, any hint of disobedience-" He put the keys in the lock, turning them slowly. "-and you will be Domhiann dinner, do you understand?"

Jonn didn't need any elaboration.

"Yes sir."

The old shit narrowed his eyes, huffed, and led them to his chambers.

Jonn rubbed at his sore wrists, never taking his eyes off that damned door.

"Now then Cayson." The door swung open. "Back to business." She wasn't here. Not now anyway. But she had been, recently by the strength of her scent, which was all over the place. What the fuck was she doing here.

"Sit." Captain pointed to the seat on the other side of his behemoth, white desk.

As Jonn looked around the room, a patch of blood – that from the streaks across the floor, had been hastily cleaned up – caught his eye.

There on the white planked floor, blood. Her blood, he determined, by the strength of her scent floating over from that direction.

The more he looked, Jonn could see that there were small droplets of it everywhere. On the white oak bedposts, on the many pieces of artwork that adorned the walls, all the way up to the twenty-foot-high ceiling.

Precious, priceless paintings that depicted scenes from kingdoms all over Myrantis, were now nearly all stained with a strange red rain.

Clenching his jaw and scratching at his beard, Jonn tried not to let his face betray any emotion he was feeling as he sat opposite the captain.

The effort to charade as his usual stoic self was harder than the performance he had given Selsie's bitch mother.

"What is our heading captain?"

The cunt didn't look up from his papers.

"Why are you alive Cayson?"

The question took Jonn by surprise.

"Captain?"

"You were captured by our enemy. A creature that should have killed you the moment you hit the water. You went to Cildraethe, a place on this planet no human has ever stepped foot in with full control of mind and lived to tell the tale. Not only that, but you also arrived back to us unharmed, as did that useless shit, Hedge. So, I ask again, why?"

Clearing his throat, Jonn refrained from shifting in his seat. Selsie's scent was distracting him, preventing him from coming up with an answer the captain would deem acceptable.

Honesty would have to prevail, after all, they were the words of his ancestors.

Though with some retractions.

Jonn leant forward, his elbows on his knees.

"Honestly, I don't know. They kept me in the dungeons, treated me... well."

Lane did not so much as blink.

"Then one day, they took me to Alboste, where I found Symon."

A scoff from the other side of the desk, silver adornments along the wood tinkling as the old git swatted the heavy wood.

"We came up with the plan of escape, and here I am."

"That's it?"

Jonn scrubbed at his neck.

"That's it. We will never get the answer as to why I wasn't killed. Maybe they wanted me for something, I don't know."

"And they just let you go?"

"I told you, I escaped. Surely Symon told you our plan when he made you wait for me off Laeth territory."

"He did."

"There you have it. You know as much as I."

Jonn stared into the grey eyes of the ugly face across the desk. He couldn't take it any longer.

"Where is she?"

A smile tugged at the corner of the captain's mouth.

"Who?"

His stare didn't falter away from the captain.

"The syren."

"How do you know she is here?"

He had to play this carefully.

"So there is a syren onboard?"

Jonn cringed at the sound of the captain grinding his teeth as the man averted his gaze to the floor to ceiling windows with an unobstructed view of the ocean behind the ship.

"We caught her. She was alone and did not even attempt to attack us. Not one sailor was lured to their death. She did not even sing one note of a song, not a hum, whistle, nothing."

"Is she alive?" Jonn dared ask the question he had been thinking about for hours. Avoiding the feeling it gave him to consider they might have killed her.

"For now. But I think I've had... *enough* of her." The captain stood up, walking towards the windows.

"Why did you keep her, why not just throw her back if she was no threat?"

"Because Cayson, she asked for *you.*" He didn't fail to miss the pointed way in which Lane spoke. "Please, do enlighten me Jonn, at how a Laeth is on a first-name basis with a man in my crew?"

Pure accusation and mistrust in the captain's eyes.

Forcing all the submission and innocence in his voice as he could, Jonn spoke.

"I was there for months, captain, sir. I had to talk to someone, or I would have gone mad."

It felt so unnatural to grovel to a shit stain of a man as Lane.

"Why did she come after you?"

Jonn shrugged his wide shoulders.

"I don't know. Laeths are not known for giving up who they think is theirs."

"And are you hers?"

Jonn did not stumble on his next words; with no need to put any falseness in them.

"No, I am not."

Captain Lane was silent for a moment, then smiled with his brown teeth on full display.

"Good, then I shall dispatch of her shortly."

His heart tripped over itself.

"Captain?" he queried, trying to mask his desperation.

"Since I no longer have any need for the creature, I shall put her out of her misery and send her back to their precious Alysee."

"Should we not show mercy to another, especially one whose own mercy is the reason I am here today?"

A sun-aged finger pointed to Jonn's face.

"If you are under syren song Cayson-"

Jonn interrupted him. "No sir I am not-"

Jonn let out a piece of information he prayed would maybe help.

"-Her syren song, the magic doesn't work."

The captain barked a laugh.

"I knew it."

Jonn could not help himself as he told him.

"She is also their heir, sir. Killing her would not end well."

Muttering curses under his breath, the captain took off his plumed hat. Jonn knew that as much as the man wanted her dead, he couldn't kill her. Not yet.

"Yes well, she can live for now. You are dismissed, Cayson."

47
Keyara

She heard their laughter behind her, thundering footsteps gaining ground as she bolted forward.

Each step echoed with the weight of the trial's climax; with each stride she was nearing the end of this particularly shitty day.

The day had been long, brutal, and her body was paying for it. With every step, her pounding feet sent wracks of pain through her body from the wound in her shoulder. The blood began blooming anew.

Running full speed wasn't an option. The Cray poison still lingered in her veins, her gait more of a jog than a run, but she powered on regardless.

To her left Fenn moved effortlessly, his strides graceful; almost as if he were gliding above the ground.

To her right, Taris moved like a bludhound in vampyre form; his strong legs, silent and relentless.

She knew both males could easily outrun her, but they were a team now. Part of her suspected they'd want to finish together – even without Jenney.

Suddenly, something whipped past her face, so fast it made her eyes sting.

"What the hell was that?" she shouted, instinctively slowing down.

"Arrows!" Fenn yelled, also pulling back.

The sky seemed to rain them, coming from every direction, too many and too fast to push forward.

"We need to move," Taris urged.

Keyara flashed him a deadpan grin, gesturing ahead with her open palm.

"After you."

He rolled his eyes, pointing past her.

"As much as *they* might enjoy your charming company, Keyara, I'd rather not stick around to find out."

From the corner of her eye, she spotted who he was referring to. Like bats emerging from a cave, the green team spilled out of the tunnel into the overcast light.

All four of them had survived.

Cinnamon swirled through the air as Fenn shattered the incoming arrows.

"Let's move!" he called to them, his voice sharp with urgency.

Keyara had to trust that his fae magic would keep their path clear, but they weren't moving as fast as she needed.

The damned poison still muddled her movements, making her slower and clumsier than usual.

From behind, shouts and manic laughter floated in the wind. Every arrow Fenn couldn't obliterate his magic deflected with a shimmer, keeping the deadly projectiles at bay.

His hands moved with fluid precision, the magic an effortless extension of his body.

Keyara found herself hoping that Jenney had made it through, wondering where in gods name she was.

There was no time for distraction, as right ahead, a low metal wall suddenly jutted up from the ground, barely knee-high.

When they reached it, the barrage of arrows finally ceased.

Taris stepped over it with ease, his long legs barely needing to lift.

Fenn followed, his movement just as smooth.

The vampyre extended a hand toward her to help her over.

She scowled, refusing the offer and making her own way across.

326

"What now?" Keyara panted, struggling to catch her breath. A quick glance over her shoulder told her the green team was closing in fast, gaining ground with every second.

One of them was even wielding a massive wooden pole, crudely fashioned from the maze walls, swinging it above his head.

"We carry on," Fenn answered simply.

They pressed forward, but after only a few hurried steps, large holes – each as wide as she was tall – suddenly opened in the walls on either side of them.

Taris's nostrils flared as he stared ahead. "Go."

"What-?" she began.

"Go, NOW," he barked.

Fenn sniffed the air. "Verzh oil."

Godsdamned shit.

That was all she needed to hear.

With no time for second thoughts, she pushed herself to run as fast as her poisoned, aching body would allow, gritting her teeth and screaming at her limbs to fucking *move*.

Just then, a torrent of slick, pitch oil poured from the holes, gushing towards them in a flood.

One of the jets sputtered, sending a wave of oil splashing in their direction.

It didn't land.

Instead, it slammed into an invisible, human-shaped barrier running alongside them on Fenn's side.

Her grey eyes reappeared first, then the rest of her. The oil clung to her form as her invisibility lifted.

"Jenney?!" Keyara shouted in disbelief, spotting her friend. Surprise was an understatement

She gave a quick wave as she ran, her movements awkward on the slick ground.

Keyara shifted closer to her, legs moving carefully, reaching out to steady the girl before she lost her footing entirely.

The girl was struggling, slipping on the treacherous surface.
Keyara hesitated, considering using her magic to burn away the
oil clinging to Jenney, but fear held her back.
Verzh oil – one of the most flammable substances in Myrantis,
prized as a heat source – could easily engulf them both in
flames if ignited.
A mere whiff of a damned candle would set it off.
Suddenly, Keyara felt a sharp sting on her exposed neck.
"Ouch!" she cried, swatting at the spot.
She heard Taris curse and slap at his face.
As she glanced behind them, she saw that the green team was
still advancing, but only three of them remained.
One was trailing behind, hobbling with an arrow lodged deep in
his leg, struggling to keep pace.
The flood of oil was on the heels of the green team, and Keyara
watched in horror as the man at the back was swallowed by a
wave of liquid night.
His scream barely reached her ears before he disappeared.
"We need to go quicker!" she gasped, realising it was her own
lagging steps that were holding them back. "Jenney, hurry up.
Don't slow yourself for me idiot" Keyara shoved the girl
forward, trying to spur her on.
Between breaths, Jenney smiled.
"I'd never leave you behind, we're a team and we finish as one."
Another sharp sting bit into Keyara's skin.
"Fucking hell!" she cursed through gritted teeth whilst slapping
at her jaw.
The ground beneath her feet launched steeply upwards, forcing
them to push even harder.
As the hill rose, she could finally make out the spectators, their
voices growing louder as she neared the top.
Fenn, Taris and Jenney were still beside her as the crest of the
hill crept into sight.
Thank the gods she thought, as the ground eventually levelled

off, her wounded shoulder still screaming at her to slow down. Once again, she glanced at Jenney to her left who met her gaze with a grin.

"Almost there!" she panted, pointing toward a distant finish line. A large gate, much like the entrance to the maze, towering ahead of them, daring them to finish.

"Let's go!" Jenney chuckled breathlessly, her words full of hope.

But before anyone could respond, Jenney was suddenly yanked off her feet, thrown through the air with a startled cry before tumbling towards the ground.

Keyara barely had time to process what happened, but Fenn reacted instantly, his magic slowing Jenney's fall just enough for him to catch her.

It was the man from the green team; the one wielding the wooden pole.

Now, up close, Keyara could see it wasn't a simple pole at all. It was a jagged, makeshift stake, crudely fashioned from the walls of the maze and sharp enough to do serious damage.

The stake had flown under Jenney's feet, knocking her off balance.

Keyara's blood boiled at the cowardice. The piece of shit had used his magic from afar to target the weakest among them.

She wanted to tear him apart herself, but as she drew closer, she saw Taris had beaten her to it.

The vampyre's teeth were bared, ready to rip into the man from the green team, who was clearly tougher than he looked.

His stocky, short build gave away his Deryn origins, and if Keyara knew anything about those people, they were tough and extremely strong.

Another sting bit into her, harsher and more spiteful than the ones before.

She realised, with growing horror, that they weren't bites at all – they were *sparks*.

Hundreds of tiny, searing specks of fire singed her skin, particularly her face and hands.

The thick leather she wore shielded most of her body, but the exposed areas were under constant assault.

It took away her attention for no longer than a few seconds, but that left enough time for her to be tackled from the side, the force of it knocking the wind out of her and sending her sprawling in the dust.

Her mind screamed at her to focus, to fight back, but the sharp, relentless pain from the sparks clouded her concentration.

Rolling in the dust on the floor, Keyara screamed at herself: *Fucking get up.*

She tried to move, but she was pinned down.

"Get the fuck off me!" Keyara growled, trying to summon her magic. The heat was there, buried beneath the pain, but she couldn't pull enough of it to the surface. The man pinning her down wasn't giving her a chance to regain control.

His face came into view; a sickly, dead-looking complexion with cold, pale green eyes that drooped slightly at the corners. It was an ugly thing to look at.

Godsdamned dead looking.

The sharp stench of sweat and rot hit her as his lank ginger hair fell into her face, and she finally recognized him.

He was a nobody she'd seen around, his face marred by a birthmark across his nose.

His eyes, rimmed red, glowed with a cruel intensity. Above his head, a glowing purple light shimmered – he wasn't part of the green team.

"You look like shit."

There was no reaction to her insult, the man just pressed harder on Keyara's shoulders, pushing into her wound.

Clenching her jaw against the pain, she refused to scream despite the agony.

They struggled in the dirt for a while, as sparks bit into her relentlessly, his magic stinging her skin.

But Keyara wasn't about to let him have the upper hand any longer.

"Eurgh, enough!" she shouted, summoning every ounce of heat within her. The force of it seared him thoroughly, and he rolled off her in an instant.

Not quick enough though.

Keyara heard him yelp in pain. She had scalded his hands, knees and forearms, anywhere his body made contact with her own.

She was on her feet in an instant, taking in the chaos that ran around her.

Jenney was nowhere to be seen.

Fenn was fending off two men, circling him like predators.

Taris was in the middle of a brutal fistfight, his punches so powerful that they cracked the ground beneath him.

Movement from her attacker caught her eye, and this time she wasn't about to be taken by surprise.

No fucking way.

What would Berran do.

Keyara made a split-second decision, like a spark from the prick's magic. Recalling advice from Berran's warriors, she remembered their words.

Fight dirty.

Fine. She could fight dirty.

She sprinted toward Fenn and his two attackers, skidding to a halt just before crashing into one of the men.

It was the one with water magic; she had seen him in action during the trial. His magic had left patches of mud in the pebbly soil, and Keyara immediately scooped up handfuls, smearing it over her hands and face.

It nearly blinded her but godsdamned it, if she needed to get dirty to fight dirty, she would.

With her vision half-obscured, she unsheathed her daggers and squared off against the man with the purple glow above his head.

She snarled, daring him to come closer.

"Come on, ugly,"

He hesitated, clearly wary of her newfound ferocity.

Keyara wasn't going to wait for him to strike first.

With a sudden burst of speed, she lunged forward, her mud-slicked hands gripping her daggers tightly as she prepared to fight dirty-just like Berran taught her.

48

Jonn

On deck, the sun forced Jonn to put a hand up to shield his eyes.

The salty sea air filled his dusty lungs, the spray from the ocean refreshing his grimy face.

His mind was awash with the conversation down below.

Confused as to whether the captain was going to kill Selsie or let her go.

"Jonn boy!" Sy bounded over to him, clapping him on the back.

"Sorry I never came back down below mate. I had other shit I needed to take care of. Sent the kid down to keep you company instead."

Jonn had no time for Symon's small talk.

"What have they done with her".

"Jonn-"

"Take me to her, now."

Sy let out a breath, shaking his head.

"Alright."

As they passed his crew, most smiled, looking genuinely pleased to see his return. A few, however, regarded him like Valhirian bludhounds, with suspicion and aggression.

"What's happened Sy?" Their steps were in tandem, whilst Sy led them to the infants' quarters, a trail of blood leading the way.

His friend took out a hefty bunch of keys from his back pocket.

"A few men on this ship ain't who I thought they were."

The door quietly creaked open. There on the floor in front of them, a net reeking of acid was tied around the feet and hands of a naked syren. A few empty vials lay scattered around her bloody frame.

She looked up at him, her emerald eyes – usually so vivid and as full of life as the sea – were wild and frantic as they met his.

The sunlight through the window and the small, empty bassinets were at complete odds with the female that currently occupied the room.

"I'll wait out here for ya," Symon said, shutting the door behind him.

The air hummed with an unspoken tension, a melody of uncharted territories.

"Selsie," Jonn rasped, his voice carrying the weight of the words left unspoken between them.

She tried to stand, an ethereal figure in the light, her gaze unwavering.

"Why are you here?" Jonn questioned, the words hanging between them like an unanswered sea breeze.

He daren't come any closer to her right now.

Selsie's lips parted. "You are mine, Jonn." She was pure Laeth standing before him now.

"Selsie-"

She staggered forward, the net audibly sizzling against her burnt skin as she moved.

"You ran away," she whispered, the strength behind them loud.

"I escaped," he corrected her.

"You left me."

Jonn raised a finger.

"I think you'll find you left me."

After he spoke the words and her face softened just a fraction, only then he realised he was not talking about his escape.

Memories of the balcony flashed behind his eyes.

Standing still as pain lanced across her bruised features, she spoke quietly.

"I came to warn you. My mother knows the song didn't work. Now, she will hunt you down, in the hopes of bringing you back to the city. Fulfilling her promise of killing us if I didn't perform the magic."

"Fuck," was all Jonn managed to say as he looked over at her again.

He couldn't bear it, her body was coated in old and new burn marks; half healed, half still raw. What the fuck was that net coated in? He had never come across such a thing.

"Why are you telling me this?" Jonn continued.

A flicker of vulnerability passed through Selsie's eyes, a brief storm in the calm sea.

"I save what is mine. I do not beg for scraps of mercy from a mother who would slaughter us both without a second thought."

He let out a breath as he took a step towards her, his brow furrowed in concern

"When will they kill me?" she asked, with something akin to sadness in her eyes.

He looked for the right words to say.

"I have convinced the captain not to, by some gods grace. You could say we are even now."

He gave her a small smile, but before he could press further, Selsie stood firm with her teeth bared together.

"Even?! Look at me Jonn. Is this even? Is this how you were treated in my care?"

Jonn could have sworn the ocean waves became higher as she spoke.

"I came to find you myself, warn you of my mother's intentions and keep you by my side, as you are still mine, my prisoner," Selsie continued.

He halted his path towards her. Despite his desperation to not see Selsie like this, he nearly laughed at her.

She was on his ship, far from her Kingdom and her syrens, wrapped in a net that was eating her alive, yet she still had the audacity, the confidence, to call him hers.

He couldn't hide the wicked grin from showing.

"I think you will find, Selsie-" He stood as close to her as he could without their skin touching. "You are mine now."

"No."

Jonn had anticipated that answer from his captain. He knew the request to remove the net from Selsie – to let her body heal from whatever poison the net was laced with – would be denied, but he asked anyway.

"Are we as cruel as those we despise for their own inhumanity, captain?"

Captain Lane's watery eyes never looked up from his desk as Jonn spoke.

"The moment that net is taken off her, she would kill the man unlucky enough tasked with the job. If we take it off, she will dive straight back into the sea and get the rest of them to be here by morning. Do you think I'm an idiot, Jonn?"

"No disrespect captain, but I think she's had plenty of chances to kill a few of us already."

"Then why hasn't she?"

Jonn sighed. He knew why, but he didn't think the captain would like the true answer, so he lied.

"It could be that the net is affecting her magic, so she doesn't want to take such a chance. But fuck, it's going to burn right through her if we keep her wrapped up in it much longer."

"Then it's a good thing she's got a tail to compensate for any loss of limb."

Jonn clenched both fists at his sides, frustration marking his heavy brow.

"Captain, what are you planning to do with her?"

"That is none of your concern, Cayson."

Jonn's expression hardened.

"As first mate, captain, I would argue it is my concern."

The captain stood up so violently, Jonn thought the man might keel over from the effort.

"As first mate, your concern is whatever I tell you it is. Is that clear?"

Specks of reeking spittle landed on Jonns face, and it took every ounce of his will not to punch the old shit square in the jaw.

"Crystal," Jonn said with a smile.

"Good. Then we are done here, ready the crew to sail home." Jonn nodded his head, back to the ever-obedient first mate.

"Yes, captain. But one more thing-" Jonn made his way to the door. "If you plan on keeping the syren alive for the next few hours, she will need more Mycillium. Otherwise, you will have a dead Laeth heir aboard your ship."

49

Jonn

Jonn knocked on the heavily bolted door, though he didn't need to. The large bundle of keys in his hands gave him access to wherever he wanted aboard the ship, except the captain's quarters.

"Selsie," he called out into the dark room as the hinges groaned, announcing his entry.

Unlike his stay in the depths of the ship, there were no candles to light the dank darkness of the brig.

He set down the candle in his grip and like the flame, his heart sputtered slightly as it saw her in the flickering light.

Selsie's long brown curls were matted with both old and fresh blood, her golden iridescent skin now dull; far too lifeless for Jonn's comfort.

The sight of her in this state was almost unbearable, but he made himself look. He was the reason she was like this, and he owed it to her to face the truth, no matter how much it fucking tore at him.

Avoiding it would be nothing short of cowardice.

"I brought you this." He set the measly plate of food beside her, watching her jade eyes flicker from him to the plate.

"I'm not hungry," she finally whispered, her voice barely louder than the summer wind drifting through Oridae.

Jonn sighed. "Eat it anyway."

Silence settled between them for a few moments.

"Jonn, I need more Mycillium."

He scrubbed a hand over his jaw. "I know. I'll get it to you as soon as I can."

She gave a faint, almost imperceptible nod.

He sat down gently against the wall nearest the door, giving her some space. She needed it, but so did he if he were honest. Getting too close to her would test every bit of his control – he'd likely rip the fucking net off her himself, and that would be no good to anyone.

He was just a man, and if the net was doing this much damage to a syren, he didn't want to even think about what it would do to his bare hands.

How the crew shifted it without dissolving into a pile of flesh and bones on the floor, he didn't know.

Selsie glanced at him. "Where are we going?"

Jonn saw no threat in telling her the truth. "We're heading home."

Selsie's shock was clear on her delicate features. "Oblitus?"

"Yeah," he said, meeting her gaze. "And you're coming with us."

Defiance flickered across her face, though something else was concealed beneath it.

"What if I refuse to come with you, what if I say no?"

Jonn let out a dry, humourless laugh, shocked at her naivety.

"They don't really give a fuck what you want, Selsie. I'm having a hard time just convincing the captain to keep you alive right now."

Those ethereal syren eyes narrowed, sharp and accusing.

"They don't care, or you?"

He opened his mouth to protest, but the door swung open before he could reply.

"I've got refreshments for our guest," Symon announced as he strolled in, two vials in hand.

Sy passed the vials to Jonn.

"Fresh from Alboste. Well, I say fresh, I got them when we all had our lovely respite there. Thought they might come in handy

one day, it turns out I was right," he continued.
Mycillium.
His friend crossed his arms, his expression tight.
"You don't even want to know what I had to give the female in the market in exchange for these."
Jonn clapped his friend on the back. "Thanks."
"Once the captain ran out of his stash, I figured he wouldn't bother getting more."
Jonn voiced a question that had been gnawing at him for days. "Why did he have vials of it to begin with?"
Sy shrugged, casual but uneasy. "Who knows? Maybe he always planned on catching one to-"
Jonn raised his hand, cutting him off with a warning glare. "Thanks again, Sy."
"No problem, mate, I'll be waiting above for ya."
With that, his friend slipped out of the brig, leaving them alone once more.
From her place on the ground, Selsie had been watching them with the wary gaze of a wounded predator.
"Is it enough?" Jonn asked her, his voice low. "For the next few days at least?"
"Yes," she replied, her voice like the lulling whisper of waves against the shore.
He brought the precious liquid over to her, knowing she could barely move beneath the net and didn't want to force her to move any more than necessary. Taking the clinking vials out of his hands, Selsie grimaced.
"I'm sorry," he muttered, the only words that came to him.
"For what?"
He paused, letting the silence linger.
"For everything."
But the apology felt hollow. It wasn't enough. The sight of her in agony gnawed at him, and
Jonn couldn't stand it any longer.

Gods be damned of the consequences. Damn Captain Lane to Hell.

"Fuck it, I'm getting you out," he said, voice firm.

Selsie didn't respond as he pulled out his pocketknife. For a split second, he hesitated, picturing the fallout if the captain discovered what he was doing. But then he shoved the thought away with a firm push, focusing solely on the female in front of him.

Wincing in anticipation, he gripped the net with his calloused hands, expecting them to melt away down to his bare bones. There was nothing.

Maybe it was so fast-acting that it had dissolved through his nerves already. He would have to work quickly. But still, nothing as the blade cut through the net's weave, the threads falling apart in his hand. Though as soon as he made the first cut, the net hissed and tightened, constricting itself around Selsie with a vicious snap.

Panic flared in Jonn's chest. *Shit, what was happening?*

Selsie began to pant, her legs contorting as the pain overtook her. Her cries grew louder, her body writhing under the tightening net. Jonn's mind raced, torn between continuing to cut or stopping.

He had to act fast.

Without a word, he jumped up, eyes locking onto a bucket by the wall. Water – likely fresh – meant for her to drink.

It was the best chance he had to ease the burning, acidic pain that was consuming her. He grabbed it, praying to the gods – even Alysee – that it wasn't seawater.

Without a second thought, Jonn tipped the bucket over Selsie's shredded legs, hoping the cool water would bring her some relief or dilute the acid-enough to endure while he worked to free her from the cursed net.

Her eyes went wide, terror flooding her gaze.

He was wrong.

The water wasn't fresh. It was seawater, taken straight from the Maolin-a bucket meant for mopping, not drinking.

A syren's tail was their lifeline, the most sacred part of their body, exquisitely sensitive. To harm it was an unforgivable offence, and in that moment, Jonn realized he had done exactly that.

He had betrayed her in the worst possible way.

Fuck.

"Gods, no. Shit, Selsie, I'm so sorry. I didn't know," Jonn cursed under his breath, yanking off his shirt in seconds in a frantic attempt to mop up the seawater. But it was too late.

He'd seen her transform only once before on Cildraethe, during one of their walks. He was still afraid of her then, in those early weeks.

She had told him how long it had been since she last felt the ocean, and how tired she was of relying on Mycillium. He remembered the awe he had felt watching her shift from human to syren, the way the setting sun lit up her golden tail like it was aflame.

This time, it was a horror. The moment her legs disappeared, and her tail emerged, Selsie began to scream. An ear piercing, gut churning scream that tore through the brig.

Her beautiful face twisted in agony as she clawed at the net, burning her hands in her desperation to free herself.

"Selsie, stop!" Jonn knelt beside her, grabbing her hands. Her tail thrashed wildly under the candlelight, her screams unrelenting. He had to stop this, Jonn had to end this suffering. He cupped her face in his hands, forcing her to meet his gaze.

"Selsie, listen. Sh sh, I know it hurts but listen, I'm going to get this off, stop moving, please!"

Her eyes, wild and unfocused, met his. But she seemed distant, not there, not really. The soul within was elsewhere.

"Please, Selsie listen to me. I can't undo the net if you keep thrashing around. I might cut you. Stay still, please."

Her screams began to quiet, replaced by whimpers and moans as she struggled to remain still.

Jonn worked with swift, careful motions, cutting away at the threads while his eyes took in every burn and wound on her tail, storing the grim details for later.

Noting to never let himself become as cruel as the men who made this net. He would rather be ripped apart by bludhounds than be a part of something as grotesque as this.

As he freed more of her from the net, she made less and less noise, until the room was engulfed in an eerie silence.

He threw the last remnants of the net on the ground.

"It's done, Selsie. It's over". But she was unconscious, gone like a light. Jonn noticed her legs had finally reappeared, red raw and covered in open wounds.

He remained in the brig for what felt like ten minutes, watching her slow, rhythmic breathing, her chest rise and fall. Only when he was certain she was stable and her wounds were beginning to heal and knit together before his very eyes, did he finally leave to find his best friend.

"That net is godsdamned barbaric, Sy," Jonn spat, tossing a shredded piece onto the floor where it landed at Symon's feet. "Where did he get it?"

Symon shrugged, taking a swig from a bottle as he leaned against Jonn's map-strewn desk.

"Fuck knows, he never mentioned it. Gives me the shivers, though, doesn't it you?"

"What do you mean?"

Symon took another swig, his expression darkening. "It's got a feel to it, like it's evil or somethin'. I don't like it."

Sy was right, Jonn thought. It exuded an aura of wrongness, as though whatever was woven into its very fibres was not meant to be there.

He also knew he should harbour no sympathy for Selsie. She

was one of the creatures that quite possibly caused his sister's death. But godsdamned it, despite his rational thoughts, Jonn couldn't bring himself to be entirely cold-blooded.

"Hm," Jonn agreed. "It didn't burn me, only her. Whatever shit is woven into that netting only works against…them"

Sy's eyebrows knitted together as he frowned.

"Strange. Where do *you* reckon the captain got it"

Dark curls dusted against his shoulders as Jonn shook his head.

"I've never read, or heard, anything about a net like it. Although it wouldn't surprise me if the Valhirians came up with it, you know what dark shit they're capable of."

"We aint been near Valhir in months Jonn," Sy countered. "And if the captain had that net since then, he would've used it during the Laeth attack in the first place."

Jonn crossed his arms, his tone gruff.

"The damned coward hid during the attack, do you remember?"

"Yeah, I remember. The rest of the crew does, too."

Jonn's expression softened as he recalled the young boy.

"Gods, even young Hary stayed on deck." He thought of the boy's terrified face, tears streaming as he watched helplessly while the adults around him perished. "Where is the boy, anyway? I haven't seen him."

The bottle at Sy's lips lowered midway through his swig, and the look on his face told Jonn everything he needed to know.

"What's he done with him?"

"Jonn-"

A calm, simmering rage rose from Jonn's stomach. "What the fuck has he done with the boy?"

His friend sighed heavily before speaking. "Captain found a conch shell in the boy's bed after a random crew search when you were in the brig. He claimed the boy was a traitor for not alerting them to Selsie's presence on the ship."

"Go on."

"Jonn, you don't wanna know mate. What good would it do?

The boy's dead. He's gone."

He never pulled rank on Sy, but now Jonn had no choice, he needed to know.

"Tell me what that cunt did, Symon. I order you to tell me."

There was a moment's hesitation, as if Symon were weighing the consequences of his next words. He must have decided he could live with the outcome.

"He had him whipped, down to the bone, before throwing him overboard. I'm sorry, mate."

A chilling calm settled into Jonn's veins, like the doldrums in the eastern sea.

"And you didn't stop him?"

"I wasn't there."

"Then where the fuck were you, Symon?"

The two men had never clashed before, not even as children. But now, it seemed, there was a first time for everything

"I was protecting the godsdamned syren!" Symon's voice was sharp, edged with frustration.

"You can't be so naïve as to think the crew would leave her alone out of the goodness of their hearts. Who do you think has been watching her all this time while you've been down below, eh?"

Shit. He had never considered that. Jonn knew what men could be like, but he hadn't expected it from his own crew, *his* men, people he shared a ship and a life with.

"You've been there the whole time?"

A fleeting shadow of guilt crossed Symon's face.

"No, I had to leave to eat, to shit, to sleep. But I left behind those I knew I could trust."

Jonn rubbed his neck, the weight of the situation sinking in.

"Fuck."

"It's been rough, Jonn. The captain's always been a miserable sod, but since the attack, he's changed."

Without hesitation, Jonn made a decision that would alter

everything-a decision he had been contemplating for some time and that he knew his friend had been anticipating ever since Jonn stepped back onto those white planks.

Symon's piercing blue eyes glinted with understanding.

"I'll tell the lads."

50
Keyara

Her body screamed for relief. She had no idea how long the fight had been dragging on, but the endless flurry of sparks from that ungodly-looking prick kept her on edge.

The mud covering her hands and face had helped reduce the biting sting from his magic, but her body was reaching its damned limit.

Every twist and turn, her shoulder throbbed, a sharp pain shooting through her with every motion, while the Cray poison continued its assault on her system.

She gritted her teeth, trying to summon more heat, more power, but fuck, her energy reserves were nearly depleted.

Each time she swung her blades, the sparks from the man's magic deflected them, forcing her attacks wide or downwards; in every direction she didn't want them to go.

His expression remained passive, not even a hint of exertion on his face.

Who the fuck is this man, she wondered briefly.

Not a single drop of sweat marred his sickly pale skin.

She kept urging her power to do something useful, but it was crying for her to rest.

Her mind flickered to Berran once more.

Would he be proud of this?

Probably not.

Reothadhs valued strength and victory.

Right now, victory seemed fucking impossible.

But would he be proud that she was still standing, even as her body threatened to collapse?

She hoped so, but there wasn't time for those thoughts.

She had to survive this.

There had to be a way to turn the tide.

Keyara feinted to the right, and as the man's sparks flared up to block her she twisted left, using the mud on her blade to blunt some of his magic's precision.

Her strike grazed his side, drawing a thin line of blood. It wasn't much, but it was something.

A mere hint of a smile pulled at her mouth.

A flame of hope ignited in her chest.

The victory was short-lived, however.

He stepped back, his eyes narrowed, and Keyara could feel the shift in the fight. He was done playing around.

Shit. She braced herself, knowing that if she didn't figure out a new strategy fast, this fight would be over – and not in her favour.

"Not tired yet handsome?" His expression did not change as she goaded him.

He lunged forward again. Keyara matched his force, but before the inevitable clash, a familiar screech echoed from below the hill.

All sounds of fighting stopped instantly.

Keyara's heart skipped a beat as she turned toward the sound, dashing to the crest of the hill.

The threat of her foe suddenly seemed insignificant compared to what was charging up toward them now.

"I thought we killed it," she muttered in disbelief.

"You did," came Fenn's voice from beside her. He was calm, his sharp thorns encasing the two men he had been fighting in a deadly, unmoving cage.

"Then how-?"

"Because I thought we could use the reinforcements," a deep voice cut in behind them.

348

Keyara turned, her eyes wide with shock as she spotted Taris standing there, a wild look in his eyes.

"I'll get it under control. Someone has to," Fenn said with a dangerous calm, his eyes locking onto Taris.

"You brought it back?" Keyara asked, her voice laced with disbelief.

Fenn's response was curt, cold. "Blood magic."

Of course, she realised.

Taris bit the Crays' ear off – he has its blood.

"Stop it, right now," Fenn said, stalking up to Taris with a predator's grace. "This is reckless, even for you."

Taris raised his hands, palms out. "I'll handle it."

Fenn clearly wasn't convinced. He walked away, his tone sharp.

"You make sure you do, or none of us are getting over that finish line. Crays are extremely adaptable. It will remember how it was killed last time."

The screeches grew louder, and Keyara instinctively backed away from the crest of the hill.

Her mind raced. She could hear the Cray's claws tearing through the ground, and she couldn't help but feel a rising sense of dread.

As she brushed past Taris, wiping the mud from her eyes, he smirked.

"Going for a new look, Keyara? Can't say it suits you."

She shot him a middle finger, too focused on the danger to engage.

Her attention was quickly drawn back to Purple, who was watching her intently, closing in on her with every step.

Not wanting to be caught off guard, she darted around the barbed cage Fenn had created.

Inside, the green team's man with water magic was already dead, a hefty thorn impaled through his neck. The other man was tangled in the barbs, his body contorted unnaturally as he tried to free himself.

Purple was closing in fast.

She sprinted toward the exit, but it wasn't enough. He slammed into her once again, sending her crashing to the ground.

Her daggers found purchase this time, the blade sinking into his flesh.

Blood poured from the wound in his leg, and Keyara couldn't help but let out a grim chuckle as the crimson river puddled onto the floor.

"With how you look," she sneered, "I don't think you'd have needed it anymore anyway."

He let out a guttural noise, a sound so similar to the Cray's screech that it made her skin crawl.

Keyara barely had time to notice that the Cray had fully ascended the hill and was ripping chunks of the wall apart with its massive claws.

Fenn's power was slowing the Crays' progress, the mountain and walls being rebuilt by green mist as fast as they were being pulled down.

Her brief distraction was all Purple needed. He seized the opportunity and slammed her to the ground once more, pinning her down.

"Fucking hell!" she shouted, having had enough of this game.

Slowly, the sparks were wearing away the mud on her face, leaving her skin exposed and vulnerable to his attack.

They danced viciously across her skin and the biting pain returned with full force.

Especially when a spark got into one of her eyes, instantly blinding.

Keyara cried out, reaching with both hands to her face. This gave the ugly prick the opportunity he was waiting for.

With his own hands coated in sparks to shield them from her heat, he wrapped them around her neck. Burning her with a sharp, relentless fire.

350

Clawing at his hands, Keyara struggled, but the sparks were tearing her flesh apart.

Panic surged through her veins as the fire at her throat grew unbearable.

It threatened to overwhelm her, but it didn't feel like her own panic.

It felt alien, like it wasn't her own beating heart and adrenaline coursing through her stomach

"Keyara, give me your hand!" Jenney's voice was suddenly in her ear.

Keyara couldn't speak to tell the girl that there was no way she would let her get near.

Jenney-like the others who were unfortunately caught in the arena's sick surprise- was covered in oil, she would go up like a summer wildfire.

She needed to urge Jenney to get away, to tell the girl to forget her and get across the fucking finish line

But the blackness was dancing in her vision, the creeping void of approaching death was overpowering, and she felt herself slipping, her throat burning as she tried to speak.

Not like this, she prayed.

Jenney's voice was soft but firm. "Give 'em hell."

All at once, Jenney jumped on top of him and touched the hands that were around Keyara's neck.

The sparks ignited the oil coating Jenney's small body.

Which in turn, had coated his body too.

The prick hadn't seen her there.

The man screamed, scrambling off Keyara, rolling desperately on the ground to extinguish the flames now consuming him, licking at his body.

But Jenney... Jenney was engulfed in fire, her invisible body turning into an inferno.

She made no sound, kept herself invisible, trying to hide her agony from the audience, but Keyara could see the horror unfolding.

"Help her!" Keyara screamed, her voice nothing more than a hoarse whisper, her throat felt as though it was lined with glass, torn apart from the sparks.

Fenn was too busy desperately trying to direct the Cray away from the crowd, his magic fighting a losing battle against the creature now tearing through the arena walls, climbing like a spider ready to devour the audience like flies in a web.

She ran towards Taris, who stood in a trance, staring at the Cray's ascent. When she reached him, Keyara pointed to where the girl was burning. She yanked on his leathers, desperate.

"Taris, help her!"

He didn't move.

"Taris, please!" she begged, pulling at his arms, trying to snap him out of it.

It hurt her pride to ask anything of this male, but she couldn't think about that. Fuck her pride.

When he still didn't respond, Keyara's frustration boiled over. She pulled out one of her daggers.

Snapping out of his trance, Taris held her by her arms, whirling her around and slamming Keyara's aching body against the crumbling wall behind them.

Boulders had tumbled down from up above, hiding them from view.

He leaned in close, his eyes locked on hers, amusement flickering in his expression.

"One day, you might actually have the balls to use those daggers for their real purpose."

Keyara looked up at him, his burgundy eyes staring at the dagger that was pointing at his side. "Get. Off. Me."

He didn't release her, his eyes narrowing.

"We need to cross that finish line. I can't control the Cray for much longer."

"I'm not leaving her," Keyara hissed through gritted teeth,

struggling in his grip.

Taris leaned in closer, his face inches from hers.

"Do you fear me, Keyara?"

She flinched as he leant into her face, close enough that Keyara could count every scar on his finely chiselled face.

"Not in the slightest," she bit back, her voice not as forceful as she would have liked.

The screams of Jenney dying in the flames echoed in the background. Taris' indifference filled Keyara with rage.

"I can't just let her die!" Tears were threatening her eyes, but she couldn't let Taris see her cry.

"The girl was an idiot, just a kid. She never would have won anyway. At least it will be a quick death." The screams from the other end of the arena said otherwise. "More or less," Taris continued.

Keyara couldn't bear to listen to it anymore.

Using every ounce of strength she had left, she summoned her magic, heating her skin to the point of burning where his hands touched her.

He let go of her arms slightly, just a fraction of a second but it gave her enough time to do what she needed to.

With a swift, practised motion, she slashed upward with her dagger and swept his legs out from under him.

Taris hit the dusty ground hard, and Keyara stood over him, dagger in hand.

Keyara wished she could have the look on Taris's face in that moment painted, just so she could look at it and laugh whenever she felt down.

She wished that a small snapshot of time could be put on paper for everyone to see.

His expression shifted from shock to a twisted smile as he glanced at his severed hand lying in the dirt, whilst licking something from his thumb

"Guess my balls finally dropped," she spat, backing away as his blood pooled on the ground.

His focus was completely on her. She looked down at her leathers where her blood was now mixed with his, a large thumbprint scored through it.

The prick started laughing. Laughing like this was the most joyous moment in his life.

In the distance, Fenn's voice called her name, but she could barely hear it over the blood rushing in her ears.

Purple was still alive, standing over Jenney's lifeless body.

A hot rage filled her.

Keyara was empty, fully spent, but the rage would be enough to kill the man hovering like a vulture over the dead girl.

Before she could make her move, strong arms wrapped around her waist, lifting her off the ground, her feet flying through the air.

Fenn.

"Let me go! I can still get him!" Keyara struggled against his grip, desperate to stay and fight.

"No, we need to go now," Fenn replied.

"Fenn, godsdamned it put me down!" she demanded as she struggled against the hold the fae had on her.

But her energy was spent, her body too weak to keep resisting.

"Sorry, Keyara, it has to be this way," Fenn said softly as the wind rushed past her ears. "Your sister would never forgive me if I didn't get you across that line."

With her body aching and her spirit burning with anger, Keyara could only watch as they crossed the finish line, leaving behind Jenney, the maze and the laughing vampyre alone in the dust.

His deep laughter followed them as they flew through the exit.

51

Berran

Berran sat quietly, watching the flickering candlelight cast shadows as it danced across the worn wooden table between them. The warmth of the Shadowfern tavern, with its low murmur of conversations and clinking of tankards, wrapped around them both like a familiar embrace.

Yet, despite the comforting atmosphere, there was a heaviness in the air, a weight that neither the fire nor the ale could lift. He silently watched as across from him, Keyara mindlessly ran a finger over the top of her glass, her eyes distant and unfocused. Her thoughts were clearly elsewhere.

Berran could see the shadow of yesterday's trial still hanging over her like a dark shadow. The grief and guilt were etched into her expression; subtle but unmistakable. He knew that look all too well. It was the same one he'd seen in the mirror after each of his own losses, the burden of a friend's death etched into the lines of one's face, memory and heart forever.

Jenney. The young girl who had sacrificed herself in the flames; invisible and unseen to most, but a hero, nonetheless. Brave and selfless beyond her years, she had chosen to give her life to save Keyara in the midst of chaos. Berran felt a pang of sorrow as he thought of her.

She hadn't been a Reothadh, not one of his kind, but in his heart, she had earned a place of honour.

"When I return to Silvanh, I'll ensure she is on the Wall of Tyrh. I'll do it myself."

Dark chocolate hair lifted.

"That wall is reserved for your own kind, for your warriors and

Kings."

Berran leaned forward.

"The wall is reserved for the bravest of souls, a place where the names of those who have given everything are remembered for all time. Jenney deserves to be there, syren or not."

The smash of a glass behind them took her attention from his words momentarily.

"You did what you could, Keyara," Berran said gently, breaking the silence that followed. His voice was low, a steady anchor in the storm of emotions he knew she was battling.

"Jenney made a choice. An... unusual choice, but a brave one. We can't change that."

Keyara nodded slightly, though her gaze didn't leave the table. Her fingers traced absentminded patterns on the worn wood.

"I didn't do anything," she murmured, her voice barely audible over the noise of the tavern. "I left her... like a fucking coward."

He felt the sting of her words but knew there was nothing he could say to lift the guilt that gnawed at her. Silence settled between them again, heavier this time. He had been through his share of loss, and damned it, he understood that no words could heal the kind of wound Keyara was suffering from. Time would have to do that on its own.

Running a hand through his hair, he took a deep breath, deciding that shifting the conversation might help, even if only for a moment.

"The last trial is tomorrow," he said, his clear eyes locking with hers, trying to pull her back from the depths of her grief. "A fight to the death was the tradition once, but things have changed, evolved. We're not as barbaric as we once were."

Keyara's gaze sharpened; the weariness momentarily replaced by a glint of something else. "Aren't we?"

A smattering of raindrops pattered over their table as a young, fresh-faced teenager ran past their table, hot on the tails of a girl his age, a palm-sized cloud rising from his hands.

Berran leaned back in his chair, fingers tapping a steady rhythm on the edge of the table, deep in thought.

"Lord and Lady Trewith have always been set in their ways, ancient traditions are followed and honoured. It wouldn't surprise me if they still sold their firstborn sons to be the broodmare for the Falkons," he mused, his voice calm. "But, in the instance of the Heir's Rite, it's not their decision to make. If the King has changed the rules about who can enter these trials, maybe he's reconsidered other traditions as well."

Keyara's gaze flicked toward him, though the light in her eyes hadn't returned.

"Doesn't mean it won't still feel like a death sentence," she muttered bitterly. "There are only three of us left. Me, Fenn and Duncann."

She said the last name with clear distaste, her fingers curling slightly around her glass.

Duncann. The human who wielded deadly sparks with cold precision.

Not only was the human wretched to look at, but he also had a reek of acid that clung to him like decay.

The memory of the maze trial was still fresh. Berran had sat with Aura, holding her hand tightly as she watched her sister fight for her life below. He'd felt Aura's fear and panic, raw and palpable, as Duncann had wrapped his crackling hands around Keyara's throat, completely indifferent to the chaos around him. Not even the monstrous creature climbing towards the audience had drawn his attention away from his prey.

Berran could still hear the audience's cries, the panic that swept through the stands as the Cray had scaled the walls. Mileya laughing at the chaos while weak bursts of human magic shot randomly into the sky. Yet, through it all, Duncann hadn't flinched. His focus had been on one thing: Keyara.

Time and time again he had told Aura that her sister would be

fine, that Keyara could handle herself. But with every moment that passed, every time the sparks flared dangerously close to Keyara's vulnerable skin, Berran had felt the gnawing doubt creeping in. He'd trained her, prepared her for this, but watching the trial unfold had tested every ounce of his composure. There was always that small, unspoken fear that whispered at the back of his mind: *What if it wasn't enough? What if he was about to watch her die?*
Keyara's voice cut through his thoughts, dragging him back to the present.
"Duncann doesn't give a shit about the rules. He just wants to win, no matter who gets in his way. Somehow, there will be a fight to the death."
Berran met her gaze, his eyes hardening with resolve.
"Then you'll have to make sure he doesn't get that chance. This final trial... it's not just about strength. It's about who's willing to see it through to the end. You've come this far, Keyara. Don't let someone like Duncann take that from you."
She gave a slight nod, her eyes betraying a flicker of gratitude. Despite the overwhelming odds, there was still a fire in her, a steely strength that Berran had always admired.
"Though, you will still need to be wary of the others of course."
Keyara's gaze remained fixed on her glass.
"Fenn won't fight against me."
His eyebrows shot up, surprised by her certainty.
"You don't know him as well as you think," he said, resisting the urge to chuckle at her naivety.
"I know enough," she replied, her tone unyielding.
He almost laughed but held back.
"You're underestimating him, Keyara. Fenn's fae. His strength, his ruthlessness-it's beyond what you've seen. The fae have power unlike anything we've ever known. He may seem calm, but make no mistake, he's as dangerous as they come."
"Then why is he even bothering with these trials?" she asked,

frustration creeping into her voice. "I haven't even seen him use his wings."

Berran knew the answer but didn't feel it was his place to share. "It's not for me to say," he murmured. "But don't drop your guard. Everyone here has the same goal. They're not in this for friendship."

Keyara grunted, clearly still unconvinced, her thoughts already shifting.

"What will happen to Taris?" she asked in a quieter tone.

A sigh escaped him whilst his fingers ran through his snowy white hair, a flicker of discomfort crossing his features. The image of Keyara severing Taris's hand played vividly in his mind. He'd nearly fallen from his seat when she'd done it, while Mileya had clapped like a seal with amusement; even Aura had looked impressed, albeit slightly disgusted.

Taris hadn't passed the trial. He and the other survivors had been dragged from the arena to godsknew where.

"Taris is the Valhirian heir and I cannot recall another Rite like it," Berran explained, his voice low. "They won't harm him outright, I have no idea what they will do with him, what they even *can* do with the male. Send him home? The presence of strong competitors this close to the end could jeopardise the future heir. If it was my castle, I'd be putting him somewhere I can keep an eye on him."

"Like the dungeons," Keyara suggested, sipping her drink.

Berran chuckled as he gulped down a large mouthful of wyne, a small grin hiding behind his glass.

"Maybe."

She snorted, her mood lightening a fraction.

"We should be so lucky."

As their conversation continued, Berran's attention drifted to the other side of the tavern, where Mileya was surrounded by children.

Despite her usual coldness, her stern demeanour softened in

their presence, a rare glimpse of her vulnerability as she entertained them. She formed small glowing bulbs of bioluminescence in her palms, the purple and blue lights casting an ethereal glow. The children passed them around gently, as if they were the most precious gifts in the world.

Not unlike the way Domhiann's viewed any offspring from any species. Priceless treasures from their great sea serpent god Uktanah; to mistreat them in any way would be an utmost evil.

"Mileya has a way with children," Berran commented, hoping to lighten the mood.

Keyara glanced over.

"She does, strangely enough, for one of the coldest people I've ever met."

Berran gave a mock look of offense. "Should I take that as an insult?"

Keyara nudged him under the table, her lips twitching into the first real smile he'd seen from her in a while.

Their conversation drifted through the evening. Berran did his best to keep Keyara engaged, trying to restore some of the confidence she'd lost after the brutal events of the maze.

Her inner-self regained strength after a few drinks and a hearty meal. The quickness of her tongue and eye rolls earning a few looks from Mileya, but Berran could see the two slowly – *very* slowly – warming up to each other. Despite the lingering shadows of the trial, the night felt lighter; as if, for a brief moment, they could forget the weight of what was to come.

It was late, and the rain poured down in heavy sheets as Berran walked with Keyara and Mileya through the winding streets towards the castle. The steady rhythm of raindrops against the cobblestones filled the air, creating a peaceful backdrop to their walk.

"I hope Aura doesn't mind that I didn't go to the library with her tonight," Keyara said, pulling her cloak tighter as they passed under another bridge, the waterfall that guarded the castle roaring in the distance.

"She's with Cass," Mileya replied. "Aura will be fine."

"I know, but she has done so much for me. I feel awful for not joining her. I shouldn't have come with you tonight Berran."

With his soaked white hair clinging to his neck, Berran slung an arm around Keyara's shoulders, giving her a playful jostle. Her body hot enough to keep the rain from settling, a gentle steam drifted off her.

"Am I boring you, Keyara? Have you finally had enough of my company after all these years?"

She laughed, the sound cutting through the rain. "Yes, actually."

They trudged through the downpour, their clothes drenched through as they neared the castle gates.

By the time they stepped inside, anyone would've thought they'd tackled the waterfall itself and failed miserably. The warmth of the castle interior enveloped them, the sound of the rain muffled as they dripped across the polished stone floors.

At Keyara's door, Berran offered her a simple goodnight. Neither spoke of tomorrow's trial, both avoiding the weight of what the dawn would bring. His Reothadh nature believed it a bad omen if he wished her a final good luck. Not wanting to tempt fate, he gave her a brief nod, hoping she understood the sentiment behind his silence.

After she disappeared into her room, Berran headed to his own chamber. He unlocked the door with his key, then melted the thin layer of ice he had formed inside the mechanism; a precaution he always took to prevent any unwelcome guests from tampering with his space. As the lock clicked open, he let out a breath and stepped inside, shutting the door behind him. His deep blue jacket, sodden from the rain, hit the floor with a heavy thud, followed quickly by his matching pants.

He stripped down and collapsed onto the bed, lying on his back with one arm tucked behind his head. One knee bent; his foot flat on the steel-coloured sheets.

Sleep would elude him, tiredness as though it was a myth. Tomorrow was monumental, not just for Eira, but for all of Myrantis. Whoever won the trial would hold the future of the kingdom in their hands, shaping the alliances and rivalries for years to come.

He sent a silent prayer to Sedna, his own god, and to the many human ones, to watch over Keyara tomorrow and help her on her predestined path with minimal harm.

Closing his eyes, he searched for a sleep that would not find him. His thoughts continued to churn, unable to find the calm he sought.

So, he turned to the familiar routine that always helped when rest was beyond reach. Rolling his broad shoulders, he shifted to get comfortable, then slid his large hand down to grip himself, his length already warm and heavy in his palm.

The thickness increased in his palm as he worked his hand up and down. The faintest traces of ice magic danced across his skin, sending sharp tingles of cold mixed with pleasure along his body. He let out a low, quiet groan; the sensation heightening as he quickened his pace, his fingers tightening around himself, feeling his cock growing harder as he was getting closer to relief.

Images of the last female he slept with flooded his mind, but none of them held meaning beyond the moment. Her body beneath his, the way she'd writhed as he thrust into her sex - it was enough to fuel his desire, to push him toward the release he sought.

His breathing deepened as Berran grabbed the sheets with his spare hand whilst he came, a final moan escaping as his release spilled across his stomach, warmth spreading as his muscles relaxed.

Exhaustion finally crept in, pulling him closer to sleep as the moon dipped lower in the sky. Bringing with it the promise of an uncertain tomorrow.

52
Aura

Aura awoke to a gloomy day, the mountains outside their window shrouded in mist and clouds. The crisp air clung to everything, a reminder that the autumn season was here.
She sighed, pulling the blankets tighter around her, knowing that once autumn truly settled in, the cold would be relentless. And she dreaded it.
She turned to her sister, gently shaking her.
"Morning, it's time to get up, your Highness," she whispered with a soft smile.
Keyara groaned, pulling the blankets over her head. Aura had heard her tossing and turning all night, restless with anticipation for the final trial. If it were Aura facing such a thing, she would've been paralyzed by anxiety. The unknown would have eaten away at her until she was nothing left but a shivering stack of bones. But somehow her sister carried it all with grace; Aura didn't know how her sister coped with the pressure.
The dark heaviness in her head was now sharp and pressing. Each spike of anxiety was more pronounced than the last, twisting inside her stomach. The heavy cloud of dread loomed over her head, so thick she was sure others could see it.
Aura padded out of bed, her feet cold against the floor as she made her way toward the bathroom. But a knock at the door stopped her just before she reached it.
"Tell them I'm not ready yet," Keyara's muffled voice called from beneath the sheets.
Dressed only in a short nightgown, Aura hurriedly wrapped a

delicate pink robe around herself.

A guard stood there, expression impassive, as he handed her a sealed letter addressed to Keyara.

"Thank you," Aura muttered, closing the door quietly behind her. She stared at the letter, feeling its weight in her hand. She held it tentatively in her hands, knowing the details of the trial would be in there; she couldn't bear to face their future just yet. Not yet.

If it really was a fight to the death, Aura wasn't sure she could watch. Wasn't sure if she could stay one more moment in the castle where her sister may potentially die at the hands of a stranger. She bit the inside of her mouth, her fingers trembling slightly as she handed it to Keyara.

"It's for you," she said, her voice quieter now.

Dark hair emerged from under the sheets as Keyara sat up slowly, and her moon-white arm reached out for the letter. She didn't open it right away, instead staring at the seal for a moment before breaking it with a flick of her thumb.

Aura perched on the edge of the bed, watching her sister closely as she read, her nerves threatening to suffocate her. The minutes ticked by in silence, Keyara's expression unreadable as her eyes scanned the page.

Finally, after what felt like an eternity, Aura couldn't take it anymore.

"So... what does it say?"

Keyara took a deep breath, her words weighed down by the gravity of the news.

"In the past, the last trial of the Heir's Rite required the remaining contestants to fight to the death until one sole victor remained. As a civilization, we have..." She hesitated, swallowing hard. "...Evolved since those times. The King and Queen, in their wisdom and good nature, have decided on a different course."

Leaning forward, her heart raced as Keyara continued.

"The last trial requires the final three competitors to plead their case before the political representatives sent by each kingdom throughout Myrantis. The democratic vote that will follow will determine the next ruler, the Heir to Eira."

Aura felt an immediate rush of relief. She felt lighter, as though an enormous weight had been lifted, the brightness of her smile could have lit up the entire room.

The emotions she was feeling from Keyara couldn't have been more different.

"Oh gods, that's such good news!"

Keyara put the letter down on her lap, her long legs crossed on the bed.

"Is it?"

Aura stared at her sister in disbelief, baffled at her reaction.

"Yes! Now you don't have to fight anyone to the death or be killed yourself."

She had never seen Keyara look so vulnerable, even during the maze a few days before. There was a raw, unfiltered uncertainty in her gold-flecked eyes. Aura grabbed her older sibling's hands, squeezing them tightly.

"How can you ask if this is good news?" Aura's voice quivered with emotion. "I don't have to lose you, Keyara. I won't have to stand there and watch you die, or-" She paused, trying to make light of her fears. "-tell our mother, 'Oh, sorry, Keyara got to the last trial, but some godsdamned man from Deryn murdered her'."

Keyara's lips twitched, but her eyes stayed clouded.

"Because, Aura, this is me." She pulled her hands free from her sister's grasp. "I'm not someone people particularly *like*."

Aura shook her head. "That's not true."

"It *is* true," Keyara insisted, her voice tight with frustration. "Back home, you were the one making friends, not me. People think I'm unapproachable, difficult... And here? Everyone thinks I'm some naïve, entitled nobody. *The bitch from Eira* is what I've heard them call me in training."

"No one thinks that!" Aura shot back, her voice rising in defence. "Berran doesn't think that, and Cass doesn't. And I'm sure Fenn doesn't either."

She pushed down the thoughts of Fenn and stored them away for later. It still didn't sit right with her that there had been a very real and distinct possibility that she would have been witness to a fight to the death between them. But that was irrelevant now.

Keyara leapt off the bed and began pacing the room.

"You and Berran don't count. You're family and Cass likes *everyone*. Fenn..." She waved her hand dismissively. "He doesn't even *know* me, and I don't know him either, as I keep being reminded."

Aura followed her, standing firm.

"Why do you care if people *like* you, Keyara? This isn't a contest on popularity."

Keyara stopped pacing and turned to her, her frustration spilling over.

"Of course it is, Aura! No one votes for someone they don't like. How can I rule a kingdom when my subjects, my courtiers, and even my allies don't want me there? Do you not think the thought keeps me awake at night?"

Sensing the deeper fear beneath her sister's words, Aura softened.

"You're overestimating the dislike people have for you. It just takes time for people to see you for who you really are. You're strong, capable, and deserving to be there. You just need to show them that."

Keyara pulled her hands through her thick hair, her shoulders still tense.

"I know. You're right."

Stepping forward, Aura pulled her sister into a tight hug.

"You've got this," she whispered, her arms wrapped firmly

around her sister's neck.

Keyara's voice was small, fragile as she whispered.

"I fear I may not win this one."

Aura pulled back and took her sister's pale hand once more, the golden current of light travelling from her fingertips, infusing Keyara with the warm, glowing energy of confidence and self-belief. Aura had always been her strength when she felt weak, her rock when the world seemed too heavy.

Within moments, Keyara's tension faded, her posture straightened, and a soft, confident smile returned to her face.

"Thanks," she said, her voice more grounded now. "But I couldn't help but notice you left Mileyakhan off that list."

53

Aura

With a heart full of hope and a head swirling with anxiety, Aura walked with her sister to the council chamber. As they made their way there, the notable absence of Berran and the other syrens did not go unnoticed by either of them.

"Maybe they didn't get the letter this morning, or they overslept," Aura suggested.

Keyara abruptly stopped, her long strides halting mid-step.

"Oh shit."

"What is it?" Aura asked, confused as her sister pulled her into a nearby alcove.

Keyara's voice lowered. "I didn't even think..."

"Didn't think about what, Keyara?"

"They're on the council."

Aura's brow furrowed. "Who?"

It took a second before the realisation hit her.

"Ah," Aura continued.

"Berran and Cass are the representatives for Silvanh in Eira, just like Mileyakhan represents the Domhiann," Keyara explained. "They'll be part of the council."

"Then surely that will work in your favour?"

Keyara paced nervously.

"It could, unless they see our friendship as a conflict of interest."

She suddenly froze, her expression clouding with disbelief.

"Taris. He's Valhir's representative-or at least Kadeen will be," Keyara sighed.

"Taris was a competitor. They can't let him be on the council, right? And you said Kadeen is fine enough," Aura reminded her.

Those golden-brown eyes closed briefly. "I hope to the gods you're right."

Aura winked., "I always am." Keyara gave her a playful shove.

"Come on," Aura said, smoothing down her sister's clothes. "Let's go, whilst you look like a future Queen."

It was not what her sister originally wanted to wear but Aura had insisted she dress as the future Heir she was, not what was comfortable. A sleeveless night blue bodice that hugged Keyara's frame, paired with matching slim trousers that accentuated her long legs. The fabric shimmered in various hues of blue, reflecting the morning light. Cass had given it to them 'just in case' something like this arose.

Aura had spent nearly all the time they had left sweeping Keyara's dark hair up onto her head, weaving in braids and some of the gilded hair pins they had been gifted. Oridae gold jewellery was around her slim neck with matching earrings dangling from her ears.

Despite Keyara's suggestion to conceal the healing Cray wound on her shoulder, Aura insisted they leave it visible-a testament to her strength.

All in all, Keyara absolutely looked the part, and with Aura's magic helping her on the inside, she really thought her sister had the win secured.

As they entered the wing of the castle leading to the council chamber, the murmurs of gathered courtiers swelled into a symphony of whispers. Guards ushered people out of their path, reminding them that each competitor could bring only one companion for support.

The hallway was adorned with intricate tapestries depicting previous battles, historic council meetings and previous rulers of Shadowfern. Along with the tapestries, ancient symbols were carved into the enormous oak doors to the council chamber. Aura marvelled at the enormous oak doors to the council chamber. There were two carvings: a great white eagle with outstretched wings, facing a three-horned ram mid-charge. The symbols of Shadowfern; eagle represented the Falkons, while the ram was the symbol of House Trewith.

The Trewith's were said to be the original family of the Vaelorns; simple mountain goat herders who founded Shadowfern to make it the force it was today.

The eagle would never be removed, forever remaining a guardian of Shadowfern. Only its foe on the other side of the frame would ever change, a constant battle with an unreliable opponent.

The hubbub of the hallway quieted, the throng of people becoming more of a small gathering.

A guard pointed them to their seats to the right of the imposing door, the two of them sitting in perfect unison.

Keyara leaned over, whispering. "I can't believe he didn't tell me."

"Who?"

"Berran. He made out like he had no fucking idea what was going to happen today, only alluding to the fact it probably wouldn't be a fight to the death. He knew this whole time that he would be sitting on a council deciding my fate whilst I rambled on about how great of a ruler I will be."

Aura sighed softly. "You can't be sure he knew about the trial. We only found out this morning."

Keyara rolled her eyes. "Come on, Aura. He knew. And if he didn't, he should have."

"What do we have here? A nobody and a syren's whore."

Aura looked up at the man who nearly murdered her sister in the maze.

Duncann's watery eyes were fixed on Keyara with a venomous hatred. Aura could have sworn he smelt bitter and acidic, but that could just be her own hatred of him muddying her senses. Keyara remained unsettlingly calm, which Aura knew from experience was a bad sign. When

Keyara was cool and collected, her hatred ran deep, woven into her very being. The lack of visible reaction spoke volumes. Aura, however, was not her sister.

With a sweet, innocent voice, she said, "Oh look, it's the most repulsive man I've ever seen. Could you move before people think we're with you?"

Duncann's head slowly swivelled toward her, and Aura felt something off in his presence. Aura could usually feel the emotions of anyone close enough to her. Most times it was calm, or happy, or tired; the range of human emotions. However, this man's energy was wrong-unnatural. Her power wanted to recoil away from him, to retreat and to find something joyful, or even angry. Just anything that felt normal. Still, she stood trying to meet his gaze, her voice steady as she spoke with all the grace their mother had instilled in her.

"Any future Heir of Eira wouldn't discriminate against anyone, wouldn't judge who any adult decided to sleep with, whether they were human or syren. I also don't think they would go around court calling women whores, do you?"

The rustling of Keyara rising to her feet followed, her taller form now standing toe-to-toe with Duncann. He finally had someone at his level staring back at him, nose to nose.

Keyara's voice cut through the tense air like a blade, her words sharp.

"I nearly killed you once, Duncann. Do you really want to risk pissing me off again?" she spat.

The name left her lips with venom, as though it physically burned to speak it aloud for the first time. Aura hadn't heard Keyara say it until now, and the weight of it felt bitter, filled with loathing.

Duncann's voice dripped with malice as he sneered.

"As I recall, it was the girl that burned. Not you."

Aura stiffened, sensing a flicker of twisted delight in his words, as if recalling Jenney's screams gave him some sick pleasure. The memory of the young girl still haunted Keyara, and Aura could feel her sister's guilt wrap around her like a heavy shroud. It had been unbearable for Keyara and Aura's empathy magnified the torment.

Before Aura could react, a flash of black caught her eye. One of Keyara's blades appeared in her sister's hand, seemingly from nowhere, the tip pressing against Duncann's throat.

"You don't deserve to even think about her, you hideous piece of shit," Keyara growled, her voice low and dangerous.

Duncann's grin only widened, but before he could say anything more, a guard intervened, stepping between them.

"No weapons in the council chamber," he said, reaching for the blade. Keyara withdrew it before he could touch it, her lips curling into a mocking smile.

"My apologies," she said, her voice tight with forced politeness as she remained nose to nose with Duncann.

The guard pulled Duncann away, instructing him to return to the waiting area for the council's verdict of his trial.

The two sisters sat back down, the hallway now silent. A few minutes ticked by without either saying a word when Aura's ears pricked up at the sound of pawprints clicking on the stony floor.

Aiza.

Fenn.

The very male appeared. One hand idly twisting and turning a small vine that was curling up his arm, the other swinging as he whistled quietly along, Aiza following his every step. Aura stood, smoothing the wrinkles from her yellow skirts as he approached.

He halted, his gaze sweeping over her, and Keyara was the first to speak.

"Fenn." She gave a small wave, which he mirrored with a half-smile.

Their interaction was interrupted by the heavy doors of the council chamber creaking open. Lord Trewith stuck his head out, his expression unreadable.

"Keyara Allis, the council is ready for you."

The two sisters shared a glance, the unspoken remaining just so. "I'll see you soon," Aura said, not wishing her luck. Keyara didn't need luck, she deserved to win from her own merit. Keyara stepped inside with her head held high and a steel rod in her back. The very air of strength radiating from her. The heavy doors thundered closed leaving behind a quiet hum of the flickering lights, enchanted in their place in the alcoves.

54

Aura

Aiza reached her first, her body so large, legs so tall, that the dog's head was up to Aura's stomach. She ruffled her pillow soft fur, stray wisps of white hair floating down to the floor.

"Hello Aura," Fenn said, stepping into her vicinity, a richness in his voice Aura would never be able to describe.

She looked up at him, her tone gentle.

"I never got a chance to thank you for what you did for Keyara in the maze."

Fenn twirled the vine in his fingers, and it bloomed into a small yellow rose. He handed it to her with a shrug.

"Anyone would have done the same."

She took the rose he held out to her, "No they wouldn't have."

"She was on my team, the trial was about working as one. Who knows if any of us would have passed if I didn't try to get at least one of my teammates across the line."

Aura felt the slight sting of a lie come from him, but she didn't push the matter, instead changing the subject.

"Do you know who is on the council? As one of the few fae who spends time in Myrantis, are you not a representative yourself?"

He grinned, his canines glinting in the flickering light.

"No, Athvar would never get involved in the politics of another kingdom."

Aura tilted her head. "Are the syren kingdoms not represented?"

He crossed his arms, "Not the Laeths, for obvious reasons, but the Domhianns and Reothadhs have a vested interest.

Domhianns need Myrantian land for birthing, and the Reothadhs' way of life in Silvanh is nearly completely supplemented by trade. They have as much of a say as the Lords of Eira in who should run the kingdom."

"And Valhir? Do you know who's representing them?"

Before Fenn could answer, a deep voice echoed through the hallway.

"Well, it certainly isn't me."

A tall figure clad in ruby red, came sauntering down the corridor, with a conspicuously missing hand. The guards immediately formed a barrier, blocking his path.

Fenn scratched his forehead, his eyes closed in exasperation.

Aura shouldered around Fenn. "What do you want, Taris?" She strode towards where Taris was hovering, behind the shimmering translucent wall in between the guards.

He smirked, his one good hand slipping into his pocket.

"Good morning, Aura, I was too late to give Keyara my best wishes I see."

Aura tutted. "Such a shame. I'll be sure to tell her you stopped by."

Taris arched a thick, elegant eyebrow. "Will you now?"

"Absolutely not," she said through a perfect smile.

He put his tongue into the side of his cheek and jerked his head at the flower in her hand, "Nice rose."

Her grip tightened instinctively as if he might snatch it away.

Taris moved forward, but the barrier held him back, a faint buzzing as the magical wall rejected him.

"Let me through," he demanded. They simply shook their heads, though Aura could have sworn she saw a dash of fear in their eyes.

Fenn stepped between them, his voice cool.

"Need a hand, Taris?"

"Tell them to let me pass, Ashverne."

Aura glanced between Fenn and the guards, disbelief creeping into her voice.

"You're not actually going to let him in, are you?"

The vampyre was a ruthless brute, who had humiliated her sister. Even though he had done one commendable thing for Keyara in the maze, it didn't redeem the arrogant prick.

Though that one thing was something she still hadn't found the right time to fully inform Keyara about.

He didn't assist Keyara when she was desperate to help that poor girl Jenney, and Aura could not forgive him for that. Nor for the fact that Keyara now blamed herself.

Fenn nodded at the guards.

"He's with me."

Grabbing at the velvet arm of his green suit jacket, she hissed at the male next to her.

"Fenn what are you doing?"

Fenn stepped forward, shielding her slightly from Taris as Aiza growled low in her throat.

"You know my bludhounds would tear your wolf to shreds," Taris commented as he walked through the barrier that was now warping around him.

"I'm sure they would, but luckily for Aiza, I have no plans on ever venturing into Valhir anytime soon. Ever in fact," Fenn said with utter conviction.

"Now why ever would that be, Ashverne?" Taris tapped a finger at his chin, "It cannot be that you're not welcome in my kingdom. My home is open for anyone who wishes to visit."

Aura watched the two males together. One dark, shrouded in danger, sex and arrogance. The other, secretive yet open with an air of allure; the power he exuded literally thrummed off his broad shoulders.

It was like watching two predators sizing each other up, and she wasn't quite sure who she would place her bets on. Aura didn't know what that made her in the dynamic.

"Why are you here Taris, what do you want?" Fenn asked with

impatience.

"I wanted to watch my fellow teammates in their last trial. Cheer them on, give them... *motivation*."

The corner of the vampyre's lips twitched, a smirk was pulling at them.

There was something tugging at Aura, like an unseen force was at play. She knew Aiza could sense it too, the dog's large pointy ears pricked up, the hackles on her back enlarged and all of her focus was on the council room door.

Then the air shifted as sudden screeching disrupted the calm. Something was terribly wrong in the chamber.

"Keyara!" Aura screamed, bolting for the door, pounding on the oak, desperate to be let in. Panic gripped her as she shouted her sister's name.

Somewhere behind her, she heard Fenn's voice, cold and dangerous.

"What did you do, Taris?"

Aura stopped her pounding, turning her head slowly towards the males.

"What *the fuck* did you do to my sister?" she demanded, her voice shaking with rage.

The doors were finally opened and Keyaras wild shrieks were now ear-splitting without the closed heavy wood to muffle them. Aura rushed over, finding Berran cradling Keyara's thrashing body, her form contorted in his arms.

Lord Trewith stood awkwardly in the threshold, and a male she had never seen before – with bright orange eyes contrasted by shockingly purple hair – was holding the doors open for Berran to go through.

"What happened, is she okay," Aura took in the scene.

Keyara's eyes were as wild as a sandcat, her face covered in scratches from her own nails, white foam coating the edges of her lips.

"Where are the healers, Lord Trewith?" Berran commanded, his voice that of the Reothadh Heir.

The lord ushered over the healers in their white garb.

"They are already here."

Berran gingerly let Keyara down into the phantom hands of the healers. Aura kept her own hands out on the chance Keyara would slam into the hard floor.

"Berran what in godsname is going on?!" Aura pleaded at him, her fingers gripping at Keyara's, using all her strength to stop her sister continuing to scratch at her already bloody face.

The syren just shook his head, his white hair falling over his eyes.

"I don't know. One minute she was fine, and then-"

Berran did a double take when he saw who was in the hallway with them.

Fenn must have caught on to the thoughts going through Berrans head, as that could have been the only catalyst to the response that came next.

A mist of green magic warped into thick vines around Taris's feet, bursting from the floor and keeping him locked into place. In a blur of white and blue and with incredible speed, Berran's fist gave a resounding crack as it collided with Taris' square jaw.

Aura would have to leave them to it, as much as she would love to see what happened next. But whatever unspoken words the three males had shared between them, would have to remain unheard for now.

She followed the healers as they carried Keyara's body, her sister's agonised cries echoing through the castle halls.

"Be still Kiki, I'm here."

55

Berran

"Godsdamn it syren, you nearly knocked my teeth out." Taris rubbed his stubble-coated jaw, fresh crimson blood dripping from his mouth.

Berran stepped closer, baring his teeth, his face inches from the vampyre's. Behind him, he could feel Fenn's presence, solid and unyielding. If Berran knew anything, it was that you always wanted a fae to have your back.

"I've been waiting a long fucking time to do that," Berran growled, his large canines itching to rip Taris's throat out.

Taris merely raised his handless arm and pointed at Berran's chest.

"Well, isn't this a frosty welcome? Glad you got it out in the end, though. It's better to voice our grievances and concerns syren. There's no need to throw around punches at our great age, now is there."

The echoes of Keyara's unravelling mind still resonated through the hallways as Aura and the healers carried her away.

"Now that's unfortunate," Taris muttered, spitting blood onto the floor, where it landed with a splatter.

Fenn, locking eyes with Taris, spoke in a low, deliberate tone. "We both know who's behind this…*unfortunate* turn of events, don't we?"

His power kept Taris confined, but the truth eluded them.

Berran knew Taris wouldn't admit anything willingly.

Taris, bloodied but defiant – and annoyingly damned good looking – responded with a deep mocking laugh.

"Do you honestly think I'd stoop so fucking low?"

Berran and Fenn responded in unison, their voices cold. "Yes."

Aiza, standing close by, growled in agreement.

The accusations hung thick in the air, like a Silvanh winter storm, ready to unleash its fury.

Taris' bronze face twisted into a smirk as he wiped more blood from his lip.

"I said I came to wish my team luck. If anyone deserved to win, it'd be one of them."

Fenn stepped closer on impressively silent feet, the vines visibly tightening around the vampyre's body.

"You're lying. I think you did it because Keyara took your hand. You wanted revenge so you took away her chances of winning. Don't think I don't smell her blood that lingers within yours."

Taris' eyes narrowed ever so slightly as Fenn spoke.

"You forget who I am, Taris. I can smell a mole in a mountain a hundred miles away. You took a small taste of her blood again before I got her away didn't you, then used blood magic against her when the time was right. You took her blood for insurance, not knowing what the trial would be today."

Berran's suspicions solidified. The moment he'd seen Taris in the hallway, he'd known the vampyre was involved in Keyara's breakdown.

"You lost and wanted to drag her down with you," Fenn said, his blonde curls catching the light as he shook his head. "How noble of you, prince of Valhir."

Taris, still pinned by the vines, shrugged off the accusation.

"Accusing me of cheating won't change the fact that your champion lost her mind. Maybe she wasn't as strong as we thought."

Berran was unwilling to accept Taris' denial.

"You've always been a damned cheat, Taris. This isn't new."

Fenn also refused to be swayed by Taris's theatrics.

"Save the lies for your people Taris and just tell us the damned truth."

Taris placed his one hand over his heart, his tone dripping with false sincerity.

"I offer nothing but the truth, my word as prince."

The vines around the vampyre retreated into the ground, and with calm predatory seriousness, Fenn crossed his arms,

"You might want to find that scrap of honesty in you Taris. Two against one never seems to work in the favour of the former".

Those deep red eyes narrowed a fraction.

"Is that a threat I hear, Ashverne?"

"I don't do threats," Fenn replied, his eyes locked on the vampyre. "Only promises."

Before the situation could escalate further, Lord Trewith interrupted.

"Fennin Ashverne, it's time. The council is waiting. Save your... inquiries for later."

The vampyre and fae did not take eyes off each other for another heartbeat. Finally, Fenn gave a low whistle to the dog before the two of them went into the council chamber.

With a final smirk, Taris slipped his remaining hand into his pocket.

Berran's voice cut through the tense silence.

"Leave Shadowfern, Taris. Take your bullshit with you, your business here is done."

For a brief moment, Berran thought he saw a flicker of hurt cross Taris's face, but it could have been a trick of the light, a passing shadow.

Clearing his throat, Taris replied.

"Perhaps you're right, syren. Autumn's on its way, and I want to be out of this miserable place before then. Tell Keyara-"

Berran didn't even turn as he interrupted whatever remark Taris was about to say.

"Choose your next words carefully, Taris."

Taris tutted but said nothing more, turning to walk away. As his figure receded into the dimly lit hallway, and with only the guards remaining in the vicinity, it left Berran alone with his brewing anger to skulk back into the council chamber.

"Well, that was a surprise-and a colossal waste of time for the male. Pity."

Berran glanced across the large oak table toward Nahese and his troupe of Akoaàns, who were chattering among themselves. As much as Berran found his patience forever wearing thin in his company, Nahese's comment rang true.

Fenn's unexpected withdrawal from the Rite had cast confusion over the entire council.

Leaning back in his chair, Berran rested his freshly shaven chin in his hand, muttering under his breath.

"What is he playing at?" He whispered the question to Mileya, seated on his left.

"I don't know," she huffed. "Typical fae."

He grunted his agreement, shuffling in his seat. The tall chairs were slightly too narrow for his bulky frame, and he had to arrange himself in such a way the damned thing didn't cut off his blood circulation.

Fenn had claimed he couldn't, in good conscience, compete in a contest where his rivals were compromised.

"Not a true win," were his exact words. Berran understood the argument in Keyara's case, but not Duncann's. The man might be cruel, perhaps even unhinged, but compromised? Berran couldn't see it.

Then again, he rarely understood Fenn's kind. Despite admiring the fae's morals, unease crept into Berran's gut. Fenn's withdrawal had shifted the council's dynamics in a way no one had anticipated. Everyone had expected Fenn to win, even if the idea of a fae ruling Eira was unpopular. But who could argue against the king's wishes?

Berran, of course, remained loyal to Keyara, barely bothering to listen as Duncann droned on in his monotone speech. From the bits he caught, it wasn't half bad.

Duncann Kasperl, the only remaining son of a lord Berran had never heard of, came from Brelia, a small town on the border of Valhir. The spit of land had been ravaged in the human rebellion against the vampyres hundreds of years before, leaving the once thriving town desolate and with the highest poverty rate in an otherwise rich country.

Not many people left Brelia, and those that did never came back.

For a brief moment, Berran almost felt sorry for Duncann. With looks and a personality like that, this council meeting was likely the most important moment of his life.

Mileya's voice pulled him from his thoughts.

"This room stinks of mould," she hissed under her breath. "And dust."

"You said that already," he grumbled.

"No, I said it was dusty. Now it smells like mould too."

Berran rolled his eyes, a habit he was sure he'd picked up from Keyara. He knew Mileya was itching to leave, not just the room, but this whole place. He couldn't blame her. It had been months since he'd seen home, and weeks since he'd glimpsed the ocean. The pull to return was growing stronger by the day.

"It'll be over soon. Then we can go home."

At the far end of the table, Lady Trewith rose, sending the room into silence. The giant urn, where they were to cast their votes, floated toward them on an invisible breeze, courtesy of Lord Trewith. Each council member would write down their choice for the heir, along with a brief explanation, and place it in the urn.

Berran watched intently as the council members took their turns, his gaze flicking between the parchment in his hand and the faces around him. King Harrold Oakstone of Deryn was next, the miserable old bastard.

Harrold was one of the most ill-tempered, prickly men Berran had ever had the misfortune of meeting. His grey curly hair was in desperate need of a cut and his scraggly beard had most certainly seen better days. Set deep in his head were navy-blue eyes with no life to them; harsh and weary, as though all they had witnessed in life was hardship.

Berran supposed Harrold led his people well enough. He wasn't particularly cruel, nor kind; though some of his policies regarding borders needed improvement Berran thought.

He was with three of his advisors, including the presumed heir to the Derynian throne – his eldest granddaughter, Ros. She stood beside him, a homely woman with red hair and the famed Oakstone strength that ran in the family. A power she had inherited through her mother, Lady Talina Rast.

Berran had met all six of the Derynian king's grandchildren, and five of them had this power. Along with the big blue eyes and dark curly hair.

Notably absent were the Coralls of Eldorhaven, represented instead by their daughter, Samari. She'd been quiet throughout the weeks, keeping to herself-though Berran recalled she wasn't so quiet in the bedroom…

As Nahese approached the urn, his fruity scent assaulted Berran's nostrils. The syren gave him a dazzling smile after dropping his parchment, returning to his seat with an exaggerated flourish.

When his own turn arrived, Berran approached the urn with measured steps. Keyara, despite her recent ordeal, deserved the throne. Yet, the uncertainty surrounding Taris' actions lingered in the recesses of his mind.

Berran placed his parchment into the urn, his letter a concise endorsement of Keyara's candidacy. He couldn't deny her resilience and strength, qualities that made her a worthy ruler.

However, doubt gnawed at him.

The room fell silent as Mileya cast the last vote, the parchment finding its place in the enchanted vessel. The urn glowed momentarily before a magical current whisked the votes away to the king's unseen chamber. It was understood that the king and queen would deliberate over the next few days before announcing their decision.

Berran, like the others, began to gather his things, ready to leave the grand room. He trailed behind Mileya, sending a small snow flurry toward the carved eagle above the door, when suddenly the urn burst with blue light. Everyone froze, no one quite believing the sight of the object glowing in the centre of the table.

Lady Trewith exchanged a bewildered glance with her husband before clearing her throat. "Please, sit back down," she commanded; though most, including Berran, remained standing, his chair far too uncomfortable to endure again.

Lady Trewith reached into the glowing urn with agonizing slowness, and Berran could have sworn he heard Mileya mutter for her to hurry up. Pulling out a single parchment, in her hands lay the king's seal, a blue songbird in flight over a golden sea. It was clear for all to see.

She unfolded the parchment, her voice ringing out over the hushed room.

"The winner of the Heir's Rite has been chosen."

She held up the parchment in her slender hands, one name was written there, one name that sucked the air right out of the room.

Everyone leaned further towards the table, clearly not believing what they were reading. Berrans stomach dropped to his feet as she read out the name.

"Duncann Kasperl."

56

Berran

Berran couldn't contain his frustration as he stormed out of the room, his mind racing to process the unexpected news.

"Duncann? How? Why?" he muttered under his breath. "We didn't vote for him. This doesn't make sense."

Mileya hurried behind him as he strode through the dark hallways, desperate to escape the stifling air of the chamber.

"You speak for everyone when you say we didn't vote for him?" she asked.

"I know most of them aren't complete damned idiots. He's not fit to lead."

Mileya's tone was calm but heavy.

"Sometimes power doesn't go to the most deserving."

He shook his head.

"This isn't right, Keyara should have won."

They stepped out into the cool dusk air of one of the courtyards, the stone beneath their feet damp from an earlier rain. Mileya sighed.

"If you want the truth, Berran, it *is* right."

His jaw tightened, the urge to snap back *'fuck off Mileya'* barely restrained.

He swallowed the angry retort, knowing full well the Domhiann wouldn't hesitate to kick him in the balls.

Mileya crossed her arms.

"She is in no fit state, Berran. They all view her insane after what happened in that room today. I'm not sure I can say they made the wrong choice in not considering her."

"She was sabotaged, Mileya. You know that-you were there,"

Berran growled, running a hand through his ruffled hair.

"I don't know that," she replied coolly. "I couldn't scent any spell or poison. You must accept that she might have failed on her own."

He couldn't. He had trained Keyara for years, prepared her for this moment. To see her fall apart in front of the entire council, while Nahese watched with amusement-it would haunt him. His anger was more than grief for his friend's loss. It was the unsettling reality of Duncann ascending as heir to one of the most powerful nations in the land. Something about Kasperl felt... wrong. Rotten.

Berran's eyes narrowed. "She was the better choice, Mileya. You can't honestly think that walking corpse is fit to rule."

"No, I don't," she admitted. "Which is why I didn't vote for either of them."

He raked a hand through his hair, now long enough that the white tips grazed his jawline. "This is fucked."

Mileya didn't respond, and after a tense silence, Berran sighed. "I need to tell her."

Striding down the corridors to the infirmary, the last dredges of late afternoon sunlight lit Berrans pathway in tones of orange and gold. This part of the castle felt lighter, more open, a stark contrast to the oppressive gray stone within.

The bustle of the castle faded as they approached the room where Keyara was resting. Berran took a deep breath, steeling himself for the sight of his once-strong friend, now weakened. The door creaked open to reveal Aura tending to her sister. Keyara's hazel eyes, once full of fire, now held confusion and vulnerability.

"How is she?" Berran asked, he knew his concern and worry was clear across his face.

Aura looked up, those big blue eyes reflecting the weariness of the day's events.

"Physically, she's recovering but...her mind... It's going to take time."

Berran nodded and approached quietly, as though Keyara might startle like a deer in Eldorhaven forest, the slightest movement spooking her back into the shadows.

"How are you feeling?" he asked softly, standing at the foot of her cot.

Keyara looked at him, her movements slow and disjointed.

"Dizzy, but a lot better," she replied, her voice barely above a hoarse whisper.

Berran pulled a wooden chair closer, sitting down with a heavy sigh. He put his elbows on his knees and tried to muster a smile.

"They'll let me come visit you in the Home for the Deranged, won't they?"

Keyara's trembling arm reached to swat at him, and Aura winked.

"We have told them to make sure your room next to hers is just as comfortable. I've also heard the Home for the Deranged has a lovely bathing pool."

He gave a tentative laugh. After a small silence that followed he began to speak.

"I'm sorry, Keyara."

"For what?" she said in a small voice.

He averted his gaze, unsure of how to tell her the truth. The suspicions about Taris, the horror of Duncann's victory-it was all too much. She continued, trying to fill the void with words.

"I felt strange the moment I stepped into that room. The nurses think it might still be the Cray poison lingering. They're testing my blood to see. You have nothing to be sorry for, it wasn't anyone's fault, it's not like you did this to me," her voice cracked. "But I swear I'm going to kill that fucking creature all over again for costing me a crown."

Berran could tell she was rambling to hide her pain-both physical and emotional.

"Although maybe they will let me take the trial again, see me in the council chamber again I mean."

He gingerly touched her hand. "Keyara…"

She rolled her head, looking up towards the ceiling that was painted to look like the clouds that grazed the peaks of the Vaelorns. The glow of sunset now illuminated her pale face on the bed. Turning the bed from white to a deep purple and pink. He had to tell her.

"It wasn't poison."

A single tear threatened to leave her eye. Though by the sheer steel of Keyaras' will, it did not fall. She knew the truth, as much as it hurt.

Aura, sensing the moment, excused herself to fetch refreshments. Just as she left, Mileya entered, her tall frame casting a shadow over the room. She stood still for a moment, as if trying to decide whether to fully commit to walking further into unfamiliar territory. He saw her contemplation dance across her night kissed face. She took a couple of seconds before she approached Keyara with a solemn expression. Her loose, deep purple trousers swept against the white tiled floor with her long strides.

Berran nearly fell out of his chair when Mileya spoke, her voice smooth and clear.

"I heard what happened, Keyara," she said softly. "And I'm… sorry."

Her apology was so unexpected and genuine that Berran had to stare at her for a moment, dumbfounded. *Mileya, apologising?* Keyara mumbled a thanks as Berran motioned for Mileya to join him in the hallway. Once outside, he confronted her.

"Now, I know you don't think I'm the sharpest male around, but don't take me for an idiot. What do you want?"

Mileya tutted, her black eyes sharp and all-seeing as she waved a hand.

"Have you told her?"

His large shoulders rose and fell with a heaved sigh.

"Not yet."

"You should. She'll find out soon enough."

"I know, but... it's going to break her. She's not ready."

"Tell her what?" Aura said to them as she rounded the corner, a jug of water in one hand, sandwiches and what looked like fresh fish on a tray in the other. "What's going on?" She asked the syrens.

Berran shot a glare at Mileya, but the syren wasted no time. "Duncann Kasperl won the Heir's Rite."

Aura blinked, her tawny eyebrows lifting in surprise. "Oh."

"We only just found out," Mileya continued. "I came down to tell her."

Aura chewed on her lip, considering.

"No," she finally said, her voice firm. "I should tell her."

He pushed his fingers through his hair, "Are you sure?"

Aura nodded. Berran opened the door, Aura dipped under his arm as she went into the sunset bathed room.

57
Keyara

Keyara lay on the godsdamned uncomfortable infirmary bed, her eyes fixed on the expertly painted clouds on the ceiling. The winner would be revealed soon, and she sure as shit knew it wasn't going to be her.

Not now.

If she lost, her sister and mother lost, too.

The thought of telling her mother about her disastrous failure at the final hurdle made her stomach churn.

It was all a damned waste of her time; tentative hopes for a better future for all of them were lost.

Taris and his blood magic had robbed her of victory.

Her days would now be dedicated to plotting all the ways she would boil Taris alive for sabotaging her.

She'd start with his smug, arrogant face.

Melt that desert-kissed skin right off.

She had to admit he was devastating to look at, his eyes capable of making any woman weak in the knees.

In another life, maybe even she would've been one of them.

But she wasn't.

Keyara knew exactly where to start her burning.

The images of the council chamber flashed vividly behind her eyes. She had told Aura all about it as soon as her mind had gotten a grip over itself.

"What happened in that room, Keyara?" Aura had asked, her hand clasped gently around her own.

She recalled the moment right before her descent into madness, the chamber feeling like a pressured pot about to explode.

Normally, her power was a loyal companion, but that day it had become something dark and malevolent, whispering vile things that clawed at her sanity.

It had felt like her very essence was boiling, a vicious storm within.

"It spoke to me," Keyara had whispered, shivering at the memory. "My magic-it was like it was possessed. It wanted me to use it against myself. It wanted to kill me."

Keyara had fought against her power, the feeling so unnatural, so wrong. It had made her claw at herself.

She had resisted the call to boil her own blood, the irresistible lure to melt her own skin of her very body.

The command to destroy herself only subsided once she was out of the room.

Even then she was not her own self. Echoes of the spell swimming within her.

Aura's eyes, usually so calm, had filled with anger and concern. "God's, Keyara, I'm so sorry. You're sure Taris did this?"

Keyara's head snapped to face her sister.

"Of course it fucking was. Who else could do this? Who else *would*?"

"I just can't understand it".

"About what? How an arrogant, entitled prince didn't want anyone else to win? Couldn't face the thought of someone else being better at him at anything?"

Aura shook her head, her strawberry curls catching the last dregs of sunset in their strands. "No, I mean maybe. But if he wanted you dead, why did he save you in the maze?"

The question had caught Keyara off guard.

"What do you mean?" she had asked.

Aura had started to explain. "Well, he-"

But that was when Berran had come in to check on her, his presence distracting them. Keyara had been furious that he hadn't turned Taris into a human icicle for what he'd done.

Now, left alone while Aura fetched food, thoughts of Taris were making her skin burn.

"Prick," she muttered to herself, tugging at the simple cotton gown she wore, her fine clothes from the trial lying neatly folded in the corner,

She was itching to fight, to storm into the council chambers and scream, *Pick me! I'm your godsdamned heir!*

But the memories of the recent few days were playing like a haunting melody in her tired mind and she was getting ferociously annoyed down here.

Fuck it, she thought, swinging her legs over the edge of the bed. She was going to find out for herself.

But as soon as she stood, the room began to spin, and dizziness threatened to pull her down.

It felt like she'd drunk three glasses of Akoaàn wyne.

Keyara put an arm out to steady herself, the spinning steadying a touch.

Not enough though.

She had to sit back down on the cot to stop her face meeting the floor.

Her ears pricked at Mileyakhan's distinctive, heavily accented voice saying her name.

In the hushed quiet of the infirmary, their conversation outside her door was impossible to miss.

They were like seagulls squawking for all the world to hear.

Ringing filled her ears, and her magic stirred beneath her skin, confused and restless after being shoved away in fear.

It had always been her greatest comfort and friend, a part of her soul. Now, after everything, it couldn't understand why she had banished it.

She had lost.

It was over.

Keyara didn't even notice when Aura and Berran entered the room.

"Keyara?" Aura's voice, soft and distant, barely registered as she placed a jug and plate of food on the table beside the cot. Keyara felt her sister sit down next to her, the weight of her presence settling on the bed. In her peripheral vision, she saw Aura wringing her small hands in her lap, her yellow dress crumpling under the movement.

"There's something we need to-"

Keyara cut her off, tone bitter.

"Duncann won, didn't he."

Berran inched forward, ready to speak.

"Too afraid to tell me yourself, Berran? Letting my sister bear that burden for you?" she spat.

He huffed in response, "Keyara-"

"Coward," she scoffed, frustration bubbling inside her like a rising tide.

Aura intervened, her voice steady. "Berran wanted to tell you himself, but I insisted, Keyara."

Keyara rolled her eyes, but the movement sent fresh waves of dizziness through her.

"How convenient for you," she said, avoiding Berran's gaze. "Letting Aura break the news for you. How brave, how noble. Fucking coward." The words were sharp, but she didn't mean them.

Not really.

Her mind was scattered, her strength drained.

She wasn't herself.

Aura stood, a flash of defiance in her eyes.

"No one *let* me do anything, Keyara. I don't need permission for anything."

Berran's face turned practically animalistic as he interrupted Aura, an icy wind blasting forth, sending shivers up her arms.

"Coward? Is that what you think of me?" His voice was sharp, cutting through the tension.

Keyara was taken aback. Berran had never raised his voice at her, not even during their hardest training sessions when her mistakes had been endless

He always had the patience of a priestess.

"Usually, no," she replied, pushing the boundaries. "But hiding behind Aura? Maybe you are. Maybe you're afraid of me."

It was ridiculous, and they all knew it.

Berran barked a short, bitter laugh.

"I'm terrified of you, truly. You're a nightmare incarnate Keyara." His temper subsided as quickly as it came, his coolness washing over him once more.

His sarcasm not completely without conviction.

She swung her legs off the side of the bed to get up again, and despite how obviously pissed off at her she was, Aura grabbed her arm to help Keyara up.

Once upright, Keyara looked at the two people she cared about most in the world.

Her resolve crumbled, and the tears she'd been holding back finally fell.

"I lost," she whispered, her voice cracking. "I fucking lost. I'm sorry."

Aura wrapped her in a tight embrace, her words soothing.

"Oh, Keyara, don't be sorry. It's not your fault."

Heavy footsteps echoed in the room as Berran stepped forward, pulling them both into a hug. The three of them stood there for a moment, silent, until Keyara's tears dried.

She rolled her eyes, managing a small laugh. "What a damned mess."

Aura smiled, grabbing a tissue to hand her.

"Not at all. Your hair stayed remarkably in place."

Keyara gave Aura a playful swat on the arm.

"Not to put a downer on this joyful evening, but there's something else I need to tell you both," Berran said as he leant against the posts of the cot.

Keyara dabbed at her face with the tissue Aura had given her.

"You've killed Taris and need me to burn his sorry arse to dust?"

Berran pointed at her. "Unfortunately, no."

"They say he's gone," Aura said. "I heard the healers talking in the kitchen"

"I can't say he'll be missed," Berran replied.

Aura's voice softened. "So has Fenn."

Keyara looked to Berran. "What, really?"

He nodded. "Yes, he left. Didn't even do his trial. Just refused and walked out."

The sodden tissue landed in the bin with a thump as Keyara threw it in, unsure how to feel about the revelation. Before she could dwell on it, Aura picked up a yellow rose from the bedside table, twirling it absentmindedly between her fingers.

"What did you want to tell us?" she asked Berran.

Berran smoothed a hand over his hair.

"We're leaving. Cass and I need to go home to report all that has happened here to my parents and the kingdom. We are expected home with the Autumn tide."

Keyara stepped towards him, panic creeping into her voice. "Autumn tide? That's in four week's time, it will take more than that to reach Silvanh from here."

"Not if I leave tonight."

The realisation hit her like a punch to the gut.

"When will I see you again?"

Her heart raced. If Berran left, it truly meant this was all over. No more training. No more guiding her.

He was abandoning her.

"Keyara," he said gently. "I need to be the Silvanh heir for a while, my warriors need me to return home. My servants, they haven't seen their families in months-years, even. I have no reason to stay in Shadowfern any longer."

Because you lost, she knew he wanted to say.

But the words didn't need to be spoken; she felt the weight of them in her chest.

A fucking loser.

"I need your help, Berran. Taris can't just get away with what he did to me. We have to do something," Keyara said.

Aura's gaze darted between the two of them, sensing the tension rising. Berran's expression hardened with concern as he spoke.

"Keyara, revenge is a dangerous path. It never ends well."

She shook her head, refusing to accept his words. "He sabotaged my win, Berran. He played with my mind like I was nothing. I won't stop until he pays for what he's done, and you should feel the fucking same."

"Of course I do, but what good will come of it? He's gone- without an arm, no less-back home. You'll never see him again. He lost too. Isn't that enough?"

"No," she muttered, crossing her arms, her eyes flickering to the pile of clothes where her daggers lay.

She could feel them calling to her, begging to be plunged into the neck of a certain vampyre.

"He can't just get away with it," she added, her voice softer than intended.

"I know," Berran said. "But you cannot let him ruin the rest of your life Keyara."

"Too late, he already did. He ruined it in that chamber."

Heavy silence hung between them until Aura broke it.

"I wish it hadn't ended this way."

A spark of inspiration flashed in Keyara's mind, and she looked at her sister.

Gods, why hadn't she thought of it before?

"It doesn't have to."

Aura's blue eyes looked puzzled.

Keyara hurriedly explained, "You could... *convince* the council to give me a retrial. Let me go again. Just say I had a momentary lapse-nerves."

Berran interjected. "No Keyara."

"Why not? She can do that."

Aura cocked her head.

"I'm not doing that Keyara, you and I are not cheating our way to a crown."

"Why not? Everyone else has tried to!" Keyara snapped, though she knew deep down it wasn't an option.

She was just grasping at anything to stop this awful reality from sinking in. The weight of the loss settled like ash in her stomach, and the thought of Berran leaving her only pushed her closer to the edge.

Berran shook his head. "You can't expect Aura to take that risk. Would you really let your sister jeopardise herself for this?"

Aura's eyes flashed with frustration.

"You both seem under the impression that you have some sort of authority over me. If I wanted to do it I would, without your permission Berran, and if I didn't want to, I do not need to give you an explanation either, Keyara. I'm not a defenceless child that needs protecting."

Keyara huffed, unwilling to push the matter further. Aura was right, and deep down, Keyara knew she didn't want to be like him- she didn't want to cheat her way to the top.

At least, that's what she tried to convince herself.

Berran fiddled with his jacket, his voice gentler.

"I don't want to argue with you, Keyara, especially when this might be the last time we see each other for a while. Please, let go of Taris. Go home to your mother. She'll be relieved to see you and Aura safe."

Keyara began to pace.

"That's easy for you to say Berran, you're going home to a palace, wealth and a kingdom that worships the damned ice you walk on."

The male scoffed but didn't disagree.

Aura turned to him. "You really don't know when you'll be

back in Eldorhaven?"

"No," Berran replied. "My time there with the warriors is over. My parents want me and Cass back in Silvanh for a while-probably to marry me off to some frozen fish of a female."

"And Mileya?" Aura asked.

He shrugged. "She wants to leave too, but not to her own syrens. She'll likely come with us to Silvanh, then... who knows. Mileya goes through life drifting to wherever the currents take her."

Keyara stayed silent. She had nothing left to say. He was leaving her, and in her mind, he could go to hell.

The awkwardness in the room became unbearable, the three of them like a puzzle with pieces missing-together, but not complete.

The tension was broken only when a healer burst through the door.

"Excuse me but I must ask for your friends to leave" The older woman said, using her authority as the castle's lead healer to dismiss Aura and the heir of Silvanh.

Berran crossed the room, rubbing the back of his neck as he approached Keyara.

"This is goodbye for now, Keyara. But I'll see you soon."

She looked at him with a blank expression. She wouldn't dare let him see how hollow it made her feel that he would no longer be by her side.

"I'm so incredibly proud of you," he said, pulling her close.

"Thanks," she said, her words muffled against the navy blue of his jacket.

As they pulled apart, he gave her a smile that promised a reunion.

"I'll come with you to the gate, to see you and the others off," Aura said, making her way to the door.

"I'm coming too," Keyara said, reaching for her clothes and daggers.

But the healer interrupted. "No, you're not. You are not permitted to leave the infirmary yet."

Keyara rolled her eyes. "Says who?"

"Me," the healer replied, using her magic to create a force that gently pushed Keyara back toward the bed.

Aura and Berran gave Keyara a sympathetic look from the threshold.

"It's fine. Go. I'll see you when I see you," Keyara said, swatting a hand at him.

Berran pointed at her. "Meet me at our usual spot."

She quirked a smile. "Wildflower meadow, moonrise?"

"See you then, Kiki," he winked, teasing her with the childhood nickname only Aura still used.

As Berran walked out the door, a tiny flurry of snowflakes brushed against her face.

"Take your clothes off please," the healer demanded, placing fresh clothing on the bed.

"You could buy me a drink first," Keyara said as she pulled the cotton shift over her head, freeing her small breasts.

She quickly dressed in the simple black tunic and pants the healer had provided.

"Why am I changing clothes?" she asked, confused by the sudden outfit change.

"These belong to the infirmary," the healer replied, bagging the shift. "You're no longer under our care."

"Then why couldn't I leave with them? Where am I going?" Keyara asked, unease creeping into her gut.

"I was only ordered to get you ready to leave," the healer said, her voice unconvincing.

Keyara didn't believe the woman one bit and by the shifty eyes the healer was sending her way, she knew Keyara didn't buy her bullshit either.

In seconds, Keyara had grabbed her discarded daggers from the floor and whirled them on the healer, the blades dangerously close to the woman's throat.

The healer tried to push her back with magic, but Keyara only pressed the blades harder.

"I won't ask again-where am I going?"

The woman seemed to be contemplating her options, the glow of the candlelight casting her face in scattered shadows.

"I do not know. All they told me was that you are to wear this and be ready to leave at moonrise."

"And where are these clothes from?" Keyara asked through gritted teeth, feeling a pang of guilt pass through her as she saw a trickle of blood trail down the woman's wrinkly throat.

"The dungeons," the healer whispered.

She lowered her blades.

"On whose orders."

Another pause, another gulp.

"Who made the godsdamned order?" Keyara's voice rose, heat building in her chest.

The healer touched the blood on her neck.

"The new heir... Duncann."

58
Selsie

Time blurred, distorted by the constant dull pain and the rhythmic rocking of the ship. Selsie lay motionless, unsure if the muffled chaos above deck was real or a figment of her fevered dreams. Shouts, the clash of steel, and the ominous creaking of the ship combined in a macabre dance that reached her ears like echoes from another world.

The damp air hung heavy with the metallic tang of blood and the acrid scent of sweat, but that could have been imagined as her mind swam in and out of consciousness.

The angry welts on her skin throbbed in time with the swaying of the floor below her. The pain was getting close to drowning her and she didn't know how much time she had left in this world.

Since Jonn had cut her from the net, her beloved tail savaged by its acidic bite, she had passed out. Her wounds were healing agonisingly slowly.

Distantly, the sea was calling her, urging her to keep her eyes open just a bit longer. To let them see the tides again, to feel the current against her fins.

She whispered back to the Maolin.

"I can't, please bring me home now," her voice a broken plea. "Take me to Alysee." But it wouldn't, the ocean was refusing her. It wouldn't take her hours ago either, when a man came down here, to visit her. To abuse her already broken body.

She couldn't recall much of what he'd done-only that the low hum of her burning skin had dulled the pain elsewhere. He had beaten her with his fists and with his booted feet, she knew that.

He had also attempted something else, something she had once only experienced in syren form with a young male under a full moon, below the waves of Cildraethe bay. Something that had been…lovely.

She would thank Alysee everyday that the man was interrupted in his…act, by another of his crew. Leaving her battered and violated body alone on the floor.

Selsie's breaths were shallow as she tentatively touched the apex of her thighs and her ribs. Her vision was blurred by pain, but her fingers confirmed the wetness coating them-blood. Her own scent drifted up into her nose.

Pulling herself off the cold floor, she leaned back against the rough wall, fighting the urge to fall back into the depths should another man come.

Selsie had been too weak to stop him, her wounds too deep, her body in survival mode. She suspected that was why a simple dousing of seawater was enough for her tail to emerge. Her body was so frail that it drank in every drop of the Maolin that it could, going against nature itself, prompting the transformation.

After a while, it had realised the mistake and hidden her tail away once more.

The man had not gotten away completely unharmed, however. She recounted her nails digging into his soft flesh.

He had been cautious at first – scared of her, the net, maybe both – taking his time to navigate the wounded predator before him. Once he had figured out she was no threat in her condition, the beating had begun. Deciding her nails scratching at his face was too much of an annoyance, he had flipped her over, trying to take her from behind, pinning her wrists down on the floor.

Selsie was sure the sea was about to flip the ship, the waves crashing against the wood. But even if it did, she was in no state to swim or escape the maze that was *The Brendann*.

Her head flopped to the side as she recalled the events, her eyes catching sight of Jonn's damp shirt lying within arm's reach. With shaking tentative fingers, she picked up the heavy material and bunched it in her fist.

It still held his masculine, fresh scent; the warm, clean apple smell of him giving her comfort in the darkness. It wrapped her up in its embrace and got stronger as heavy footsteps neared outside the door.

Then, a large shadowy figure crashed into the brig. He was bloodied and bruised, the discarded shirt had been replaced and was now red and torn.

Jonn stood before her; his deep blue eyes met hers. They were marred by exhaustion and something she couldn't place. Selsie's mind, still fogged by the day's torment, struggled to comprehend his words.

"Selsie," Jonn called, his voice roughened by hurried breaths. "Let's get you out of here."

Selsie's lips parted, but her parched throat yielded no words. His eyes ran over her, seeming to make sure she really was here.

His eyes froze on her fingers and their bloody tips. He then looked to the inside of her thighs, where not only welts and burns appeared, but the bruising and fresh crimson that was painted across her caramel skin.

The ship seemed to groan in response to the unfolding events inside it. The distant clang of swords – once reverberating through the ship like lightning strikes in a raging winter storm – now calmed to a lazy spring shower.

Jonns eyes however, had taken that storm within him, brewing it into a hurricane, turning ever more violent.

Selsie scented something shift in his soul. He didn't say a word as he ever so gently walked over and squatted next to her fragile body, his rough calloused hands gentle as they brushed against her fevered brow.

"Come on, let's get you up." He took the shirt out of her hands, helping her arms through the long sleeves and buttoning it up around her.

Selsie staggered to her feet, her limbs trembling with exertion as she clung to Jonn for support. Together, they stumbled towards the door.

She forced a few dry words out.

"You're bleeding."

"I'll be alright" he replied, holding her tight around the waist. His hands grazed her sore ribs but she wouldn't ever dare complain. His close touch registered in her even through the pain.

Selsie looked at him to her side, his face was set in stone, his jaw which was framed with his usual dark stubble was tightly clenched. Over these months Selsie had seen him frustrated, angry, calm, even…at times… happy, but this was a fury she had not seen.

What had happened on the ship to make him so?

They reached the stairs that led above deck, where she had been brought down to the brig. "Careful" he gently said to her, keeping close behind as she made her ascent, keeping a firm grip on the wooden rail.

The sounds of battle had faded, replaced by the distant chatter of men at work. But as they emerged into the sunlight, Selsie knew it wasn't over.

The air was thick with the scent of blood and death, so walking felt like wading through the shallows. The wood beneath her feet was groaning under the weight of the conflict that drifted in the air, settling on their shoulders.

The hazy morning sun reflected off the blood pooled on the deck, glistening like scattered rubies in a jeweller's box.

Her eyes quickly adjusted to the light she had been deprived of for many days, her senses settling in once more.

She turned her head to the left, her eyes falling on rows of men kneeling with their hands bound behind their backs. Many of them, like Jonn, were bloodied and bruised. She quickly counted twenty men in the first row, and the line stretched back several rows deep.

Symon stood at the ship's rail, sword in hand, muttering something to another man whose weapon was also drawn. Selsie could sense the gravity of what had happened here-something significant had unfolded.

Jonn's hand rested gently at the small of her back, urging her forward toward the kneeling men. The touch made her flinch, her mind flashing to unwelcome memories of other hands that had once wandered too freely.

A few had already spotted her, looking up through sticky lashes with hate in their fearful eyes. The other men, who were unbound and walking about the ship, looked at her in stunned silence; a wariness emanating from them.

The ship itself was in a state of disarray. Though Selsie had no other vessel to compare it to, she could tell that something had torn through this place, leaving chaos in its wake. With his hand still on her back and his fingers brushing ever so gently in a steady rhythm, Jonn brought them to a halt before those bound men.

"Mornin', Selsie," Symon greeted her with a bright smile. She managed a small smile in return but couldn't shake the unease tightening around her fins.

Scanning the faces of the men below her, she couldn't find the one she was sure to recognise.

Selsie couldn't smell him either, though she was certain that his scent would make her stomach vacate what little contents it held. She took a large breath in through her nose, clinging onto the familiar scent of the sea. Though all she could sense on the salty breeze was the whisper of change.

Jonn began to talk, and Selsie listened to every word, hanging onto his voice in the clamour of the ship's surroundings.

"Where have they put him?" he asked Symon, his tone calm but commanding.

"Marc's got him tied up against the main mast," Symon replied with a snort. "The old bastard tried biting-damned fool. I'll go get him."

Selsie watched Jonn nod his head at Symon, who saluted before making his way below. She looked to the man beside her, his dark hair blowing in the wind. It looked so soft, Selsie nearly begged to touch the curled ends.

"Jonn, please, what has happened?"

For a human, Jonn was unusually large, towering over her even though she was tall herself, as all Laeths were. Yet in his presence, she felt smaller than she ever had before.

He removed his hand from her back, the warmth of his touch leaving a lingering absence.

"There's been a change of leadership on board."

59
Keyara

With little time before the guards came for her, Keyara had managed to coax as much information as possible about Duncann from the healer.

The woman had whispered about the unsettling rumours circulating among the servants, deep within the bowels of the castle.

Duncann had arrived as an ordinary-if ill-tempered and seedy-man; even considered fair-looking by some.

But over the weeks, he had transformed into something almost rotten, inside and out.

That was why Keyara barely remembered him from that first dinner.

He had become notorious for beating his attendants regularly and threatening to toss them over the waterfall for the slightest mistake.

Worse still, the servants were forced to use what little magic they had to put on humiliating performances, enduring constant belittlement.

But the strangest thing of all? He didn't eat.

The man had no hunger beyond that of feeding from human suffering.

By the second or third day of his stay, he hadn't touched a scrap of sustenance.

"Has Lord and Lady Trewith been told about this?" Keyara had asked her.

The healer nodded.

"Yes, but Lord Trewith doesn't seem to care. It's all very

strange."

Keyara's jaw clenched, and her gaze turned steely.

"Thank you for telling me. You can go."

The old woman left silently, the door closing behind her with a soft click. The lock turning on the other side sealed Keyara's fate.

The clouds above her head moved with the flickering candlelight, and Keyara stared at them for a moment. Yearning to feel the sunlight on her skin that peeked behind their softness in the day.

I won't be seeing the sun for a while, she thought, glancing at the moon hanging high in the sky.

The hour was getting late, they would come for her soon.

But not today.

She tossed the uneaten sandwiches into the laundry bag the healer had forgotten.

As she gathered the bejeweled hairpins scattered across the floor, her hand paused over one of her daggers. She turned it over, catching her reflection in the blade-a shadowed, haunted version of herself.

There was no room for hesitation. She sliced through her long, dark hair with the dagger, the sharp blade cutting through the chocolate strands effortlessly.

Bending down, she gathered the fallen hair, letting it melt to ash in her blazing palms.

Her magic seemed to whisper a thank you in her ears as it was finally allowed back to the forefront of her being.

She walked over to the small slit window, opened it as far as it would go, and released the ashes to the breeze.

Her reflection in the window caught her by surprise, her now shoulder length hair making her look so much like their mother it almost brought her to damned tears.

She shook the feeling off, her gaze falling on the medical supplies neatly arranged on a silver tray by the windowsill. She shoved them into her bag.

There was one more thing she wanted to do.

Keyara sat down to lace up the leather boots left for her eventual trip to the dungeons, taking her time even though she knew she was stalling.

The next thing she had to do would hurt.

A lot.

But time was slipping away, and hesitation wasn't a luxury she could afford.

"Come on Keyara," she hissed at herself, psyching herself up for the task ahead.

She placed the hilt of one of her daggers in between her teeth and summoned her magic, concentrating it into her fingers.

She couldn't think too hard about what had happened earlier- about how her power had nearly consumed her.

Now who's the coward? she thought bitterly.

There was no time to rethink her plan.

"Not me," she growled through clenched teeth, biting down on the dagger so hard she feared her teeth might crack.

Her magic held its breath within her, knowing that she had finally had no choice but to let it free.

Inside, a part of her body that protected her from her own heat retreated. A shield she had implemented from a very young age. After nearly immolating herself one too many times

Her scalding fingers brushed beneath her eyes and along her cheekbones.

Godsdamned, is this what it feels like to others?

The burning pain shot through her like wildfire, and though it only took a mere few seconds, it felt like an eternity.

It fucking hurt.

But now, with the promise of a swollen face, shorter hair, and the cover of darkness, Keyara hoped it would be enough to conceal her identity.

Here we go. She gathered the last bit of mental strength she had left, as she melted the doorknob between her hands.

60
Selsie

She must have looked confused.

Jonn's voice, strong and steady, cut through the restless murmurs of the crew.

"Listen up, men!"

The sailors who remained free from shackles, assembled before the man beside her. The old captain, who Selsie immediately recognised, was bruised and bound, brought forward by Symon and another large dark-skinned man.

Jonn began to speak, his words cutting through the air like a call to arms.

"For too long, we've suffered under a captain more interested in his rum and the company of married women-" A few men jeered, jostling the disgraced captain. Jonn pressed on. "-than the safety and lives of his crew. A man who hides in the face of danger and shows no mercy to those who deserve it most."

The men murmured their agreements, their faces telling stories Selsie couldn't yet grasp.

"Last night, I spoke to each of you. I couldn't stand by any longer. This ship deserves better, *you* deserve better-and most of you agreed."

He gestured toward the men closest to him, faces bright with support. Then, his sword pointed to those kneeling on the deck, their expressions hard with distrust and fury. Jonn's eyes were cold.

"Some of you made the wrong choice."

Cutting through the sudden silence on board, Symons' laugh

drifted on the breeze.

"The captain," Jonn gestured to the dishevelled figure beside him, "will be placed in the brig. I've chosen not to follow the same merciless path he took with young Hary. Mercy, even for the undeserving, is what will set us apart from this rotten, old, cunt."

Cheers erupted, and Selsie watched Jonn closely. There was a weight to him now, the mantle of leadership settling onto his shoulders. He wasn't merely a usurper who had staged a mutiny; he was a liberator, a beacon guiding them through the stormy seas of change.

As their eyes met, she glimpsed the complexity within him: the burden of command, the regret of past choices, and the final decision to chart a new course. In that moment, she saw herself in him-her mirror and her opposite.

Marc and Symon restrained the captain as he thrashed, spitting at Jonn's feet. As they led him away, Jonn raised a hand.

"Hold on." The men stopped, still holding the struggling figure.

"I'll be taking this, thank you," Jonn plucked the captain's large, plumed hat from his bald head and placed it on his own.

"Ah, suits you, mate. Very handsome," Symon quipped with a wink.

Jonn chuffed a laugh. "Get him out of my sight."

"Aye, Captain," Symon replied, as they dragged the old man below deck.

On the ship, the crew seemed frozen in place, awaiting orders, as if the sea itself had paused. The waves barely whispered against the hull of *The Brendann*.

Now adorned with the captain's hat, Jonn strode toward the sailors.

"Now, back to wo-" He stopped mid-sentence, his eyes double taking at the look of horror upon Selsie's face. Jonn narrowed his eyes to the man among the kneeling group, the man who was the cause of her expression. In a few seconds, Jonn had leant over and grabbed the man by his torn collar and pulled him over the rest.

It was *him*-the man who had visited Selsie in the night. His beady eyes found hers, and he sneered, his too-large teeth gleaming in the hazy sunlight.

Long, angry scabs ran from his forehead to his chin, marking where she had scratched him in her delirium. Perhaps that, along with her cracked nails, had given him away.

Or maybe Jonn just knew. Selsie would never know.

"Seize him," Jonn ordered, his voice deadly calm. "And tie him up." The surrounding sailors moved swiftly, tying the man up with lightning speed.

"Where?" One of them asked, ropes twisting in his hands.

"Against the rail," Jonn replied, his voice full of dark promise. Selsie stepped back, leaning against the mast. Out of the corner of her eye, she saw Jonn glance at her. She gave him a small, confirming nod.

There was an overwhelming part of her that wanted to rip the man who had harmed her to absolute shreds. She yearned to tear him apart with her teeth slowly, put a spell on him to prolong death, to make sure he stayed alive long enough to feel everything that was happening to him.

But she knew this was Jonn's moment. This was about more than just her-it was about the ship and its crew.

She also knew she wasn't in any condition to summon her magic, much less fight. She had failed to do so mere hours before.

Once the man was bound, Jonn stood before him.

"What are you doing to me? What the hell is this?" The man spat at Jonn, who didn't flinch. A collective hush fell over the Brendann, all waiting for their captain's reply. But if they wanted an answer that told all, they would be disappointed. Jonn locked eyes with her between the distance that separated them. The man, his bravado now replaced with a stark realisation of his impending fate, began to protest.

"You're punishing me for a fucking syren? She's a killer-a man-eater!"

With deliberate calm, Jonn removed the captain's hat and placed it aside. "The fact of your mortality seemed to have escaped your mind when other thoughts took its place," he said quietly.

Phlegm landed at Jonns booted feet, some of it landing on the polished leather. Selsie winced, her mother would have rewarded such behaviour with a swift throat removal if that were one of her pod.

The man's eyes widened in terror as Jonn approached him with a penknife in hand.

"I don't need men like you on my ship. Let this be a warning to you all." The man's hollow screams filled the briny air as Jonn enacted his judgement. Selsie was unable to look away, as Jonn severed the source of the man's intended cruelty.

The act of retribution was intimate, visceral-a stark declaration of justice.

Jonn's large hands stopped midway through their sawing. Wiping off the penknife with the hem of his shirt, he didn't look up as her name was called from his lips.

"Why don't you finish this off. My knife is unfortunately becoming too blunt."

Selsie couldn't deny the satisfaction that tinged the edges of her being.

Jonn's gaze, as he turned to address the crew, hinted at the complexity of his decision. The risk he took in showing anything but indifference to her was a dangerous game. She was an enigma to them all and perceived as a threat, a harbinger of chaos. The crew's murmurs reached a crescendo, threatening to erupt into violence at any disruption to the harmony within the ranks.

Walking forward with her back as straight as one of the

towering masts, she approached them both. Selsie's instincts flared, her Laeth nature rising within her. Her mother would have been proud. The man, now tiny and insignificant in the morning sun, was trembling in fear.

He should be.

She could vaguely hear the man's screams echo in her ears as she ripped off the remaining flesh dangling between his legs, with her bare hands. The sea seemed to churn in response. Selsie tossed the severed parts overboard, in a symbolic cleansing of the ship. In return, the Maolin below sent large waves spraying onto deck, sending cool splashes of water onto her face as though it recognised the gift as recompense for what he had done.

The man, now deprived of both pride and dignity, was unceremoniously thrown into the unforgiving embrace of the ocean. It was a pity he had fallen unconscious; she would have liked to have seen him watch as his parts were thrown overboard like nothing more than rotten fruit.

Selsie hoped the Domhianns wouldn't do as they normally did and eat his body that had sunk to the ocean floor. The deep ocean syrens saw human flesh as a gift from their gods and always worshipped the food they were about to consume.

He was not worthy of their thanks.

She prayed to the Domhiann serpent god, Uhktanah, hoping he would not accept this unworthy offering and did not reject a prayer from a Laeth.

The man's comrades, who had opposed Jonn's mutiny, watched in stunned silence. Not a sound stirred aboard *The Brendann*— only the whispering sails and the gentle lapping of the waves. Jonn placed his hat atop his head once more. Selsie waited for him to readjust himself before she padded over to him on her bare feet. She reached her hand up to his face, where a few drops of the man's blood had sprayed across his nose.

Her finger gingerly wiped over the stain, she could hear his breath hitch upon the contact. Selsie did not look away from him as she placed the tip of the finger in her mouth.

The taste of human blood was new to her, and by Alysee it was unlike anything she had tasted before. It was a firework in her stomach, a bomb had exploded in her mind, and she had never felt more syren than in that moment.

Jonn blinked as Symon cleared his throat, stepping forward. Every ounce the captain now, he addressed the crew with a possessive edge in his voice.

"She is mine. No one touches her or goes near her without my say."

He was making it clear-Selsie belonged to him, and no transgression against her would go unanswered. Her soul was telling her that she belonged to no man, the ocean was her master, but she couldn't be seen to disagree, otherwise the men would most likely rally against her at this very moment. A small growl of defiance escaped her, nonetheless.

Jonn turned to the remaining loyalists, still bound on the deck. "You lot, think about the consequences of your choices. Take them to the brig with their captain."

Symon saluted. "Aye, Captain Cayson."

The rabble were led away by Symon, bound for the brig-their fate sealed by their choice to remain loyal to an unworthy, cruel human. The older man had beaten her in his chambers, jabbing at her with anything sharp he could get his hands on.

He also stole the bag that Neesh had given her. The contents of which she prayed to Alysee he had not destroyed before she even had a chance to look at herself.

Selsie had still possessed her syren strength when the captain had first taken her, her fists, feet and nails kicking and scratching at him. But it had quickly waned as the net did its job, her magic too eluding itself from her grasp, not readily coming forth into her hands.

The crew dispersed, leaving behind only change and salt on deck.

61
Jonn

As dusk bathed the horizon in golden hues, Jonn leaned against the carved railing outside his captain's quarters. The wind whispered of a sea that bore witness to both chaos and change, whipping through his dark hair.

Behind him, the large doors were open, revealing a bustling white room as his crew cleared away all traces of Captain Lane. He could smell her before he could see her.

Jonn turned to see her bathed in the fading sunlight. Despite her dishevelled state she glowed with the setting sun. Her long curls were slightly matted on her head, those enormous jade eyes were ringed with shades mauve. Her usually strong body was somewhat withered away and covered in welts that were all at different stages of healing.

She was still the most beautiful female he had ever seen, but something was stolen from her.

His jaw clenched at the memory, a flash of rage bubbling up. He wished he could rip that bastard's dick off all over again-ten fucking times over.

She stepped closer.

"What now, Jonn?" she asked, her voice a soft melody in the stillness of the night.

He had to physically restrain himself from touching her, crossing his arms tightly as he leaned back against the rail. She absentmindedly twirled a strand of her hair, and he couldn't help but recall the way her lithe fingers had traced his face not long ago, the way she had sucked on the tip of one-the memory had caused Jonn to eventually become so fucking short tempered with those around him, he had needed to excuse himself from deck.

"Jonn?" Her voice took him from his thoughts. He exhaled slowly, considering her question. "We're heading to Oblitus-home," he began. "But first, we need to stop at Silvanh."

"Oh?" She looked surprised.

"Captain Lane has control of the ship's purse. He has access to the money through his connections that I don't have. At this point, I can't pay for a crew to man a rowing boat, let alone a ship."

He scrubbed at his jaw; his stubble was getting too long for his liking.

"Silvanh has one of the busiest and best markets in the world," he continued. "Which is where we need to trade."

Selsie nodded, her deep, golden-brown hair catching the light. "Trade for what?" she inquired.

"Supplies, provisions, and anything else we might need for the journey. I need to take the ship through One Bridge crossing, so there are...*things* that we need to prepare."

Only the Reothadhs had the weapons they would need to deter anything in those waters.

She looked at him, her syren's eyes piercing through the impending darkness.

"And what about me?"

Jonn had been contemplating that very question since the moment he freed her from the brig. There was only one answer he could live with.

"You're free to leave, Selsie."

Her head quirked to the side.

"I'm free to go?"

"Yes," he replied. "But on one condition-no attacking my ship or my men, and tell your mother there will still be repercussions for the vow your kind broke."

His eyes darkened at the memory of the Laeth's attack, the men he'd lost and the threat she had posed to those infants. He would never forget it in his damned life.

Just like he would never forget Selsie, when she inevitably left him. Some part of his soul begged her to stay; hell, he even felt like begging on his fucking knees for her to not leave him. Though he couldn't, wouldn't, do that.

She considered his words for a moment before speaking.

"I think I want to stay."

His heart stopped.

"What?"

Selsie's eyes softened, and she looked out to the open sea.

"I'll stay. I think maybe it's time for a change. Besides, I've never been to Silvanh, and I've heard the Reothadhs are very…."

Jonn raised an eyebrow.

"Are very what?"

She looked at him from the side, a wicked smile on her face.

"Welcoming, despite the tension between our kinds."

He chuffed a laugh, turning to lean on the wood beside her.

"We won't cause trouble in Silvanh. Can you promise me that? I want to remain as low key as possible."

Her eyes glinted with a mischievous spark.

"I can't promise that," she replied, a faint smile playing on her lips.

"Of course you can't," he muttered with a soft laugh. "We'll be there in four or five days, depending on the tides. It's going to get cold soon. If you plan to stay in this form, I'll need to see if we've got any furs for you, though none of them will fit."

The thought of the icy winds of Silvanh made him shiver. He could handle cold and stormy seas, but Silvanh's winters were brutal, and they were heading straight into autumn's harshest winds. The scarce heat their summer sun provided would be gone by the time they got there.

He didn't know how anyone could survive the winter on the ice.

"What are you going to tell the crew, about me?" Selsie asked.

He sighed deeply.

"I don't know yet. Men have been taught from birth to fear you, to hate you. I'm asking a lot from them to share their home with you."

Selsie said nothing, waiting for him to continue.

"But they trust me," Jonn said quietly. "They trust my decisions. I can only hope their loyalty holds."

Most of the crew had been loyal during the mutiny, but the others were new recruits picked up in Noran after the Laeth attack. They were mostly criminals or desperate men, drawn to the promise of money and a hot meal. They had been promised a fair wage if they sailed under Captain Lane to Oblitus, from there they would be released from service.

"They're fair men," Selsie said softly.

"Even Sy?" he teased, a faint smile tugging at his lips.

She rolled her eyes, glancing up at the sky. "Even Symon."

A few moments of comfortable silence passed between them, the stars beginning to rise in the changing sky.

"Will we need to make port, to get you any Mycillium?" he asked her, mentally sifting through the ports he could recall from memory along the northern tip of Deryn. She shook her head.

"No," she replied, her voice quieter now.

Jonn frowned, moving unconsciously closer to her. She shifted slightly away, and he remembered the way she'd flinched at his touch when he'd first brought her on deck. He promised himself then that he would never touch her again unless she asked.

He felt disgusted at himself, how could he have been so careless.

Jonn studied her for a moment, the last of the light playing on her features. Selsie began unbuttoning his shirt, which she was still wearing.

"I won't need the Mycillium," she said as the fabric fell to the floor.

Before he could respond, she was over the rail, diving with perfect form into the churning sea below, without even creating a splash. Her syren form flashed beneath the waves, a blur of gold moving swiftly alongside the ship.

He lost sight of her in moments.

Hours later, as the moon hung high in the sky, and taking a bite of a green apple, his exhausted body flopped onto the embroidered white bed that was now his. It had been a long, hard day. Himself and Sy had been up the night before planning the mutiny and convincing the sailors to join their cause.

It hadn't taken much convincing, most of them had been disgusted at what the captain had done to Hary. They were also not too keen on how the rotten old man had cowered in fear during the Laeth attack.

Lying on the comfortable bed, a cool breeze from the open doors worked it's damned hardest to clear out his heated, conflicted senses.

He took a large bite of the fruit as he stared up at the painted ceiling. The various stars and constellations of the sky above Myrantis depicted in glittering gold against the paper white ceiling. He could feel his heavy eyelids begin to fall, the weight of the day taking its toll.

"Good night Selsie," he called out, hoping she heard him in her realm beneath the starlit sea.

424

62

Aura

Opening the door to an empty room didn't surprise Aura. Though she doubted her sister was strong enough to wander far, this was typical of Keyara.

The cool, sterile air of this wing of the castle clung to Aura's senses as she drifted through the long corridors in search of her sister. Faint male voices echoed from a nearby room where most of the healers had gathered.

Peeking around the doorframe, she spotted three Shadowfern guards. A sinking feeling fell through her body. Something wasn't right.

One of the healers noticed her, and the room fell silent. Aura could taste the tension in the air, the sickly-sweet hint of secrecy hanging on her tongue. The guards regarded her with disdain, as though she were nothing more than an irritation-a pebble in their boots. Assholes.

The healers exchanged uneasy glances behind the armoured men.

"Where is she?" Aura demanded, her voice cutting through the air like a whip. The curvature of the low ceiling amplifying her voice. The room remained silent and frustration surged within her. "Where is Keyara? She is not in her room."

Finally, one of the guards spoke. "Go back to your room." Aura's eyes narrowed.

"Have they taken her?" She fixed her gaze on one of the healers.

"We cannot disclose that information," replied the youngest, her voice without the strength of her male counterparts.

Aura's patience was wearing thin. She never liked to use her power to manipulate those oblivious to her power. It made her feel sticky, devious, and fed the darkness within her that told her she was a bad, wicked person.

But this was different.

She focused her magic on the healers and guards, a subtle but irresistible force compelling them to answer her, to relax in her presence and to trust the pretty young woman in their company. Though not as potent as physical touch, it was enough.

"Now, where is Keyara?" Aura asked again.

Under the influence of her power, the healer's resistance crumbled.

"We don't know," she mumbled, unable to resist the compulsion.

Aura's heart sank. "What do you mean, you don't know?" She asked the room.

One of the guards answered this time.

"Keyara Allis is gone. We were ordered to take her...*somewhere* else, but she has since vanished."

The healers averted their eyes, confirming what Aura had feared. She could feel the taste of uncertainty on her tongue, heavy and metallic.

Aura turned to an older woman she recognized.

"Did she say anything before she left?"

They all shook their heads, and dread settled deep in Aura's gut.

Crap.

She had half a mind to order the guards to scour every inch of the castle, but a nagging thought kept surfacing-an instinct, like a mole digging its way to the light.

As they stood in uncomfortable silence, that thought finally burst into clarity.

She knew where Keyara had gone.

Aura just hoped she was still in the castle, in Shadowfern even, just so she could stop her sister from doing something stupid. Aura needed help, she sent a silent prayer to the gods that the people she needed had not left just yet.

Without hesitation, she turned and sprinted out of the infirmary, her dandelion-colored skirts billowing behind her.

Keyara was not in their rooms, neither had she left a note.

Aura's heart raced. If her sister had slipped away unnoticed and without a word, it meant she didn't want to be followed.

Because whatever Keyara was about to do was something Aura had feared the moment her sister regained her senses, realized what had happened to her in the council chambers, and who was responsible.

Sprinting through the corridors, Aura's mind raced. Berran was not in his room, where she had left them. Neither was he with Lord and Lady Trewith, who were hosting the celebratory ball that Aura had skipped in favour of her sister's company.

She finally found him in the courtyard, his deep blue cloak billowing as he and his companions prepared to leave. Cassidae stood beside him in a matching cloak, smiling, while servants loaded their luggage into a striking blue and gold carriage hovering in the air.

"Berran!" Aura called out, breathless.

Cassidae's laughter tinkled as she approached the syrens.

"Couldn't bear to see us go, or are you coming with us, dear Aura?"

Berran turned, surprise flashing in his eyes. "Aura, what's wrong?"

"Keyara," she gasped. "She's gone."

Mileya stepped forward, her expression sharp. "Gone where?"

Aura hesitated, unsure whether to reveal her suspicions to those who didn't always think the best of her sister. She had to choose her words carefully.

"I don't know. I went to the infirmary after saying goodbye to you all, and she was... just gone."

Cassidae placed a gentle hand on Aura's arm, her voice soft and like a hummingbird.

"And you're sure she's not anywhere in the castle? Have you checked your room?"

"Yes," Aura replied, shaking her head. "She's not there. The guards don't know where she is either-no one's seen her."

"Have you checked the dungeons?" Mileya asked, her eyebrow raised.

Aura shot a look at the night-black syren, puzzled by the suggestion.

"Why would she be there?"

Mileya folded her arms.

"Why not, she cut off the hand of a prince, I'd have her thrown in the dungeons too."

Aura glared at the syren, even though she knew Mileya couldn't see the expression thrown her way. Maybe she knew where Keyara had really gone. The syren was incredibly intelligent, her blind eyes never missing a thing.

Berran pushed a large hand through his hair, his expression torn.

"I have to return to Silvanh, Aura. I don't know if I can help you."

She took Berran's large muscular arm in her small hands.

"Please, Berran."

He paused, meeting her wide, pleading eyes. She was trying to convey what words couldn't.

After a moment, he pulled her aside, his voice low.

"What's really going on?"

"I think she's gone to find him."

The male lifted his face to the cloud covered skies, a small sigh of exasperation escaping him. "Are you sure?"

She bit her bottom lip.

"She will never rest until she gets her own justice for what he done to her."

He grunted in agreement, his jaw tight.

"I really can't stay, Aura. You know I would help if I could. But if you want my advice-go find Fenn."

"Fenn?" Aura echoed, confused.

"He's the best tracker I've ever known, he can sniff out a mouse in a mountain a thousand miles away."

"But he has no reason to help me," she said, doubt creeping in.

Berran's lips quirked into a small smile.

"I don't think he needs a reason, Aura."

She took a steadying breath.

"Fine. Do you know where he is?"

"He can't have got far. I suspect he's still in Shadowfern. Ask around-he's not exactly the most inconspicuous male."

Aura nodded, finally releasing his arm. Berran turned to his sister, who had been watching silently.

"Let's go."

Cass said nothing as she kissed Aura on the cheek, embracing her. It was a sisterly embrace that held a world of unspoken understanding for her newfound friend. Mileya's dark eyes followed Cass's every move like a hawk. Never letting the female out of her unseeing sight.

Stepping into the carriage on featherlight feet, Cass held the door open for Mileya, who gave Aura a nod goodbye.

Berran's expression hardened as he turned back to Aura.

"Be careful."

"I will be."

"No, I know, but around him... be careful. He is a decent enough male for a fae, but he is still one of them."

She smiled, thinking of all the men in her life who had rallied toward her.

"I can handle him."

Berran pulled her into a tight hug, their earlier farewell now feeling distant and hollow. As he climbed into the carriage, Cass blew her a playful kiss through the open door.

Aura waved at them all, the anxiety of being left alone tearing up her insides. She knew Berran had to leave for his own kingdom, but the closing door behind him still hurt.
The Carriage moved away towards the gate and out of view, where the waterfall crashed beyond, Cass's laughter carrying on the wind.

63
Keyara

Keyara moved swiftly through the castle toward the main courtyard, her every step calculated to avoid detection.

The ridiculous grand ball being thrown for the corpse of an Heir had been her cover, providing the perfect distraction to slip away undetected.

Most of the guards were in attendance, and even the maids and servants had been invited.

She wondered what the creep thought of that, sullying himself with the help.

Still, there was one silver lining to the crowd: with so many people gathered, fueled by goblets of wyne and countless honeymeads, loose lips would be inevitable.

Just as she was about to threaten a teenage gate watchman on his break in the guard wing, three noblemen staggered past her.

Leaning against a tapestry, she feigned a drunken stupor.

Not hard for her to do, worryingly.

"…The male was last seen with a woman in his lap and another on his face," one of them slurred.

"Is that jealousy, Mikael?" another laughed.

"Most certainly not! I don't need to hire the services of a Shadowfern whore; the women here are more like men," Mikael retorted, prompting more laughter.

"The prince of Valhir will find the women of Oridae more appealing, that's all I'll say," one of the others chimed in.

"Maybe he prefers mountain goats; they're warm and welcoming," the trio continued as they wandered off, discussing women in a manner that made Keyara want to cut their cocks off.

Despite their ignorance, the idiots had revealed something crucial: Taris and his court were bound for Oridae.

The night was her ally as she navigated the labyrinthine corridors of the castle, skilfully avoiding the prying eyes of courtiers.

Once or twice, she was sure a stray guard had recognised her, and her arse was about to be hauled back kicking and screaming straight to the dungeons.

They could fucking try, she thought.

Keyara jogged down a corridor whose purpose was solely for the servants of the castle. Discreet and not to be seen, built only for those who are to conduct their business undetected.

It was bustling with energy down here, everyone seeming to have somewhere to be and something to do.

She slipped towards the kitchen out back.

Godsdamned, it was hot in here, even for her.

Shouting and clattering filled the air as pots and pans flew around, food soaring over her head as the cooks used their magic to transform raw ingredients into lavish meals and drinks.

The large serving doors loomed behind the fire.

Keyara traced the walls, keeping her head low.

The doors were open, the servants trying and failing to let the night's cool air bring the temperature of the kitchen down. But autumn had only just begun to crawl in, with a trace of warmth still holding on.

No one paid any attention to the woman amongst them. All too busy to notice as she climbed into an empty supply cart and under the protective sheets.

She prayed the guards wouldn't look under the sheets, hoping they would be too busy with the ball.

Come on, she urged silently. Duncann would have been notified of her disappearance by now, and she wanted to be long gone before the night was out.

The last thing she needed was for her escape to become more complicated.

She lurched with the cart as someone climbed into the front.

Horses whinnied and neighed as they were clipped on.

Shit.

Horses meant the cart would go no further than Shadowfern itself.

She was going to have to make her own way down the mountain. But she would get past the waterfall at least.

She remained concealed as the wheels creaked and the cart rumbled towards the gate, her senses attuned to the sounds and scents of the night, anticipating any potential dangers.

They trundled along for a few minutes, the sounds of distant music echoing. Keyara's ears pricked as the crashing of the waterfall became louder, the party became barely audible.

Suddenly, the cart jolted to a halt. From beneath the sheets, she heard the driver speaking to a man in muffled tones.

Please don't look under the blankets, she silently pleaded to the gods, who seemed to pick and choose when to listen to her.

To her surprise, they did this time.

Rolling forward, the cart moved on, the clamour of the castle growing quiet behind them. Roaring water steadied with magic beneath the cart, its wheels creaking as they rolled over the bridge.

Shadowfern was sleeping as they made their way through the town. The clacking of the horses' hooves against the cobblestones bouncing off the houses as they moved along.

Peeking out the sheets, Keyara wondered how long it had been since they left the castle. The moon was on its lonely descent towards the horizon, stars at their brightest.

Gods forgive me Aura.

The betrayal would inevitably shatter something in their relationship, a bond that had remained strong throughout their lives.

Nothing could come between them.

But this could be the knife that cuts the tie that bound her to Aura. Keyara couldn't dwell too much on that now, she had to get out.

"Whoa!" The driver called out, the cart crawling to a stop.

As she felt the man get out of the cart, Keyara took the moment to lunge forward as quietly and quickly as she could.

The driver was either deaf or blind because he did not notice her as she whipped the sheets off and ran from the vehicle.

Her surroundings was completely unfamiliar.

Shit, they were on the very outskirts of Shadowfern, near the main gates.

"Fuck," she hissed to herself, realizing that the gates would be crawling with city guards

Her planning would need some serious work. Action without thought was stupid and she couldn't afford to waste precious time.

They would find her as soon as the sun came up.

The towering Vaelorn peaks loomed overhead, judging her, waiting for Keyara to make a decision.

She concluded that she had no choice; the decision had been made for her.

Moving on hurried feet, Keyara skirted along the enormous wall that encased Shadowfern.

In the shadows she pulled out her daggers, clenching the engraved pommels in her calloused hands.

They would remain hidden until absolutely necessary; Keyara aimed to avoid detection, to remain as unnoticed as a gentle summer breeze.

Her back remained against the wall as the gates came into view. She eyed the men and women stationed atop them, their stern faces illuminated by torchlight.

Keyara inhaled deeply, filling her lungs with the biting night air. The temperature had dropped significantly since leaving the castle, as if the enchanted wards around it had dissipated at the waterfall's edge.

The gates became taller and taller as she walked towards them.

The path beyond beckoning her on, telling her to hurry.

"I'd like to pass through," she called out into the night.

One of the women atop the gate replied.

"The path down is dangerous at night; wait until morning."

Keyara bit back a frustrated retort. She was just a nobody trying to pass through.

"Thanks for your concern, but I'd like to go through the gates."

The woman squinted down at her, keen eyes scanning her from above.

"What's the hurry?"

Many others were now interested in their exchange, faces of gall kinds staring down at her.

She doubted they had received orders to look out for a dark-haired woman with hazel eyes just yet.

Unless the guards had a way of communicating without being in each other's presence.

She had to move.

"The Heir's Rite has ended, there will be thousands of people leaving here in a few hours and I'd like to give them a wide berth. I've had enough of crowds." She let her words hang in the air, hoping they would resonate.

The woman waved a hand, and the gates began to creak open.

Praise the gods, Keyara thought, as she slid her daggers back into their holsters.

65

Keyara

The rocky horizon was barely visible in the night.
Keyara moved stealthily through the shadows; her senses
heightened. Her straining eyes caught the faint glimmers of
moonlight reflecting off the treacherous mountain paths.
As she descended deeper into the heart of the Vaelorn
Mountains, her thoughts raced.
Taris' decision to visit Oridae had set a plan in motion, and she
intended to follow his trail.
Her resolve burned within her, a flicker of something real
amidst the inky darkness.
She would never let him get away with what he had done.
Images of him dying by her hand sent satisfied shivers through
her, as the winding paths tested her agility, her legs burning
with exertion along the way.
She had made good progress, refusing to stop for even a
moment.
Keyara couldn't afford to slow down-not with that prick and his
court already ahead.
The whispers of the night and distant echoes of nocturnal
creatures accompanied her descent. Those sounds kept her
company throughout the night.

With the moon having long left the peak of the skies above, the
howls of the mountain dwellers quieted as dawn threatened the
inky sky.
Walking to Oridae would take weeks – months, even. Taris
would be moving by horseback and Valhirian steeds were fast-

extremely fucking fast.

If they were moving with carriages and carts loaded with his many suits, she might have a chance of catching up; but only if she too could find a horse.

The wind whipping off the two lakes grew nippier, a sure sign that she was nearing the base of the mountains.

Her newly cropped hair blew around her face, obscuring her eye line.

Keyara quickly fished out two hairpins from her bag and secured her dark strands away from her features.

She had stuck mostly to the path on the way down, not wanting to risk a broken ankle or smashed hip if she traversed the unmade mountain side. The risk of injury was far greater than the risk of being spotted by anyone also treading the path.

As the sun began to rise the path levelled out beneath her, revealing the lakes that now framed her view.

Keyara desperately needed transportation; the descent down the Vaelorn was starting to take its toll.

Exhaustion clung like a heavy cloak, threatening to pull her into the depths of weariness.

At last, Heim embraced her, its tall wooden buildings a welcome sight after hours and endless hours of hiking.

The small town began to stir around Keyara as she navigated the side streets, aware that she needed to act quickly while most were still slumbering inside their homes.

She would have to abandon the quiet alleyways and make her way to the main road if she hoped to find what she was looking for.

As she left the lazy shadows of the morning behind in the alleys, she spotted a cluster of sturdy-looking horses tethered near a makeshift stable.

Raised in the mountains, they boasted stocky legs and thick, flowing manes.

Grazing from the shallow trough outside a blacksmiths, the

horses snorted when she approached, shaking their white and grey manes.

Keyara had not been around horses much; her family was too poor to own one. But Berran had shown her the basics on his own horse, a beautiful snow-white mare named Belle, whom he had left in Eldorhaven for the local children to ride, as they all loved her dearly.

These horses were no Belle, but they would do.

There was nothing quite as disrespected as a horse thief, and Keyara knew the penalty for such a crime was a swift removal of one's foot. She needed to hurry.

Untethering one of the horses, she quickly swung herself into the saddle. The horse whinnied and shuffled slightly, questioning its new rider.

"Come on, girl, or boy," she coaxed, patting its soft, ashy mane and urging it forward.

But the animal refused to budge from the trough.

Godsdamned horses were so stubborn.

She rolled her eyes, bringing heat to her hands.

Causing harm to any animal was abhorrent, and Keyara would rather kill a man that hurt them; but for this, she had to make an exception.

With a swift pat to its rear, her red-hot hand spurred the animal into a run.

Rhythmic pounding of hooves echoed her frantic heartbeat.

The world passed in a blur, the wind bringing tears to her eyes as she pressed the stolen horse to its limits.

Heim rushed alongside her, the buildings growing in numbers before falling again, the horse making quick work of removing them both from the town.

Her hands clung onto the reins for dear life, her lack of experience in the saddle obvious.

She knew the horse felt it too.

The summer bleached grass blurred in her vision either side of her, the landscape becoming more barren as she made her way westward.

The horse tried to slow down a few times, but Keyara only had to bring her heated hand close to its behind for the animals to speed up once more.

They rode like that for a while until Keyara was certain she had made it far enough from town to allow the horse to slow down. She wasn't going to let the animal run itself to death.

Her thighs were sore from the chaffing, her back twinging in pain with every step the horse made, but she couldn't stop. Not yet.

Epilogue…

"The net has been transferred to the hands of the human captain, my queen."

Queen Adne's pointed wings remained still behind her on the throne, the news of his successful venture seeming to neither displease nor satisfy her.

Adne had sent him to the far western shores of Myrantis, to deliver the cursed net to some piss-stained human. He knew her weavers had been working on it for years, had been forced day and night to craft a net that would disable a syren.

Though why his queen wanted it the hands of a human, he didn't have any fucking idea. The fae queen would rather clip her own wings than help the humans in any way.

But he could never ask her as to why; he had lost that privilege over twenty years ago.

His ongoing disgrace would follow him until he passed over to the Everealm. A burst of pale orange hair flashed in his memory. As did the scent of fresh bed linens and fruit. He could almost feel it upon his tongue.

It tasted soiled, rotten, dead.

Just as she was.

That woman with the babe of raven hair.

"What of our friend in the Vaelorns?" His own black wings bristled at the mention of his former friend.

"I've no news to tell you my queen, I have not yet ventured into Shadowfern. I thought it best to keep a fair distance from his…senses."

Those golden eyes narrowed ever so slightly, "Keep him in your sights Dax. I want to know that he is true to his orders and does not steer from his course."

Dax bent his head in acknowledgement, his long dark ash hair falling over his face and grazing the weapons at his waist.

"Now go, before your presence is sensed."

Without uttering a word further, he turned and left the airy throne room.

He strode to the veranda outside, the clouds skipping along the trellis below. Fluttering his black wings, he pushed off into the sky, heading west to Myrantis once more.

ACKNOWLEDGEMENTS

My gosh.

Here we are, at the beginning of a journey I HOPE you are all ready to embark on. It has taken years of hard work, tears and crippling anxiety to get this story into your hands.

I would do it all again in a second.

First, I want to thank Maire Gerrad my editor, who without- this book probably never would have been coherent enough for my eldest son to read! Let alone you guys. She deserves an award for her generous offering of time and patience.

Next, the love of my life, George. You inspire me every day, and I am not sure this book ever would have been conceived without your unwavering encouragement and support.

Mum, you were the first person to hold me, and the first person to hold my book in your hands. I love you to the moon and beyond.

And finally, to you.

Holding my book in your palms whilst on the train, in bed, or on a sun lounger by the beach, wherever you are, without you to read it- the story remains untold. Myrantis remains undiscovered and our characters journey ends before it can begin.

I love you all very much.

Thank you.

ABOUT THE AUTHOR

From the age of 7, Ebony was writing love stories about the fairies who lived in the flowers at the end of the garden, and who brought gifts to the human children.

Along with writing those stories, she always had at least three or four books on the go from her school library.

Her mum always catching her reading under the covers, or holding the book up the crack in the curtain, just to get the last dregs of sunlight onto the pages.

Now her nights are filled with her two rambunctious children, soppy cat and 6'4 hunk of a husband in the south east of England.

(O) ewilkinsauthor

(♪) @ebonybowyer

Printed in Great Britain
by Amazon

61580680R00251